HOCUS
CORPUS

James Tucker

AN ONYX BOOK

ONYX
Published by New American Library, a division of
Penguin Putnam Inc., 375 Hudson Street,
New York, New York 10014, U.S.A.
Penguin Books Ltd, 27 Wrights Lane,
London W8 5TZ, England
Penguin Books Australia Ltd, Ringwood,
Victoria, Australia
Penguin Books Canada Ltd, 10 Alcorn Avenue,
Toronto, Ontario, Canada M4V 3B2
Penguin Books (N.Z.) Ltd, 182–190 Wairau Road,
Auckland 10, New Zealand

Penguin Books Ltd, Registered Offices:
Harmondsworth, Middlesex, England

First published by Onyx, an imprint of New American Library,
a division of Penguin Putnam Inc.

ISBN: 0–7394–0402–4

Copyright © James Tucker, 1999
All rights reserved

REGISTERED TRADEMARK—MARCA REGISTRADA

Printed in the United States of America

PUBLISHER'S NOTE
This is a work of fiction. Names, characters, places, and incidents either are
the product of the author's imagination or are used fictitiously, and any resem-
blance to actual persons, living or dead, events, or locales is entirely
coincidental.

For my family
Peter, Brad, Scott
and Kim

ACKNOWLEDGMENTS

The more I write the less I seem to know. I'm astounded by the number of people whose expertise helped shape *Hocus Corpus*.

I must thank Joe Dominick at the Coroner's Office and Rob Askew at the Allegheny County Crime Lab. The Fox Chapel Police Department generously helped whenever I called. Drs. John Buzzato, Chris Harner, Steve Strelec, Jean Harwick, and Andy Urbach offered technical advice on medical and dental matters.

My friend Patty Wilkosz spent more time helping me understand the intricacies of Jell-O than either of us probably cares to remember. Dan Liberati taught me the finer points of picking a lock, Bob Cicco and Paul Gertner advised on sleight of hand, while Tony Schaffer was, what can I say, Tony Schaffer.

Mark Shiffman and Frank Dermody solved every legal conundrum I could throw at them, Alan Weiskopf served as an architectural consultant, and Mark Koenig was my bowling guru. Jeanne Baseman, bursting with suggestions, never let me down.

As always, my wonderful parents encouraged, commented, and gave me their valuable perspective.

Before I started writing I could never have imagined how important an agent could be, but without Jake Elwell of the Wieser and Wieser agency, this would not have been.

I am honored to have such a supportive and bright editor as Dan Slater. He truly made the book better.

Finally, it is most important to me to thank my family. My boys, Peter, Brad, and Scott, are a constant source of inspiration. Kim, my wife, was the first I trusted to look at *Hocus Corpus*. The first read is of course a difficult one, smoothing out the rough spots, but she whipped it into readable shape, and I am eternally grateful.

PROLOGUE

Tory Welch couldn't clear her mind. What she needed was a good run, but her doctor had forbidden it, so she sat in the small kitchen of her Aspinwall home, absently rubbing her wrists. If there was any pain, it was only in her mind's eye, but she massaged away as she tried to focus her thoughts. For the moment, the assistant district attorney in Allegheny County propped her feet on Jack Merlin's chair, paying no attention to the prattle coming from the tiny TV sitting on the counter across from her.

Twice she'd run through the channels. Nothing had made the news yet, but it was only a matter of time. Somehow she'd neglected to turn the set off, leaving it on a talk show known only by the first name of the host. No matter how outrageous the topic, it couldn't compete with the nightmare she'd just witnessed.

As the talk show paused for a commercial, Tory went back to the TV, realizing another fifteen minutes had gone by. It was almost noon; a bright splash of sunlight came through the window, beckoning her for a run. This time Tory thought about it seriously.

Each day it took more and more effort to follow her doctor's advice. Naturally her thoughts drifted to Merlin. Whenever she thought about him the corners of her mouth turned up ever so slightly. Her lips parted ever so subtly. And anyone watching would know she felt dreamy.

Merlin was the first guy with whom she'd been in love. Although he was not her first lover, Tory insisted that he was far and away the best, playfully teasing that she was comparison shopping before she met him. For the last year they had lived together in her small, two-story house. Merlin was the chief resident in surgery at the Pittsburgh University

Medical Center, and Tory knew he would be tied up in the OR for at least another hour.

While the TV blared a furniture commercial, Tory dialed the operator at the Medical Center and asked for Merlin to be paged. Instantly she was clicked on hold. Instead of music, however, she was treated to a recorded voice explaining the importance of preventive health care. Then she heard about mammograms, cholesterol, and the benefits of pre-exercise stretching. That got her attention.

Soon she was balancing on one foot, pulling her ankle up behind her until she could feel the quad tighten. By the time the operator clicked back onto the line—blandly informing her that Dr. Merlin was in OR and couldn't possibly be reached—Tony had already finished with her hamstrings and was leaning against the sink to work on her calves.

I tried to reach you, but you were in the OR. Didn't you get the message? Tory rehearsed silently as she headed up the stairs. There was a large mirror in a wooden frame just outside their bedroom door. When she spotted herself in it she paused. Her dark hair was longer now, just as Merlin liked it, falling past her shoulders. Before tying it back in a loose ponytail, Tory unbuttoned her blouse, never once taking her eyes away from her reflection. Her fingers worked smoothly, pulling the silky fabric from her skirt as she undid the last button. Slowly, she slipped it off her shoulders and stood for a good long while. There were still some bruises on her chest, but they were fading. Hesitantly, she turned to the right. Her eyes moved down her torso, coming to rest just below her rib cage. Gently, as if for the first time, she traced the pink scar with her index finger.

Leo Lieberer was a veteran of a hundred jobs and a thousand bar fights. He was mostly a small-time crook who'd never done any real time, but you'd never know it talking to him. Twenty-six years old, muscular, but not in that Gold's Gym bloated sort of way, Leo was the tough guy permanently perched at the end of the bar during football season. A master of turning idle conversations into friendly arguments, Leo juiced them into verbal wars until the veins on his neck popped out like vines on a tree. Closer and closer he would get, breathing all over the guy he was talking to, until his victim would break sweat and quickly offer to buy Leo a drink.

Surprisingly, despite all the fights, Leo was a good-looking guy, sort of a Redford in the rough. But Leo thought his best asset was the tattoo: Leo's Sex Club, Sign Up Below. As much as possible Leo wore short sleeve shirts. That way the tattoo got noticed.

Now he was sitting on the ground, freezing his ass off, hidden from view in a cluster of bushes on a gentle hillside overlooking a small park. The only noise Leo could hear was the faraway sound of traffic way down on the Highland Park Bridge. This time of year the park was usually empty, no more pickup softball games or picnics, just a large field of grass with several acres of surrounding woods. A winding dirt path meandering through the oaks still attracted a few dedicated runners.

It was cold for October. Leo's breath came out in little puffs. He played with them, sometimes pursing his lips tightly, sending out a long thin squirt of condensed moisture. Whenever he took a drink of coffee he could see his breath better, so Leo sipped away, wasting time, checking his watch, feeling for his gun, checking his watch again, and generally hoping she'd get the hell to the park before he froze or fell asleep. He tried opening his mouth wide, letting his breath out slowly so the white vapor would rise past his eyes like a sheer curtain.

"Whaddya got, bad breath or something?"

Leo looked up. It was Tommy, dressed in dark slacks and a light-weight jacket zipped all the way to the neck. "Hey, Tommy, I didn't know you were coming. How's the arm?" Leo asked, eyeing the empty right sleeve of Tommy's jacket, hanging limply at his side like a sausage casing waiting to be filled. Without waiting for an answer he resumed his watch across the park, concentrating on a small cluster of oaks just starting into the reds and oranges of autumn.

"Not too bad." Tommy squatted down. His movements were deliberate, as if he were in pain. When he got all the way down, he set a container of coffee on a flat patch of dirt, then looked across the park and nodded. "The sun's out."

"Good, I'm fuckin' freezing."

Tommy looked at Leo. "No one been by?"

"Uh-uh. Just like I said. One or two early morning joggers, besides that the place's deserted."

"When did you dump him?"

"This morning, nine-thirty. Just like you said."

"Anyone see you?" Tommy asked.

"Nah. Came up through the woods, dumped him, and circled back through the woods to get here."

"You sure she'll see him?"

"See that stump off to the left, behind those weeds? I been following her. Late morning, just before lunch, she walks over. Never here before eleven-thirty. Same thing every time. After she gets to the park she sits there, retying her shoes. Then she stretches before she goes for her little walk. I laid him out real nice, like he's lying on the beach getting a tan, right behind the tree where she stretches. If she was blind she'd see him.''

"What about from the path? Can you see him from there?'' Tommy asked as he produced a napkin from his pocket and began to wipe the dirt from his black shoes. These weren't fancy wing tips like his boss wore, but plain black shoes with thick rubber soles, the kind a clerk in an auto supply store might wear as part of his uniform.

"Nah, only if you go over to the stump. It's perfect. Hey, if you look real close you can sorta make out his feet,'' Leo said and pointed with a nod of his head.

Tommy squinted across the park, then looked at Leo. "Better not.'' He smiled.

Leo realized his mistake. "You know what I mean.''

Tory pulled on a long-sleeved T-shirt, silky running shorts, and her beloved Sauconys. Just before heading out she grabbed a huge Milkbone from a box by the front door and walked out onto her porch.

Mrs. Kincaid, Tory's next-door neighbor and landlady, was puttering about in her yard. The two exchanged greetings while an ugly mutt tore across the yard to accept the treat from Tory.

"You wanna take Pepper with you?'' Mrs. Kincaid called across her yard. "You know she's a good watchdog.''

"I'll be fine, but thanks,'' Tory said, bending over to stroke Pepper a couple of times.

"You should have company when you go for a walk,'' Mrs. Kincaid offered again, pulling her jacket closed around her.

Tory smiled. "I'm not walking today,'' she said softly.

"What?'' Mrs. Kincaid sounded surprised. "Does Merlin know?''

"Of course,'' Tory lied. "I'm as good as new.'' Then she patted Pepper one more time and headed down Ninth Street in the direction of the little park while her landlady shook her head in disapproval.

As Tory crossed Center Avenue she began to jog, tentatively at first, catching her stride just before she got to the park.

"How long you been here?'' Tommy asked, settling his gaze on Leo, reminding him who was in charge.

Leo stroked his upper lip where his mustache used to be. "Like you said, since nine-thirty.''

Tommy looked at his watch. "Got you some coffee.''

"You have it,'' Leo offered as he reached down for a cup which had been sitting outside Tommy's view in the dirt. "Already got one.'' He held out a yellow cup emblazoned with the Wendy's logo as if he was making a toast, then sipped carefully so as not to burn his mouth.

Tommy looked at his watch again. "So you been here, what, two and a half hours?"

"Something like that. Maybe I got here a little before nine-thirty," Leo said, holding his gaze across the little park, setting himself up for an attaboy, letting Tommy know how seriously he took his watch.

"You didn't need to leave or nothing . . . take a leak?"

"Nah. I'm cool." Leo took another sip, making a quiet sucking noise, pulling in a little morning air with the hot java.

"You have a Thermos of coffee hidden away, or what?" Tommy shifted his weight, wanting to put a knee down but opting to stay taller than Leo. When he saw Leo's breath quicken he knew he had him, but he held his tongue, letting Leo stew for a while.

Hearing the question made Leo feel uneasy. He repeated it several times to himself. For an instant he was back in school, listening to the sister say accusingly, "Leo Lieberer, what did you do during recess?" His breathing quickened, taking little puffs that disappeared quickly, but his breath rate was the last thing he was thinking about. "What?" he asked hoarsely, feeling trapped.

"You got here at nine-thirty—"

"Nine-thirty, quarter to ten. I don't know," Leo said, his mind numb with confusion.

"Okay, a little *after*. So how'd ya keep the coffee warm?"

Shit. Leo took a deep breath. "Look, I got really cold. Took me five minutes to run over to Wendy's. The park was empty. Christ, she never gets here 'til after eleven-thirty. Now that she's back at work—"

"She's home."

Leo thought about this. "Oh."

Tommy rubbed his face. He was tired of looking after his fuckup. "Lookit how you're dressed. Leo's Sex Club," he read aloud from his biceps in a condescending tone. "How the hell do you think that's gonna look when you got some kids of your own?" Tommy picked up the coffee he'd brought, popped a hole in the plastic lid, and took a sip.

Leo looked down at himself. His black sweatshirt had the sleeves cut off so the tattoo showed. He wore jeans that snugly hugged his narrow waist. Whenever he moved or stretched, his sweatshirt lifted up, exposing a tight flash of abdomen. And he wore boots, hand-tooled cowboy boots that cost more than everything on Tommy's back.

As hard as Leo tried, he couldn't think of a damn thing to say. The silence was growing, driving Leo more crazy than anything Tommy could say. He didn't even know what to do with his hands so he wiped his mouth, checked his watch, and patted the bulge in his hip pocket.

Tommy smiled, knowing the bulge in Leo's pocket was a gun, wedged in tightly enough so anyone could tell it was a revolver from the outside. But what really tickled Tommy was the thought of Leo almost having to slide his pants down any time he needed to pull out his weapon. "How's your gun?" Tommy asked.

"Huh?"

"What are you calling it today? You know, your roscoe. Your piece."

"Oh," Leo said in a little voice, "I didn't hear you."

"Maybe if you ever wise up you'll thank me for not letting you shoot that thing off last night, but I doubt it."

Leo looked confused.

Tommy continued with a warning. "Remember, don't ever shoot that fuckin' thing near me."

"I know. I know. What's the big deal, anyway?"

"Forget it, just keep it away from me. Wise up, okay? Partnering with you wasn't my idea, but dumping you will be," Tommy said flatly.

Suddenly Leo blurted out, "Hey, over there!" signaling with a quick upward jerk of his head toward the entrance to the park, directly across from where the body had been dumped.

Both men ducked down.

A little girl, no more than four or five, was walking into the park, doing her best to control a large dog.

Tommy thought it was a collie.

Leo thought it was great there was something else for Tommy to worry about.

The little girl struggled to walk the dog around the grassy field, but the canine wouldn't cooperate and pulled his preschool master straight across the field, toward the path that led into the woods.

"Shit, she's going toward the path. The dog'll smell him. Shit! Shit!! Shit!!" Tommy hissed. "Okay, get down there, fast."

"What difference does it make who finds him? He's gonna get found eventually."

"I want *her* to find him. Get off your ass and do something! We want to make sure he gets recognized."

"What about his driver's license?"

"This is why I had to come check up on you." Tommy pulled out a calfskin wallet from his jacket pocket and flipped it on the ground in front of Leo. "I parked next to you. Found it behind your car."

"Must've slipped out when I pulled him out of the trunk."

"I don't want it to take a week while they confirm he's really dead. Now get the fuck down there and do something."

"Then why didn't we just leave him in his house?"

"Because I want to make sure she sees what we did to him. Now take care of the kid," Tommy demanded.

"What am I supposed to do? Kill her?"

"Go down and call her dog. Whistle or something. Yeah, whistle; call the stupid mutt over and pet him. Maybe throw a stick or something and get the dog away from where you dumped him."

Leo pushed himself up and started down the grassy slope toward the little girl. He gave a short series of whistles, each starting in mid-range and rising in pitch until the sound disappeared from his lips. "Here, boy," he said encouragingly.

The dog and the little girl must not have heard him because they kept heading toward the woods.

By now a second person had entered the park. This time it was a jogger.

Tommy recognized the runner and immediately started calling, "Pssssst. Psssst," to Leo. Then he snapped his fingers, like he was trying to get a waiter's attention in a restaurant.

Leo turned around and watched Tommy's hand signals motioning him to get back in the bushes, but Leo wrinkled up his brow and spun around to see what the hell was going on.

Tory's side was barely hurting, so she slowly picked up the pace. After taking her pulse—ninety-seven—she jogged into the park, planning on a couple of lazy laps before heading into the woods. The day smelled wonderful, and she pulled air in through her nose, releasing it through her mouth. Her face caught the sun, and she picked up the pace some more. Everything was falling into a groove as Tory concentrated on the soft sound her Sauconys made on the thick grass.

Then she heard the scream. Not a squeal or a yell from a skinned knee. A scream. A loud, piercing, high-pitched sound of utter terror, making the little hairs on Tory's arm stand at attention.

Someone had seen the devil.

She stopped running and saw the little girl drop the leash to the ground, her back toward Tory, looking down into the brush where her dog was nosing around. The screams continued. The terrified child stood frozen, staring at the most frightening thing she had ever seen.

Tory was at her side in seconds, putting her hand gently on the child's trembling shoulders. "Hey, sweetie, what's wrong . . . my God." Before her thoughts took shape she saw the body lying in the brush. It was a man, obviously dead. Tory felt a terror in her gut and fought the urge to scream a duet with the little girl. Instead, she put her arm around the frightened child. "All right, sweetie, everything's gonna be okay. Everything's okay. You live around here?" Tory babbled.

The little girl nodded, then vomited on the grass right in front of Tory.

"You run home and tell your mother to call the police. Go!"

The little girl, grateful to be dismissed from the horrible scene, turned and ran, forgetting about her dog, not noticing the blond-haired man settling himself back down in the bushes on the little hill as she sped by.

Tory swallowed and inched closer. *Please don't get sick. Let me get through this.* The body was supine, dressed in a suit, dark blue with subtle white pinstripes. The jacket lay open. The label was clearly visible: J. Press.

The shirt was bloody, stained so dark that Tory couldn't tell what color it was supposed to be. The dog was sniffing the body, licking at a crimson clot of blood that looked like a glob of dark gelatin.

He had no hands. *My God, where are his hands?* The sleeves of the jacket had bloody shirt cuffs sticking out but ending limply, giving them the appearance of being hugely oversized, like a kid wearing his dad's sport coat.

Involuntarily, Tory began to massage her wrists. Her eyes furiously looked around, flitting about in search of the missing hands. First the bushes. Then the tree stump and the surrounding woods. Finally back to the body. Nothing.

Her eyes wandered down his legs. It was almost no surprise to see he had no feet. A bloody stump protruded from one of the pant legs and some grassy strands stuck to the clotted blood.

Then Tory looked at his face and felt a rush of acidic bile come charging up her esophagus, filling her mouth with a sour burn. Her body dumped adrenaline in her bloodstream, and her heart rate soared. The man had been severely beaten, his face swollen and dark purple. The nose was flattened, a black curd of blood sat beneath it like a tiny mustache. His forehead was bashed in, making his hairline recede, and his eyebrows were almost pushed down to meet his cheekbones.

But the strangest part was he seemed to be smoking a little cigar. A stogie, three, maybe four inches long. It was a sick joke. Someone actually thought it was funny to beat the life out of this guy, chop his hands and feet off, and make sure he was sucking on one of his favorite cigars.

In the distance the sirens could be heard. It would be another minute or two before they arrived.

The body's features were so terribly distorted he should have been totally unrecognizable. Tory walked closer, drew her breath in, and bent down to take a look at him.

That's when she realized it wasn't a stogie hanging out of his mouth. It was a severed finger. She felt faint, quickly dropping to her knees to keep from passing out.

Tory Welch knew exactly who this man was. There was absolutely no doubt.

1

Sixteen days earlier

It had been an emotionally exhausting week for Jack Merlin, the worst during his tenure as chief resident in general surgery. There were three postop surgical deaths. All three were unexpected.

No matter how many times a doctor witnessed those last agonal breaths before the EKG went silent, it never got any easier. Somehow, though, when a patient's condition gradually deteriorated while treatment after treatment failed, it was tolerated.

But when a patient was lost who should not have died, the very thought of it ate away at the soul of everyone involved. It was true even for the physicians who spent a good deal of energy posturing and rationalizing in order to fit the casualty into a more convenient category.

There was a tradition in the department of surgery at the Medical Center. Each week every member of the department, from the lowly medical students assigned to hold retractors in the OR to the most senior attendings, showed up for Morbidity and Mortality Rounds. It had gone on for as long as anyone remembered and often provided quite a show.

Everyone convened in the small surgical amphitheater—a fifty-seater with severely banked sides so even the back row had a great view. If you dropped your pen and bent over to retrieve it, you'd get a mouthful of hair from the person one seat below. By convention, it was the responsibility of the chief resident to chair the meeting. This was a time surgeons bared their souls.

Morbidity and Mortality Rounds was a brutally honest, occasionally ruthless, discussion of the surgical failures and disasters of the preceding week. The most pointed barbs often came from Jonathan Olsen, the pompous and brilliant chairman of pathology. More than anyone else in the department, Olsen, ballooning his way up to 270 pounds, stood out during the proceedings with his bald cranium and salt-and-pepper beard. An unlit pipe was as much a part of his image as his freshly laundered three-quarter length white coat. The ass-pinching seats in the amphitheater were unkind to his form, but that didn't stop him from squeezing into one each week.

While surgeons routinely made decisions in the operating room and rarely got a chance to sit around and cogitate about the next cut of the scalpel, Olsen had all the time in the world. If a particular specimen was confusing, he could get a cup of coffee with several colleagues who would offer up their opinions. By the time Morbidity and Mortality Rounds rolled around each week, Olsen came prepared with every answer to every question and never hesitated to be openly critical of his surgical colleagues' actions in the operating room.

The preceding week had seemed like a recurrent nightmare. Three STAT pages to surgical postop floors for patients in septic shock. Three unsuccessful cardiac resuscitations. Three unexpected deaths. All were from overwhelming bacterial infections. Not one of the patients had responded to IV antibiotics.

One of those patient deaths belonged to Merlin.

The conference always started late. Therefore Merlin didn't even approach the chrome-and-glass lectern until ten after the hour. He had been in the OR early and was now dressed in a blue scrub shirt and white pants.

Each case was presented by the chief resident, succinctly and without editorial comment by way of body language or subtle inflections of his voice.

The first case had been a fifty-seven-year-old man with severe chronic lung disease. He had been back and forth between the hospital and his home multiple times each year for any number of problems. This time he had been admitted to the hospital for surgical treatment of bedsores. Four days after the minor surgery, he was dead from a Staphylococcus infection.

A stylish doctor named Duncan, hair plugs sprouting from his scalp like newly planted grass in the spring, was the attending surgeon. Duncan always sat near the door and had a standing arrangement with his secretary to beep him out at precisely twenty minutes past the hour so he could get back to his own lucrative practice.

Today Duncan had requested his case be presented first and sat rather stiffly with his leather briefcase on his lap. When Merlin finished the case presentation Duncan spoke up. "Everything went smoothly. Skin-to-skin in less than forty-five minutes. Sterility was never broken, and I performed a routine debridement of two decubiti that never should have been there." Duncan paused momentarily and looked several rows down, taking comfort in the fact that Jonathan Olsen wasn't turned around in his seat glaring at him. Never mind that his office was filling up with patients and that conference time wasn't billable. He had some momentum going. "Hell, I even covered him—"

Duncan's beeper went off, causing several wrists to turn simultaneously, so the accuracy of their timepieces could be checked. One surgeon even took his watch off to reset it.

Without looking down, Duncan silenced his beeper and continued. "—with prophylactic antibiotics, the first dose administered in the recovery room. In my opinion, he was getting second-rate care at home and probably should have been in a nursing facility. His family probably never got him out of bed, for crissake." Duncan looked around at his colleagues, making certain he wasn't laying it on too thick. There was no eye rolling or head shaking. "He probably came in here with a deep wound infection that we would have been chasing for weeks." The room was silent. Duncan gave Merlin a little nod, indicating the chief resident should move on to the next case.

Merlin looked around. Under different circumstances, maybe sitting in the back of the amphitheater with a group of residents, he would have whispered, "Let me translate that bullshit. The patient was asking to die and already had enough surgeries in the last year to pay off Duncan's Lexus, so it didn't really matter." But the top brass of the department were sitting right there, and Merlin let the thought go.

Jonathan Olsen cleared his throat, his uncomfortable seat squeaking under the strain of his doughboy body. "Let me make a comment or two, Duncan, if you can spare a minute. Indeed the Staph I recovered was multiply drug resistant, a pretty nasty bug we haven't seen before. And I concur it was a wound infection. But I have no way of knowing whether the patient came into the hospital with it or developed it here." Duncan seemed to breathe a sigh of relief just before Olsen added, "And, Duncan, you tell your secretary next time you see her, she was almost four minutes late with her page."

Now there was some laughter and eye rolling. Someone rubbed his thumb against his fingers in a greedy gesture, but no one leveled any criticism of the way the case had been managed. In fact, Merlin thought the quality of the surgical treatment had been very reasonable.

Duncan chose to ignore the teasing, actually seeming relieved no one had any more comments. As he left his chair he muttered a brief, "Thank you," and shot out the door.

*   *   *

Tommy and Leo drove up to the Friendship Club, a small, green, cinder block building by the railroad tracks on the fringe of a blue-collar neighborhood. They were in Tommy's big old Chrysler, a ten-year-old monster guaranteed to make a statement whenever he drove through this tired neighborhood. Tommy did a lot of things for the boss but mostly ran special errands. Any trip to the Friendship Club concerned one of those special errands.

The two had met for the first time only an hour before at Ritter's Diner near Oakland. Tommy was waiting outside when his new partner arrived. Immediately Tommy knew who it was by the tattoo but didn't introduce himself until Leo was seated in the back.

"You've gotta be Leo," was all Tommy said as he slid into the booth.

"You're Tommy. You must've spotted my tatt," Leo said, pleased he had something going for him that got him instant recognition.

Before either could say another word a cute waitress with big hair, her blouse opened one more button than it should have been, appeared. "What can I get you guys?"

"Just some coffee," Tommy said, but the waitress was staring at Leo's biceps, unable to take her eyes off the tattoo, standing there like a schoolgirl in the presence of a movie star.

Leo nodded his head, a sneaky smile crossing his lips, encouraging her to say what he knew she was thinking.

The waitress was smiling at Leo, wiggling her pencil back and forth like she was dying to make the next move but sensing he was trouble.

For the moment Leo forgot why he was in Ritter's in the first place. He tugged at his blond mustache where it curled around his mouth. "How 'bout some coffee and fries with gravy."

She read Leo's biceps again and bit her lower lip.

"I'll just have coffee." Tommy's voice had an edge.

"Where do you sign up?" she finally asked, her cheeks turning a coy shade of pink.

"I'll bet you'd like to know," Leo began. "What's your name?"

"Wanda." She tapped her oval name tag with her pencil and giggled.

"Look, why don't you write me down your number. Maybe I'll call you and show you my dotted line."

Wanda giggled again and scribbled her phone number on a scrap of paper. "You said fries with gravy and coffee, right?"

"That's right, cutie-pie." Then Leo looked at Tommy. "You said coffee."

"Forget it. Just give me some water," Tommy muttered. While Wanda disappeared, Leo watched her ass moving beneath the white bow of her waitress apron. "If all you want is a piece of that, I'm outta here."

"What?" Leo sounded surprised. "I'm not gonna call her. Just fooling with her."

"That's not the point. This is business. Keep your dotted line in your pants."

"Okay, okay," Leo said with a tone that seemed a little condescending to Tommy.

"Watch how you talk to me, asshole."

"Hey, take it easy, Tommy. We're working together. You're the boss—thanks, Wanda," Leo said as Wanda placed a plate full of french fries smothered in gravy and a steaming cup of black coffee in front of him. "So what's going on here? Things are hopping and you need some help, right?"

"Something like that." Already Tommy was having doubts about his new partner.

"Well, you're sitting with the right guy to make things happen."

"Listen to me, you little shit." Tommy leaned forward on both elbows as he whispered coarsely, "Quit acting like you're some fuckin' James Bond. You're not running the show. And you better keep your mouth shut and stay in line."

"Hey, all I meant was I'm your man. That's all. You're the boss, okay?" As Leo stabbed the fries, sopping up as much gravy as possible, he ticked off as many of his accomplishments as possible. Steelworker. Bouncer. Rent Collector. Bouncer. Barkeep. Even a stint at Kennywood guessing people's weight. "You done any time, man?"

"Jesus Christ," was all Tommy would say.

"Just in case you're wondering," Leo added, "I've done it all. So I can handle whatever it is you need me to do. Lemme show you what I carry."

Tommy whipped his head around. The restaurant was filling up. "Forget it."

"That's the beauty of it. No one will notice."

"Not here," Tommy said like a father reprimanding his child in the restaurant.

"What do you carry?" Leo wanted to know.

There was one more fry on Leo's plate. "You finished?" Tommy wanted to know, evading the question.

"Yeah, yeah, I'm done." Leo gulped some coffee. "Don't you carry?"

"Not unless I havta."

"You know what I got? Smith and Wesson loaded with .38 caliber Special plus P hollow points. It'll stop a rhino."

"Whaddya, memorize that shit from the box? Hey, big shot, you ever shoot it at anybody?"

Leo hesitated just a second, long enough for Tommy to wonder if he was full of shit. "Fuck yeah," Leo said, watching for a reaction from Tommy. "It hides very well." Leo scootched forward in the booth so that he could stretch his legs out.

Tommy glanced around. "I said, not here."

"It's small, Tommy. Not to worry. These jerks won't have a clue." Now he was sliding his fingers down into the hip pocket of his ultra-tight jeans.

"Don't be a jerk," Tommy said and looked around, craning his neck all the way back toward the cash register.

Leo shifted, wiggling back and forth, trying to get hold of the gun. His body was stretched out until his feet were under Tommy's legs, his butt cheeks resting on the very edge of the red-padded bench while his shoulder blades rode the top of the booth. Evidently Leo needed to see what was going on in his pants, because he twisted his head around uncomfortably, trying to look under the table.

By the time he fished the weapon from his pants, Tommy was gone, a crumpled buck for the water on the table. Leo had to sprint out of Ritter's cupping the Smith and Wesson in the palm of his hand so Tommy wouldn't drive off without him.

Merlin then presented the second case. This one involved a middle-aged woman with ovarian cancer. Although her chemotherapy was nearing a successful completion, she had been admitted with incapacitating constipation, a complication of her previous surgeries which left scars in her abdomen that kinked her bowels and blocked her intestinal flow. A simple laparotomy was performed to release the adhesions, but she had died three days later.

The preliminary diagnosis after her autopsy was overwhelming E. coli infection, resistant to antibiotics.

Her surgeon, a nerdy fellow named Ford, wearing thick-framed glasses, sat up stiffly in his seat. "Ken," he said with a tone of superiority, looking around to find one of Merlin's senior residents, "I think you can speak about this case." And just like that he was off the hook.

Ken shifted in his seat, surprised to be called upon. "Actually the case went smoothly. We released half a dozen adhesions, ran the bowel, and sent her off to recovery in excellent condition. She was septic within forty-eight hours."

Now Ford chimed in. "Everything went well—perfectly—just as Ken reported. Of course I scrubbed out before closure, so whatever happened after I left, well, I trust Ken did his usual high quality work."

A doctor in the back asked, "Any possibility you nicked her bowel?"

Ford stared at Ken as if he, too, had wondered whether Ken had unleashed the deadly bacteria from the intestines.

"I worried about that," Ken began, "so I went down—"

Olsen shifted around in his chair, straining the nuts and bolts that held the seat together. His eyes bore into Ford. "Ken made the effort to come down and watch the autopsy, Ford. Ken asked *me* to run the bowel and look for peritonitis. Everything looked okay."

"Oh," Ford said, embarrassed by the one-upmanship.

"You'll be interested to know I got some pus from the suture line," Olsen continued. "Looked like a wound infection. Those bugs didn't come from the bowel. A bit of a mystery perhaps, but with her immune system weakened from the chemotherapy, any infection could get out of control."

Olsen sent Ken the briefest of nods then looked over at Ford. "By the way, Ford, I faxed your office directions to the morgue. Next time I'll expect to see you when I do the post."

"Thank you, Jonathan." The words oozed from Ford's mouth. "I might just take you up on that."

Finally it was Merlin's turn.

"The final case is mine, that of John Gonzales," Merlin began, his voice thick. "This was the second time I'd operated on Mr. Gonzales. Fifty-two years old, an insulin-dependent diabetic for thirty years. Unfortunately he didn't watch what he ate and was always out of control. A wonderful person but a terrible patient. This time Mr. Gonzales came in with gangrene of his lower leg. We did a below-the-knee amputation and covered him with antibiotics. He spiked a fever, and we added a second antibiotic. Twenty-four hours later, he went into septic shock. It was Staphylococcus, resistant to every antibiotic the lab can test for."

Although Olsen had little to add to this case, he couldn't resist an opportunity to be didactic. "This was a classic case: a diabetic in poor control with bad vascular disease. Perfect setup for sepsis. I pulled some pus from the wound, grew out Staphylococcus. Not much you can do with drug-resistant Staphylococcus. Look, folks, I sense we'll all be happy to put this week behind us. These superbugs should terrify every one of us. This isn't the first time we've dealt with them, and it won't be the last, either. But it doesn't mean we as a department should do anything different. Treat infections properly. The indiscriminate use of antibiotics should be avoided because that's what got us in this predicament in the first place.''

When Jonathan Olsen finished speaking, the conference broke up. There was no chitchat afterwards. These were busy people, and the room cleared quickly.

Tommy flipped open the glove compartment and took out a small cardboard box, opened it under Leo's nose, and checked the contents. Nestled in a bed of toilet paper was a condom, double-knotted halfway down. Inside the rubber were a couple of teaspoons of light brown liquid.

Not wanting to say, "Hey what's that?" and have Tommy not answer him back, Leo waited for the man to tell him exactly what was going on.

Before he got out of the Chrysler, Tommy dropped the condom with the light brown liquid back in the box.

The mystery was killing Leo. What the hell was in that box? *What the fuck is up with that shit?* They were walking up to the Friendship Club, getting closer to the front door, and he didn't want Tommy to be in the middle of an explanation when they got inside. The goddamn thing was driving him crazy.

Finally, as Tommy reached for the door, Leo said, "Hey, yo, wait a second, this ain't a clinic for artificial inspermination or anything, is it?" And he laughed, like he'd said something funny, so Tommy wouldn't jump all over him.

"Nope, it's a private bar," Tommy answered, not bothering to hold the door for his new partner.

It took a few seconds for their eyes to adjust in the dim light of the club. Leo was still thinking about the box as their pupils doubled in size and the club came into view. The Friendship Club amounted to a collection of junk, an eclectic array of kitchen tables fitted with an equally mismatched assortment of chairs. A handsome oak bar that was too big for the space looked as if it might have been salvaged from an old tavern when it was torn down. Behind the bar was a guy who stopped eating from a plate of eggs when he saw Tommy and Leo walk in. From all the way across the room, Leo could see his massive neck. If the top two buttons of his shirt hadn't been left open, it would have hung over his collar.

Half a dozen guys—the regulars—sat around a Formica table, playing a little acey-deucey. When they saw the visitors they immediately switched to three-card monte. Tommy walked over to the bar. The bartender with the neck was working on a piece of bacon. Between chews he said, "He ain't here yet. He called."

"What do you got to drink while I wait?" Tommy asked, letting the bartender know he was staying, whether or not he was invited.

"Shot'n a beer."

"That'll work."

The bartender reached under the bar and brought out a shot glass with a little chip missing from the rim. He poured from a label Tommy didn't recognize, then pulled a bottle of Iron City from an old Frigidaire.

By now Leo had wandered over to the card game. One of the regulars was acting as dealer, working the three cards on the table. Each card had been given a longitudinal fold, so that when they were placed on the table facedown, they looked like three pup tents, all lined up. Two of the cards were numbered, the third was the queen of hearts.

At the beginning of each hand the dealer made a point to show the queen. Then he placed the three cards on the table facedown and casually changed the order of the cards by sliding them around the table. Sometimes he would pick them up and throw them back down on the table with a flourish, but mostly he slid them around.

The other guys at the table, pretty much ignoring Leo, were putting down five and ten dollar bets on where they thought the queen was. Leo didn't say word one, but he could find her every time. Three hands were played, and he stepped closer and closer. It seemed so obvious. At one point an old guy wearing a topcoat, sitting nervously behind a ten dollar bet, started to point to the wrong card. Leo couldn't resist. "Yo, Mister I-don't-pay-attention, try one card to the left."

Topcoat listened to the advice and collected ten bucks from the dealer. First he offered a nod of thanks to Leo. Then he put a fiver right in front of an open chair at the table and used his foot to slide the chair away from the table.

That was all the invitation Leo needed. He bet the fin, smiling at the regulars as he watched the cards change positions, tapping a card with his thumb, and doubling his money. Cocksure of himself, he wanted Tommy to see him now, but he was still over at the bar talking with the bartender, draining his beer.

Leo let the ten ride. His was the only bet this time, but Leo didn't seem to take notice. The game was too exciting.

As the dealer worked the cards slowly about the table he squinted at Leo's arm. "Whatcha got there? Leo's Sex Club," he read with a tone of admiration. "Bet that gets you laid all the time."

"Ya got a couple of hours?" Leo asked, and everyone let out one of those group laughs that men always do when someone tells a good dirty joke.

All this time the cards kept moving across the Formica, sliding past one another. When the laughter died down, and Leo had swiveled left and right in his chair so that everyone could read the tattoo for himself, the dealer picked up one of the cards so that he held it between his fingers at one end and his thumb at the other. He even turned his wrist so he could show Leo what card he was holding. The queen. A freebie.

A second later he snatched one of the other cards in the same hand, then immediately threw them back down on the table, one at a time.

Leo assumed, as he was supposed to, that the second card picked up—the numbered card—would be the first card thrown down. But the longitudinal fold in the cards that made them so easy to manipulate also made it easy for the dealer to throw down the top card first.

In the blink of Leo's very blind eye, the cards, now facedown, had changed order.

The problem with street corner three-card monte—and the reason no magician would ever go one-on-one with a three-card monte dealer— is that there are any number of ways to cheat. Too much happened too quickly. If you were sitting there with ten bucks on the table, your heart thumping loudly in your head, you couldn't possibly tell which card was the queen, even if you knew some kind of cheating was going on.

Casually, Leo tapped a card with his thumb, the one that should have been the queen, the one that *was* the queen every time the cards had been dealt before. And when the dealer flipped Leo's card over, Leo did a classic Looney Tunes double take, his eyes bulging as if they might pop out of his head.

No one made a sound or looked around. The hum of the Frigidaire behind the bar and the clock ticking on the wall suddenly seemed very loud. For one terribly long moment there was a hint of doubt in each of the regulars' eyes that Leo would pay up without making trouble.

But Leo muttered, "Damn," and got out his wallet.

Topcoat even helped out, muttering something like, "Sonovabitch, I thought you had it," while Leo bet ten dollars of his own money.

The cards were moved around. The dealer accidentally dropped one of the cards halfway through the routine, giving Leo a little peek at the queen. When the cards stopped moving, Leo picked the wrong one. Again.

Two more rounds, and Leo was twenty bucks lighter in the wallet. Finally Tommy tapped Leo on the shoulder. "We gotta go."

"What about the guy?"

"Came and went. Let's go."

"One more hand," Leo said, then turned to the dealer. "Deal. Deal! DEAL! I don't have all fuckin' day." Leo ripped open his wallet and pulled out everything he had. "Nineteen bucks. Let's go, c'mon. Deal."

"Why don't we call it an even twenty," the dealer said, and put a buck of his own in front of Leo.

The cards were moved around quickly, picked up and thrown on the table several times with a lot more flourish, this being the last hand. Leo sat forward and studied the table. The cards stopped moving and Leo studied some more. He needed a glass of water. The game had grown deadly serious for him, and he had absolutely no idea where the goddamn queen was. His lips were suddenly so dry that he rubbed furiously at them.

"C'mon, Leo, we gotta go," Tommy urged.

"Gimme a sec. I *know* it's one of these two," Leo said, pointing his finger at two of the cards. "Motherfucker. This was a lot easier before." Leo slammed his hand down on a card.

The dealer flipped it over. Seven of diamonds.

"SHIT!" Leo slapped the table.

"Look, you're a nice guy," the dealer said. "Tell you what. Two cards left. Put another bet down. Fifty-fifty chance. Win some of your money back."

Leo turned to Tommy. "Gimme some money. This is a lock. I know which one it is."

"No fuckin' way. You don't know what the hell you're doing."

"I'll pay you back, man. I'm not going outta here with these jerks having all my money."

Tommy opened his wallet. "It'll come outta your pay."

"How much you got?" Leo snapped, more as a statement than a question. He lifted his head to look inside Tommy's wallet. "Gimme thirty, no, make it fifty."

Tommy threw three tens on the table. Leo slapped the other card hard, shaking the table. Hungrily, Leo grabbed the card, crumpling it in his hand as he turned it over. Nine of clubs.

Tommy shook his head and walked toward the door.

Leo grabbed for the third card.

The dealer's fat hand slapped down hard, beating Leo's bony fingers to it.

"I wanna see it."

"You pay to play, pal. Put a bet down, you see the card."

Leo looked to the door. It was closing slowly and Tommy was gone.

"You know I'm tapped out."

"Then you better go ask your buddy for some spare change."

"Tommy. TOMMY!" Leo waited. "Fuck." He looked at the dealer, his fat fingers covering the down-turned card. "And fuck you, you cheater." Leo stood up and worked his hand into his pocket, using his fingers in the confined space like a pair of tweezers, barely grabbing the butt of the Smith and Wesson. He worked it up through the fabric like he was delivering a baby.

The thick-necked bartender said, "Hey, buddy, you won't make it to the door."

Leo stopped. No one was showing a gun, but suddenly he was scared in there all alone. He looked at the dealer with his fat paw on the card and the bartender with the neck standing behind the bar with a white dish towel over one shoulder.

"I'll be back!" he screamed as he stormed out, but before the door closed, he heard them all laughing.

2

The STAT page reached Merlin just as he came out of the OR. Because he was the chief resident, Merlin scrubbed on the most challenging cases. It was now mid-morning. Already he'd been in surgery for more than three hours repairing a ruptured aorta. He hadn't had time to see any of his own patients.

The voice belonged to a female, broadcast from a tiny speaker on his yellow beeper. "Dr. Merlin, STAT to Ten South. Cardiac arrest. STAT to Ten South. Cardiac arrest." Although the voice from the beeper was calm to the point of being blasé, the message was taken seriously. No time for a quick call to Ten South to verify what was going on. In fact Merlin's first instinct shot him down the hallway, past the elevators, and up three flights of stairs. Before Merlin reached the tenth floor it hit him: he was not being paged to a routine cardiac arrest.

Every cardiac arrest that occurred in the Medical Center—regardless of whose service the patient was admitted under—was attended by a team of doctors and nurses called the STAT team. Although a medical resident typically was in charge of the resuscitation, several other specialties were required. An anesthesiologist was needed to intubate the patient, and a surgeon was always available to perform a cutdown for venous access if the patient was in shock and no IV could be established.

At the Pittsburgh University Medical Center it was the responsibility of the second-year surgical resident to respond to the STAT pages. Not the chief resident.

Merlin realized he wasn't being paged as part of the STAT team. Something deep within his gut told him he was being summoned by Mr. Blaine Huffman. This was not the first time Merlin had been called to the bedside of six-year-old Katherine Huffman.

* * *

Two days earlier he had been cornered by the chief of surgery and informed that Blaine Huffman, *the* Blaine Huffman, requested a personal consultation with the chief resident. After spending forty-five minutes reviewing the six-inch-thick medical chart on his new patient, Merlin had gone to Katherine's room on the tenth floor. Dressed in his typical blue surgical scrub shirt and white pants, he politely knocked on the open door before stepping inside to find six-year-old Katherine sitting cross-legged on her hospital bed, surrounded by her vast collection of Beanie Babies. It was a large corner room, one that had two views of Oakland. Colorful, vibrant flowers filled the wide windowsills, and a cluster of silver balloons was tethered to the side rail of the bed.

Katherine was thin and pale, her skin an orange hue usually associated with waxy Halloween candy.

Mrs. Huffman dutifully stood by her daughter's bedside, looking smart in a suit from one of those one-name designers favored by wealthy housewives who insisted on overdressing no matter what the situation. Her delicate wrists were adorned with enough gold and diamonds to guarantee that even the visually impaired would notice.

Mr. Huffman was at one of the windows in tie and shirtsleeves, giving Merlin a view of his back, talking rapidly on his cellular phone. Merlin guessed him to be about fifty, but he was trim enough to be mistaken for forty. Even standing by the window, staring out at the campus of the University of Pittsburgh, Blaine Huffman projected an unmistakable aura that went along with the ability to buy anything his eyes could see.

For a moment Merlin wondered what Huffman would say if reminded cellular phones were not permitted in the hospital. "Hi, are you Katherine? I'm Dr. Merlin."

Before the child could possibly say a word, Mrs. Huffman turned to greet Merlin, her matching triplet of heavy gold bangles clanging against each other expensively. "Dr. Merlin, I'm so glad to meet you. I'm Mrs. Huffman, but please call me Cynthia. We've heard so much about you. And this is our precious little girl. Kit, dear, say hi to Dr. Merlin."

"Hi," Kit said, and broke into a wide smile. Kit, despite being horribly jaundiced, was adorable. Her hair was in two tight braids that just made it to her shoulders. When she smiled, Merlin couldn't help smiling back, and he helped himself to a seat on the bed.

"Which is your favorite Beanie Baby, Kit?" Merlin asked, about to launch into a discussion of the popular plush animals that would win him a place in his young patient's heart.

"I like this one best," Kit answered, holding up a white dog with black splotches.

Merlin hunted through Kit's expensive pile of Beanie Babies. "You know which one I like?"

By now Mr. Huffman had finished his phone call. Never imagining Merlin could possibly be doing something important, he immediately interrupted. "Kitten, why don't you line up all your Beanies. I'm sure Dr. Merlin will look at them later. Now I've got to talk with Dr. Merlin before I go back to the office." Kit did as she was told while Mr. Huffman gave Merlin a perfunctory handshake. "I appreciate your coming up, Dr. Merlin."

"Hey, call me Merlin."

Cynthia took her place by the bed, letting the men conduct their business. She touched one of Kit's braids softly, making a gentle adjustment so her daughter looked perfect.

Before the handshake was over, Mr. Huffman was talking. "Listen, what I wanted to talk to you about is this central line they want to put in Kit this afternoon."

"I reviewed your daughter's chart and—"

"Kit was born with biliary atresia—I assume you're familiar with the condition—"

Merlin nodded. Biliary atresia was serious, often life threatening, the result of a massively clogged system for draining the bile from the liver.

"—and had surgery—the Kasai procedure—that, unfortunately, has failed. Now she's waiting for a liver transplant—top of the list, incidentally—and she needs to be in the best possible nutritional shape so she's fit for surgery. She's got no appetite, so her doctors want her on hyperalimentation. Ergo, Kit needs a central line."

The procedure Huffman was talking about—placement of a central line in one of the larger veins of the body for nutritional support—was relatively simple. Merlin was confused why he had been consulted, but recognized Mr. Huffman's tone as he finished speaking. Huffman was clearly the type who expected Merlin to say, "Gotcha," and speed off to make preparations for his daughter. But Merlin wanted to understand his role in Kit's case, so he said, "And I understand it will be done in the OR because of her—"

At once Huffman held up his hand to silence Merlin. He had an agenda and was evidently on a tight schedule. "My daughter's got no PT or PTT. You've gotta make an incision rather than poking it through the skin so any bleeding can be controlled."

Merlin was impressed. Although Mr. Huffman had the wrong idea about PT and PTT—which measured how quickly her blood clotted and were both abnormal in Kit's case because her liver disease inhibited the production of clotting factors—he was obviously well informed and not in the mood for a physiology lecture. "May I ask you a question?"

Before Huffman could respond there was a soft ringing sound, and like a soldier snapping to attention with a salute for a superior officer, the cell phone was at his ear and he instantly became engrossed in some aspect of an important financial deal.

Merlin turned to Cynthia. "I'm curious why you chose me to do the procedure. Kit has a superb group of doctors looking after her."

Cynthia smiled and took a small step forward. "Well, as you can see, Mr. Huffman is very organized. He spoke to the chairman of surgery. You came very highly recommended. He even arranged with the insurance company to cover some sort of an experimental drug so Kit's body won't reject her new liver—"

Huffman snapped his fingers two times and held his hand out with one finger pointed up to the ceiling. *Give me a minute, please.* Then he showed them his back and looked out the window, forcing Merlin and Cynthia to wait in silence and listen.

"Look, I don't care what you heard, Europe is the target. Screw Asia. It's Europe—"

While Mr. Huffman clicked off a series of orders about seemingly important minutiae, Merlin sat back down on the bed. He reached into one of his pockets and innocently pulled out two small squares of silk, a blue one and a red one, each the size of a Kleenex. "Wanna see a magic trick?" he whispered to Kit.

Kit looked at her mom. "Sure." She clutched a Beanie Baby that looked like a kitten to her chest and gave her attention to Merlin.

"Okay, watch closely. These are like handkerchiefs, but they're actually magical. First I'll put the blue one in my hand." Merlin made a loose fist with his left hand and carefully stuffed the blue silk inside until it completely disappeared. "Now I'll put the red silk *on top* of the blue one." And the magician did the same thing with the red silk, pushing it in tightly, right behind the blue one. "Here comes the magic. I'll shake my hand"—Merlin gave his hand a wiggly kind of shake— "and . . . presto! They've *switched places.*" Merlin pulled the blue silk from the *bottom* of his fist, followed by the red one. He ended with a triumphant smile.

Kit smiled, too, pleased to be able to figure out the trick so easily. "Hey, you put them in the *top* of your hand but you took them out the *bottom* of your hand."

Merlin frowned. "No, you *think* that's what I did, but the silks changed places in my hand. It was magic. Let me do it again."

Kit was enjoying herself, and Cynthia was content to watch her daughter smile.

Then her dad's voice became louder and filled the room. "How about this. I should be leaving the hospital in about ten minutes." The billionaire, catching a glimpse of the magic show from the bed, checked his watch. "You get the money boys on a conference call at, say, eleven-thirty our time, and I'll handle 'em myself." And with that he hung up.

Merlin hesitated, assuming he would have to finish the trick later, but Huffman was already on to another call before the magician's hands had cooled.

What was perhaps most impressive to Merlin was the fact that Huffman must have had the private numbers of everyone he needed because he never seemed to go through a secretary or voice mail. "Hello, Carl. Here's what I need you to do. I want you to show up—" And just like that he focused his eyes out the wide expanse of glass, a king gazing out at his kingdom.

This was a window of opportunity for Merlin. He repeated the trick once more, taking advantage of the same phony technique Kit had so easily exposed. As the fumbling magician pulled the silks out of the bottom of his hand for the second time, Kit squealed with the delight of discovery. Huffman turned to his daughter and gently scolded. "Kit dear, Daddy's doing a really big deal and you need to be quiet."

Confident that his command would be heeded, Huffman turned back to his telephone conversation, never noticing the obedient little nod Kit gave him.

Merlin took advantage of the momentary diversion to slide his right hand into his pocket and slip on a waiting thumb tip—a realistic-appearing, hollow plastic thumb, allowing him to hide small objects inside—that fit snugly over the magician's own thumb.

Merlin spoke quietly, holding the two colorful silks between his right thumb and forefinger, the thumb tip not two feet from Kit's eyes yet invisible as if it weren't there at all. "Okay, Kit, gimme one more try. I'll bet this time I can really fool you."

"She's very smart, Dr. Merlin," Cynthia added helpfully.

"Oh, I can see that. That's why I need three times to fool Kit." Merlin began the trick one last time, first pushing the blue, then the red silk into his left fist, pushing them in hard, dramatically using his thumb to jam them down. "Now, I really want to prove to you that this is magic, so how 'bout if instead of having the silks change places, I have them melt together?" Merlin said the last two words dramatically and was rewarded with a smile from Kit.

"Wow, that would be great, Dr. Merlin!"

Merlin shook his left hand up and down and then sideways for a bit. Finally he reached two fingers into his balled up fist, which contained the two crumpled silks, as well as the thumb tip which had been deposited there only seconds before. A third silk had been secreted inside the plastic thumb tip, which Merlin now pulled out very slowly. "Now, Kit, what do you think of this?" he asked, showing off the blue-and-red-striped silk.

"Oh, my, what do you think of that, Kit?" Cynthia said appreciatively.

"That was great. Really, really great. Do it again, oh, pleeeeze do it again," Kit begged.

"No, dear," Huffman said, gaveling the meeting back to order with the smart snap of his cell phone closing. "I've got to talk with Dr. Merlin."

Merlin stood, and the two men were now face-to-face.

"Listen, Dr. Merlin, I really don't have much time. I heard you ask my wife why we selected you. Very simple. Kit's got liver disease, but she's also got hospitalitis. When it comes time for the transplant we're going with the full team. Don't you worry. But for a central line we thought you'd be perfect. You juggle or something?" Huffman made a little motion with his hand to show Merlin that he didn't know anything about Merlin's magical skills and didn't care to. Merlin was just a sideshow.

"Daddy, he's a magician, a *real* magician."

"That's nice," Huffman said to quiet his enthusiastic daughter. "I'm sure Dr. Merlin will do lots of tricks for you after I leave." Then to Merlin, "Anyway, whatever you can do we'd appreciate it. Oh, as far as informed consent goes, we know the routine: I-fully-understand-the-risks-of-infection-and-damage-and-most-importantly-the-risks-of-bleeding," he said quickly, reciting it like a hungry child saying a prayer before a meal. "Cynthia will take care of signing whatever you need. We fully understand the risks."

"Well, then, I'm happy to help."

Huffman watched as Merlin pocketed his magic props. For a moment the billionaire had a flash of doubt. What with all the paraphernalia, was Dr. Merlin too silly to entrust with his daughter? "I assume you can handle this procedure."

"Absolutely. I've put in more than—"

"Fine," Mr. Huffman decided, not wanting to hear Merlin's credentials. "You'll take care of it today."

"If I can get Kit on the OR schedule."

"That's already been taken care of. She's on for two o'clock." Huffman slipped on his finely tailored jacket. "Well, that being decided, I've gotta go." As he turned to leave he blew a kiss to Kit. "You're my best girl. I'll be thinking about you, Kitty." Then he gave Cynthia a quick kiss on the cheek. "Cind, I can't take this hospital food. See if the club will send something over for us. Caesar salad maybe. I'll be back by seven-thirty."

Then he was out the door and gone.

Merlin stayed for another ten minutes and explained everything that would happen to Kit in detail. Then Cynthia signed the informed consent papers and the begging began.

"Dr. Merlin, pleeeeeze. One more trick. I promise to be a really, really good patient."

Then Cynthia chimed in. "I'm certain Kit would truly appreciate one more of your marvelous tricks."

And the magician complied, taking out a single bright red sponge ball from his pocket, handing it to his audience of one for examination. When Kit was absolutely certain there was nothing sneaky about the sponge ball, Merlin first took it in his right hand then innocently seemed to place it in his left. But actually, he made a false transfer, retaining the ball in his right hand. "Now, Kit," the surgeon said, holding out his balled up left fist for her approval, "put one of your hands on top of mine." Kit obeyed. "And put your other hand underneath." Again, Kit did as she was told. "Now I want you to blow on my hand very gently, and the sponge ball will disappear from my hand and won't reappear until after the operation. It will be waiting for you, right under your pillow, when you get back to your room." As Merlin began to open the fingers of his left hand, he reached around Kit with his right and handed off the sponge ball to Cynthia, who immediately caught on and slipped the ball in a pocket of her jacket.

Finally, after nearly forty minutes—twice as long as the simple procedure would take—Merlin said his good-byes and started to leave. Before he was out of earshot Kit said to her mother, "I really like him."

Cynthia stroked her daughter's hair and agreed. "So do I, sweetie."

The operation went smoothly. At two o'clock—precisely two o'clock—Kit was wheeled into Merlin's operating room and helped onto the narrow operating table. The room was a flurry of activity. The circulating nurse acted as a conduit for the delivery of sterile supplies. First she opened a large plastic bottle of saline and poured it into a metal basin that waited on a small green-draped table, called a Mayo stand. Then she brought three packages of gauze sponges, each ten-sponge unit packed in a white plastic tub, sealed on top with special sterile paper. Delivery was actually quite simple. All the nurse had to do was peel back the paper, invert the white tub, and dump the gauze squares onto the Mayo stand.

Through all this Kit concentrated on a Beanie Baby she had brought with her. Merlin allowed her to hug it while the anesthesiologist prepared a syringe of ketamine, the anesthetic used for central line placement.

Kit's eyes were locked on the syringe as the ketamine was slowly drawn.

"Hey, Roland," Merlin said to the anesthesiologist as he took one of Kit's hands in his, "be really gentle, Kit's a good friend of mine."

The little girl smiled at Merlin, then winced momentarily when she felt the prick of the needle. It took less than two minutes for Kit to fall into a deep, peaceful sleep. As Merlin prepped her skin, painting it with a brown coat of Betadine, he noticed the little girl's relaxed breathing. It was quite possible, he surmised, that Kit's only true peace came with sleep.

Once the prepping and draping were completed, Merlin chatted with Roland and Nick Bello, his surgical scrub nurse. Having operated as a team so many times made them feel very close, and their idle chitchat in the OR was usually of a nonmedical subject. This was especially true with a simple procedure like the insertion of a central line. The atmosphere in the room was relaxed.

Roland took his place at the head of the table, concentrating on Kit's blood pressure and oxygenation. Merlin stood on one side of the table, Nick Bello on the other. Most of what was needed for placement of a central line came in a clear plastic prepackaged tray with a series of formed compartments that held the various components. The only additional items Bello needed were a few hemostats, a scalpel, and several stacks of white squares of gauze.

First Merlin made two incisions, each one-half inch in length, one at Kit's right collarbone, a second below her right nipple. Merlin and Bello worked flawlessly together. As the scalpel made each incision, Bello handed a white gauze square to Merlin, who applied pressure to the bleeding wound.

During these moments of inactivity, the surgeon and scrub nurse picked up the conversation. "So, what do you know about this family?" Bello asked Merlin.

Merlin rolled his eyes. "Pretty high-powered pain in the ass. Dad treated me like a flunky. Like I was a scrub nurse or something." Merlin's eyes, the only thing not covered by his scrub cap or surgical mask, twinkled.

Bello looked up, shaking his head. "I heard from the supervisor he had some other case bumped so his darlin' daughter could go today."

"He also called me a juggler."

The anesthesiologist smiled and said, "Mother of Jesus. You magicians are a very sensitive lot. Thank God he didn't call you a sword swallower."

Bello laughed, and Merlin released the pressure on the incision. He then performed his trademark OR sleight of hand: making the bloody square of gauze vanish only to become a perfectly white one.

Confident that the bleeding was under control, Merlin created a "tunnel" from the lower incision to the upper one, working a blunt instrument that separated the skin from the underlying muscles. The tissues separated quite easily, not much different from peeling the skin off a chicken breast. Once the tunnel was established, the silicone tubing of the central line was threaded through. It would run four or five inches just beneath the skin, securing it against accidental tugs from an active six-year-old.

In a stepwise fashion Merlin used a metal trocar, a thin guide wire, and a peel-away to insert the catheter in the large subclavian vein. It now ran from below the right nipple, tunneling under the skin to the collarbone and into the subclavian vein. The two incisions were sewn up, and the procedure was over in seventeen minutes.

Despite Kit's bleeding problems, there was minimal blood loss. Merlin's postoperative note reflected no problems in the OR.

Kit was returned to the recovery room in good condition.

The next day, the first thing Merlin spotted as he ran down the hallway on Ten South were the Huffmans, standing in the hallway. Cynthia was crying, clutching the wall for support, desperately watching everything happening to her daughter.

Mr. Huffman, standing behind her, covered his mouth with one hand, holding Cynthia's shoulder with the other. If time could be frozen, the Huffmans would trade their vast fortune to freeze it, for it was obvious by the looks on their faces that they knew these were the last precious moments of Kit's life.

"What happened?" Merlin asked, talking well before he reached the anxious parents.

"That's what I want you to answer, Doctor." Huffman faced the surgeon. "Kit developed a fever this morning. Then they said it was probably an infection. Where the hell were you? Someone gave her some medicine for it, but the fever got higher and higher. One second she was complaining of a headache, the next she stopped breathing. *Now* you arrive.''

"I was in emergency surgery," Merlin said gently enough to set the record straight without sounding defensive. "Let me see what's going on."

Huffman winced as he spoke. "Why don't you go inside and save our little girl."

Without further discussion, Merlin went into Kit's room to witness a full code in progress. Half a dozen doctors and nurses were at work. A male nurse had one knee on the bed and was performing chest compressions, thumping out a steady rhythm.

THUMP! THUMP!

Kit was intubated, a strap of white tape running over her cheeks to secure the breathing tube. An anesthesiologist stood at the head of her bed squeezing a clear plastic bag, forcing oxygen into Kit's lungs.

THUMP! THUMP!

A resident stood at an EKG machine reading the wildly erratic tracing as the strip of paper flowed out onto the floor.

"Give me another two cc's of epi," the resident in charge called out over the commotion. A nurse quickly drew up the adrenaline, a heart stimulant, and handed it off to the resident.

THUMP! THUMP!

Merlin looked at his young patient. Naked, her pajamas cut from her frail body, the central line catheter bounced up and down with each forceful compression. No longer was Kit's skin orange. Her Halloween color was lost to the overpowering purple mottling of a patient whose heart had stopped beating.

The resident in charge immediately noticed Merlin at the bedside. As she grabbed the bouncing catheter to inject the medicine, she called to him. "Septic shock. Fever earlier today. They hit her with Vanc and Fortaz, but she went into shock anyway. Any trouble putting the line in?"

THUMP. THUMP. The nurse continued his cadence but seemed to be letting up on the chest compressions ever so slightly.

Merlin ran his hand absently across his face. "No. A breeze. How long's the code been going on?"

The resident looked at her watch. "Twenty-three minutes."

"You get a gas on her?"

A nurse handed Merlin a sheet of paper with the results of Kit's blood gas. The most telling statistic—a pH of 6.6—indicated Kit had become severely acidotic and had no doubt suffered brain damage.

The resident continued, "Her pH is too low, I know. We can't get it up, and we've already done three rounds of meds on her. What do you think, we call the code?"

They were ready to give up. Every person in the room could feel it. Everything that could be done had already been tried. *Thump. Thump.* Merlin looked out the door, saw the Huffmans watching the tragic scene, and slowly looked back at Kit. It was horrible for parents to watch the demise of their child as they stood in the hallway, helpless to do anything.

Thump. Thump.

The worst was about to happen. The Huffmans were about to witness the code on their beloved daughter terminated. Even though Kit was probably already dead, the flurry of activity around her bed did suspend time, if only momentarily.

thump. thump.

But they were about to see a team of highly skilled physicians and nurses give up, admit defeat, and walk out of the room. And as the emotionally drained doctors and nurses dragged themselves down the hallway, the Huffmans might even overhear someone say, "God, do I need a shower." And the realization would hit them smack in the heart: while their pain was just beginning, a simple shower would end it for these people.

thump. thump.

Merlin spoke in a controlled voice. "You'd better call it—"

thump.

"—but let me draw the cultures, okay?"

The resident in charge put her hand on the nurse who was doing chest compression.

thum—

Then she said to the anesthesiologist, "That's it, I'm calling the code. Thanks, everybody."

Somehow Merlin ended up in the hallway, positioning himself between the Huffmans and the lifeless child, hiding that awful moment when each member of the STAT team disengaged from Kit. Behind him, someone was already pulling the sheet over Kit's face.

Doctors and nurses slowly filed from the room, self-consciously looking away from the parents. Cynthia Huffman gave out a little scream and collapsed in her husband's arms.

Merlin spoke to the Huffmans very quietly. "I'm sorry we couldn't do more to save her. Maybe we should go to the lounge and sit down together."

"That won't be necessary, Dr. Merlin. I'll handle Mrs. Huffman," Huffman said, more anger than grief in his voice.

Regardless of the barriers the family threw up, it was Merlin's obligation to talk with them. "They did everything possible."

"It wasn't enough," Huffman said, looking Merlin dead in the eye.

"I don't know how she got so sick so suddenly. Kit seemed to develop an infection, one that didn't respond to the antibiotics she was given. I don't know why, but I'll get some cultures and hopefully we'll have some answers."

"Can I go in and see her?" Cynthia managed to get out between sobs.

"I'll go with you." Merlin stepped aside.

"No, you won't. We're fine," Huffman said, dismissing the surgeon.

Merlin retreated to the nursing station as the Huffmans said goodbye to Kit. An hour later, long after the family went home, Merlin returned to Kit's room to remove the central line and place it in a sterile container for culture. He also inserted a needle into each of the incisions, pulling back a small amount of fluid into a syringe for analysis. Finally Merlin inserted a long needle directly into Kit's heart and removed ten cc's of blood.

Then Merlin spotted it. The red sponge ball was on the floor, under the bed. For some reason, he suspected this was just the beginning.

3

Frederick Graham was staying late in his office, enjoying being CEO so much it was sometimes hard to go home. Things were happening so quickly that he often felt dizzy, but he was loving the view from the top—the top being twenty-two floors above Grant Street, a swank office in the executive suite of the Western Insurance Company of Pennsylvania, affectionately known as WIP. He leaned all the way back in a plush brown leather chair that had been special-ordered for him by the medical director so he wouldn't get lumbago. The new leather smelled great. He turned his head into it and breathed the smell of success deeply into his lungs.

Lately he'd taken to a tumbler of scotch as he reviewed the daily numbers, never pouring a drop until the last secretary had disappeared for the night. Casually, he worked the glass around, listening to the merry sound the ice cubes made as they bounced around the empty glass. He reached for the bottle, took a moment to read the label, and poured himself another.

If there was one thing that wasn't perfect, it was the way his wife kept reminding him he wasn't the same as he was three years ago. Well, of course he wasn't the same, he would say. Three years ago he was president of a no-name tiny hospital sixty miles northeast of Pittsburgh, a rinky-dink operation that paid him sixty-seven five and left his evenings free for his family, except for his once-a-month community outreach meeting at Denny's. He was lost in a dead-end job, authorizing the receipt for three dozen doughnuts every time the doctors had their medical staff meeting.

One day, though, someone noticed his hard work. A letter arrived from Western Insurance inviting him down to Pittsburgh for an interview. Wearing a new suit, Graham drove his Chevy down to the city and spent nearly three hours interviewing with the top management of Western Insurance. Three weeks later Leonard Silverman, the medical director, was showing him around, introducing him to everyone, including his new personal secretary.

He didn't need his wife to tell him he had changed. Christ, she had changed, too. Now they were in a spanking new house with a stiff mortgage. He was pulling in a hundred seventy thousand dollars a year, driving a new Acura, and looking across the breakfast table at a wife in a tennis outfit who couldn't wait for their kids to get on the bus so she could get to her game.

All too often, when the sky had gotten dark and the scotch grabbed him the right way, he would get his calculator out and run the numbers just for fun. Temporarily, he put down the drink and punched in: one-seven-zero-zero-zero-zero. "One hundred seventy thousand big ones." Then he tapped the keypad some more, making a quick calculation to figure out how much money he would ultimately have, then hit the equals sign. "One *million* three hundred sixty thousand dollars," he whispered to himself as if he'd just scratched off a winning lottery ticket. That was the carrot he was working for, what the board of directors called his Golden Clause, and it seemed so close he could almost spend it. Hell, every time his wife started bitching about how he was always missing dinner he reminded her about the Golden Clause, and now she was spending it on tennis lessons and some colorist who charged seventy-five bucks twice a month to make her hair look like melted butter.

"Okay, a million three invested at"—his fingers tapped out his future as he announced the play-by-play—"twelve percent is—are you ready for this, sports fans?—a hundred sixty-three thousand, give or take." He frowned. No way would he be able to retire and keep his stylish wife clothed and colored on a measly hundred sixty-three.

"Don't panic, no reason to worry. Take that million three and invest it a tad more aggressively," he went on, reaching for his drink and enjoying the way the scotch burned its way down his throat. "Say, at fourteen percent." He punched the keypad numbers as he spoke. "A hundred ninety thousand, give or take." *Maybe we could squeak by on a hundred ninety.* "Heh, heh, heh, heh, heh," Graham chuckled. Podunk Hospital and his sixty-seven five salary were back in another lifetime, so it was okay to laugh. Flipping the little calculator back on the desk, he sipped the scotch the way it was supposed to be sipped. Slowly.

Whenever Graham sat alone in his office and looked around, he couldn't help but smile. The desk he sat behind was uncluttered, clearly the workplace of someone in charge, someone who had a competent lieutenant to handle the mundane workaday details. He rapped his knuckles on it several times, enjoying the sound of the solid mahogany surface, not some cheap, wood-grained laminate like they had for him at Podunk.

There were the requisite framed photos of his kids adorning one corner, a computer workstation, a mug stuffed full of pens and pencils, and one folder. Exactly one folder, right in the middle of his desk. That's what his secretary did at the end of every day, made certain the folder was on his desk right where he wanted it. By the time he opened it each night, he knew his family was probably sitting down to pork chops and little potatoes sprinkled with parsley. He savored this moment like it was slow sex.

The Current Status of Inpatients. Three typed pages of names and numbers that was the icing on his day.

Admissions were up one percent from the previous week. That was the bad news. Graham always followed a discipline of taking the bad news first.

Then he turned the page and scanned the good news: the discharges. As long as patients were home it was much cheaper for the insurer. It wasn't free, but it amounted to a fraction of the cost. The primary care physicians made do with a monthly capitation check that covered all their services. Those dollars were already figured into the WIP budget, so it didn't matter how sick the patients got or how many times they visited their doctor. As long as they stayed the hell out of the hospital, it cost WIP exactly the same. Discharges were up almost two percent. *Good ol' Silverman, he could really light a fire under some of those internists.*

Finally Graham flipped to the third page, the recent deaths. Not that he could ever let himself think of deaths as good news. But it certainly wasn't bad news, and with the boys from Connecticut poring over the numbers, it was better to have good news than bad.

A name jumped from the page: Katherine Huffman. Over and over, Graham read the little summary describing her rapid demise. One day she was on the inpatient column; the next she'd jumped two pages. Rocking his chair forward so he could put down the scotch, he tapped several keys on his computer and pulled up the data on the Huffman family, needing only a moment to find what he was searching for. He closed his eyes and rubbed them hard. *Oh, shit!* Graham felt sick, like he might vomit scotch all over the mahogany. *Where the hell is Silverman?*

Just as the zeros on his solar-powered calculator quickly faded after he snapped out the lights and headed for the elevator, they also disappeared from his mind. He felt numb, like this would somehow undo all the months of meetings and negotiations. How he got from the executive offices to the parking garage was a blur to him. *Katherine Huffman. Blaine Huffman.* He couldn't shake the two names from his head. *Not now, goddamn it, not now.* He hardly knew Blaine Huffman, having met him only once at some charity event. But he sure as hell knew his reputation.

Blaine Huffman could make waves. Anytime he wanted.

The parking garage was underground, dark and full of echoes. Graham sat in the Acura working himself into a full panic. Maybe he should place a call, alert someone and get this thing settled. But who should he call? Maybe he should call Blaine Huffman and show some concern, to make sure he wasn't going to cause trouble. *That's it, just call him,* he decided. By the time he picked up the phone, his breathing had quickened and the ends of his fingers tingled as if they were asleep.

Suddenly his penis burned like he had to go to the bathroom. The urge was tremendous. Not wanting to wait for the elevator and go all the way back up to his office, he snuck behind the car and unzipped himself, but nothing happened. He just stood there, wedged in the little space between the back of his car and the cement wall, hunched over so he wouldn't go on himself. Nothing. A dry well. He tried to relax, looking at the vanity plate on his car, CLAUAWS. Somehow his private little joke didn't seem so funny tonight.

Graham zipped up and got back in the car. Once again he picked up the phone then slammed it down in the receiver. *What the hell am I going to say?* He rubbed his bleary eyes. "Will you please tell me why you're calling Huffman?" he said aloud, rehearsing what Silverman was more than likely to ask. "What the hell is wrong with you? How can he hurt you?"

Then he dialed Silverman's home number and let it ring until the machine picked up. "Uh, Lenny, I . . . uh . . . wanted to bring you up to speed on a prob . . . never mind, I'll catch you tomorrow."

Again, he started thinking about the boys from Connecticut. Would they care? Of course not. Why should they care? What possible difference could Katherine Huffman make to them?

Graham thought hard, closing his eyes and seeing a disaster in the making. Blaine Huffman would make a public stink about the crappy care his daughter received. The Pennsylvania Insurance Commission would be forced to examine WIP to make certain all its doctors had been properly credentialed. And the boys from Connecticut would sit on the sidelines and wait for the dust to settle.

By that time he'd be smothered in debt, and all hell would break loose when his wife found out she'd have to go back to being a brunette playing on the cement courts at the high school.

Maybe he should call Huffman. Once again he picked up the phone, then hung it up. He didn't even have the number.

His hands went up to his eyes and he rubbed them hard again, then moved on to his head, finishing with a vicious massage of his temples. *Don't call. Thank God I don't have the number. What would I say? "Please don't make trouble for us with the insurance commission?"*

"Get control of yourself. You're okay. Think logically." He was talking to himself again. "Silverman would probably say, 'This can't hurt the deal.' That's exactly what he'd say. This can't hurt the fucking deal."

A half hour later he started the car and drove home.

The next morning Merlin skipped ICU rounds and went down to the morgue. After the elevator deposited him in the basement of the new wing, it was quite a walk, down one long hall, then another. Bright fluorescent lights hung in clusters every thirty feet so that he could watch his shadow rise and ebb like the tides.

If you were taking this walk you knew where you were heading. The little creature comforts that decorated the rest of the hospital probably wouldn't brighten your mood.

For a moment, maybe a good bit longer than a moment, Merlin hesitated at the heavy metal doors of the morgue, reminding himself, *Don't let him get to you.*

The morgue was harshly lighted, not a shadow in sight. The unmistakable stench of death hung in the air, thick as a wool blanket on a hot day, fighting the efforts of the ventilation system. If you thought about it—really closed your eyes and concentrated—it was some dreadful combination of stool and urine, but there was also the metallic odor of blood, strong enough to taste in the back of your mouth. There were two autopsy tables; one already had a work in progress.

Jonathan Olsen was hunched over a corpse: a little girl, naked, and so small on the huge metal table that she looked horribly out of place. It had to be Kit.

Merlin heard the door close behind him, but the pathologist didn't react. Kit had been opened with a "Y" incision, the cuts having been made from each collarbone to the sternum and from the sternum down to the groin. The sternum had already been removed along with several inches of each rib and bright red muscle. It had been placed, skin side down, just below Kit's feet.

Without looking up, both his gloved hands delving into the little girl's abdomen, Olsen said, "Been expecting you, magic man." Then the chairman of pathology stood to his full height, the thick strings of his butcher's apron straining to stay tied around his waist. His lips slowly curled into a home-turf smile. Right away he seemed pleased with himself for guessing correctly who had just entered his morgue, but also because Merlin had to come to him for answers. Especially, though, he loved saying "magic man" in that condescending tone of voice of his.

"Any surprises, Dr. Olsen?"

"No. Pretty much what I expected," he answered. "A wound infection."

"The infection spread quickly. Probably a multiply resistant bug."

"This one's different from the others last week."

Merlin took a step closer. "Different?"

"She shouldn't have died, magic man." Olsen looked at Merlin for a reaction. "Waiting for a liver transplant, you don't die getting a central line put in."

Instantly the room became hot and stuffy. Merlin desperately needed a mouthful of fresh air. His ears burned and felt as if they must be glowing. Olsen was going to make this as difficult as possible. "That's why an autopsy is so important."

"When I opened up her chest wall where you tunneled the catheter there was gross evidence of infection throughout the layers. This was a wound infection, pure and simple. You sent the catheter for culture?"

"Of course." Merlin nodded. "Anything from micro?"

"Blood cultures from yesterday morning, before she coded, look like Strep."

"What kind of Strep?"

"The preliminary suggests Group A. Strep, goddamn it, like you find in eight-year-olds with sore throats. What'd you do, sneeze on her, for God's sake?"

"Strep." Merlin paused, thinking. "The moment she spiked a fever she was started on antibiotics. The bug must be virulent as hell. It didn't respond to vancomycin."

"By the time she spiked a fever it was probably too late, even though this little girl had a decent immune system. She was top of the transplant list, goddamn it!"

"Did you get surface cultures from her throat?"

"Yesssss," Olsen said, pulling the word slowly from his lips, reminding Merlin who was chairman of pathology. "You don't really think this is a Strep throat gone mad, do you?"

"I don't know," Merlin answered, shaking his head.

"Well, it's not. Do you have any idea the expected mortality from putting in a central line?"

"If you've got a point, make it."

"I've never seen one here. I've been doing this for a lot longer than I care to remember, and I've never seen one."

"You say it as if the fact that it is rare makes it impossible to happen. Infection is one of the risks of any procedure, and the family was well aware of all the risks. It's horrible that a little girl died, and I feel for her family. But I have no idea how she got Strep."

"The hospital is open to all kinds of liability on this one. The father is—"

Merlin's voice was getting louder in frustration. "If you want to lecture me on your results, fine. But I know who the father is. You do not need to inform me of the medicolegal consequences." Sweat was collecting on Merlin's brow. "I've dealt with Mr. Huffman a couple of times now. But tell me one thing, is Kit's death any more of a tragedy than the three postsurgical deaths we had from infection last week?"

"It sure as hell is. She was a six-year-old girl having a minor procedure, and her father is Blaine Huffman. It is *very* different." Olsen turned back to the small body and hesitated, as if trying to remember where he was when he was interrupted. "Before I forget, Merlin, did Banks Wickford find you?"

"Banks Wickford?" Merlin frowned. "Now I see where this is heading. Banks Wickford couldn't care less about any of the patients in this place. But he sure as hell cares about money and publicity."

"Watch it, Merlin."

"For crissakes, he's a hospital administrator, what do you expect from him? He doesn't give a crap about people. Everything is about money with him."

"You're on thin ice," Olsen warned. He turned away from the surgeon and placed his hands into the open abdomen. Instantly he busied himself examining the intestines.

"Why don't you scratch a little deeper and see if there are other possibilities? This isn't a case of one little girl dying. There were three last week. Maybe there were others before that. Go below the surface, and see what you find."

"We're done, Merlin. Run along."

"No, not until you've heard me. Get up on the front lines, make a difference in someone's life. When you do there will be occasional failures, but your successes will be all the more sweet. But I'd bet you'll never go for that, because then you wouldn't have the last word anymore."

Olsen turned his big bald head to look at Merlin. "Okay, magic man, vanish. I've got work to do. Banks Wickford wants to see you."

On the second floor of the Pittsburgh University Medical Center, safely insulated from the annoyances of the paging system and the hordes of filthy patients who came by bus to the emergency room, was the executive suite. The small cluster of offices was excessively well-appointed, the most lavish one belonging to CEO Banks Wickford. His passion was golf, and he kept his set of bookshelves laden with polished hunks of walnut festooned with shiny brass figurines swinging golf clubs. A prominent corner of his huge desk was reserved for his most recent acquisition. Whenever a visitor would notice the trophy, Banks would pick it up reverently and launch into a detailed description of every hole on the course and recount how he nailed his seven iron on the sixteenth.

The Medical Center had flourished under Banks's tenure. His was a personality designed to be in charge. Although he prided himself on never lying to anyone, at one time or another he misled even his top lieutenants. Whenever bullshit was called for he could sling it like a farmhand late for a Saturday night date. Each year at the charity ball, knowing damned well he looked splendid in his tuxedo, he delivered a ten minute toast to the celebrants that he made sure was widely quoted in the society column.

Just before Merlin was ushered into Banks's office by a suitably proper middle-aged secretary, the chief resident caught a light burst of laughter through the door.

Banks was standing behind his desk and immediately came around to introduce Merlin to Knox Pincus, the Medical Center lawyer, and Carter Forsythe, the chairman of the board of trustees. These were the heavy hitters. "Banks, Knox, and Carter" was most often said as if it were one word, one person with three heads.

After the briefest of greetings, including the perfunctory eye contact afforded underlings several rungs down the ladder, Knox and Carter headed for the door, their work apparently finished, confident that Banks could handle Merlin. *Banks, Knox, and Carter,* Merlin mused to himself, noticing the expensively drab clothing they wore.

Once they were alone, Banks motioned for Merlin to sit down on his sofa, choosing a green wingback chair for himself. Never in a hurry when dealing with such an important matter, Banks took a moment to pick up his coffee cup from a side table before he spoke. "As I'm certain you're aware, I've already been briefed by Jonathan Olsen about this Katherine Huffman case. A tragedy, no doubt, but while I leave the medical issues to you and your residents, unfortunately there are other issues we must deal with today." Banks sipped some coffee. "That's why we wanted to meet with you, to see exactly what kind of a problem we're facing."

Merlin noticed Banks was deliberately using the word "we," as if Knox and Carter were still in the room. "I assume the issue you are concerned with is Kit's father," Merlin said.

"Let's not get ahead of ourselves." Another sip of coffee. This time he placed the cup on its matching saucer. "Let's look at this thing in its various elements." Banks struck a pose, legs crossed, looking like a statesman. "When children die . . . unexpectedly, I might add . . . it affects people in an emotional way that is sometimes difficult to explain. I think you and I both understand this." Banks nodded his head, as if he were used to people agreeing with him. "Katherine was a very stable patient awaiting a liver transplant. If Katherine had died during her transplant, well, people could understand that." Banks paused before starting again. He chose his words very carefully, wanting to put the precise tone into each thought. "In Pittsburgh, we know a great deal about transplants. I don't mean just the medical community. I'm talking about soccer moms and bus drivers and the little guy who carries my golf bag. We're transplant savvy in Pittsburgh, but we still respect what putting in a new liver means. It is a big deal. Now, I know Katherine had some bleeding problems. If there were complications from hemorrhage when you put her central line in, well . . . there would be a certain logic that her family could accept. They might not like it, but they could accept it. You following me?"

Merlin nodded.

"But I've been informed the risk of infection from central line placement is minuscule. Olsen tells me he's never even seen a case like this before." Banks stopped talking and held the silence until he saw Merlin's lower jaw move as if he were about to say something. "I want to be honest with you, Dr. Merlin. We have grave concerns about the outcome of this case. How do you feel about the situation?"

"I feel horrible that her parents had to walk out of here yesterday knowing their struggle is over. It made me sick. Unfortunately, medicine isn't perfect and results are never guaranteed. In fact, Mr. Huffman dictated to *me* the informed consent for the procedure, including the risk of infection. Sometimes circumstances like these force us to look at cold statistics that we would rather not deal with. Both parents knew the risks even with a relatively stable patient like their daughter."

"But you would agree, Dr. Merlin, this was an unexpected death."

"What kind of a doctor expects his patients to die? I've examined every aspect of this case, and I can honestly report to you everything went smoothly. I can't imagine at what point the infection was introduced.''

"Nor can we," Banks said thoughtfully.

"Are you aware that there have been other deaths, all in the *unexpected* category, within the last two weeks?"

Banks frowned. "Dr. Merlin, this morning we are going to focus on the death of Katherine Huffman."

"I care about Kit Huffman. Not as a statistic, but as a child I did magic tricks for. But more than one patient has died. Maybe the responsible thing to do is look at these patients as a group."

"Not today. Let's try to stay focused."

"I'm interested in John Gonzales, too."

Banks cocked his head to let Merlin know he had no idea what he was talking about.

"Mr. Gonzales was a diabetic who died from a drug-resistant bacteria after I amputated his leg. And there were others. The fact that I didn't operate on them doesn't make me any less interested."

"Once we've dealt with Katherine Huffman we can look into this Mr. Gonzales."

"What if there is some problem with the sterilization technique we use on the surgical instruments? What about the ventilation system in the OR? Could it be spewing out bacteria? Suppose the water that the nurses in recovery use to wash their hands is contaminated?"

"Not now, Doctor. Once we have some answers about Katherine Huffman, I'll make it priority one to have all your concerns addressed."

"Then you have no objection if I start now."

Banks's tongue flitted out of his mouth and licked his lips. "We have people in the Medical Center to do that. If you'll leave their names with my secretary I'll personally see that it gets investigated. Let me be blunt, Dr. Merlin. Is there any possibility you may have overlooked something you might have done?"

"I was there, skin-to-skin, and nothing went wrong. Kit developed sepsis so quickly that I'd guess she somehow got a hefty dose of Strep. I've made mistakes. If a doctor says otherwise, don't let him near you with a blade. But I can't think of a single moment when something happened. There wasn't even a medical student in the room who might not know how to scrub."

"Then maybe you can enlighten us where the responsibility should fall."

A heavy silence filled the room. Merlin knew exactly why he was there. If he wouldn't take the fall, then he was expected to name someone who would. Merlin did not want to launch into a discussion of all the people who have contact with a surgical patient. The list was dizzying.

"Dr. Merlin, quite frankly we are at war with another teaching hospital across town. That's no secret. When they have a problem that makes it into the evening news we see an uptick in ER visits and admissions. Blaine Huffman is a very powerful man. I don't need to remind you of that. In my mind it is not a question of *if* he brings a lawsuit, it is a question of what form the suit will take. It could be very public. Quite frankly, I don't know how the Medical Center could survive a very public lawsuit." Then Banks looked up, reading an imaginary headline floating in front of his eyes. "Six-year-old dies from a minor procedure while awaiting liver transplant," he said melodramatically.

Merlin cleared his throat. "His daughter had a routine procedure that carried a small but definite risk, and he understood it."

"But, Dr. Merlin, Huffman is a man who doesn't let something like a little informed consent get in his way. Maybe he'll find someone who will say you tied one on the night before, or some nurse will testify you seemed unsure of yourself in the OR, or your girlfriend wouldn't sleep with you. Who knows? We're quite worried about the Medical Center, but we're also concerned about you."

"Why is this discussion being handled by you and not the chairman of surgery? If the quality of my work was in question, my chairman would have chewed my ass off. The fact that you're doing it makes me think there's an entirely different agenda." Not waiting for a response, Merlin walked out of the room.

Five minutes later Merlin marched into the morgue. Olsen had just finished, and a technician was beginning to sew the chest wall back in place using heavy thread. Kit's chart was on a metal stand near the autopsy table. Merlin picked it up and said, "You finished with it? Banks wants it now, and they want your report in the A.M.," and strode back out before Olsen could say a word.

A quick trip to medical records, and Merlin had the three charts of the other patients who had died of overwhelming infections.

4

Merlin snuck out of the Medical Center early, his backpack four patient charts heavier than when he entered, breaking the sacrosanct rule: hospital records must never leave the Medical Center. Had he been caught, Banks Wickford might have considered it a wonderful way to rid himself of Jack Merlin. Who but the most guilty steals evidence?

Earlier he had taken a quick glance in Kit's chart as he sat in Medical Records waiting for the other charts to be pulled. A terrible thought struck him. What if someone removed the informed consent from Kit's chart? What if the Huffmans claimed that Merlin hadn't mentioned a word about infection as part of the risks? What if they said they had no idea what was going on?

Merlin flipped through the pages, his hands working too quickly, not finding it right away, fumbling with the pages that stuck together, going backwards for a second look. For the first time since Kit Huffman had died, he felt frightened. The chart was thick, hundreds of pages divided among three brown folders, too many pages describing a life taking place within the confines of the Medical Center instead of a sandbox.

It was gone.

The goddamn informed consent that he had watched Cynthia Huffman sign was not in the chart. *Shit.* Did Banks already know there was no informed consent? Did Olsen? Now he started over, his hands shaking. One by one he turned the pages. Unable to control his fingers he grabbed at the pages, crinkling them so no two could stick together.

Suddenly he found it, stuck to the back of a lab data sheet. A tiny fold had been placed in one corner and they had become wedded. The informed consent, with Cynthia's signature was right where it was supposed to be. He felt foolish. *You're paranoid, Merlin. Watch it.*

Admitting he was being overly suspicious didn't stop him from walking over to a Xerox machine in order to make a quick copy of the informed consent. In fact it seemed a perfectly natural thing for a paranoid person to do.

He arrived home on Ninth Street to an empty house. Before he popped the tab on a can of beer he spread the purloined charts out on a small coffee table in the living room. He picked up the first one, the thinnest of the four, put his feet up on the edge of the table, and began reading about his diabetic who died after an amputation. The case was exactly as he remembered, and he was tempted to skip portions of the chart that seemed redundant. But he forced himself to be disciplined, flipping through the chart until he came across the physicians' notes, including the exhaustive account of the cardiac arrest and failed resuscitation. That was followed by the more exhaustive nursing notes that detailed every bowel movement and sneeze the patient had. Then came the orders and the endless pages of laboratory reports. Finally he read the last page of the chart, which contained Mr. Gonzales's personal information, including everything important to the billing office: phone numbers, place of employment, insurance information, and home address.

Of course, Merlin could not tell whether or not Mr. Gonzales owed the hospital any money from any previous hospitalizations. If he needed that information it would be available only on the central computer system.

The second chart belonged to the woman with ovarian cancer who had been operated on for abdominal adhesions. Again Merlin proceeded in order. Doctors' and nurses' notes. Orders. Laboratory. Personal information.

Merlin closed his eyes and tried to enumerate all the similarities between the two patients. Unfortunately there were many, but nothing in particular jumped out at him. Nothing sinister. In fact, up until the patients developed fevers, their hospitalizations had been fairly routine. Each had had a chronic illness that brought them into the hospital frequently. The number of doctors whose names appeared in both charts was astounding, because on nights and weekends, physicians on call were expected to cross cover. Six surgeons had their signatures in each chart. Nine nurses. Not to mention the dozens of behind-the-scenes people who interacted with everybody indirectly. The insurance carrier of both patients was the same, they lived in the same community, they had the same telephone exchange, and they were within seven years of each other's age.

Merlin groaned. Already it was becoming tedious, and he was just getting started.

Tory pushed the front door open and walked in with a bag of groceries. "Quit loafing and unload the car."

While Merlin spent the next five minutes helping Tory, he recounted the details of his experience with Banks Wickford. Tory jammed the freezer full of things that were starting to melt. Finally, as he finished his chronology, Tory joined him at the table but ignored the beer he had poured for her. Banks Wickford frightened her.

"What an asshole," she declared. "He's looking for a scapegoat."

"There's one other thing," Merlin said, leaning on his elbows. "I mentioned to Wickford that there were three deaths last week, all from overwhelming infections. I asked if he thought there might be some connection. He gave me some bullshit lip service about leaving their names with his secretary."

"And you didn't."

"Of course not. I'm going through the charts myself, maybe talk with some of the families, see if there's any connection."

Tory frowned as she walked over to the counter and began to stock the shelves with canned goods. "Why do you think the cases are related?"

"They're so similar. Each involves a patient sent back to the floor after successful surgery only to develop an unstoppable infection with a superbug."

"Same superbug each time?"

"How the hell'd you know to ask that?" Merlin queried.

"One of those highbrow medical journals you leave lying around the bathroom. I think it's called *Newsweek*."

"They were different bugs," Merlin answered.

Tory thought a moment. "How could they be related? I mean, aren't there dozens of operations performed daily?"

"In the last ten days there were probably, oh, a total of two hundred fifty operations. That would include orthopedics, gynecology, ENT, and thoracic surgery. I'd bet almost half are general surgery. So these would be three percent."

"Burgers on the grill okay for dinner?" Tory asked, changing the subject.

"Sure," Merlin said.

"Go start the grill," Tory said.

Merlin smiled. Tory couldn't fool him. "Aha. You think I'm nuts, but you can't say anything because we live together and I might snap and kill you or something. I'm safer outside with a bottle of charcoal lighter.''

Tory laughed uneasily as Merlin headed off to the backyard. Half an hour later they were eating at the kitchen table, talking about everything but the Medical Center. When they finished and she settled down on the sofa with the evening news, Merlin tackled the third chart, the patient with chronic lung disease and bedsores. It weighed in at more than four pounds. By the time he'd dispensed with the physicians' notes, Tory was into a rerun of *Seinfeld*. The nurses' notes were next. Merlin was having trouble keeping his eyes open. Orders and Laboratory. Now Merlin could have sworn the writing must have been smudged.

He finished with the last page of the chart.

"Wait a minute!" he exclaimed, quickly grabbing Kit Huffman's chart. Opening it to the last page, his eyes found the information right away. "Tory, listen to this. All four patients have the same insurance carrier. Western Insurance. You ever hear of them?"

"Yeah, I see their billboards. They're new."

"Exactly. They're not one of the behemoths like the Blues. These are the new guys in town. They couldn't possibly have that many patients. That changes everything."

Tory shut off the TV with the remote and repositioned herself right next to Merlin. By now, he had all four charts opened to the same page. As he reread the insurance carrier from each front sheet he noted, "WIP. WIP. WIP. WIP."

"I'm sorry I thought you were nuts. But tell me what it means."

Merlin smiled. "I have no idea. Four patients with WIP insurance, each with a serious illness, each dead within ten days of one another from an overwhelming infection."

"It would feel more significant if these patients *didn't* have such serious illnesses, you know? Healthy people dying after having a mole removed."

Merlin hesitated before answering. "Maybe, but this is what we've got. WIP insurance is just too small to have four patients die of life-threatening infections. Can we really accept this as a coincidence?"

"Even with what you're thinking—and I know just how you think— what are you going to do next? You can't go to Wickford. He'll have you committed." Tory walked across the living room to a set of bookshelves and pulled out a book. "You didn't read this, *The Bible Code,* but I did. They did some fancy computer analysis of the Torah. Looked for patterns of letters, looked at the text forwards, backwards, up and down. And you know what? They found all sorts of incredibly accurate predictions about twentieth-century life. The Gulf War, Bill Clinton.

That sort of stuff. Is this for real? Is it a case of if you look at anything long enough you can squeeze your eyeballs and see something that isn't really there? Don't get me wrong. I'm on your team. But please don't give Wickford reason to say you fabricated this to avoid whatever blame he's trying to put on you. I'd bet anything he'd use it against you if he could."

"How's this sound? What if tomorrow I mention to a couple of people what we found—"

"*We* found. Ahh, so I'm in this also."

"It wouldn't be fun without you."

Tory leaned over and kissed him. "Go on."

"Nothing clever. Just a little mention to some people I work with. See how they react. Maybe someone else has some suspicions. But don't worry. I'll be subtle. And I promise not to say," and Merlin dropped his voice to a very low whisper, "conspiracy theory."

Frederick Graham was ensconced in soft leather, the tumbler of scotch comfortably cradled in his hand, reviewing his daily copy of Current Status of Inpatients. He had been waiting all day for Leonard Silverman to show up and now was ready to forget it, take the final sip of scotch, and leave a nasty message on the medical director's voice mail.

"Freddy baby, what's up?" It was Silverman, breezing into the CEO's office like he owned the place, never bothering to knock. Not one to break tradition, he streamed in with all the confidence in the world and plopped himself down on a small leather sofa that sat across the room from Graham's desk.

Silverman was the type of guy who loved to tell stories at parties in a booming tone of voice that made people in other conversations feel compelled to shut up and listen. His sartorial trademark was one-of-a-kind, handmade ties. "What are you drinking? Scotch? Not that cheap piss, I hope."

Already, Silverman's obnoxious bravado made Graham feel better. Showing off the label and getting a cocky smile of approval, Graham poured a drink. "Didn't you get my messages?"

"Don't skimp on the booze. Gimme another finger." Graham poured the scotch slowly, wanting his confidant sober. "A little more . . . that's it . . . almost . . . more . . . stop!"

"Didn't you check your voice mail?" Graham asked as he handed him the drink.

"Yep." Silverman took a slug of his scotch. "Ohhh, that's good. Freddy boy, once you get used to this shit you never go back. You'll be drinking top-shelf from now on. Maybe get you a Mercedes instead of that Aaaaacura you drive. Hey, I know. What about a little apartment stocked with the bimbiest of bimbos?'' Silverman moved his hips erotically and laughed.

Graham watched the amber drink develop whitecaps in Silverman's glass.

"Hey, watch the drink, will ya? The leather.'' Graham didn't know how to react to this kind of talk. Zeros on a calculator were one thing, but air-fucking some bimbo made him kind of nervous.

"Can I show you something in a nice, tight twenty-two-year-old?'' Silverman said, imitating a salesman in a clothing store.

"Whatever you say, Lenny,'' he said quietly, hoping to silence his medical director.

"I say,'' Silverman declared with his glass held out in a toast, "we're gonna be rich when the sale goes through. Rich enough to have anything we want.'' He put the glass down, resting it on one knee. "You been following the numbers?''

"That's my job,'' Graham said sarcastically.

"Well, you're doing one hell of a good job because they look terrific.''

Graham couldn't control his smile. "Medical costs are down almost three percent this quarter.''

"By Christmas this is a done deal, and I'm outta here. My ex-wife's lawyers can look all they want, but I'll be in Bimini fucking everything in sight.''

"You heard about Katherine Huffman?''

"Who?''

"That little girl . . . waiting for a liver transplant—''

"Oh, yeah. Obnoxious father who got you to okay any and all experimental drugs. I meant to ask you, why the hell did you do that? We don't pay for *experimental* drugs. Shit, why not give away the house? What's the story? You know the guy or something?''

"I met him once. I told you. Anyway, there was a death.''

"Who? The guy?'' Silverman asked, concentrating more on his drink than what Graham was saying.

"No, the girl.''

"Ooooh. The little girl. No. I just look at the numbers, don't follow the actual cases. That's why we pay our PCPs the big bucks, so I don't have a silly stethoscope hanging around my neck getting tangled up with my neckwear.'' Silverman looked down at his tie—a colorful silk he had picked up in Italy—and smoothed it vainly against his shirt.

"Well, I wanted to talk with you about Katherine Huffman. About her death. Something about having a central line put in."

Silverman sat up and leaned toward Graham. "What are you, upset a little girl died? Don't get emotionally involved. She's not your kid. She's a statistic on a piece of paper."

"I'm not emotionally involved," Graham said confidently. "It's just—"

"Then why the hell do you care? Kids who need transplants die all the time."

"Ordinarily I wouldn't even notice. But her father is Blaine Huffman. He's—"

"Shopping malls, a small airline, an NFL team out west, blah, blah, blah. Hey, you think the Pens can do it without Lemieux?" Silverman said, ready to change direction. "I don't."

"Blaine Huffman is a powerful man."

Silverman's eyes squinted down to slits, and the smirky tone disappeared from his voice. "So what? I mean it. You think he's gonna sue? Let him. So what if he grabs a couple of mil from the Medical Center. Who gives a flying fuck if some overpaid schmuck surgeon's malpractice carrier loses some dough. It doesn't affect us, or the deal."

"What about publicity? Would that frighten the Connecticut Insurance Brokers?"

"Jesus Christ. Listen to me, Freddy. I mean, get a hold of yourself. If the president of WIP starts to pee his pants publicly, *that* will scare Connecticut off. For one second shut your mouth and let me be a greedy bastard and say exactly what you know to be true. Here it is in a nutshell. As far as WIP is concerned—and you and I *are* WIP, don't forget that—the Huffman girl is better off dead." Graham's jaw dropped open. "You heard me right. She's better off dead. Don't be shocked. She would have cost us a small fortune," Silverman said, expertly balancing the scotch on his knee as he hooked both thumbs in his lapels, puffing his chest out a bit. "You know, that felt pretty good. C'mon, don't look upset. You know me, I'm all heart. Shit, a kid dying is the worst. Okay? You feel better?" He looked at Graham, who didn't know what to think. "Now," Silverman said, rubbing his hands together like he was hungry, "let's get some takeout. See if they can send some deep-dish pussy up here right away."

5

This was an end-of-the-day phone call, and Banks Wickford didn't want to be interrupted. He believed he would be able to chart a path that would satisfy everyone.

A sheet of paper—"From the desk of Stephanie Wickford" across the top in raised purple script—had the number printed carefully, copied straight from the club directory. Already, his hand had reached out toward the receiver a half dozen times, and each time he had withdrawn, wiping away the little drops of moisture that collected on his upper lip. When he finally picked up the phone—his first successful uncradling—his bladder went into some kind of spasm and he made a quick trip to his private bathroom. Tucking himself in, Banks stood at the sink, staring at his reflection in the mirror. Somehow, the way his lip was sweating and his five o'clock shadow was showing, he realized he looked a little too much like Richard Nixon. Furrowing his brow and raising his hands in a double peace sign, he proclaimed, "I am not a crook," but he sure as hell felt like one. Grabbing a washcloth and soaking it in cold water, Banks wondered if he could muster the nerve to make the call. Then he held the washcloth to his face, breathing through it, taking in the cool moist air like he was on a lake after a morning rainfall. It felt wonderful. When he pulled it away he even felt a brief flutter of confidence. "Blaine? Oh, hi, Banks here." *No. Too clubby.* "Hello, Blaine? Banks. Just wanted to let you know how dreadful—" *Don't go into a big speech.* "Hello, Blaine. I'm just sick about Katherine." *Horrible.*

His phone rang. The washcloth got dropped in the sink. Banks walked to his desk with long strides and stood next to it rather than taking his seat. It made him feel like he was running a meeting.

"Hello? . . . Oh, Knox, it's you. . . . No, I haven't reached him just yet. His line's been busy. . . . I'm just going to tell him, you know . . . the truth. . . . Knox, calm down. It's under control. . . . Yes, yes," he said, sounding irritated that he was getting advice from someone who would never have the nerve to handle the dirty work. "Just what we discussed, Knox. Sympathy without guilt. Look— . . . No, Knox, this needs the right spin. You wouldn't have the nerve to handle it. . . . Of course I know him . . . From the club. I told you. . . . Right. Okay, I'll call you back after."

That was all he needed. Hearing the words "from the club" come out as comfortably as a sand wedge from sixty yards made it clear. He and Blaine were at the same club. Members. Equals. Of course he should be the one to call him.

From somewhere deep inside, a surge of confidence grabbed control of the situation. The room seemed brighter. While his fingers danced across the numbers he whispered, "Blaine, you old son of a gun." *That's it. You can go one-on-one with anyone.*

"Hello." It was Huffman, abruptly answering on the second ring. He accented the first syllable heavily—HEL-lo—almost offering it as a challenge.

"Blaine, oh, I'm glad I got you. It's Banks. I just wanted—"

"Who?"

"Banks. Banks Wickford." He kept his voice strong, pausing for just a second, anticipating Huffman saying something like "Oh, Banks, sorry, thank you so much for calling."

But there was a hollow silence at the wealthy end of the phone. One. Two. Three. Four. Five seconds that seemed like five minutes. All Banks could do was hold his breath and pray he hadn't made a huge mistake.

"Banks . . . Banks Wickford," Huffman said, again trying to put a face with the name.

"From the club," was all his dry mouth could get out. He meekly considered slamming down the phone and running out of the building.

"Oh, yes, the golf committee. Listen, Wickford, this isn't a good time."

Think, goddamn it, think. Don't let him hang up. "That's why I'm calling. Uh, listen, I don't know if you know, evidently I guess you don't, I'm the—" Banks babbled.

"What *is* it, Wickford?" Huffman demanded.

"The Medical Center. I'm CEO, and on behalf—"

"Enough. I hear you. You want me to finish your little speech?"

"Oh, it's nothing like that." *Change direction.* "Actually, I'm calling as a friend. I wanted to call and tell you how deeply—"

"How deeply what? How deeply worried you are I'll sue you? Does that about sum it up?"

"Evidently I've called at a bad time."

"No, now that I've lost my daughter I've got lots of time, and I've got you and your staff to thank. Actually you called at a great time. Saves me from wondering what your reaction will be when you hear from my pack of rabid lawyers."

Banks dry-swallowed. "Blaine, the reason I called is confidential. I have information that may be important. I believe I have uncovered . . . a significant problem." Banks spoke quietly, tipping off Huffman to the weight of what he had to say.

"Hold on." There was the scratchy sound of a hand covering the receiver, some muffled voices, and the sound of a door closing. "What!" Huffman said, not as a question but as some type of command.

Banks tried another swallow but nothing happened. Never again would Blaine Huffman forget Banks Wickford. They would be friends, soul mates forever. This was the cement that would bind them together and virtually guarantee that all the Medical Center's problems would disappear.

"There may have been a problem in the OR."

"May?"

"Was." This was it. The absolute point of no return.

"You've got my attention. Don't blow it."

"Look, I want to be forthright with you, but I don't want to destroy the Medical Center in the process."

"So why'd you call?"

"I want to be pragmatic. I've got information that I want you to know. But I don't want innocent people hurt."

"I presume what you've got involves a certain individual."

"It does."

"Listen, Wickford, I don't make deals without knowing every god-damned fact. But I don't want to drag my wife through all the legal bullshit if I don't have to."

"My thoughts exactly. So we have . . . an understanding?"

"Something like that."

"I am not confident that the surgeon—" Banks began.

"Dr. Merlin."

"Yes, Dr. Merlin. I'm not confident he took your daughter's case as seriously as you would have liked."

Now that the cork was off, Huffman sat silently and listened.

"As soon as I learned about Katherine I interviewed Jack Merlin at length. During my conversation with him I found him to be quite defensive. At one point he said that Katherine's death was just a statistic." Banks paused, hoping for some verbal encouragement from Huffman.

"We called her Kit, not Katherine."

"Sorry."

"That's it?"

There was no turning back. "Uh, no. There's more. When I talked with the anesthesiologist—separately, of course—all he remembered was Merlin saying during the surgery that you, uh, were a pain in the ass."

"A pain in the ass," Huffman murmured contemplatively. "Go on."

"And the scrub nurse. He—" Banks grabbed a glass of water and spilled half of it on his shirt trying to take a quick gulp. "The—uh—scrub nurse in the OR said that Merlin did a magic trick during the operation with a piece of gauze."

"WHAT!? During the surgery?"

"Some kind of a magic trick. I don't know. I could find out more about it if—"

"Is that it?"

Banks said, "Well, yes. Of course we fully intend a formal investigation in this matter. He will most likely be—"

"Wickford, you will do nothing of the kind. Am I making myself clear?"

Oh, shit. He's gonna sue the whole fucking Medical Center. SHIT!
"Yessir, you are."

"Is everything you just told me absolutely true?"

"Absolutely."

"You goddamn better be right." Huffman said nothing while he thought, then added, "Tell your board members they can exhale."

"And what do you want me to do about Merlin?"

"Nothing. Stay the hell out of my way." And then Huffman hung up.

Banks held the phone a good long time. *I didn't lie. Nothing was a lie.* His hands were shaking, and he missed the cradle, letting the phone drop to the floor.

Every word was true. He looked at the little note card on his desk with the short list of items he had recited for Huffman. Some had been culled from his unsatisfying conversation with Merlin, others from the surgical team who unquestionably gave Merlin high marks for his performance in the OR. They only made the incriminating remarks when asked pointedly, "We're worried that Dr. Merlin may have been under extreme stress during the surgery. Did Dr. Merlin seem relaxed or uptight in the OR?"

6

Merlin's beeper went off just as morning rounds ended. The female voice implored Merlin to call an extension on Ten South, STAT. The call was unnecessary. It was becoming routine. A nurse would answer the phone in a panic and then race to get her words out without stammering.

Merlin ran to the stairs and bolted up flight after flight, streaming past a group of giggly candy stripers and bursting onto Ten South. A cluster of white clothing was the beacon that immediately led Merlin to the correct room. In lieu of looking at the patient who was being covered by a sheet, Merlin snapped, "What was the surgery for?"

"He had a deep abscess on his leg that we drained," came an anonymous voice. "This morning he spiked a fever, we covered him with meds, but he—"

"Was he otherwise healthy?" Merlin interrupted.

"Yeah."

Then another voice said, "Except for his spina bifida."

"Spina bifida. Where's the chart?"

"Where is Mr. Mardigian's chart?" someone with a female voice asked loudly, assuming responsibility for finding the chart.

A nursing student, wedged in a corner of the crowded room, handed Merlin the chart, a three-inch tome. It took the briefest of moments to scan the information sheet. "I'm taking the chart," was all Merlin said as he walked away from the crowd and stormed toward the elevator.

This time Merlin didn't even notice the thickly carpeted hallway leading up to the executive offices. Banks Wickford's secretary sat at her prestigiously uncluttered desk, looking up from her word processor as

Merlin approached. Without changing her perfect posture, she glanced briefly at Banks's day planner. "Oh, Dr. Merlin," she said in a carefully selected tone that warned him she didn't see his name on the schedule.

"I need to see Mr. Wickford."

She took a second look at her book, just to make it look good. "I'm sorry, Doctor, I don't see that he has an appointment with you today."

"Is he in?"

"Of course, but his schedule doesn't look good." She turned back to her typing, confident that her imperious tone would make the unwanted visitor scurry away.

In a second Merlin had crossed the remaining feet of carpet. Banks's office was protected by a heavy wooden door, floor-to-ceiling, and the chief resident aggressively opened it. The CEO was on the phone, leaning way back in his chair, one foot up on the corner of his desk, having what could only be described as a relaxed happy conversation.

Five charts, the four Merlin had reviewed at home and the new one from today, were flung on the massive desk, sliding over one another, slapping loudly on the imported wood and knocking over the golf trophy that stood sentry on the corner of the desk. It tumbled onto the floor, snapping the brass golfer in two, revealing his insides to be nothing more than white plastic.

One of the charts, a thick one weighing in at almost four pounds, made it all the way across the desk, skimming across the smooth surface like a flat rock on a glimmer-glass lake. It was still moving quickly when it whizzed off the opposite side and caught the telephone cord, ripping the phone out of Banks's hand, sending it bouncing to the floor.

"Another one! Another one, goddamn it!" Merlin yelled.

"Calm down, Doctor. Why don't you sit down and tell me what's wrong." Banks spoke like he was talking to a kindergartner who was upset about some minor incident at school.

"Another postop patient died of what is most definitely sepsis. It's one of those *unexpected infections* you were so worried about the other day. The only difference is—"

"Mr. Wickford, would you like me to show Dr. Merlin out?" It was Banks's secretary, standing at the doorway.

"Of course not, Emily," Banks said, sitting up in his chair, evidently forgetting about his phone call, the cord running tightly across the desk and over the edge where it disappeared, "Dr. Merlin and I were just discussing a problem we're having in the surgical department. That's just fine." Then, turning to Merlin, he asked, "Coffee?"

Merlin didn't react.

"No?" Then back to the secretary, "I guess we're fine. You can close the door," Banks said, pleased with his genuine equanimity.

The secretary retreated, silently closing the door.

"Sit down, Dr. Merlin," Banks said, indicating the same sofa Merlin had occupied during their first meeting.

"That's okay, I'll stand. This situation requires that we admit there is a real problem here. I took these charts home and found out what links each patient. They are all insured by WIP insurance."

"WIP. That's Western Insurance, right?" Banks picked up one of the charts and casually flipped through it, looking for the information sheet. "So you've worked this through. No deaths from any other company?"

"I don't believe so."

Banks put down the chart he was holding and picked up another one, this time finding the information sheet more quickly. His head nodded subtly as if it was difficult for him to admit Merlin might be right. Finally, when he confirmed exactly what Merlin had just told him in the two charts remaining on his desk, he said, "Okay, Merlin. Let's get some people together and talk this thing through. Who do you suggest?"

For a second Merlin was taken aback, never guessing Banks would believe him or that his opinion would in any way be sought regarding how to approach the problem. "How about Jonathan Olsen?"

"Olsen? I thought there was some bad blood between the two of you."

"He is already aware of the problem, understands microbiology, and, although I disagree with his methods at times, I believe him to be honest."

"It's your call. Let me get in touch with Jonathan and maybe Knox Pincus as well. We'll meet in the conference room here at, say, noon tomorrow?" Banks looked at a gold watch on his wrist.

"Noon," Merlin confirmed.

When Merlin left and Banks Wickford was once again alone in his office, he retrieved the phone from the carpet, drawing it up hand over hand like he was pulling in a fish. Putting the phone in his ear he said, "You hear all that?" Then there was a pause and Banks chuckled, "That's Merlin for you. Just like Chicken Little."

Seven P.M. and he was in the Friendship Club having his third beer, playing a little acey-deucey. The drab atmosphere always seemed a little less dingy when you were winning. In fact, he was so hot all he could concentrate on was the nice little pile of ones and fives in front of him. Maybe the losers had time to let their eyes wander around the room and notice the red and green MERRY CHRISTMAS cardboard sign still up from last year, but his eyes never left his loot. When the phone behind the bar rang he certainly didn't hear it. The bartender with the thick neck waited for the hand of acey-deucey to be over before he held out the phone, never mind covering the mouthpiece, and said, "Hey, Brooklyn, someone calling for you. You wanna talk or should I have 'em call back?"

"Who is it?" the man known as Brooklyn asked, bringing the game to a standstill. The dealer with the fat fingers gathered up the cards, working slowly, not wanting to miss a thing.

"Who is it?" the bartender said into the phone. Then he held it out again. "Dr. . . . Verkorian or something." Brooklyn seemed surprised. Without a second's hesitation he went over to the bar. As he was handed the phone, the bartender asked, "Hey, you want another one?"

Brooklyn nodded, then looked back at the table with the regulars as he spoke into the phone.

"Yeah, what?" The thick-necked bartender handed him an Iron City. "No. I don't think I can anymore. Things have changed. You know, heated up." He took a good slug of the beer, then talked quietly, barely above a whisper. "Then I can return the money." Again in an inaudible whisper he said, "I said, then I can return the money." Now he spoke in his normal voice. "Look, is there someplace maybe where we can meet?'' Again he looked at the regulars, all turned around in their seats so they could hear everything. "No, not here." Brooklyn looked at his watch. "See ya."

Brooklyn drained his beer, walked over to the kitchen table where the acey-deucey game was on hold, scooped up his pile of winnings, and walked out of the Friendship Club.

Tommy drove the Chrysler down the increasingly narrow streets. Leo sat in the front seat and put his boot up on the dashboard, looking cool.

"Get your foot down," Tommy demanded, taking a swipe at Leo's leg.

"Hey, Tommy," Leo said, wiping a smudge of dirt from the leather dash with the palm of his hand, "who's this doctor you said you were, anyway?"

Tommy was just about to launch into an explanation but took one look at Leo with his blond hair and vacuous tough-guy expression and knew it would be a waste. "It's nothing."

Leo said, "Lemme talk with him. I can handle guys like this."

"You wouldn't know what to say."

"Try me. That's why you brought me on, right?" He leaned back, the cocky tough kid, proud to think of himself as the muscle. Then he forgot what he was doing and started to put his foot up on the dashboard, his tight jeans riding up, showing off a little cowboy boot. "That him?" Leo asked. "Looks like a deer caught in the headlights."

The window on Leo's side opened silently as Tommy worked the button. "Yep, that's him. Keep your fucking foot down. And you're not ready to do any talking. Try doing the listening for once, okay?"

They had arrived at the Friendship Club, and Tommy swooped the car across the street and pulled up right where Brooklyn was waiting on the curb. As the car came to a stop, Tommy told Leo to hop in the back. Leo gave him a pissed-off look but was already getting out of the car. The look was just for show.

Tommy ignored him.

It was cool outside, one of the first evenings that promised winter was just around the corner. Brooklyn had on a red satin jacket that always felt cool and slippery. It had his real name on the left breast in fancy script. On the back it said "Brooklyn Turkeys" over a picture of bowling pins being knocked over.

No greetings, no words of any kind. This was business. Tommy didn't even look at him as he got in. Instead he hit the accelerator as soon as Brooklyn's butt hit the leather upholstery. Brooklyn had to hold on and reach for the armrest on the door as the car lurched away. Soon they were doing fifty on the little side streets. Tommy hit a button, and the door locks snapped shut loudly. Brooklyn made a little turn of his head and looked at his door. Then Tommy pressed a second button, and the window on the passenger side closed. When the wind stopped moving his hair around, Brooklyn turned his head one more time and looked uneasily out the window, shifting in his seat.

"That's Leo, in the back," Tommy said and made a movement with his head toward the backseat.

Brooklyn made a half turn. "Leo."

Leo nodded and sulked in the backseat.

"Brooklyn Turkeys," Tommy said. "Tell me again what that's about."

"It's nothing, a bowling joke. That's all."

"Hey, Leo," Tommy said, looking in the rearview mirror. "You see anything funny in the name Brooklyn Turkeys?"

"Nah."

"That makes two of us. Okay, Brooklyn, now tell me what you were whispering about on the phone," Tommy said as he took a couple of turns too quickly. Each time Tommy jerked the car, Brooklyn sat up a little straighter, his knuckles on the door rest became a little whiter. Tommy took in everything, pleased he had his passenger's attention.

"I said that I'd return the money you gave me and not do it anymore."

A stop sign stood at the end of the block. Tommy gave it a little gas, hitting the brakes hard at the last second. "Okay, give it to me," Tommy said, taking his first good look at Brooklyn while he held his hand out.

"I . . . I don't have it with me. I'll get it to you, gimme a week."

"So what's the problem?" Tommy said.

Brooklyn looked down at his jacket. He felt like a kid just before the fight started. "Someone started asking me questions about the infections."

Leo grabbed the back of the front seat and pulled himself up so he was talking right in Brooklyn's ear. "When?"

"Today. We were in the OR and someone said, 'Hey, you know there's been four patients die after surgery from infections?' "

"What'd you say, man?" Leo demanded.

"Leo," Tommy said and hit the accelerator hard, pushing Leo back in his seat. "Hey, Brooklyn, it's a *he,* right?"

"Yeah, I think it was a guy," Brooklyn said, choosing his words carefully.

"Well did he say anything else?"

"Something about WIP insurance. I didn't know what to say, so I said nothing. What's he talking about, WIP insurance?"

"Don't have a clue. Listen, he don't know anything. Trust me. This whole thing is just for a month or two more, then you get the rest of your money."

"I don't care. I don't want to do it anymore."

"Turn around and take a look at Leo." Brooklyn turned around in his seat and squinted to get a good look at the passenger in the backseat. When Tommy was satisfied Brooklyn had studied Leo long enough, he continued, "I don't want to have Leo talk to you. Leo's hard to control."

For the first time Leo smiled.

Brooklyn swallowed. "Look, I'm scared. They're gonna be watching closer."

"It's easier to be careful than have Leo show up at your house and chat with you in front of your wife, huh?"

They drove in silence for a couple of blocks, taking it in. Finally Brooklyn said, "Okay." His voice was weak. "I'll do it."

Tommy stopped the car. "Open the glove box."

Brooklyn found the box and checked out the condom tied in a knot, the light brown fluid sloshing around inside.

"What's this guy's name again?"

"Who?" Brooklyn wanted to know.

"The guy who said something to you in the hospital." Tommy spoke slowly, trying to control his temper.

"I don't know. One of the guys in the OR."

"In the OR?"

"Right. Some guy in the OR."

"Some *doc* in the OR?"

Brooklyn cleared his throat. "Yeah, I think."

"And you don't know him?"

"I didn't really notice who said it. You know, everyone wears a mask and everything. Sometimes it's hard to tell."

"What the fuck's his name?" Tommy snarled. Brooklyn didn't say anything for the longest time. "WHAT THE FUCK'S—"

Finally Brooklyn mumbled, "Merlin."

"Merlin, huh." Tommy hit the brakes. "See ya."

"What?"

Tommy raised his voice. "Get out!"

"What, here? Where are we?"

"I'm not your driver. And don't forget the rubber."

After Brooklyn was out of the car, Tommy cut a harsh look at Leo in the backseat. "This Merlin is a problem we're gonna fix tomorrow.

8

It was just before six when Tory shut down her desktop computer, closed her office door, and changed clothes. If office particulars were any indication of rank in the district attorney's office, then Tory had positioned herself squarely in the middle of the pack, which was an accomplishment in itself for someone less than two and a half years out of law school. Although she enjoyed one of the smaller offices in the hallway, she was thrilled to have two windows with an eastern exposure that invited a warm swath of morning sunshine which nurtured a tiny garden on her windowsill.

Several times a week, Tory hopped a ride to work with a friend, packing her running clothes in a lightweight backpack in anticipation of a run home. The weather was changing, and it wouldn't be much longer before it would be too dark to run the seven miles home at the end of the day.

Wearing a sweatshirt and silky running shorts, Tory slowly jogged down Grant Street from the Allegheny County Courthouse, adjusting the straps on her backpack that she filled with personal items. It was overcast and some of the cars already had their lights on. Since coming to Pittsburgh five years earlier she had become a confident city runner, learning how to negotiate the traffic and the other pedestrians. Grant Street was usually difficult, the traffic always heavy. Just as she started across the wide expanse of cobblestone, a big car thundered through the intersection, accelerating to beat the yellow light.

Tory stopped abruptly, keeping her legs going, rhythmically lifting her feet just a few inches off the ground to stay loose.

For some reason as the car roared past, the driver took the time to look right at her. It was a man with blond hair, turning his head hard to ogle her. She could feel his eyes snaking over her bare legs. For a second Tory became furious and shot a look back at him. The whole thing took less than a moment. Then he was gone. Several women started across the street, commenting loudly on how rude the drivers were in Pittsburgh. Tory trotted the rest of the way across Grant, trying not to devote too much thought to what had happened. If she had gone over it in her mind she would have concluded it wasn't that much different from what happened on any given day of the week. Guys checked her out all the time, tried to buy her drinks whenever she arrived at a restaurant before Merlin, and occasionally slowed down their cars and provocatively lowered their sunglasses before giving her that leering smile.

This was really nothing. Just some jerk showing off. But he'd left the air thick with oily exhaust, and the only thing Tory really concerned herself with was holding her breath until she hit the sidewalk.

Over the next several minutes Tory made her way past Heinz Hall and down toward the Seventh Street Bridge. As traffic was usually heavy around the cultural district, Tory's run was filled with starts and stops as she kept waiting for red lights to turn green. Finally, just when she was about to cross the river, the traffic seemed to thin out, and for the first time she hit her stride. Even with the gradual incline of the bridge Tory maintained her six-and-a-half-minute pace, running easily, her breathing relaxed, enjoying a good long look at one of the monstrous river barges inching its way up the Allegheny.

A noise to her left caught her attention. A growl, but not something from an internal combustion engine. No, this was a sound from a human larynx. It startled Tory. She whipped her head around and saw the taillights of a big, brown car speed off. Was it the same car? Tory couldn't tell. But hearing that growling sound made her feel as if she were running through the streets naked. Harder and harder she pumped her long legs, pushing herself across the bridge to the less hectic North Side of Pittsburgh.

Another runner's presence would have been nice.

Out of nowhere a silent ambulance flew by with its lights going. It made her think of Merlin, but this one was probably heading toward Three Rivers General Hospital, which sat on a gentle hillside not far away.

Once she was off the bridge, the streets on the North Side were quieter. With less traffic, the air smelled a little cleaner. Another ambulance sped by. Tory was feeling stronger and was ready to pick up the pace when it happened.

A car—the same car that had just growled at her—came out of nowhere, swerving sharply. It got too close to the sidewalk where Tory was running, and the tires scraped up against the curb. It seemed huge, a Chrysler maybe, like the one her dad had driven ten years ago. This one was big and brown, swooping out of the dusk and scaring the shit out of her. The driver got close to her, less than four feet away, near enough for Tory to get a good look at the little grille ornament. But the car missed her, never actually leaving the street. It didn't slow down, either, but tore around the next corner, disappearing as quickly as it came.

First her legs stopped working, feeling like useless rubber appendages barely able to hold her up. Her breathing came in loud gulps, heaving her chest. She looked around for someone, anyone, on the street, just so she wouldn't feel so alone.

Unfortunately, she was alone. The sky was growing darker by the minute, and the buildings, while not as tall as the ones across the river, dwarfed her.

The big, brown Chrysler was gone, and for more than a minute Tory leaned against the brick of a small office building, taking refuge in a puddle of light from an overhead streetlamp.

When she had her wits about her and her legs came back to life, she started running, slowly at first, craning her neck every which way, trying to convince herself that everything was all right. *Who the hell was that?* Tentatively, she jogged another half block in the direction of Aspinwall, hoping the driver was just another jerk having some redneck fun.

Off in the distance, a block and a half away, she spotted the headlights of a car poking out of an alleyway between two buildings. Again Tory stopped cold, stepping back into the shadow of a small luncheonette that was already closed for the night. Even if it had been thirty degrees cooler, the air could not have felt more icy. *Turn around and go back over the bridge. Now. Get the hell out of here and go back to the courthouse and call a cab.* The voice in her head repeated itself, getting louder and louder until she found herself turning around, trotting back toward the Seventh Street Bridge.

Her heart was beating frantically in her chest. Every few steps she spun her head around to grab a quick look over her shoulder. The combination of running forwards and looking backwards sent her staggering down the street like a drunk. But the nose of the car never moved from the alley, and Tory's confidence started to come back. Slowly she picked up the pace. The ramp of the bridge was less than three blocks away.

Another look over her shoulder. The car remained in the alleyway.

Tory felt herself relaxing. As she lengthened her stride, her breathing slowed. The view across the river was beautiful, the small cluster of tall buildings lighted against the ever darkening sky. *Maybe I'll forget the cab and just call Merlin.* Tory was running well.

One more look over her shoulder, and she almost stumbled.

The car that had been safely tucked into that little space between two big buildings was now creeping along the curb not thirty feet away from her. This was the same big, brown Chrysler, and it was getting closer and closer.

Tory picked up the pace, sprinting down the street, feeling the backpack bouncing around clumsily between her shoulder blades. Again and again she looked over her shoulder, struggling to keep from weaving down the sidewalk.

The car was gaining and she could barely make out the face of the driver. The jerk was giving her a smile.

Now she was running all out, racing past a heavy brick building, knowing she could only keep up this pace for another block or two. No way could she cross back into the city at a sprint.

Around the corner, Tory said to herself, and leaned into the turn as she whipped around the corner and onto an empty side street. This was virgin territory and, seeing how dark it was, she immediately regretted her decision. Her feet pounded the pavement, slapping loudly against the concrete as she began to tire.

Before she knew what was happening the street exploded in bright light. A long shadow appeared at Tory's feet, and she was bathed in the glare of the Chrysler's headlights as the car followed her onto the deserted street.

She felt trapped and stopped running. Dropping her shoulders one at a time, she let the backpack slide to the ground. Instantly she formulated a plan. Standing her ground, she would wait for the car to pull up beside her. Then the window would roll down and the driver would lean across the front seat and spew some horribly lewd comment at her. That's when she'd make her move, running back the same way she'd come from, leaving him to either chase her on foot or try to turn his big car around on the narrow street. Yep, that's exactly what she'd do.

But the Chrysler seemed to be picking up speed. As it approached, it veered slightly, heading right for her. When it jumped the curb there was the horrible sound of metal banging off concrete.

It never seemed like slow motion. Everything was coming so quickly. Tory knew exactly what was going to happen next. She was going to get hit. There was no time to jump out of the way. The headlights came closer and closer, and Tory stood frozen, her hands out clumsily to cushion the blow and *THWAAACK.*

The right headlight smacked into her belly, knocking Tory backwards onto the sidewalk, arms and legs flailing everywhere like a rag doll rolling down the stairs.

She had screamed for a second, no more, but loud enough to leave her vocal cords ragged. There had been the horrible noise of the car smacking her, and the dull thud of her body crashing into the concrete. Now it was quiet, and for just a second there was a fleeting calm that set in knowing it was over.

Then the pain started. Not slowly like a stomachache from eating too many jalapeño peppers. This pain grabbed her in the gut and twisted hard. Searing pain. Throbbing through her belly, worse than anything she could imagine. Pain that made her want to die.

She was lying on the curb, one arm in the gutter, flat on her back. Each breath became increasingly difficult. The air at street level reeked of tar, and all the sounds of cars off in the distance frightened her. When a horn sounded Tory winced.

Merlin. Tory saw Merlin walking toward her . . . her mother touching her hair . . . Merlin . . . her father in his police uniform. . . .

Spinning. Sick spinning like she needed to vomit. Then her eyes rolled up and everything was dark. Quiet sounds became loud noises.

"Miss, you okay? You alive? I'm gonna pick you up and help you," a man's voice said.

Other voices screamed on top of one another. "Call an ambulance." "Don't move her. She'll get paralyzed." "Someone call 911." "Who hit her? Did anyone see who hit her?"

But the man's voice said, "I saw. It was a truck, a white bread truck. Came right up on the sidewalk. She better get to the hospital quick; I'll take her up to Three Rivers Hospital." Tory felt herself being picked up like she was a little baby. *Who are you? Tell me who you are.* The man was strong, like her dad, picking her up effortlessly. Then she was eased onto something cold and uncomfortable. Something was sticking into her back. There was a loud bang, then a second bang, the sounds of car doors closing.

Please talk to me. She could feel movement, slow movement at first, the engine purring and the bumps in the road barely noticeable. Her eyes opened just a crack, but it was too dark to see.

Soon they were going faster, making some turns, rushing over potholes, the horn sounding a couple of times. Moaning was just about the only response Tory could make as the car moved through the streets. She wanted to scream, "What happened?" but the agony of her neurons firing in the pain center of her brain was unbearable.

Seconds went by.

Then minutes.

Where is the hospital? We should be at Three Rivers by now.

She could see out of the window now, and the telephone poles were flying by too quickly to count.

Breathing out. Breathing in. Breathing out. Breathing in. Out was easy. In was hard, a horrible spasm gripping her belly with each inspiration. *Maybe I'm bleeding. Oh, God, am I bleeding?* Amazingly, she hadn't even thought about being cut. The thought of her belly slashed wide open terrified her. It took several seconds to steel the courage and send her fingers creeping down the right side of her abdomen. What if there was a big hole and she put her fingers right inside her stomach? Delicately, like a butterfly alighting on a flower, Tory's fingers floated along the surface of her skin. Then she slowly brought her fingers up to her face, moving them around to get them in focus, looking for blood.

It was too dark to see. She opened her mouth and tasted the end of her finger.

Suddenly the car stopped. A little squeal came from the tires, and Tory had to put her hand out, pushing against the front seat to keep from falling. *A car. I'm in a car.* All this time she had thought she was in an ambulance. Without saying anything the driver got out and slammed his door. "Where am I?" Tory said in a hoarse whisper. *Am I alone? Is anyone else in the car?*

The door by her head opened, and she could feel the rush of cool air. "Okay, upsey-daisy," the man said, and large hands reached under Tory's shoulders and slid her out of the car.

Again the pain. Her belly was exploding, probably bleeding heavily. All she could see were lights. Lots of lights. Bright lights hurting her eyes when she brought her hands up to look for blood. But they were clean. All of a sudden it dawned on Tory that she'd been here before. But the spasm worsened as the man shifted her in his arms, the muscles in her face tightening until her eyes closed off in little slits, and Tory forgot about trying to remember where she was.

He was carrying her, walking quickly. There was something digging into Tory's shoulder, something hard. It probably hurt but the pain pulsing from her belly made it impossible to tell. *Maybe he's a cop.*

The man must have been getting tired. He shifted his arms and Tory's knees jerked up toward her chest, the hurt coursing through her body. It was rapidly becoming hard to see, the lights fading to dull brown, darker and darker until they were tiny dots of bronze in a black sky. Then they disappeared.

Merlin was sitting in his office making his last phone call of the day. The noon meeting had become an excuse for an elegant private luncheon in the executive conference room. Of course Banks had arranged for Knox to be there, but Olsen was late, so Banks suggested they start eating while they waited. Knox rhapsodized about the baby mesclun salad, taking time to name each of the varieties of lettuce as he popped them into his mouth. When a cold salmon was served with a mustard dill sauce, Knox declared that it rivaled the Four Seasons in New York. In forty-five minutes they made it to dessert, a cold lemon soufflé with raspberry sauce drizzled over the top. Not one word of business had been discussed. Just as Banks was making little smacking noises with his lips to savor the delicate flavor of the soufflé, Jonathan Olsen made his appearance, rushing into the room with a stack of charts, all five of them under one arm. His apology was brief. At once he seated himself, placing the charts where his dessert dish should have been.

Knox seemed particularly glad to see the chairman of pathology enter the room. He checked his watch and raised his eyebrows as if surprised at how the time had gotten away. "Well, Olsen, you missed quite a meal."

"Don't worry," Banks reassured, "I had yours wrapped."

"It took me quite a bit longer to go through these charts than I anticipated."

Knox stood. "I've got a meeting across town. Give it to me straight. Is the sky falling like Chicken Little here would have us believe?"

Banks smiled. Merlin did not.

Knox turned to Merlin. "I was on the receiving end of the phone you knocked out of Banks's hand."

"I don't think I'd say the sky is falling—" Olsen began.

"Good," Knox said quickly, interrupting him.

"But," Olsen continued, "if we're using analogies—we don't want to sit in a hospital made of straw when the big bad wolf comes around."

Now Merlin smiled.

"Fair enough." Knox shook hands with Banks. "So can I assume this is a . . ." he paused, searching for the right word, "little situation . . . that requires a further look-see?" he asked, not wanting to use the word "investigation."

"That's exactly what I propose."

"Then it's settled. I'll expect to hear from you if anything turns up. Now, if you will excuse me, gentlemen." Knox Pincus headed for the door. "You know," he said, not forgetting his manners, "I'm just going to pop in the kitchen and tell them what a wonderful luncheon they prepared."

"Well," Olsen declared after Knox made his hasty exit, "I've read through all five of the charts Merlin delivered to us. I've also reviewed the autopsy results. To be honest with you," he paused and looked first at Merlin, then at Banks, "I can't say we *don't* have a problem. Statistically speaking, Western Insurance is too small an insurance company for this many infectious disease deaths in such a brief time period."

Merlin leaned forward as if he were about to say something when Olsen continued, "But . . . I don't want to go off the deep end, either." He looked over at Merlin.

"Hear, hear." Banks nodded in agreement. "So what do you suggest we do?"

"First, *we*," Olsen said and motioned with his hand to indicate that he meant only those in the room, "do some investigating. Have there been any deaths of patients insured by other carriers? I'm certain one of the computer whiz kids could tap into our information system and come up with that answer in five minutes."

"You'll talk with them?" Banks wanted to know.

"This afternoon."

"Excellent. Keep going."

"I want Chicken Little here to contact his counterparts at other area hospitals to see if they have noticed any similar clustering of recent deaths."

"Done," Merlin said.

"Uh-uh," Banks said. "No way. This has got to be kept in-house."

"We've got to know. I can inquire without tipping our hand," Merlin offered.

"No. This is exactly the kind of thing Three Rivers Hospital would love to leak to KDKA and turn into a public relations nightmare for us. Remember, we don't know for sure that this isn't an unfortunate coincidence, do we?"

"I can't believe we're dealing with a coincidence," Merlin responded.

"Give me one concrete piece of evidence something nefarious is going on. Show me the smoking gun," Banks snapped.

Merlin held his tongue.

Then Banks looked to Olsen. "Anything else?"

"I'd like to track all patients who are admitted to the Medical Center with Western Insurance for the next month, follow the medical as well as surgical patients."

"Good," the CEO said.

"And I want Merlin to create a database of the recent deaths, listing what OR the patient had been surgerized in, what personnel were involved, and the type of diagnosis. Then we can see if there really is a trend."

"Thank you, Jonathan," Banks said, getting up from the table. "Let's get together one day next week when you've gotten all the information together. I remind you both not to discuss any of this outside this room."

The three headed for the door.

"One more thing, Merlin," Banks said, patting him on the back in a friendly fashion, trying to end the session on a light note. "I hope you'll make do with sandwiches next time."

Merlin chatted on the phone with the surgical chief resident at Three Rivers General Hospital. It made sense to find out if other hospitals were experiencing similar problems, and as far as Merlin was concerned, Banks's financial concerns were ridiculous.

As Merlin started into a thinly veiled explanation of the situation at the Medical Center, his beeper sounded. Instantly he ran down the list of patients he'd operated on in the last few days. *Shit, I hope it's not a postop.* There was no doubt in his paranoid state what he was about to hear. *Dr. Merlin, it's Mrs. So-and-So on Ten South. She's developed a fever and now*—Merlin saw himself dashing up to the floor only to find the STAT team thumping on her chest. So certain was Merlin about his message he hung up the phone without so much as a good-bye.

The anonymous female voice began talking to him from the miniature speaker on his yellow beeper. He plucked it from his belt and held it to his ear. *Please don't let it be postop. Anything but postop.* "Dr. Merlin, STAT to ER. Merlin, STAT to ER."

Merlin smiled.

Imagine that. The chief resident was grateful to be STAT paged to the ER. Whatever it was, at least it wasn't a postop patient.

Any time Merlin responded to a STAT page he went full speed. Running. No time for elevators or last bites of sandwiches. There was nothing that infuriated him more after he'd raced up six flights of stairs than some cocky third-year resident sauntering in five minutes late looking like he just stepped out of a soft drink commercial. When you arrived at a STAT page you'd better be out of breath.

Over and over, like an echo in a canyon, the page was repeated from the overhead speaker system. "Dr. Merlin, STAT to the ER." Merlin started to run faster.

Whenever a nurse was waiting at the door to the ER it usually meant time was critical. The charge nurse, an overweight woman who had known Merlin since his medical student days, started yelling to him when he was thirty yards away. "Merlin! Quick, it's Tory. She was hit by a car!"

He ran by the nurse, and she tried to keep up as they talked.

"Is she conscious?"

"She comes in and out."

"Bleeding?"

"Just scrapes."

Merlin whipped open the white drape that surrounded Tory. The growing crowd of doctors, nurses, and onlookers parted with Merlin's arrival, allowing him his first glimpse of Tory.

She was naked, except for a couple of towels that someone had thoughtfully placed over her breasts and pubis. An IV ran into one of her arms, and a technician had just finished drawing blood from her other arm. EKG leads were taped to her chest, the cardiac monitor showing a steady heart rate. Someone in a white coat was bent over her chest listening with a stethoscope, while someone else gently pulled her eyelids open and shined a tiny flashlight to make certain her pupils were the same size and contracted when exposed to the light.

"Head trauma?" Merlin asked, his clipped tone demanding quick, accurate answers.

"No," came the reply from the person examining the eyes. It was an ER resident Merlin had worked with before.

"So she's neurologically okay," Merlin stated, wanting to hear the words come out of his mouth, praying the ER resident didn't correct him.

"So far so good," the resident said. "Reflexes are intact, down-going toes, sometimes she wakes up and follows some directions. She's out again. I'm pretty sure it's just her belly."

Tears trickled down Merlin's face. *Oh, God, thank you.* Merlin immediately went down on one knee, face-to-face with Tory. He brushed some stray hairs from her face and said, "Hey, Tor. It's me. Open your eyes for me."

Tory could hear the voice talking to her, but it was far away. She felt like she was asleep, her muscles having a mind of their own, disobeying any and all of her commands. She desperately wanted to wake up and look at who was talking to her, but her eyelids wouldn't budge. Something touched her face gently, stroking her, soothing her. She could barely make sense of the words, a whisper in the dark, a radio in the next room playing softly in the middle of the night. *Open your eyes.* And she tried, but she couldn't put the tiny muscles in motion. Then she caught a word, "Tor," and got excited. Only one person ever called her that.

Merlin whispered, "Can you hear me? It's safe now. You can open your eyes. Hey, ya gotta talk with me."

Merlin! It's Merlin. Merlin! Oh, don't leave, Merlin. Take care of me. Slowly, her eyelids fluttering at the bright lights, Tory opened her eyes. The world was out of focus, but she looked in the direction of his voice.

He smiled and let his fingers brush her lips. She responded with a weak pucker and kissed his fingertips.

The ER resident waited patiently. "Merlin. She was hit over on the North Side. Some good Samaritan put her in his car and drove her here."

"From the North Side?"

"Said they were near Three Rivers Hospital, but Tory insisted that he bring her across town here. BP's low, Merlin. Started at a hundred over sixty, now it's eighty-five over fifty. Lungs clear. Her belly's pretty tender. Maybe she's bleeding internally."

Merlin's hand gently slid over Tory's abdomen, palpating here and there. When he got to her left side she winced in pain and cried out. "Her spleen. Look at where the abrasion is." Merlin glanced around. "Where's the guy? The guy who brought her."

"I'll get him," one of the nurses said and broke from the crowded bedside.

Merlin borrowed a stethoscope and listened to Tory's lungs. Hearing clear, symmetrical breath sounds, he proceeded to her belly. At even the slightest pressure of the stethoscope Tory would turn her head and moan softly. For at least fifteen seconds Merlin concentrated on those grunty-groany noises a happy intestine makes as it digests its food. There was nothing. Absolute, complete silence. He closed his eyes and tried to block out the din of the ER. Gradually he heard a noise, a tapping sound that was the rhythmic pulsing of the blood through his own ears. Otherwise Tory's abdomen had shut itself down.

"No bowel sounds. Gimme a nineteen-gauge Angiocath and hook it up to a bag of normal saline."

This ER functioned like a well-oiled machine. Hands seemed to come out of the attentive crowd as if it were one living, breathing being. First a pair of Merlin's seven-and-one-half gloves appeared, then some Betadine preps which Merlin quickly used to clean a small portion of belly.

Finally he was handed an Angiocath, a small flexible plastic sheath—the catheter—with a sharp needle running through it. The needle would pierce skin and clear the way for the soft plastic catheter to follow.

"Tor, gonna feel a little prick."

Her eyes opened and she heard what he said, but she wasn't expecting the pain that followed.

Gently, but with confident hands, Merlin pierced Tory's abdomen with the needle and catheter. When the Angiocath was buried down to its plastic hub, Merlin withdrew the needle and left the catheter in place. A nurse was ready with a long plastic tube which Merlin used to attach a bag of sterile saline to the plastic catheter. By hanging the bag on an IV pole the fluid quickly ran into Tory's belly. In several minutes the bag was empty.

"Merlin. He's gone!" The young nurse who had gone in search of Tory's ride to the hospital had returned, breathless, and blurted out, "The unit clerk said he left as soon as he dropped Tory off. He told her—he told everybody—that Tory had demanded that she be brought here and that only you operate on her. Some young guy with blond hair. Dressed in a dark suit."

By now the empty bag was removed from the IV pole and unceremoniously dropped to the floor. Immediately, the fluid began to drain back out of Tory's belly under the force of gravity.

When it went into the belly, the fluid was as clear and colorless as fresh spring water. Now, it was dark pink. There was an audible gasp from one of the nurses.

"It's got to be her spleen," the ER resident said confidently. "And, Merlin, her BP's slipping."

Free blood in the abdomen. A surgical emergency. The trauma from the car had ripped or ruptured something. It was a good bet that it was Tory's spleen, a small and fragile organ that God had tucked up under her left lower rib cage for protection. Unfortunately, it was a vascular organ, loaded with blood vessels. When traumatized, it could bleed uncontrollably.

The surgical decision was easy. It didn't require a series of tests or X rays, and with Tory's blood pressure falling, waiting for X rays could prove deadly.

"I'm gonna take her to OR."

It was like flipping a switch. Once again things began to happen quickly, and a systematic chain of events took place. Someone called the seventh floor and told them that an OR team had to be assembled, STAT. More blood was drawn from Tory and cross-matched for a transfusion, just in case. People from admitting appeared out of nowhere with lots of questions about insurance. Meanwhile Merlin slipped from the crowd, found a phone in the nursing station, and made a quick call to Tory's dad, telling him a sanitized version of what had happened.

As he hung up it hit Merlin. The guy, the good Samaritan, who had quite possibly saved Tory's life had simply disappeared. That was odd. No one just scooped someone off the sidewalk and dumped them in the ER and bolted.

It felt wrong to Merlin, who had always trusted his instincts. Why the hell would anyone go to all that effort, show up way across town, and disappear in the blink of an eye?

Merlin was getting himself going. He was upsetting—no, terrifying—himself. Everything was reeling out of control. Nothing made sense.

Why would someone make the effort to drive Tory to the ER and then leave? Maybe the good Samaritan was the same guy who hit Tory but didn't want any trouble with the police. If so, disappearing from the ER was almost like a hit-and-run.

What the hell was going on?

He saw them wheeling Tory out of the ER, right past the desk where he was sitting. Her eyes were open, and she seemed to be looking about, searching for him. Merlin raced to catch up with her stretcher and walked alongside.

"Oh, Merlin, you're here. I'm so glad—"

"Tory. Why did you make that guy drive you all the way here?"

"No, Merlin. No."

"No what?"

"I didn't make him. I couldn't even talk."

"You sure? You didn't tell him—"

"No." Her voice was weak, almost a whisper. "He swerved. Came on the sidewalk. He swerved to hit me—"

Time was flying. A decision had to be made quickly. They were at the elevators. *Think, goddamn it, think.* When the doors opened they wheeled Tory on. Merlin gave her hand a little squeeze.

Before the elevator started to move, Merlin was back on the phone. Nervously he dialed, his eyes darting around as he waited for someone to pick up. When his connection went through he hunched over, creating privacy where there wasn't any. Immediately he identified himself in a tone that was professional, no friendly chitchat or even an explanation for his unusual request. While he dictated his concise list of orders he stole a glance around. Not taking any chances, everything was repeated.

As a surgeon who had faced numerous emergency situations, Merlin had never been afraid to make a decision. While time was of the essence, the only thing worse than making a bad decision was the inability to focus and make any decision.

Tory needed surgery. That much was easy. But there was one nagging question: Was Tory's accident really an accident or did it somehow fit into a bigger picture? Merlin might be a committee of one, but he was absolutely convinced the series of deaths was not a coincidence. And now this incident with the good Samaritan disappearing from the ER and Tory claiming she never demanded to be brought to the Medical Center was eating away at him. What he needed was time to sort things out. Time to investigate. Maybe even call the police.

But Tory was bleeding and if he fell prey to a revolving loop of introspection Tory would certainly go into shock.

If he was wrong—and he hoped he was—then he would be the joke of the Medical Center for the duration of his chief residency.

If he was right, then his paranoia might keep Tory alive.

Merlin made one more phone call, this time to hospital security.

The seventh floor was finally quieting down except for one or two late cases. There were a few nurses and doctors lingering in the nursing station, chatting away before heading home.

Tory beat Merlin to the operating suite by several minutes. By the time Merlin arrived at OR Four, his home court, Tory was being transferred from the stretcher to the operating table. An anesthesiologist—not his friend Roland, who had probably long since gone home—was preparing the equipment at the head of the table. Working feverishly to assemble the hemostats, forceps, needle holders, and scalpels was Nick Bello.

Nick Bello? At nine P.M.?

The circulating nurse was racing around the room, fetching packages of sterile instruments and dumping them on the Mayo stands for Bello to organize. Then she poured Betadine into a small metal bowl and sterile saline in a large metal basin. Three scalpel blades were dropped in a little pile. Bello clicked each blade securely into its own handle. Knowing this could be a bloody operation, the circulating nurse grabbed four packages of four-by-four gauze squares. Just as she approached the Mayo stand and fumbled momentarily with the little tab on top that would peel the paper from the white plastic tub, Merlin interrupted her.

"Would everyone please STOP!" Merlin commanded in a booming voice.

Instantly the room became quiet, and the circulating nurse stood frozen in her tracks. Nick Bello looked up at Merlin. The anesthesiologist stood to have a better view.

"Nick, you pulled a double?"

"Yeah. Someone called off. I don't mind." He looked down at an unruly pile of hemostats as if they beckoned him.

Speaking to the circulating nurse, Merlin said, "Please bring that stretcher over to the operating table." Merlin waited for a few seconds.

All eyes were on the nurse who clumsily guided the long stretcher around the crowded room. "If we can get some help, I'd like to load Tory back on the stretcher."

"What?" Bello asked, sounding amazed.

"It's okay, Nick. Everyone, please don't take this the wrong way. I'm going crazy with paranoia. I'll allow you all a good laugh behind my back when this is over, but I'm taking the patient."

"Merlin," Nick said, "you can't take her. She's bleeding."

"Her BP's eighty-five over forty. It's not safe to move her," the anesthesiologist added.

Tory was confused. Nothing made sense, and everything that was happening frightened her. Although turning her head to look around was uncomfortable, she made one failed attempt to find Merlin before wincing in pain.

The circulating nurse, clearly pissed off at racing around for nothing, flipped her unopened packages of gauze right onto one of the Mayo stands and stormed out of the room.

"I understand the clinical situation, Nick. I'm going to take her to surgery, but I don't think I can do it here. I've made other arrangements."

Silently the anesthesiologist and Nick Bello helped Merlin move Tory back onto the stretcher. Merlin tucked a light cotton blanket around her, then her IV bag was rehung on the pole attached to the stretcher. "Okay," Merlin said as he took his place at Tory's head. "Would you both please clear the room. I'll arrange for cleanup later. Please . . . just walk out." Merlin waited while the anesthesiologist and Bello walked out of OR Four. When they were alone Merlin took Tory's hand and whispered softly into her ear. He hoped the wait wouldn't be long.

"Excuse me. You can't be dressed like that on this floor," one of the OR nurses said. There was a no-nonsense tone to her voice.

"Where's Merlin?"

"Excuse me. You'll have to wait in the lounge." The nurse eyed the large black man standing in front of her.

He was from hospital security and went by the name Big John. Briefly looking down at himself he nodded. "He said it was kind of an emergency."

"I don't care what Merlin said, we have rules."

Expecting Big John to cause a commotion, Merlin raced out of OR Four when he heard his voice. There he was, 230 pounds of muscle packed tightly into his blue uniform, a service revolver dangling from a thick black belt around his narrow waist. With his shaved head he looked menacing, as if he would feel more comfortable in a boxing ring. But he and Merlin were friends, and sometimes one friend does a favor for another.

"Merlin," the nurse said, sounding relieved. "You know he can't come up here dressed like that."

"It's okay," Merlin said. "We'll get out of the hallway in a second." Big John made a point of nodding politely to the nurse before following Merlin toward OR Four.

"Okay, Merlin, what's going on?" Big John wanted to know as soon as they were alone.

Merlin pushed open the door to the OR and went to the stretcher. "You remember Tory. Like I told you on the phone, she needs surgery, but I don't feel safe doing it here. I know it sounds crazy, but trust me."

"So what do you want me to do, Merlin?"

"Just stay here. No matter what, don't let anyone in. I'll come back as soon as possible. Do whatever you have to do."

"Just sit here, huh."

"That's it. I'll run back after I'm done."

"I don't know, man. I've got to make my rounds."

"John, listen to me. You know I wouldn't bother you if it wasn't important. I trust you. What else can I say?"

Big John smiled and sat down on a tiny stool. "Then you better get going."

Nick Bello stood in the empty hallway watching Merlin head down the hallway with Tory. As Merlin boarded the elevator, the scrub nurse took a walk over to OR Four. He glanced through the little window in the door and immediately caught Big John's eye. Wandering back toward the nursing station he pulled down his surgical mask and slipped off his cap, wondering what the hell was going on.

A two-floor elevator ride brought Merlin to the obstetrics floor. This was alien territory for him, but an OR was an OR. With the help of several nurses, he was ushered into a waiting operating room.

Nine minutes later Tory was asleep, put under by a nurse anesthetist who specialized in OB-GYN cases. Somehow the fact that Merlin had never seen her before seemed strangely reassuring.

The scrub nurse was also new to him, but once they got started they seemed to work well together.

"Hemostat."

"Yes, Dr. Merlin." A hemostat was slapped into Merlin's upturned hand.

"I'm gonna need two more of those," Merlin said crisply, and each time his hand went out a hemostat was ready.

A comfortable rhythm developed. First a nine-inch up-and-down incision was made in the middle of Tory's belly, the only deviation from a perfectly straight line was a half-moon curve around the belly button. Layer by layer, Merlin descended. When the peritoneum was incised, the belly was overflowing with a watery fluid the color of Hawaiian Punch. What remained of the saline solution had been further darkened by continued bleeding.

Using a plastic suction tube like a mini-vacuum cleaner, Merlin cleaned out the abdominal cavity and began the meticulous process of checking each organ for signs of bleeding.

In a matter of thirty seconds it was obvious the spleen was indeed the source for the bleeding. Blood was a tremendous irritant. When splashing freely about the abdomen, it caused great pain.

Fortunately, the laceration was actually quite small, less than a centimeter, but the vascular spleen was notoriously difficult to suture. Instead, Merlin filled the opening with a cotton-candy-like material called Surgicel that quickly bonded to the splenic tissue. Then Merlin put gentle pressure on the wound for several minutes.

The bleeding stopped.

Merlin reexamined the rest of Tory's abdomen. The liver, stomach, small and large intestines. All clean. The source of bleeding—the only source of bleeding—had been the spleen. Once Merlin double-checked his work it was obvious the Surgicel was holding. He touched it gently, satisfied his repair was successful. In less than ninety minutes the skin was sutured closed, Tory was begun on the antibiotics vancomycin and cefazolin, and, as the anesthetist began the process of waking up his patient, Merlin went to the wall phone. He telephoned Mrs. Kincaid, their landlady. She listened as Merlin explained what had happened. Not once did she utter, "What!?" and make him repeat everything over and over. When he was finished talking she promised to hurry.

Once in the OB recovery room Merlin waited until Tory was awake, then entrusted her care to the small nursing staff there.

Back on seven Big John maintained guard in OR Four. The long hallway seemed much darker now, every other light panel in the ceiling being out for the night. Only a skeleton crew remained.

Armed with several dozen sterile swabs—a nine-inch version of a Q-tip—Merlin went into the OR. After a brief explanation of Tory's successful surgery, Merlin began the tedious process of compulsively swabbing and culturing everything that would have come in contact with

Tory during surgery. First the tangle of hemostats and scalpels. Next the endotracheal tube that would have been put down her throat. Then the suction tubing, and a squirt from each of the IV medications the anesthesiologist was planning to use. Each swab was used for a single sampling, then was handed off to Big John, who inserted the swab into its own sterile container and labeled each one.

Merlin dipped one of the swabs into the metal basin filled with sterile saline and handed it off. The package containing sterile gauze—never opened—sat on the Mayo stand next to the metal basin. Merlin picked up the package and examined it. It was a large blister pack containing several inches of white gauze. He looked at it more closely, holding it up to the light. Just as he was about to rip it open, he was hit with a sudden burst of inspiration. Could the package have been tampered with? Submerging it in the basin full of saline, Merlin gave it a little squeeze.

A tiny stream of bubbles rushed out of the pack and raced to the surface of the water in a silvery line.

"We've got something. Hey, grab me another blister pack from the shelf. Just like this one."

Big John brought three packs instead of one. All three were given the underwater squeeze test. None emitted bubbles.

Going back to the first blister pack he examined it again, looking for a pinhole that was too small for the naked eye to see. Eventually Merlin relieved Big John of the swabs he was holding. "I owe you one," he simply said.

Twenty minutes later, after depositing the cultures in the microbiology lab and instructing the microbiologist to run a series of cultures on the gauze squares, Merlin waited on one of the hospital loading docks.

Tory was with him, on the stretcher, awake and terribly confused, breathing in the cold night air. Three blankets failed to keep her warm. Her entire body shivered. Every time she moved, her toes poked out, and Merlin passed the time tucking her back in. An IV bag hung from the metal pole that was attached to the stretcher.

The wait wasn't long. Merlin spotted the Buick station wagon working its way down the long driveway toward the loading dock. Although a great and loyal friend, Mrs. Kincaid was a terrible driver. Three times she scraped up against a brick wall, making a horrible noise that certainly should have attracted attention.

After an unexpected hug from Mrs. Kincaid, who immediately charged up the stairs to the loading dock, Merlin gently began the torture of transferring Tory from the stretcher to the backseat of the wagon.

Any movement produced excruciating pain. Over and over, Tory moaned and winced as Merlin picked her up, one arm supporting her neck, the other under her legs. For a few moments she settled down as he whisked her down the stairs to the waiting Buick. But getting Tory into the backseat of the car was a different story. First Merlin placed her as far into the car as he could manage. While Mrs. Kincaid supported her legs, Merlin raced around the car, then carefully slid her all the way in. Tory was in tears. Merlin fussed over his patient for several minutes, wrapping her in the blankets, tenderly brushing a clump of stray hair from her face, and telling her how much he loved her. Only when she was settled down did Merlin insist that Mrs. Kincaid let him drive. It was cold, so he ran the heat full blast.

"You okay back there?" Merlin asked, smoothly backing the car out of the long driveway.

"Why are you kidnapping me?" Tory said and bravely tried to smile.

"I'll tell you in the morning. Just try to go to sleep."

"No. This is the second time I've been kidnapped today. I need some answers, Merlin."

Merlin obliged, continuing to drive as he talked over his shoulder. He explained that the guy who had driven her to the hospital had said that she demanded to be brought across town to the Medical Center. Then he had abruptly disappeared. "Maybe you were set up. I was afraid to operate on you with the usual team and equipment. So I made a last minute switch to the OB operating suite."

He finished with an explanation of how he had cultured all the sterile equipment and found that the blister packs of gauze had been tampered with.

"Then why are you kidnapping me now?"

"Just because."

By two A.M. Tory was asleep in Mrs. Kincaid's guest room, Merlin snoozed on Mrs. Kincaid's sofa, and Mrs. Kincaid sat worriedly by Tory's bedside.

9

For the next twenty-four hours time stood still for Merlin. He and Mrs. Kincaid took care of Tory, monitoring her vital signs, squirting vancomycin and cefazolin into the IV tubing, and hanging a new IV bag each time one ran out. Mostly, though, it was sitting with Tory and watching Mrs. Kincaid's favorite programs on the tiny black-and-white TV in her guest room. Periodically, Merlin pulled out his stethoscope and listened to Tory's belly. Gradually her pain was easing, but the incision line continued hurting every time she rolled over.

By early evening, when Tory had watched a continuous stream of eponymous talk shows and was nearly ready for a dose of Prozac, Merlin heard her bowels making happy grunting sounds for the first time. An hour later he kissed Tory good night and made the short walk next door and straight up the stairs to bed.

Merlin was up early the next morning, making a predawn house call. While he removed the bandages and examined Tory's belly, Mrs. Kincaid busied herself in the kitchen preparing Jell-O. His patient had one request. There was no way she could take another day of talk shows and wanted to go home to her own bed. Merlin was pleased with how Tory looked. So, with Mrs. Kincaid in tow carrying a bowl of hot runny Jell-O, Merlin took Tory's arm and patiently helped her home and up to bed.

It was still dark when Merlin came back down the stairs. Mrs. Kincaid was already busy, straightening up the living room while she listened to the local news on TV. Then she reassured Merlin everything was under control, the Jell-O was already in the fridge, and, promising to call him if there was a problem, insisted that he go to work.

* * *

Wanting to stay on top of every unusual admission to the Medical Center, Merlin was always the first to arrive on the surgical floors. This morning he slipped through the empty hallways unnoticed, planning to conduct work rounds as usual and still be in the OR by eight-thirty. He had left voice-mail messages for the chief of surgery explaining his twenty-four-hour absence, but his erratic behavior called for a face-to-face later in the day. There was also the information he had to gather for Olsen and culture results to check in the microbiology lab. If the sterile gauze squares tested positive for bacteria, then his outrageous behavior would certainly seem less suspicious. He decided to hit micro before he talked with his boss.

The office of the chief resident was on the eleventh floor, wedged in between a lavatory and a service elevator. Lacking windows, the office always seemed dark. Merlin automatically flipped on the lights as he pushed open the door, flipping his keys on the desk. With one foot he caught the door and kicked it closed.

"I was afraid you weren't coming in today."

The voice came from behind him, and Merlin jumped. Jerking his head around, he immediately recognized the uninvited visitor, sitting quite comfortably in the corner.

Blaine Huffman.

"What are you doing here?" Merlin demanded, his voice coming out louder than he expected.

"I was here yesterday. Drove all the way in from Cleveland. Sat for almost an hour. You didn't show, so I went back empty-handed. Where the hell were you?" Huffman questioned. His voice was unusually quiet, but he had a way of phrasing his words so that they demanded full attention. He had chosen a heavy wooden spindle chair with nice thick armrests, and he looked smart wearing a tweed blazer over a brown turtleneck. His legs were crossed in a casual manner, and he seemed surprisingly relaxed for a man who had recently lost his only child and had just broken into Merlin's office. A roaring fire and a brandy snifter would have completed the image.

"How'd you get in here? What do you want?" Merlin asked, firing two questions in rapid succession.

Huffman smiled. Already he had Merlin rattled and that would work to his advantage. Ignoring both of the surgeon's questions, Huffman shifted in his seat. He slipped one hand into the patch pocket on his tweed jacket, casually hooking his thumb on the material so that it kept his hand from disappearing all the way into the pocket. This was an affectation few men could pull off as gracefully as Blaine Huffman.

The showy display was not lost on Merlin. Of course he took notice of the heavy bulge in Huffman's pocket, correctly assuming it was a weapon he'd secreted there. After a deadly long silence, Merlin held up his jacket so Huffman could see he wasn't planning anything sneaky, then slowly turned toward the door and hung his jacket on the back of it. "You've got quite a James Bond thing going."

Huffman looked down at himself and smiled. "Maybe Bond's got quite a Blaine Huffman thing going." Again Huffman said little, not wanting things to get too chatty.

"So that was you the other night. It never occurred to me."

"What are you talking about?"

"You tried to run Tory over to get back at me. It didn't work, so now you're here."

"Tory?" Huffman said, obviously confused.

"Quid pro quo. You went after the most precious person to me."

"I don't know what the hell you're talking about, Doctor. I'm here to deal with you, man to man. That's the way I do business. If you and I have a problem I come to see you. I wouldn't touch your daughter."

Daughter? Now it was Merlin's turn to be confused. "Look, I don't know what's going on."

"We're going to talk, Dr. Merlin. Have ourselves an honest conversation about what really happened to Kit. Then I'm going to decide how to deal with you. But I'm getting ahead of myself. We've got some time," Huffman said, glancing at his Patek Philippe. "Lots of time. Go ahead, sit down." Moving his hand around, Huffman called attention to the bulge within his pocket once again.

Somehow hearing that Huffman wanted to talk gave Merlin a hopeful feeling. Once in his chair, Merlin asked, "If you're here this early you really know my schedule."

"Oh, I'm not actually here," Huffman bragged. "I'm really in Cleveland right now, asleep next to my beautiful wife. Yesterday, I addressed some of my stockholders at the annual meeting there. I made excellent time here today, beat yesterday's by sixteen minutes. Poor Cynthia's still asleep. I popped a couple of Valium in her cream sherry last night." Huffman hesitated briefly, working his hand in the pocket. "I could probably shoot off a small handgun right next to her, and she wouldn't wake up. I'm due at a breakfast at nine. My car's right outside."

"So you said you want to know what really happened to Kit when I operated on her. You didn't need to break in."

"The other night I had quite a conversation about you."

"With anyone I know?" Merlin asked.

"Of course."

"There were only three other people in the OR. The anesthesiologist, scrub nurse, and circulating nurse. I hope you got firsthand information.''

"Confirm if you will, Doctor. Did you tell Banks Wickford that Kit's death was just a statistic?"

"Banks Wickford. Oh, my God."

"Surprised?"

"No. That's exactly what I would expect from him."

"Did you tell him Kit's death was just a statistic?" Huffman's voice had taken on an edge, as if he could lose control without notice.

"*Just* a statistic? No. But I did explain to Wickford that there are statistical risks with any procedure. The same risks you outlined for me the first time I met you. The same risks I went over with your wife before she signed the consent." Before he said another word he made certain to lock eyes with Huffman. "I would never say any patient is *just a statistic.*"

Huffman studied the young surgeon's face. "During the procedure on my daughter did you talk about me?"

Merlin recalled the conversation in the OR and knew if Huffman was asking he probably already knew exactly what was said. "Your name came up just as we were getting started."

"What did you say about me?"

"I said you were a pain in the ass the way you treated me when I met you. I didn't care for it."

Huffman could not suppress a smile. "You tell it straight, don't you?"

"I'm not ashamed of anything that happened in the OR. Your daughter was genuinely likable. I spent extra time with her—not because of who you are—but because I enjoyed her company." Merlin took a deep breath. "If you want to know the truth, you made me feel like a novelty act you hired for her birthday party."

Huffman sat back and gave Merlin's comments some thought. "What about the surgery itself? Any problems?"

Merlin didn't hesitate before he spoke. "No. I don't know what Wickford told you, but the surgery went smoothly. Blood loss was practically nil, nothing unexpected happened, and at no time did anyone break scrub."

"Excuse me?"

"There was nothing that occurred that might have led to contamination of the field. Again, here's the truth. If there had been a problem you would have heard about it from me when Kit was still in recovery. Talk to the other people who were there."

"Any hanky-panky in the OR?"

"What?" Merlin exclaimed.

"You know . . . funny business."

"Of course not."

"There was no fooling around?" Huffman asked, drawing out his words.

"No!" Merlin said firmly.

"How about any magic tricks?"

Merlin didn't fidget or make any facial expressions. Instead he opened his drawer.

Immediately Huffman stood up, springing to his feet like a madman. "DON'T!" His hand was out of the pocket, holding a gun, aiming it at Merlin's chest. The weapon was entirely matte black, sleek in design like no other that Merlin had ever seen. The barrel was enhanced by a silencer that extended it an extra four inches.

Reflexively, Merlin's hands shot up in the air like a common criminal caught in the act by the police.

"Let me tell you about this gun. Got it in Germany, custom-made. A little boutique in Stuttgart that specializes in high-end weapons. Teflon bullets that'll go right through you. Untraceable. Never bothered to register it."

"There's something in the desk I want to show you."

"Careful." Huffman took a step closer to the desk so he could look into the shallow pencil drawer. Then he motioned with the gun for Merlin to proceed.

Moving in slow motion, every movement carefully planned, Merlin sent one hand into the drawer and plucked out a single red sponge ball. "Okay." His voice was shaky. "Pretend this is one of those little gauze squares we use in the operating room." Holding the two-inch ball in his right hand, between thumb and first finger, he continued, "Now, imagine I've just made the first incision, and I used this to stop the bleeding. When I knew the bleeding had stopped, I handed the gauze from my right hand to the left." Merlin effected his trademark sleight with the sponge ball, pretending to transfer it from one hand to the other, then holding his left hand tightly closed as if it contained something. "And as you can see the gauze disappeared." Merlin held up his left hand and opened it, one finger at a time, showing it to be empty. As the magician worked, the manipulations seemed to calm him down.

His relaxed style must have been convincing, because when he was finished Huffman said, "That's it?"

Merlin noticed the gun was no longer pointed at him. "Yep. I do it all the time in the OR. When things are going well, when the case is proceeding smoothly, I make a piece of gauze disappear. It's my way of smiling."

Huffman collapsed back down in the chair, looking tired. "It went that well, huh." There was a loneliness to his voice as his eyes went misty. It was obvious that he was thinking about Kit. Taking his hand off the weapon, he said, "I wasn't going to use it. I'm just . . . so upset . . ."

Abruptly the door opened. Only 6:45 in the morning and Merlin's office was hopping. This time it was Banks Wickford. Merlin was stunned, unable to imagine what was going to happen next.

Banks looked straight at Merlin, not acting as if he was expecting anyone else to be in the room. "I figured I'd find you here. What the hell were you thinking with that little stunt you pulled the other night—"

"We were just talking about you," Merlin said casually.

The CEO quickly scanned the room.

Huffman seemed to regain some of his strength, sitting up straight, but slipping the black weapon inside his tweed jacket. "What are you doing here?"

"Blaine. Oh, no, it's not about that. I didn't realize—" Banks was flabbergasted to see Blaine Huffman sitting in the corner.

"Is there something I can do for you?" Merlin asked.

"Uh, no. It can wait. When you finish with Mr. Huffman—"

"I bet you'd like to see me."

Banks looked at Huffman but spoke to Merlin. "Just to go over what happened with your girlfriend. She's okay, isn't she?"

"She's fine. I don't think we'll be too much longer. Mr. Huffman has an early meeting."

Banks nodded. "Blaine," he said with a lilting tone that turned the billionaire's name into a smarmy salutation. Then he backed out the door, closing it silently.

Once Banks disappeared the two sat without talking for a good while. Huffman sat very still, staring off into space. Finally he spoke. "I loved her so much."

"I know."

"I wish like hell I could get out of this gracefully. When Banks called, he really got me going. For the first time in days I had . . . something to grab on to." Huffman made a fist. "Someone to hate, and it felt good. With the way I was led to believe you behaved in the OR, I wanted to ruin your career."

"Let's start over. There's something I bet Wickford didn't tell you. Kit was one of five patients who died within a ten-day period."

"Patients die all the time. I care about only one of them."

"Kit was special. But everything went so well I have to question why she died."

"What are you saying?"

"Kit had two things in common with the other four who died. Each had a chronic illness, and all five shared the same insurance carrier."

"You mean Western Insurance?"

Merlin nodded.

"Are you suggesting these deaths weren't accidental?"

"Don't know. To be honest, I don't know for certain the clustering of deaths means anything at all. It just seems suspicious."

"Who else knows this?"

Merlin smiled. "A bunch of people have heard my theory. Everyone thinks I'm crazy. Just give me some more time."

"What about Banks Wickford?"

"What about him?"

"You're not suggesting he's somehow mixed up with the deaths?"

"No way," Merlin said confidently. "He's a hospital administrator, a rat who cares more about the institution than anyone inside it."

"After the way he set you up, how can you be sure?"

"I've seen him work."

"I'm not ready to let him off the hook. Before I deal with him I need to know more about what's going on at Western Insurance."

"No!" Merlin asserted. "I'm assembling some data. Western Insurance may be as much in the dark as we are."

"Sometimes it helps to stir things up a little."

"Things are already stirred up. My girlfriend was run down by someone a couple of nights ago."

"And that's why you weren't here yesterday."

"Right. I should have proof later today, but I believe the OR I almost took her to was set up to give her the same type of unstoppable infection Kit died from."

"She okay?" Huffman asked softly.

"She's fine. Wickford is in a snit because I snuck her out of the hospital to recover at home."

"They ran over your girlfriend," Huffman thought aloud. "What do you know that they're so worried about?"

"That's what scares me. I don't know."

"You know my reputation. I can't sit on my hands."

"No way," Merlin said with a tone of authority. "You're too emotionally involved. Right now this takes grunt work. Examining each of the deaths to see which personnel were involved. Even though I don't know what progress I've made, I've got someone's attention. Give me some time."

"Kit was *my* daughter."

"And that's why you've got to back off. Look at you, coming in here with an unregistered gun, shooting off your mouth about giving your wife sleeping pills. Hell, you're not thinking straight. Listen to me. Right now I'm the only one taking this mess seriously. You start making waves and whatever's going on might disappear. Then we'll never find out what the hell happened."

Huffman slapped his armrests, announcing the meeting closed. Then he stood. "Two weeks."

Merlin gave a little nod.

Huffman offered his hand to Merlin. "You'll keep me posted."

"When I've got something."

"I'll stop by Banks's office, get him off your back."

10

"Brooklyn. Where you been? We've been calling you, Brooklyn."

Nick Bello had just locked his car and was heading toward the Friendship Club. It was five-thirty but seemed later because of dark clouds hanging in the Pittsburgh sky. He always looked forward to colder weather so he could wear his bowling jacket wherever he went.

Tommy and Leo popped out from behind a couple of oak trees on the other side of the sidewalk. Tommy started walking alongside Bello as he headed for the Friendship Club. This was a meeting Tommy had hoped wouldn't be necessary, but he came prepared to handle whatever the situation demanded. Immediately he got cozy with Bello, putting his arm around the startled man's shoulder.

Lagging behind, Leo shivered in his sweatshirt with the cutoff sleeves. Although he would never admit to being cold, the skin on his arms was mottled with purple blotches. As he rubbed them he stood for a moment staring at the license plate on Bello's car, whispering to himself, "One-oh-P-I-N-S. One oh pins. One oh pins. One opens." Suddenly, a burst of inspiration: "Ten! Ten pins. Yeah, bowling." He smiled and repeated "ten pins" several times to himself while he double-timed it to catch up.

"Sorry, didn't get any message," Bello said and kept walking up the sidewalk toward the bar. He didn't like Tommy's arm around his shoulder.

"Didn't get a message. Hear that, Leo? Bello, here, didn't get no message," Tommy mimicked, taking his arm back and jumping out in front of Bello, walking backwards so he could look him in the eye. He reached out and picked up the lapel of the red satin jacket where the fancy script writing was. "Still wearing that fancy-dancy jacket. Brooklyn Turkeys on the back, Nicky B on the front."

Nick Bello stopped walking.

"Nicky B," Tommy said, his voice low and menacing, letting the "B" ooze from his vocal cords so the individual vibrations could be heard as a deep staccato.

Bello didn't like where this conversation was going. "Well, whaddya want, Tommy?"

"First I talked to your wife. Then the guy in there with the weird neck. I even called the hospital. Where you been, Nicky B?"

"Nowhere. You know, around." His voice was coming out shaky. Nervously he looked about, hoping to see someone walking down the street he could call to. A car crossed the intersection a block away. Then a door slammed off in the distance while a dog barked far away. "I was sick the last couple a days. That's all."

"We went to a lot of fuckin' effort to set things up. Paid you some serious dough. You chicken out?"

"Yeah," Leo said, sounding tough.

"Look, Tommy, you never said nothing about healthy people. You said they would all be better off dead. That they'd thank us if they could. That doctor you talked about, what's his name?"

Tommy knew what Bello was talking about. Jack Kevorkian, the doctor who had made a name for himself assisting people commit suicide when they had terminal illnesses. "Kevorkian."

"Yeah, you said this was the Kevorkian Society. Helping people who didn't know they needed help."

"You think you were the first person we tried that Kevorkian crap on? You were the one who wanted to believe it. I told you what you needed to hear. You wanted the money, you knew what we were doing was illegal, but you needed something to make it seem legal. You want your ass in jail?"

"No. But you told me it was the best thing for the patients."

Tommy grabbed hold of Bello's silky jacket. "Bullshit. You didn't need no arm-twisting."

"Why did you have me do that little girl?"

"She was gonna spend the rest of her life living in a goddamn hospital hooked up to some IV. Remember? Remember what you said? You said that was no life, kids should be at school with their friends. Now we got to keep going. Things got a little complicated, that's all. In order to cool things down we gotta do a couple more people. There's still a lot of money."

"I don't care about the money anymore."

"That's all you cared about in the beginning. A thousand wasn't enough. You wanted two. Remember? We gave you two. Then you started talking about three."

"I made a mistake doing this. I thought it was mercy."

Tommy pulled Bello close enough to give him a whiff of the alcohol on his breath. "Maybe you thought it was about mercy to make it easier. But the first thing you said to me was, 'What's in it for me?' 'Member? 'What's in it for me?' It was always about the money, Nicky. Admit it."

"I don't know. Maybe I'm mixed up, but I . . . I know I don't want to be in it anymore."

"Let's take a walk, Brooklyn."

"Yeah, let's walk," Leo said.

"I can't . . . I'm meeting some people."

"Okay, you're meeting some people, but you're gonna be late."

Leo took one step forward, got right in Bello's face, and said, "Listen, fuck-face, take a walk with us so I don't have to kill you." Then Leo pushed his Smith and Wesson that he had finally wiggled out of his pocket hard into Bello's gut.

Merlin arrived home hours earlier than usual. He was carrying a shoe box size package and seemed surprised that Tory was downstairs on the sofa, watching TV in her terry cloth robe. He made an effort to stow it behind the rickety wooden TV stand, but any attempt at subterfuge was a waste of time.

"Whatcha got?"

"You're supposed to be in bed," Merlin said evenly, hoping to change the subject.

"I thought you were getting home at seven. I would've been in bed by then. You're early."

"I've gotta be going back for rounds. I just wanted to see you. Hey, maybe you're ready for some real food when I get home."

"What's in the box, Merlin?"

"A surprise for later."

"Oh, my," Tory exclaimed, feigning a love-struck girl about to get an engagement ring. "It must be huge. At least a thousand carats."

"Okay, okay. You weren't supposed to be downstairs to ruin the surprise, but—" Merlin said and reluctantly brought the box over to Tory.

One look at the writing on the box and she said, "Take it back, Merlin. I don't want it."

"Just take a look at it."

"No." She sounded mad and put the box down on the sofa next to where she was sitting, then used the remote control to make the television louder.

"Tor, just let me explain," Merlin said softly, sitting on the sofa, the box in between them.

"No, Merlin. No guns in this house."

"It isn't for you. It's for me. I love you. You know that. And you've got to do this for me."

"No."

"I operated on you, just like I thought you wanted. Not for a second did I want it otherwise. Now you do this for me."

Tory brushed the hair from her eyes. "When did you buy it?"

"The day after you were run over. Remember that county sheriff I operated on? He sped things up with the background check. The permit arrived today."

Tentatively she opened the box. Inside was a .25 caliber Beretta with a clip. Semiautomatic. It was small, almost petite, weighing less than a pound, obviously chosen with Tory's small hand in mind.

"I had them load it. See, this is the safety."

"Merlin, please. My father—the cop—always said when amateurs play with guns they never hit whoever they're aiming at, but someone always gets shot."

"If you love me, you'll think about it."

Tory started to cry.

"Thanks," Merlin said, leaning over to kiss her.

They walked through an empty lot, Bello flanked by Tommy and Leo, around back of the Friendship Club where a green Dumpster sat.

Each time Leo poked his Smith and Wesson in Bello's ribs, the scrub nurse jumped sideways, knocking into Tommy. While they had been waiting in the bushes, Tommy—on a hunch—told Leo three times not to hurt Bello. "We need him," he'd said. Three times. "Scare him if you have to, but don't hurt him." Then they'd stood waiting for Bello more than an hour, Leo rubbing his arms, denying he was cold every time Tommy asked. The colder Leo got the more pissed off he seemed. "Where the fuck is that asshole?" he kept saying. Tommy briefly wondered why Leo didn't wear a jacket but didn't care enough to listen to some bullshit explanation. Leo was a punk. No matter what he said it was bullshit, and Tommy didn't need it.

The first thing Tommy noticed when they were behind the Friendship Club was the stench. Bello smelled it, too, saying, "Hey, it stinks out here. Let's go inside, sit at a table, have a sausage sandwich or something.''

That sounded pretty good to Leo, but he didn't want those assholes inside to laugh at him. Instead he took it on himself to check things out, walking around the Dumpster like he owned the place, waving his gun around, making sure they were alone. Across the empty lot were a couple of houses. Fortunately there were trees in the way, and unless someone wandered through the lot, they would have privacy.

"All right, Nicky, you're a card-carrying member of the Kevorkian Society," Tommy said.

"All right. So what. I did it for the money. It's over for me. Get someone else.''

"It's not that easy. You're in, and you don't leave until we say so. Why didn't you go through with it the other night?''

"I did. I injected the shit into a package of gauze just like always. The nurse grabbed it and was walking over with it when this doctor— Merlin, I told you about him—switched ORs at the last minute. He figured it out or something. I mean, he even got some security guy to guard everything like he knew what the fuck was going on. He knows, I'm telling you. Maybe he don't know it's me, but he knows.''

"Then if he don't know it's you, we're still in business.''

"No, please, you gotta listen to me. I swear I can't do it anymore.''

"Lemme see," Tommy said. "Instead of gauze, we'll try something else." He gave Leo a little nod. Frantically, Bello started turning his head left and right, terrified that Leo was going to shoot him. Then he heard the click of the hammer as Leo cocked the weapon and pushed it deeper into his gut.

Tommy was standing on the other side of Bello. When he realized what Leo was doing he jumped out of the way. "Leo, Jesus Christ, what's wrong with you?" Tommy yelled. "That thing goes off it goes through him and into me. Give it to me.'' Tommy sounded pissed, holding his hand palm out, opening and closing his fingers partway to hurry Leo. "You're dangerous with that thing.''

Tommy grabbed the gun, not bothering to aim it at Bello, but held it down at his side while Leo produced a small tin-snips with yellow plastic handles from his pocket.

"What the fuck is going on here?" Bello demanded and turned to run.

With one hand Tommy grabbed the back of Bello's bowling jacket and yanked him hard. "Scream and I'll kill you." He got him in a choke hold, tight enough to make it impossible for Bello to breathe. "Listen good, you sonovabitch. You gonna help us?''

"He knows," Bello said, his voice straining to get out of his throat. "Merlin knows. Ahhhhh. I . . . can't . . . breathe."

"Leo, here, is gonna cut off one of your fingers if you don't say yes. And every day we'll track you down. And every time you say no he cuts another."

This was Leo's cue. He came alive, feeling like the most powerful fucker on earth. Roughly he grabbed one of Bello's wrists and caught the index finger between the blades of the snips.

Bello's eyes almost popped out of his head trying to see what Leo was doing. "Get . . . get him away from me. Lemme talk. Please, Tommy. Listen to me. I got some of the money in my pocket, the rest at home. Take it." Bello started to sob. "Take my car. Don't hurt me."

Leo smiled. The guy was begging, becoming more and more pathetic. Leo couldn't resist tightening the tin-snips a little and watched Bello's other fingers tighten into a ball.

Tommy never raised his voice. "It's not over 'til I say it's over."

"No, please. Listen to me. Let's sit down."

"Tell me you're in, Nick. Leo's a crazy fucker. Tell me you're in, Nick. Please, tell me you're in so I can get Leo off you."

"Get off me, goddamn it!" Bello screamed. "For chrissakes, okay. Okay, okay, yeah, I'll do—"

Tommy's face broke into a smile. He started to loosen his grip around Bello's neck, but the scrub nurse was wild, frantically pulling his hand away from Leo's tin-snips.

Fingers tightened. Handles drew closer. The lever worked, blades sliding across one another. First through skin and nerves.

The first jolt of pain, sharp as an electric spark jump-starting the brain. Then little slips of muscles and tendons, pinched tight between the blades, slicing in two.

Bellow drew the stench of garbage into his lungs and opened his mouth wide. His eyes bulged out of their sockets trying to explode from his skull.

The sharp blades continued, quickly severing rubbery arteries and delicate veins.

In the end, a quick crunch through bony cortex, more pain receptors, and a smidge of marrow.

All that in a tenth of a second.

"Ahhhhhh!!!" Bello screamed.

Leo jumped back and took a good, hard look at the tin-snips in his hand. The sharp blades were clamped tightly shut. Dangling loosely from the tempered steel, tethered by a thin flap of skin, was Nick Bello's index finger. "He moved! The sonovabitch moved, goddamn it," Leo screamed, taking two steps back from Bello. Still screaming, he demanded, "Why the fuck did you move?"

Like a powerful little hose, blood was squirting from Bello's hand, pulsating wildly. The pain was ferocious, like nothing he had ever imagined. Initially he thought the tin-snips were still attached to him, biting his finger, and he whipped his hand back and forth, desperately trying to shake it loose. Red droplets shot all over the three of them, polka-dotting clothing and skin. When Bello finally looked at his hand he couldn't believe what he saw. Once there had been five; now there were four. A huge gap existed between his thumb and middle finger. For several seconds he was too stunned to talk. Then he started screaming. "My finger! My finger! Shiiiit! You cut off my finger!" Panicking, he turned his hand to look into the stump and squirted blood all over his face.

Then he began to scream nonsense.

By now Tommy and Leo had moved back a safe distance. Leo held one handle of the tin-snips between two of his fingers, letting it hang there like a dead mouse dangling by the tail.

As Nick continued to scream he clamped his left hand over the wound, squeezing it tightly until the bleeding slowed to a tolerable ooze. "You fuck!" he hissed at Leo. "I said I'd do it. But now I can't work, you shit. I don't have a fucking finger!"

"Leo, give him the finger." Tommy watched Leo hand Bello the tin-snips with the index finger still flapping in the breeze.

Instead of plucking his finger from the tin-snips, thereby sacrificing the little flap of skin that had become squished between the blades, Bello carefully worked the handles apart, taking care not to allow his finger to fall to the ground. He held it for a few seconds in the palm of his good hand, contemplating it. Seeing something that had been a vital part of him rolling around the palm of his good hand frightened Bello until tears rolled down his cheeks.

"How's he supposed to work, Leo? You think they make surgery gloves with four fingers?"

"I thought he was breaking away. It was his fault. He shoulda stayed still."

"He said he would do it. Didn't you hear him? It worked. Like I told you, scare him but don't fucking hurt him."

"Sorry."

"Oh, that makes everything better. What're you, nine years old? Sorry." Tommy pocketed Leo's gun. "Hey, Nicky," Tommy said. "It don't make it any better, but it wasn't supposed to happen this way."

"Fuck you," Bello hissed, squeezing the stump to dull the pain.

"You're off the hook, Nick. But say one word to the cops, and Leo goes for the other nine." Tommy walked away.

When they were back in the car, after driving three or four blocks, Leo finally remembered, "Hey, Tommy, what about my piece?"

"You know what you are? A dumb fuckin' blond. And you know what else? You coulda killed me, you dumb fuck."

"C'mon, man. Gimme the gun."

"Didn't you hear what I said?"

"Yeah, I heard you," Leo said contritely.

"You're not getting the gun 'til I think about it." And the gun stayed in Tommy's pocket.

A half hour later Nick Bello walked into the ER at the Medical Center. The pace was picking up, families having nothing to do after dinner, streaming into the waiting room with screaming kids. Every seat was taken. It was just before seven.

He'd been through the automatic doors of the ER twice each day, every shift he worked, for four and a half years, but not once as a patient. For a few moments he just stood there, looking lost, waiting for someone to tell him where to go. He was a mess. Tiny red dots of dried blood covered his face. Clumps of sticky hair went this way and that. And he was sporting a bare midriff, his shirt having been pulled out of his pants so he could wrap the tail around his seeping hand.

The automatic doors opened behind him. A gush of cold air made him shiver. An old woman with a dirty scarf hiding her hair slowly walked in, shuffling her way past Bello on a meandering path toward the registration desk. He followed her and waited in a long line that snaked its way back into the waiting room.

In Bello's left hand was a large white Styrofoam cup filled with crushed ice. As he inched forward in line, an idiot grin crept across his face. He was thinking back to when he was a kid, sitting on the front stoop, whining to his mom that he didn't have nothing to do, driving her so crazy she would challenge him to try to touch his elbow with the same hand. Then he would bend his hand until it hurt, trying so hard to bring the tip of his middle finger down to the crinkly skin of his elbow that he would start to spin around like a dog chasing its tail. Faster and faster he would go until he would fall down on the sidewalk in desperation.

When he realized he was smiling, the line had moved and there was a big space between him and the woman with the dirty scarf. Gently he shook the cup back and forth, loosening the top layer of ice until it spilled out onto the floor. The tip of his index finger poked out from the pink ice. Placing the cup for safekeeping between his legs for a moment, Bello used his good hand to work the bloody sleeve of his bowling jacket and shirt as far as he could manage. With a delirious little giggle, he grabbed the Styrofoam cup from below and brought it to meet his right elbow. For a few seconds he enjoyed the cold of the ice, smiling at what his mother would have said if only she knew.

The line was moving once again. He took a quick step forward this time, bumping into the old woman, who wasn't paying any attention. Of course she turned around with a scowl on her face, took one look at Bello, and screamed.

Now everyone was looking. A couple of kids wandered over. This was Nick Bello's nonstop ticket into a trauma room—coincidentally the same one Tory had occupied. Instantly, an orthopedic surgeon materialized, whipped on a pair of gloves, and began to examine Bello's hand.

"Sir, what happened to you?" the orthopedic surgeon asked, probing the wound.

"That hurts."

"Nick, what happened? You okay?" It was Merlin, just arriving in the ER, jacket still on, backpack over his shoulder. He listened to one of the ER nurses reciting Bello's blood pressure and pulse.

Before Nick spoke, before he uttered one single word, he realized he hadn't thought up a story. Like an idiot he was writhing about on a narrow stretcher, having absolutely no idea what to say. The last thing he wanted was the police. Tommy and Leo would leave him alone if he kept quiet, but the thought of Leo coming after him again with the tin-snips was terrifying.

"Hey, Nick, it's me."

"Oh, Merlin, it really hurts. What are you doing here?"

"Someone said you were here. What happened?"

"Uh, I fell. I, uh, was cutting some sheet metal and—I was on a ladder, you know—yeah, the ladder wiggled, and I kinda caught my finger on the metal and sliced it off."

"What were you doing with sheet metal on a ladder?"

"Some gutter thing on my house."

By now the orthopedist was examining the finger with a magnifying glass, turning it slowly in his gloved hand.

Merlin noticed Bello's satin bowling jacket and dress shirt. "Wearing a nice shirt and pants?"

Bello looked down at himself. He seemed stunned. While the orthopedic surgeon went back to examining the hand, Bello touched his nice shirt, running his fingers from the collar to the tail.

"Mr. Bello," the orthopedist said, "I'm Dr. Carroll. I'm with orthopedics. I think I can save your finger, but we've got to operate tonight."

"It'll work and everything?" Nick sounded surprised.

"We'll have to see. The wound is clean." Then the orthopedist fired a series of questions at Nick, asking how the accident had happened, did he have any allergies, was he up to date on his tetanus shots, how healthy was he in general, and when he ate most recently.

Bello looked at Merlin. "What do you think?"

"Dr. Carroll's the best."

"I never had surgery before. I wish you could do it."

"You know it's not my area. But I'll keep you company."

Surgical reattachment of a finger was difficult and tedious, involving pin placement to hold the bones together and delicate microscopic suturing of arteries and veins that were barely larger than strands of spaghetti.

Merlin had a funny feeling about Bello and waited in the ER until the patient had been taken upstairs. He found Dr. Carroll writing his admission note in the nursing station.

"Something doesn't fit," Merlin said.

"You're right. Looks to me it was cut off by a scissor-like device. No way his finger was sliced off by a piece of sheet metal," the orthopedic surgeon said matter-of-factly.

"How can you be certain?"

"If you look at the point of amputation, the tissues—skin and muscle mostly—are pressed into the bone on the top *and* the bottom. If it was a single blade cut, the tissues would compress only in the direction of the cut."

"Then he's lying."

"Absolutely. Hey, what difference does it make? It's his business what happened. All I gotta worry about is putting the pieces back together."

Merlin drummed his fingers on the table. "Let me ride up with you."

While two orderlies managed to undress Bello and transfer him to the black operating table, Merlin did a little ear bending out by the scrub sink. As luck would have it, the anesthesiologist on call was his friend, Roland, but even with a buddy, there was a limit to what you could ask someone to do. Merlin was requesting something patently unethical. The anesthesiologist kept saying, "Gee, I don't know, Merlin. I could get in a lot of trouble." Then, turning to the surgeon scrubbing at the sink, he looked for support. "What do you think?"

The orthopedic surgeon, rinsing the last of the soap from his hands, shrugged his shoulders. "What the hell difference does it make? Whatever you do, I don't want to be here all night." Then he pushed the door open with one foot and quickly walked into the OR.

"This better be good," Roland said, a tone of irritation creeping into his voice.

Roland drew up a syringe of fentanyl—a narcotic that would spread a wonderful warm glow as it flowed through Bello's veins—and squirted it into the IV tubing.

As the pain melted away, Bello slowly relaxed, his breathing quieted down, and the tension in his shoulders eased. Roland drew up a second syringe and began a series of Pentothal injections—old-fashioned truth serum, the stuff used in World War II by the Nazis to loosen the tongues of Allied POWs—twenty-five milligrams every thirty seconds.

Just before the sixth injection Bello started to mumble, incomprehensible at first, sounding like a drunk babbling on a street corner. Patiently, Merlin waited. Bello blurted out, "I won't talk." His eyes were wide open, staring up at the ceiling.

Merlin leaned in close, whispering quietly right in his ear. "Nick, talk about what?"

"Kevorkian. I won't tell anyone . . . I won't."

"Tell me about Kevorkian, Nick. What does that mean?"

"The Kevorkian Society. No, no!" Bello's voice became louder. "No police. Don't cut off my finger. No, no. Don't cut off my finger. I won't tell. Not my finger."

"What happened, Nick? Tell me who hurt you."

Bello's eyes were closed. His words dissolved into quiet mumbles that made no sense. The anesthesia was taking effect. Nick Bello became silent.

Merlin tried a couple of times to get him talking again, but Bello was out. As the surgery began, Merlin walked out of the operating room, silently repeating, *The Kevorkian Society. The Kevorkian Society.*

11

Tommy arrived at Busy Beaver just as the manager was unlocking the door from the inside. The first customer of the day. Back in aisle twenty-one, where the paints and brushes were stacked floor to ceiling, Tommy found the glue and cement section. Elmer's Glue. Liquid Nails. Contact Cement. Epoxy. Rubber Cement. Superglue. Twenty-three selections, mostly in toothpaste-like tubes, some bigger than others. An employee wearing a red smock that matched his flaming auburn hair happened by. He noticed Tommy struggling with all the choices and asked him why he wanted the glue.

"Usual repairs," Tommy said casually.

"Then the best thing you can get is this," the employee said as he grabbed a fancy type of epoxy that came in a wide syringe with two plungers sticking out the top. "Ninety-minute setup time, no mixing. It's what I use."

Tommy examined the unusual syringe through the clear plastic bubble on the package. It looked perfect. Both syringes depressed simultaneously, releasing the two gooey chemicals that automatically mixed together and turned rock hard.

Then he noticed the bottom of the syringe. There were separate nozzles that released the two epoxy components about an eighth of an inch apart. He thought about it and realized he'd have to get a tiny funnel to direct the goo as precisely as he needed. As slick as this was, it wouldn't work for the one and only reason he was buying glue.

First he'd thought about chewing gum, how cool it would be to buy some Double Bubble and ball up a little piece so it would slip in with no one the wiser. But gum hardens slowly, and the pink wad would always be visible.

No, he needed epoxy, and the helpful guy with the smock was now at the other end of the aisle advising another customer. So Tommy kept searching, not realizing his answer was right next to the double-plunger syringe. He eventually spotted it, also an epoxy, but this package, Depend II Industrial Strength Adhesive, came with two individual syringes. First you squirted some of Part A, then Part B. Perfect.

"I wouldn't recommend that one," the guy with the red smock said, walking back up the aisle. "Setup time is about ninety seconds, no room for error."

"I don't plan to make a mistake."

"May I ask what you plan to use it for?" the salesman said, trying hard to be friendly and polite in the face of a suspicious-looking customer who didn't really want his advice.

"To prevent death from accidental gunshot."

"Oh, no, sir, I wouldn't recommend using the product for that. It's strictly for home repair. Sir? Sir?"

But the guy in the smock was talking to Tommy's back as he headed to the cash register with exactly what he needed to do the job right.

"Huh?" Nick Bello muttered sleepily and opened his eyes. When he realized Tommy was standing next to his bed he instantly curled up into a fetal position, protecting his bandaged hand.

"Stay cool," Tommy warned. Terrified at what was going on, Bello looked around to see if Leo was also in the room, but the two of them were alone. Tommy put one hand on the IV pole that held the bag of fluid running into Bello's arm and leaned forward, his dark suit jacket hanging open slightly giving the patient a perfect view of his gun. "Didn't have time to get you a card or anything. You recovering okay?" he asked in a strong voice.

Bello shifted himself around in the bed nervously. "Look, I told everyone I fell," he said simply. "I don't know why everybody keeps asking me about it, but I kept saying I fell, cut myself on some sheet metal. Why's that such a big deal?"

His hand looked like it was inside a white boxing glove. "I hear they put it back on."

"That's right. Probably'll be good as new."

Tommy looked at the door. "So . . . Bello . . . what are you gonna say when the real heat comes down?"

"I fell off a ladder! If that story doesn't satisfy you or anyone else, tough shit!"

"That's what I like to hear," Tommy said with a hint of a triumphant smile. "How's our old friend Merlin?"

Bello's eyes darted nervously about the room. He craned his neck to look out the door and swallowed hard. "I know Dr. Merlin's real upset about all the deaths around here, and he's asking questions. Maybe you should talk to him."

"Well, I'm real upset about it, too. Take care of that finger. If your tongue loosens up, don't worry, I'll be back."

Before Tommy was off the floor, Nick Bello was out of bed, starting to get dressed, threading his bloody shirt around the IV tubing attached to his good arm just to speed things up. Within an hour he'd signed out of the Medical Center "against medical advice," promising to call the orthopedic clinic for an outpatient follow-up appointment.

12

It had been five days since Merlin had repaired the rent in Tory's spleen, and she was recovering nicely, feeling less pain and more boredom on a daily basis. Although Merlin still maintained his frantic workload at the Medical Center, he had been staying up later than usual with Tory. Tonight they were watching Letterman, the forbidden fruit of the crack-of-dawn surgical world. They sat on the old sofa, propping their feet on the simple wooden coffee table they had picked up at a garage sale. It had cost all of seven bucks.

By the time the monologue was over and Dave was dashing out of the studio to the pizza shop next door in a valiant effort to re-create the insane magic that once distinguished him as the king of zany spontaneity, Tory was asleep, curled up next to Merlin so comfortably he hesitated to wake her. As soon as he reached for the remote, and the TV went dark, Tory stirred and they headed upstairs. Each day she moved with less difficulty, and Merlin marveled at how easily she ascended the stairs, holding the railing gently, not even taking a breather halfway up.

The night was cool. Merlin cracked the window on his side of the bed just before turning out the lights. Tory wore a thin cotton nightshirt; Merlin a pair of blue boxers. In the soft light from a streetlamp, Merlin lay on his side, watching her as she fell asleep.

Theirs was a quiet neighborhood. The sound of Mrs. Kincaid's dog Pepper, barking away next door, was the only noise to break the quiet of the night. Pepper had a huge, ugly face and sad eyes. Although Merlin didn't care for canines, Mrs. Kincaid had insisted he get to know Pepper if he was going to live with Tory.

Anything could get Pepper going. A chipmunk. A fire siren. Someone arriving home late at night. Anything. Usually Pepper barked wildly at the annoyance only to settle down after a couple of minutes. If she didn't, Mrs. Kincaid would push open the kitchen door, unleashing her dog to scare away the bogeyman. And once again, everything would quiet down.

It wasn't long until Pepper settled down. Merlin was exhausted. His pillow felt cool and comfortable. His eyelids were heavy. Sleep came quickly.

The last several nights Merlin had slept horribly, never allowing himself to relax enough for the deeper stages of sleep. Every time Tory rolled over and moaned softly, his eyes opened wide and he would stay awake until her breathing became relaxed again.

Descending quickly to a deep dream state, his body tried to make up for lost time.

"Merlin, you hear that?" Tory said, pushing on his shoulder.

Now Pepper was at it again, yipping and snarling louder than usual. Merlin sat up in bed, needing a moment to get his bearings. He checked the time on the bedside clock—2:17 A.M. Tory wasn't one to react to sounds in the middle of the night. Patiently, Merlin concentrated, supporting himself with both arms pressing into the mattress behind him. Other than the excited bark of Pepper, it was quiet. The longer the barking continued, the more he expected to hear the loud wooden bang of Mrs. Kincaid's screen door as she let Pepper out. But the slamming of the wooden door never came and eventually the barking quieted.

"Musta been a cat or something," Merlin said.

"Maybe something happened at Mrs. Kincaid's. What if she's sick?"

Merlin got out of bed and went over to the window. "Her lights are off."

"Maybe she fell or something. You think we should call her, see if she's okay?"

"Pepper's quiet. Whatever was bugging her is gone. Betcha it was a deer. Why don't we let her sleep. Tor, you need anything?"

"I need to get back to work."

"Not yet," the surgeon said.

"I love Mrs. Kincaid, but I don't think I can take another day of her TV schedule."

"You're not ready. Go to sleep."

Tory gave him a quick kiss before she rolled over, being careful of her stitches, and when she was settled under the down comforter, Merlin scootched in nice and close, the Yang of his anterior fitting perfectly with the Yin of her posterior. Tenderly, his lips brushed the back of her neck, his chest pressed against her nightshirt, his legs intertwined with hers. This was the first time he was venturing into their wonderfully comfortable sleep position since the surgery, and Tory wiggled her bottom gently into him. Then, carefully, Merlin slid his hand around Tory's side, up under the nightshirt, and found her breast. She murmured softly, fighting off sleep so she could enjoy the moment. Several minutes went by. Merlin's breathing slowed as he drifted back to slumber.

TEEEEK.

A high-pitched squeal cut through the silence. It was clear and crisp, as startling as a knife going through an electric sharpener. Not more than a second or two in duration, but it seemed to linger in Tory's ears, getting louder and louder until she opened her eyes and her breathing quickened. At first she couldn't place it, but the sound was so familiar. She knew this sound. Tory pulled away from Merlin and listened. All she could hear was her own breathing.

Noises were part of life in an old house. The wooden furniture and floorboards creaked every night as they cooled down, and Tory had gotten used to them long ago. As long as Merlin was home with her, even if he was dead asleep, Tory hardly noticed the sounds of the night. Any time she did hear one, she usually blamed it on Merlin.

But whenever Merlin was away at a conference, those little creaks and groans of their aging house frightened her terribly, ruining any attempts she made at restful sleep.

This noise had a familiarity. One that was a fixture in their world. All at once she was struck by a horrible realization: *That's the kitchen door.*

She froze. Only their kitchen door made that particular squeaking sound, nothing more than a rusty hinge whining every time the cheap pine door was opened. When the hospital kept Merlin past midnight, Tory would wait in bed for him, listening for that noise. *TEEEEK.* It meant Merlin was home. To her, the sound was like music, and she would feel safe.

TEEEEK. The sound was wired in her brain. But with Merlin dozing right next to her, it took on new meaning. No doubt about it. This was for real. Thousands of times before she thought she'd heard demons, and even though each one had frightened her, there was always a germ of doubt that it was only her imagination. Not this time.

Her brain was racing. It took every bit of self-control to keep from screaming.

There's someone in the house. Not a monster. Not a demon. Not a figment of her imagination. But a person—probably a man—and he was inside.

CRRREAK. The floorboard in the living room. The one you couldn't possibly miss as you walked from the tiny kitchen into the living room. First the rusty hinge, now the loose floorboard. Someone was walking toward the stairs, coming closer, and panic tightened around her throat like a hangman's noose.

Tory's heart beat out of control, pounding rapidly in her chest, making so much noise she felt deaf to everything else. *Wake up, Merlin!* Her mouth was parched, so dry she couldn't swallow or utter a single word. Silently, she looked out at the hallway, terrified of what she might see. It was almost pitch-black, only a slip of moonlight filtered through the bathroom window across the hall. Her eyes betrayed her. She saw movements in the shadows. *Do something. DO SOMETHING!!*

Desperately, she found her voice, a thick whisper. "Merlin, wake up. Someone's downstairs. Someone's in the house."

"Huh?" Merlin said sleepily.

"Shhhh. Someone's in the house. I heard the kitchen door. Listen."

Merlin listened quietly.

Nothing.

Nothing.

Nothing.

Nothing.

CRRREAK.

"Where's the gun?" Merlin said. That frightened Tory even more. Some part of her had held out hope that Merlin would say, "You're hearing things," and he would be right, and nighttime would turn into day.

But Merlin sounded dead serious.

Tory started to cry. "Oh, God, it's downstairs, in the box."

"Stay cool. Call the police." Merlin said and slipped out of bed. Then he did the strangest thing. He put on his pants, then a T-shirt. Someone had broken into his house, and Merlin wanted to be dressed.

"No dial tone," Tory whispered as she watched Merlin looking around the bedroom for a weapon.

Coming up empty, Merlin instructed, "Lock yourself in the bathroom, and don't come out." Then he slipped out of the room.

Merlin proceeded slowly down the dark hallway. Trusting his ears as much as his eyes, he stopped every few steps and turned his head this way and that, listening. Finally he made it to the top of the stairs just in time to see a spot of light dancing on the wall next to the front door. It appeared to be from a small flashlight, as if Tinkerbell was flitting about the room.

Without a weapon, Merlin hoped the intruder was only interested in robbery. Maybe he would grab Tory's purse and take off.

If he came up the stairs, which seemed more and more likely as Tinkerbell grew smaller and smaller on the wall by the landing, at least Merlin would have the element of surprise in his favor. For now, all he could do was wait at the top of the stairs.

The second floor of the small house was laid out quite simply. Coming up the stairs there was a small study off to the right, and to the left was a short hallway. The left side of the hallway had a tiny linen closet and the bathroom where Tory now hid. The only door on the right led to the bedroom.

Merlin took refuge on the floor of the entrance to the study, squatting down on his haunches. From time to time he heard the creaking noise of the intruder's steps one floor below.

RRRRRIT. The muffled sound of a foot on the first step. The intruder was coming up to the second floor.

Ideas flew into Merlin's head. What about screaming? A loud, piercing cry that would scare the sonovabitch and hope he'd run for his life.

But since the intruder took the time to take the downstairs phone off the hook, he probably meant business, and a scream wouldn't faze him.

RRRRRIT. Another stair.

Tinkerbell danced on the wall right in front of Merlin's eyes.

Merlin waited, knowing everything would happen in the next few seconds. *Swish, swish.* A wispy noise, light as air, made its way to Merlin's ears. *Swish, swish.* The guy's pants, thigh rubbing against thigh. He was getting close.

Like the two claws of a predator about to grab a small animal, Merlin's hands tensed as they waited. Then Tinkerbell disappeared. Once again it was dark. As Merlin's pupils adjusted he realized the intruder had put one foot on the top landing, a large foot, wearing some sort of boot. For the first time Merlin knew for certain he was dealing with a man.

The foot remained in the same place for a good long while, less than a yard from Merlin. *What is he waiting for?* Then Merlin looked up and saw it. A gun. The guy had a gun. Medium-sized, but the barrel seemed huge. *Wait. Wait until he comes up.*

Merlin started rocking back and forth gently, like a tennis player getting ready to return serve. *One. Two. Three. Four.* Merlin counted the seconds, relaxing his breathing, getting into a zone.

He heard a soft sound off in the distance. It was Tory. She was crying. *Five. Six. Seven.*

The second boot joined the first on the landing, pointing toward the door of the bedroom.

Eight. Nine. Ten. NOW!!! In one quick move Merlin grabbed both of the guy's ankles and yanked them out hard, standing himself up as the intruder crashed to the floor loudly. *The gun. Get the gun.*

Instinctively, Merlin understood there would be a brief opportunity before the intruder realized what had happened and started shooting, maybe a second or two. Like a cat, Merlin hopped over the guy's legs, lunging for a vague shadow in the darkness that was the intruder's right hand. First Merlin grabbed flesh. They struggled briefly, Merlin on top, in control of the situation. Maybe it was luck, but the young surgeon quickly got his hands on the gun, violently twisting the weapon away. "Move and I'll kill you," Merlin snapped, pushing himself to his feet.

The guy remained silent.

"You alone?" Merlin demanded, waiting two seconds for an answer. "Hey, Tinkerbell, you alone?"

"Fuck you."

Right away the gun felt comfortable in Merlin's hand. Keeping one eye on the stairs for whoever else might be charging up, Merlin flicked the dim hallway light on. Tinkerbell was facedown on the floor. He had blond hair and wore a sweatshirt with cutoff sleeves. "Tory, c'mon out. It's safe."

The door to the bathroom opened slowly. Tentatively, Tory walked out into the hallway and let out a little gasp.

"Get up, Tinkerbell. Now!" Merlin yelled.

Slowly the intruder stood up. Blond mustache. Tight jeans. A tattoo that read, Leo's Sex Club, Sign Up Below.

"You just made the mistake of your life, asshole," Leo grunted.

"I don't see you with the gun, so shut up!" Merlin looked at the weapon in his hand. A revolver. It looked new.

"Keep the fuckin' gun. I was jus' looking for some quick cash."

Merlin kept his distance, motioning with the gun as he spoke. "Bullshit. Who are you?"

"I'm Tinkerbell," he said with a snarl.

Merlin waited. "Okay, Tink, down the stairs. Slowly." Merlin cocked the gun, making sure Leo watched. It was set on single action and thus could be fired that much more quickly.

Leo wanted to say "Fuck you," and beat the shit out of Merlin, but he just stood there defiantly, letting the world know he wasn't scared.

There was a standoff. Merlin knew if there were any signs of weakness or uncertainty in his actions, his intruder would take advantage. So in a dramatic TV posturing, Merlin wrapped his left hand around his right wrist, raised the gun up in the air and slowly brought it down, aiming it directly at Leo's face.

Leo turned and started down the stairs. Not because he thought Merlin would have the balls to shoot him. And certainly not because he was scared. He figured there was more space in the living room, so maybe he'd try a spin kick and bolt for the kitchen door.

Acting like he didn't give a shit, Leo took his time going down the stairs, trying to piss Merlin off as much as possible. When he passed by a framed picture on the wall Leo took his index finger and pushed the picture, sliding it up the wall so it rode an arc around the nail holding it. When he released the picture, it swung wildly back and forth, a pendulum out of control. Merlin, several steps back, kept repeating, "C'mon, let's go."

In less than a minute, Leo stood in the living room, his back to Merlin. Tory lingered halfway down the stairs, leaning forward to improve her view.

"Just so you know," Merlin said, "I'll put a bullet through your knee if you so much as move. I'm a terrific shot." He turned and caught Tory's attention for a second. She rolled her eyes at the bullshit. "Put your arms straight out in front of you."

Leo slowly obeyed, stretching his arms out in front of him, hands balled up with only the middle fingers extended toward the ceiling.

Carefully, Merlin approached Leo, the gun resting confidently in his right hand. Mindful of keeping a safe distance, Merlin grabbed his prisoner's sweatshirt in the back and pulled him backwards to a stuffed chair with sturdy wooden arms.

Once Leo was in the chair he checked the surgeon out with baleful eyes. Merlin came around front. "Okay, who the hell are you?"

Leo thrust his lower jaw forward, his eyes squinty with venom. "Your mother."

Merlin burst out laughing. "Your mother? *Your mother?* You musta dropped outta school in about the ninth grade. That's a junior high insult. Listen, pal, if you want to piss me off you gotta do better than that. Maybe say something like 'I'm gonna suck out your eyeballs and eat 'em.' Try that."

"Okay, tough guy," the prisoner said, "you got the gun. Why'nt you put it down and you'n me go at it."

"Not until you answer a few questions. You weren't here for quick cash. You coulda done that any day of the week when we were at work. You took the phone off the hook. You've got this cowboy gun, and you walked right past a purse on the TV stand over there. Who sent you?"

"I'll sit here all fuckin' night. You'n me both know you ain't gonna cap me sitting here in the chair. So you might as well call the cops, big shot. I'll be home for breakfast.''

Merlin knew the guy was right. He looked over toward Tory, standing on the bottom step, barefoot in her nightshirt, like a child sneaking a peek at her parents' dinner party. "Tory, hold the gun on him for a second.''

Reluctantly, she walked over to Merlin, almost embarrassed to be asked to participate. Merlin handed her the heavy Smith and Wesson, not once taking his eyes off Leo.

"I'm okay," Tory said, aiming the gun at the intruder who sat defiantly in the chair.

"Be right back," Merlin whispered, then dashed to the kitchen and retrieved a twelve-foot extension cord from the tool drawer next to the sink.

Unraveling the unruly white cord as he came back to the living room, Merlin stood behind the chair where Leo sat. It was not Merlin's intention to tie him up so that he couldn't get away. All he wanted to accomplish was to make it difficult for the prisoner to make any quick attempts at escape or physical confrontation.

"Put your arms down at your side. That's it. Sit up straight. No, *straight*.'' When he was satisfied his directions were being followed, Merlin took the cord and created a small loop in one end with a simple knot called a bowline. Next he took hold of both ends of the twelve-foot cord and flipped it over Leo like a cowboy using a lariat. Then he tightened the cord, pulling it back hard, wrapping it around Leo a second time. Then, maintaining pressure, he fed the free end through the bowline loop and pulled the cord taut, even putting his foot on the back of the chair to brace himself, yanking the extension cord so tight it dug into Leo's skin. As a magician, Merlin was an expert with knots, finishing his work with a couple of half hitches. Once completed it was called the trucker's hitch, a wonderful knot used to secure unruly loads on big rigs. Even if the prisoner wiggled about, a trucker's hitch wouldn't come loose.

When it was all done, Leo sat stiffly in the chair, his upper arms cinched tightly to his side. Tory handed the Smith and Wesson back to Merlin. Her job finished, Tory drifted out of the way and quietly slipped over to the TV by the front door.

"I like your gun," Merlin said and sniffed the barrel. Then he sniffed it a couple more times. "It looks brand-new. Hmmm, Smith and Wesson," Merlin read aloud. "You ever shoot this thing?''

"Yeah, I shot it.''

"Merlin, let's just call the police," Tory suggested.

"Doesn't smell like it. Smells new. You ready to talk?" Merlin asked as he fiddled with the weapon until he found the button that released the cylinder. It was fully loaded. With the cylinder out of the weapon Merlin sighted down the barrel, like he knew exactly what he was doing.

"Merlin," Tory said, "forget it, let's just call the police."

"Our friend Tinkerbell's right. We call the police, he gets a little slap on the wrist. I want to know what he wants." Merlin smiled at Leo, then held the weapon up to the light for the second time, squinting down the barrel, turning the gun in his hand this way and that, surprised that he could not see any light coming through. "I guess you're not counting on the Miss Congeniality award at the annual thug banquet." Evidently satisfied with what he saw, Merlin inverted the pistol, and all five bullets fell into the palm of his hand. The .38 caliber bullets were big and fat. When he moved his hand around, they bounced against one another, tapping dully. "One," Merlin said as he dropped a bullet to the floor. "Two," Merlin said and dropped another. "Three," when the third bounced and rolled in an aimless arc. "And . . . four."

Merlin took the fifth bullet and rolled it between his fingers. "Number five." Then he turned slightly so his captive audience could see exactly what he was doing. With the tip of his index finger he slid the cartridge partway into one of the chambers in the empty cylinder, pausing for a moment to allow his prisoner ample time to view the bottom of the brass cartridge protruding ominously. Again Merlin used his index finger and the .38 Special plus P hollow point slowly slid home.

Finally, taking all the time in the world, Merlin inverted the weapon as he snapped the cylinder back inside the gun.

Merlin took direct aim at his prisoner's head.

"Oh, wait. Let's make this fun." Merlin pulled back the hammer partway with his thumb so the cylinder could rotate freely, then spun it provocatively. *Tick-tick-tick-tick-tick-tick-tick-tick-tick-tick.* The cylinder clicked around, slowing finally to a stop. "Now we're ready. I hope you're feeling lucky." Merlin took aim at Leo's head. As he squeezed the trigger with his index finger, the hammer drew back slowly, working its way further and further. *CLICK.*

Leo winced and jerked his head to the side, as if a bullet to the side of the head was more desirable than one between the eyes.

"Okay, that's how we play the game. Question number one. Who the hell are you?"

Merlin's captive was now sweating visibly. "Leo."

"How appropriate, Leo. You're the fifth sign of the zodiac, and there are five chambers in your gun. That's what they call poetic. But I still want to know *who* you are and *what* you're doing here."

"It's just fuckin' Leo. And I already told you. I was jus' looking for some cash."

"What are you doing here?"

"Shit, why don't you listen? I ain't telling you again."

Merlin took aim with the gun. "Yes, you will." Leo turned his head to the side, but his eyes never left the revolver. Again Merlin worked the trigger back until it clicked on another empty chamber.

Leo let out his breath slowly.

"Two down."

"Hey, man, that's not how you play it."

"Play what?"

"Russian roulette," Leo said, pausing between words for a quick breath. "You're supposed to spin it each time."

"This isn't Russian roulette. It's *rushing* roulette. We don't have time for the full game. Now, one more time. Who sent you?"

It was working. Leo was breathing hard. He tried to bring his hand up to wipe his face, but he had to flex his neck all the way for the two to meet. "Look, I don't know. I don't know! Okay?"

"Then why were you sent?"

Leo shifted uncomfortably in his seat. "To scare you. The man wanted me to give you a message. To tell you to stay the hell away from this shit in the hospital with the people dying."

Suddenly, the room got incredibly quiet. Jack Merlin instantly felt more frightened than his prisoner. "Why?"

" 'Cause it's none of your goddamn business."

"They're my patients. It *is* my goddamn business." Leo clamped his mouth shut. "Okay, Tory, now you'd better call the cops." Merlin waited for Tory to get her cell phone from her purse, press the little button to get a dial tone, and start dialing before he worked the trigger a third time. Squeezing it as slowly as possible, Merlin pulled the trigger until the hammer traveled all the way back—

"No, man. Stop!" Leo pleaded.

Merlin released the trigger before the hammer fired. "I'll stop when you talk."

"No. They'll kill me."

"Then either way you're gonna die." Merlin pulled back the trigger until the hammer fired. *CLICK.* "Two to go."

Merlin got closer, the barrel now inches away from Leo's cheek.

"Look, man, I told you what you wanted. LET . . . ME . . . GO."

Taking advantage of Leo's wide-open mouth, Merlin slipped the gun inside like an anesthesiologist intubating a patient, working it all the way back until Leo was gagging on it, saliva running out of his mouth.

Although Leo's neck was extended all the way back, Merlin kept pushing the barrel further and further, as if forcing it down into his lungs.

"Ahhhhhhh. Eh, eh, eh," Leo gagged violently, his entire body joining in the spasm. Breaths of air were a luxury that he couldn't afford right now.

"Tell me now, Leo. What the fuck is going on?"

"Ake ih ou. Ake ih ou," Leo pleaded, his chest heaving violently. He started to retch again.

"Talk or I squeeze the trigger." Merlin eased up on the thrust but left the end of the barrel resting on Leo's lower teeth.

"I just do deliveries. Deliveries. I deliver rubbers with germs inside to some guy from the hospital. I don't know his name, I swear. That's *all* I do. That's it."

Suddenly, a loud bang emanated from the kitchen. All three looked that way as the kitchen door swung open wildly, smashing against the counter next to the sink. Tommy, hidden behind a ski mask covering his entire face, strode into the room with a large semiautomatic weapon in his hand. "No one move," he said in a deliberately low and gruff voice.

Leo sat up. "All right, Doc. Payback time. Untie me."

"Put the gun down," Tommy said, and brought his Sig Saurer .45 to a firing position, shoulder high. "Take a look at your chest."

Merlin looked down and saw a tiny dot of bright red light dancing over his heart.

Leo laughed. "Shoot him."

Tommy said, "First, put the gun down on the table."

Merlin laid the Smith and Wesson on the coffee table.

"Now untie him before I have to use it," Tommy demanded.

Off in the distance the sirens of the Aspinwall police could be heard as the squad cars sped up Center Avenue.

Slowly, Merlin walked around the back of the chair and undid the knots. Before he fully unwrapped the cord, Leo flipped it over his head and bolted from the seat. The first thing Leo did with his new freedom was take a swing at Merlin, but he missed.

"Forget it. Cops are coming. Let's go!"

Reluctantly, Leo came around the chair, heading for the kitchen. Almost as an afterthought, he grabbed his Smith and Wesson before following Tommy out of the living room.

Just as Tommy reached the kitchen door, Leo turned back toward Merlin. Sirens were in the air, getting louder, and he knew there wasn't much time. Standing in the doorway to the living room he raised his gun and took aim at Merlin. Before Tory or Merlin could react he pulled the trigger. *CLICK*.

Tommy yelled over his shoulder as the hammer fell harmlessly, "Cut the shit, man. The cops are out front." Then he disappeared.

"This is it asshole. Number five." Leo wrinkled his lips into an angry snarl.

Merlin had pulled the trigger three times, Leo once. Tory knew the next squeeze of the trigger might kill Merlin. Watching Leo aim his gun at Merlin brought out primal feelings. Tory wanted to kill him, but her hand was shaking so badly she didn't know if she could lift the small Beretta she had kept hidden in the folds of her nightshirt.

She wasn't even sure whether she'd clicked the safety to the on position or the off position.

Fortunately, while Leo was retching, she'd racked the slide, using the noise he made to camouflage the sound. It only weighed a pound, but even with a light gun, Tory knew she would need two hands to squeeze off a shot accurately. Maybe, if she was lucky, she could get off a quick shot in Leo's general direction and the blast would cause him to miss.

How could the last twenty minutes boil down to one shot?

Merlin, on the other hand, was fishing around in his pants pocket with one hand as he stood calmly, eyes on Leo, watching him waste time, hoping the cops would charge in the back way and surprise him. But Leo steadied his aim, sighting right between Merlin's eyes. *CLICK*. The Smith and Wesson, its five chambers absolutely empty, clicked harmlessly. Leo's mouth fell open in shock.

Ever the showman, Merlin proudly displayed the fifth bullet between his thumb and index finger, just as Tory jerked her weapon up and squeezed off a round as soon as it was pointed in Leo's direction. *BANG*. Tory's Beretta made an awful noise, especially loud in such a small room, and for a moment the ringing in her ears made her deaf.

When Merlin heard the blast from the Beretta, he nearly jumped out of his pants. The bullet, palmed before he'd closed the cylinder and secretly slipped into his pocket, popped out of his hand and dropped to the floor.

Of course Tory missed Leo, the bullet going wide left by a good eighteen inches and straight through the screen on the back door. It didn't travel much beyond that. Tommy's right shoulder got in the way, and the bullet ripped a clean hole through the black warm-up suit and lodged itself within his thick deltoid muscle.

By the time the Aspinwall police ran up the wooden steps to the front porch, Leo and Tommy had run through half a dozen backyards and were piling into Tommy's car. His right shoulder hurt with a dull burn, and he could feel the trickle of warm blood running down his arm.

Leo took the wheel, flooring it as he pulled away from the curb. Tommy put his hand to his shoulder. Even in the dark he could see it was covered with blood.

"Hey, Tommy, you want to go up to the hospital?"

"That's exactly where the cops'll be looking."

Leo kept driving, wanting to ask how the cops would know Tommy had gotten shot. But he'd fucked up enough for one day. For once he kept his mouth shut.

13

When the police arrived, guns drawn, Merlin shouted out that they were okay, and that the two intruders had run off. He then directed their attention to Tory. Four cops stayed for over an hour, hearing the details about how Leo had broken into the house looking for money, examining the hole in the screen door, and helping Merlin hammer a couple of nails in the kitchen door to secure it where a crowbar had been used to pry it open. Three times they listened to Merlin's explanation of why a twelve-foot extension cord was still tangled around an easy chair in the living room.

Not one word was said about the delivery of bacteria-filled condoms to the Medical Center.

Tory sat on the couch wrapped in a comforter, her feet tucked underneath, watching the activity around her. The Beretta was on the coffee table in front of her, and she was having trouble keeping her eyes off it. A cup of hot chocolate had appeared in her hand—probably from Merlin—and she sipped it while the police made the effort of taking prints. No usable ones were found.

Before they left, the police stated they were going to step up patrols in the neighborhood for the next week or so. They even offered to put a man outside their Ninth Street home if it would make Tory feel better.

But Tory said no; she and Merlin would be okay.

Once they were alone it was hard to feel relaxed enough to go to sleep, so they sat close together on the sofa pretending to watch some old movie on the TV, trying to pass the time.

Scaring the shit out of Leo had felt wonderful. Silently, Merlin went through every detail of what had happened. Tory, who was occupied with quite different thoughts, struggled with the realization that she'd been willing and ready to kill someone. The Beretta remained on the table, where it seemed to call to them. It had become the focal point of the room.

Finally Tory broke the silence. "I saw my dad kill someone once."

She sniffled a couple of times, and Merlin tightened his grip around her shoulders, suspecting she was about to reveal a secret.

"Some guy came to the door one night while my mother was still alive. He asked for my dad, but he wasn't home yet. I was seven. I was standing right behind my mom when he pulled out a gun and aimed it at her and pushed his way into our house."

Merlin felt his eyes get wet. He was frightened to hear the details but hesitated to say anything.

"He must have known what time my dad got home because about three minutes later he walked in. The guy was behind Mom, you know, with his arm around her neck. Mom was crying, and"—Tory sniffled some more—"my father talked to him very calmly, but the guy started yelling . . . screaming at my dad. I just stood there knowing the guy was gonna kill my mom. I never felt so helpless. It was the worst feeling I ever had.

"Then the guy told my dad to take out his gun and drop it on the floor. My dad was plainclothes at that time and wore one of those shoulder holsters. It was just like slow motion. His hand went into his jacket so slowly.

"Then there was this incredibly loud bang. It stung my ears. I didn't know what had happened. The guy didn't just fall down, he flew backwards like he was hit by a truck or something. That was it. My dad had less than a second to aim his gun and hit the guy. And he did it. Some time after that, my mom started drinking. But she always looked at my dad different, like he was a real hero. Even when she was dying of liver failure, all my dad had to do was walk into the room, and her eyes would light up."

They were both crying now.

Tory wiped her eyes. "I'll never forget that helpless feeling. Seven years old, watching that guy wave his gun in her face. Oh, God."

"You weren't helpless tonight. If there had been a bullet left in his gun you would have saved my life."

"I knew I wasn't going to hit him. I wanted to, but there was no way."

"Then maybe we should practice. Take a drive tomorrow, way out in the woods, and do some target shooting."

"I don't need to practice. Believe it or not, I'm a damn good shot. I started to go to the range with my dad when I was twelve."

Merlin spoke gently. "Tory, you missed him by three feet."

"It was the first time I'd touched that gun. You've got to get used to a pistol. The way it feels in your hand."

Merlin didn't believe a word she was saying. "Maybe you're a little rusty."

"You're not listening. I don't want to get into guns. Don't you see? We've had enough guns to last a lifetime. The answer is no."

He could sense how brittle her emotions were. "I don't want to fight with you, Tory. Let me go on the record, counselor, that I saved your life in the OR—"

Tory gave out a little laugh. "You said it was a small laceration. I love you for operating on me, but you're not the only surgeon at the Medical Center who could have operated."

"*I* was the one who figured out the operating room was rigged."

"Touché," she said and turned her face to kiss him on his salty cheek.

"*And*—a big and—I caught an intruder tonight—an armed intruder, no less—with my bare hands."

"You know you're my hero." Another kiss.

"How 'bout this? A simple wager."

"A wager?"

"Right." Merlin went over to a small cabinet where he kept his magic supplies and selected a deck of cards. "Here's the deal. You name a card—any card, as they say—and I'll cut the deck once. If it's your card we shoot tomorrow."

For the first time Tory smiled. "You think I just tumbled off the turnip truck. No way. That's one of your fancy rough and smooth decks, and it's designed to do exactly that. With a rigged deck any two-bit magician can cut the deck to any specific card."

"What kind of a wager would you be comfortable with? Maybe some poker. Hey, I know, we'll play strip poker. If you lose we take a drive tomorrow after I go see Banks Wickford."

"Every time you lure me into strip poker you deal off the bottom of the deck—"

"No, I don't. I stack the deck as I'm shuffling—"

"Whatever. No strip poker. I've got stitches, remember?"

"I was hoping to accumulate some credits, like a gift certificate. You know, I could pull them out some evening and you'd have to—"

"Forget it." The only way to shut him up was to agree to a bet of some sort, so Tory came up with a ridiculous wager. "Here's the deal. *You* name the card, and we'll shoot tomorrow if I cut to your card."

Merlin smiled. "Ahhh. Heads I win, tails you lose. Nothing like a sure bet, huh?"

Smiling right back, Tory was pleased with her one-in-fifty-two odds. Merlin shuffled the cards several times.

"Hey, I'm supposed to do that," Tory said without much of a protest. Merlin handed over the deck. Tory shuffled twice, then squared up the deck and placed it on the coffee table.

Merlin scratched his chin, playing the role of stooge. "Okay, I say you cut to the seven of—oh, I don't know—diamonds."

"Seven of diamonds, okay." Tory cut the cards and held up the top half of the deck for Merlin to see.

"How do you like that," Merlin said with a hint of glee. "Seven of diamonds! Think of the odds."

Quickly, Merlin reached out and scooped up the bottom half of the deck from the coffee table, then innocently held out his hand for Tory to give him the rest of the cards.

"Wait a second," Tory said with a tone of frustration in her voice. "I want to see the cards." Flipping the half-deck in her hand over, she riffled through them. "Merlin! They're *all* seven of—oh, I don't know—diamonds," she said, mimicking Merlin's innocent tone of voice as he hazarded a guess. "You cheated!"

"Me?" Merlin said, pointing his index finger at himself. "*Moi?* Hey, who called the bet?"

Tory knew she'd been had. Of course Merlin knew that she knew about the rigged deck. And of course he wasn't stupid enough to try a trick she already knew. "You win. I'll go—for one hour. But you answer one question for me. How the hell did you know I would let you name the card while I cut the deck?"

"I know everything you're gonna do before you do it." Merlin flexed his fingers and held them up so that his nails were right in front of his mouth. Then he blew gently on his nails to polish them in a deliberately obnoxious show of bravado.

Tory smiled. "What am I gonna do next, hotshot?"

Merlin rubbed his hands together. "First, let me tell you what you're *not* going to do. You're not gonna put your arms around me and drive me crazy with your tongue. Instead, because you realize I can read your mind, you're so angry that you're just about to march up those stairs in a huff and pretend to go to sleep, even though you'd love to make out down here for a while."

Tommy and Leo were back at Ritter's Diner, sitting in a warm beam of sunlight at a window booth. Seemingly immune to the close call he had had the night before, Leo was sopping up brown gravy with his french fries and working on a double cheeseburger. Tommy sat stiffly in the booth, adjusting his shirt with his left hand so it wouldn't pull on his bandaged shoulder.

"You oughta see a doc or something," Leo offered helpfully and jammed two large fries in his mouth.

"It was a popgun. It'll heal," Tommy said quietly, sipping some hot coffee.

"There's a slug in you, man."

"Keep it down," Tommy said, checking around to make sure they weren't being overheard. Wincing from a bolt of pain, he continued. "Look, my dad came home from Nam with a slug in his thigh. It was never removed, and not once did he complain about it. I'm okay. It's even hurting less today. I took a couple of Percocets when I got home and a couple hits of Jack Daniel's and I slept pretty good. Bleeding's stopped. Forget it. Where's the paper?"

Leo slid the *Post Gazette* across the table. It took Tommy one look to find the article on the first page of the Regions section. He scanned it quickly then reread snippets for Leo. "It says here, attempted armed robbery . . . Aspinwall . . . two   men . . . guns . . . surprised   by . . . Jack Merlin, a surgeon . . . here it is . . . one of the men identified himself only as Leo." Tommy looked over at Leo before continuing, "Blond hair and a blond mustache . . . a successful escape."

"That don't sound so bad," Leo said, feeling optimistic. "Then they don't know you were shot. That's something."

"Maybe they know but aren't saying, like to get me to go to the ER. Try to think for once."

"There's a million Leos in the world."

"Shave the 'stache, blondie."

"What?!" Leo exclaimed, reaching up and smoothing the hairs growing over his upper lip.

"Off today."

Leo looked down at his food like a scolded child.

"One more thing. You tell them anything else?"

Looking directly across the table at Tommy, Leo said, "You know, I could go back there tonight, kick the fuckin' door in, and shoot them before they knew what happened."

"What if they're waiting for you with the gun? Give it up, Leo. You blew your chance. Now what else you tell 'em?"

"Nothing. He was gagging me and sticking the gun in my face. I had to tell him something 'til you came in."

"You couldn't have thought of any other name, huh?"

Leo smoothed his mustache. "What'd you tell the boss, Tommy?"

"There's nothing to tell. I wish I could find out what the hell's going on in the Medical Center."

"I'm not through with the broad that shot you."

"Don't fool with her, Leo."

"I'm just gonna follow her, get to know what she does now that she's been out of work, 'cause when we're through with this thing, I may come back for a visit."

While they were driving away from Pittsburgh, Merlin couldn't resist. "Hey, great make-out session on the couch last night," he said, slipping a naughty look at Tory, who, up until now, was enjoying her first outing since her surgery.

"Exactly what did Banks Wickford say when you told him about last night?"

"It was typical. He didn't care if we were hurt. All he wanted to know was whether we told the police anything. When I told him we hadn't, he let out his breath like the Medical Center had dodged a bullet."

"So he ordered the ORs shut down?"

"Yeah, right," Merlin answered sarcastically. "You think they're going to cut out a major source of revenue? Besides, everything's done by committee. He had to meet with the Medical Center attorney and the chairman of the board."

"Don't make me ask. What'd you do?"

"I told him we hadn't said a word to the local police so that the announcement could come from the Medical Center. I gave him twenty-four hours. If he doesn't take action, I go to the press. As long as he acts responsibly, I promised to stay out of it."

"What about the police?"

"All he would say was he would act appropriately. I'm sure there will be a press conference tomorrow if he cancels surgery for the Medical Center. If he doesn't bring the police in, then I'll call them myself."

"What about Bello trying to sneak out of the hospital, then signing himself out against medical advice?" Tory asked.

"Wickford already knew about it."

"What did he say?"

"Nothing. Maybe he'll form a committee to look into it."

Tory looked out her window. "I'd sure like to have a talk with Nick Bello."

They drove for almost an hour before finding an old abandoned farm that would be perfect for target practice. The farmhouse was missing a wall. All the windows were broken, and there was a barn that was hidden from the road. No neighbors were in sight. Merlin parked near the road. Up the rutted dirt drive and around the house, the two walked toward the barn. Merlin carried a roll of white paper that looked like wrapping paper. Tory had the Beretta in her bag.

It was a day pretty enough for a picnic. "Okay, Merlin," Tory said when they reached the barn, "what are we shooting at?"

He held out the white wrapping paper. "I brought a target." Holding the paper at one end, he let the roll go. As it unfurled Merlin looked down at it with a smile, knowing what Tory's reaction would be.

"What is that?" Tory asked incredulously.

Drawn in thick blue marker was a rendering of a person that looked like the chalk outline the cops might draw of a slain gingerbread man. But this one was adorned with block print words written in the appropriate places: SHIRT. PANTS. BRA. PANTIES. SOCKS. SHOES.

"Strip target practice," Merlin said, walking the twenty steps toward the barn and fixing the drawing to the wall with a couple of pushpins he'd brought. "What do you think? Anything you hit is like a—"

Tory rolled her eyes. "I know, I know. A gift certificate."

"Right. I'll go first. Any item of clothing I hit, I collect at my discretion." Merlin took aim with the Beretta.

BANG.

Tory squinted. "Ooooh, you hit the barn. I'll promise to take off my barn the next time you want me to."

"Just warming up."

BANG.

"I'd better buy some more barns. You'll have me ripping them off all the time." Tory giggled.

"Watch it. In a couple of seconds you're gonna need six layers of clothes to stay warm this winter."

BANG. BANG. BANG.

"Two barns and that little tree over there. And you told that nice young man you were an excellent shot. Poor old Leo."

"You knew that was a bluff."

"My God, Merlin, with the gun shoved in to his tonsils you still would've missed him."

BANG.

"Help, I'm living with a foot fetishist." Tory was having trouble talking she was laughing so hard. "You got a shoe. Hey, what the heck, let's do the stripping now."

"It's too cold."

"No way, a bet's a bet."

Merlin swept his right hand out, gallantly allowing Tory to proceed. Obliging him, Tory put her bag down on an old bench near the porch of the house. She then used the toe of her left Saucony to hold down the heel of her right, wriggling her foot until she stepped out of it.

"Your turn." Merlin popped the clip and reloaded it.

"My foot's a little cold," Tory said.

"Remember, a bet's a bet. Let's see how you do," Merlin teased, snapping the clip in place. Then he handed over the gun.

Tory turned toward the target, slowly bringing the weapon to a two-handed firing position. Not the grab-your-wrist stance of TV cops, but the steadier cup-and-saucer technique, her left hand acting as a base upon which the butt of the gun and her right hand rested. Wrapping the fingers of her left hand up around the right, she was ready. Taking care to slow her breathing, Tory squeezed off her first round.

BANG.

A bullet hole appeared in the paper, several inches to the right of the gingerbread man's chest.

"That's not bad," Merlin offered. "Better than last night." He chuckled.

Tory didn't look away from the target. "Just getting to know my Beretta. *Now,* I'm ready."

BANG.

"I bet you'd call that a lucky shot, huh? Take off your shirt, anyway," she said.

BANG.

"What do you know? Gimme your pants."

Merlin hadn't finished getting his shirt over his head.

"C'mon, Merlin, quit stalling. I wanna see some skin."

BANG.

"Now your panties, you chauvinist. How come you didn't put 'boxer shorts' on the target?"

BANG.

"How about a shoe?"

BANG.

"How 'bout another shoe?"

"Okay, okay, you win." Merlin said.

"Let's go, you're not naked yet. I've got one more bullet."

BANG.

"Your bra. I want to see your bra. No, naked. I want you completely naked." Now the gun was empty. Tory blew across the end of the barrel, showing she could be an obnoxious tease also. "Like I told you, I learned to shoot when I was twelve."

"You really want me to strip?"

"Now. And when I relate this story to your friends—and believe me I will—I promise not to mention you asked any stupid questions."

"Can I get dressed now?" Merlin asked as he flipped his boxers to Tory.

There, in the middle of an abandoned farm on a beautiful Autumn day, Jack Merlin was completely naked. His hands made a poor substitute for fig leaves, and Tory had never seen Merlin so nervous, or so small.

"I'm a good shot—but I couldn't hit that," she observed.

Daring only a quick glance down at himself, Merlin said, "My underwear."

One by one Tory flipped his clothing to him. He dressed quickly. When he was fully clothed Merlin said, "You're a terrific shot. But if it wasn't a target, could you still hit it?"

"You mean could I kill someone?"

"If you had to."

Tory thought for several seconds. "I wanted to kill Leo last night."

"But you missed," Merlin said while reloading the Beretta one last time.

"One, I never shot the gun before. And two, there wasn't time for a two-handed grip. I'm not strong enough to hold it one-handed. And three, why are you reloading the gun?"

Merlin looked around and spotted a big brown rat nibbling at something by the barn. "Could you hit the rat?"

Tory was getting irritated. "I'm not going to."

"Listen to me, goddamn it, I want to be able to sleep at night. It's a rat, for God sakes."

"Then we go home?"

"Then we go home." Merlin handed Tory the gun.

Slowly she raised the gun, cup-and-saucer style, but Merlin could see the short barrel making little circular movements.

BANG.

A sliver of wood splintered off a loose plank, the rat scurrying away. Merlin looked like he was going to cry when he admitted, "I'm sorry I pushed you. C'mon, I'll take you for a late lunch before I go back," and put his arm around her.

"I don't know if I'm hungry."

Together they walked to the car, like mourners leaving a funeral, Tory lost in thought, holding the Beretta down at her side.

They were almost at the car when Tory remembered, "Oh, my God, my bag! Be right back."

Looking up at the clear sky, Tory walked back up the drive, thinking about that night when the devil came into their house. So many times over the years she'd gone back, yet it always felt the same. Horrible. Helpless. Too many hours of sleep had been lost. Too many what-ifs had been considered. The way he talked, saying terrible lies about her dad. The way he smelled like whiskey and needed a shave. Picturing her mom was even easier, so pale she looked like she was already dead.

Three years later she *was* dead.

By the time Tory rounded the farmhouse she was breathing hard. Seven years old, standing behind her mom, watching that man wave his gun around. The whiskey on his breath. Her dad's hand moving up to his holster . . .

The big brown rat was back, nibbling by the side of the barn.

. . . the horrible man rocketing backwards . . .

BANG.

Merlin heard the gunshot. He was sitting in the car with the motor running, feeling like a jerk for upsetting Tory. Before he knew it, he was running up the driveway, terrified at what might have happened. Harder and harder he pushed himself, wondering what he would do when he found her. Whatever had happened was his fault. He had pushed her too hard and—

Just then Tory walked around the corner of the farmhouse and gave Merlin a smile.

"What happened?" Merlin asked, breathless.

"Nothing," Tory said brightly and kissed him on the cheek. "I'm starved. Let's go."

14

An emergency staff meeting convened in the large auditorium so that Banks Wickford could address the entire medical staff. Television news cameras were invited, and the room was packed. Standing at the heavy podium with the crest of the Medical Center carved right into the wood, Banks looked splendid in a tailored suit. Seated near him were Knox and Carter. Jonathan Olsen and several other heads of departments flanked the big three on stage.

First, Banks announced the discovery of bacterial contamination of the sterilization process used for the surgical instruments, stating that all surgeries were temporarily being canceled. Emergencies and minor procedures would be farmed out to the Medical Center's outlying community hospitals. All others would be postponed until the problem was solved to his satisfaction.

Immediately, hands went up around the room. From the second row a female voice could be heard above everyone else's. Sandy Keller, the KDKA reporter who thrived on Medical Center intrigue, was going to have the first question whether anyone liked it or not. "Mr. Wickford. How long have you known about this problem?"

"Last night I met with key physicians. As soon as we understood the situation, all surgeries were immediately canceled."

Sensing he had completed his answer, hands shot up.

"Follow-up question, Mr. Wickford. Has patient safety been compromised in any way so far?"

"Miss Keller, we have no definitive proof that safety was compromised because of the bacterial contamination. The reason surgeries have been canceled is a precaution. Of course, we're launching our own investigation into the matter, and our results—whatever they may be—will be fully disclosed. Dr. Olsen here will head the committee.''

"One more question, if you will—"

But Banks had already pointed to a surgeon in the front row who wanted to know exactly how it would be decided which cases would be postponed and which would be farmed out.

A few more questions were taken from the floor, then Banks finished on a strong note. "As long as I'm responsible for the lives of the patients and the reputations of the physicians, I will rely on my judgment. The integrity of the Pittsburgh University Medical Center will never be compromised.''

Sandy, smelling a story with her tiny bobbed nose, sidled up to Merlin as he made a quick exit. Oversized earrings had once been her trademark, but as her success and bank account grew, Sandy had taken to more expensive and heavier jewelry. The once tiny holes in her earlobes had expanded over time into sizable openings which had caused her to look like something out of *National Geographic*. Having recently seen a plastic surgeon who repaired the damage, her lobes now sported a series of tiny black sutures, forcing Sandy into a moussed-up hairstyle that almost covered the surgeon's handiwork.

"Hey, Merlin, what can you give me?"

It would have been too easy for Merlin to tell Sandy the truth. If Banks hadn't canceled all surgeries he would have blabbed in a minute. Banks was a worm, puffing himself up and covering up a series of murders, but at least he'd taken action. More importantly, Merlin didn't want to be on the news. There was no reason to give Leo and his friend cause to come back. For now it would be smart to let Banks Wickford grab the spotlight and let the police begin a quiet investigation.

"Not much. I'm happy that Mr. Wickford had the courage to do what was right," Merlin said, playing the role of loyal citizen of the Medical Center. "The safety of our patients is top priority. How many other CEOs would react so quickly and not wait for a disaster?"

He excused himself and dashed down the hall.

Tory arrived home from her daily walk in the park just as the phone rang. This was her longest walk in the park since her surgery, and the last thing she wanted was for Merlin to find out.

The first thing Merlin said was, "You see the news?"

Tory was relieved that he hadn't said something about trying to reach her for a half hour. "Sure did. Do you think he was more interested in preserving the Medical Center's reputation or his own?" Tory asked.

"Probably his own. This is just the beginning of a cover-up. After what I told him, I'm sure safeguards will be in place so no more deaths occur. But the press will never know what really happened. I mean, what if Bello was running the operation from the inside and got spooked? Now he's gone, and Leo knows he told us enough that we're onto the scheme. No more unexpected infections. In three weeks the whole thing'll be forgotten."

"What do you suggest?" Tory asked.

"You free for dinner tonight?"

"You mean a date?"

"Yeah, there's a bar I want to check out called the Friendship Club. Probably's very casual."

"The Friendship Club? Never heard of it."

"It's a bar Nick Bello used to hang out in. I remember he used to go on about it."

"You think you should call the police?"

"No. Maybe they've already been there. But if they haven't, I don't want the cops flashing their badges around and scaring everybody. You'n I can get a burger and casually talk with the waitress. You know."

"Shall I bring . . . protection?" Tory asked and laughed.

"Yes," Merlin said, dragging out the word, emphasizing that it was understood she should always bring her gun.

By five o'clock Tory was dressed casually in jeans and a sweater. She was so excited at the prospect of going out for dinner she even put on a hint of lipstick.

By six o'clock Merlin was half an hour late. Tory paged him. The operator said there was an emergency in the ER and he wasn't answering his page.

Tory sat in the kitchen, looking at an empty stove. When it hit her that dinner was about to be macaroni and cheese, she pulled out the phone book and checked the address for the Friendship Club.

It took a while for her to find the Friendship Club. She cruised in her Saab up and down the narrow streets, eventually stumbling upon the small cinder block building. Above the door, sticking out several feet, was a metal sign hanging from a rod that allowed it to swing in the breeze. There was a fixture above the sign with places for two light-bulbs, one to light each side of the sign. One of the lightbulbs was out, so it only could be read from one direction. Taking one look at the place Tory figured the bulb had been out for a while, and when the other one went, nobody would be in a hurry to replace it.

Under one of the few trees on the street, Tory parked halfway down the block, the only car without Ford or Chevy on the back. Walking up the sidewalk, something told her to slip off her gold bangle bracelet and drop it into her bag. The necklace Merlin had given her, a single diamond set in gold, the one she never took off, was tucked under her blouse and safely out of sight.

Nervously, Tory waited outside, mustering her courage, feeling incredibly conspicuous. A pair of headlights headed up the block toward her. It was a pickup—"Built Ford Tough"—and two guys hopped out, already reeking of beer. They could have been twins. Long hair, black T-shirts, and tight jeans with huge belt buckles. One of them carried a pack of Camels, which looked odd, but he probably couldn't get them in his pocket without crushing them. As if scripted, he opened the door, holding it briefly as he eyed Tory up and down, and mentioned something about having a beer with them. But he acted polite, not pissed off when she shook her head and said she was waiting for someone. Instead he smiled and disappeared inside.

Eventually, after pacing up and down in front of the cinder block building for another ten minutes, Tory—way overdressed in jeans and a brown sweater—entered the Friendship Club.

15

Once inside the Friendship Club, it was too dark to see much of anything right away. As Tory's eyes slowly adjusted, she noticed a string of Christmas lights that probably stayed up year-round, a dartboard surrounded by a million little pockmarks in the wall, and a pathetic crooked shelf teaming with bowling trophies and photographs of the Friendship Club regulars in their red silk jackets.

This was a hangout for men, definitely not a waitress kind of bar. If a woman had walked in, Tory thought it a safe bet that she would be showing a tattoo.

At the far end of the room, a long walk for a woman with a dozen sets of eyes locked onto her breasts, was the bar. Only one customer was seated there, wearing a bulky camouflage coat, hunched over his drink. Standing off to one side was the bartender, his shirt unbuttoned to accommodate his vast expanse of neck that creased into half a dozen chins whenever he looked down. Always operating in slow motion, he was wiping a small beer glass with a rag he had slung over his shoulder.

It was quiet. No jukebox, no hidden speakers. Just a bar and tables, and all but two were empty. The pickup twins were at one of the tables, drinking beer straight from the bottle. A group of guys were gathered around a larger table playing cards. Some of them had dollar bills in their hands; others had bills stacked up neatly on the table, ready for action.

"Hey, how 'bout that beer," one of the pickup twins offered as Tory walked by their table.

Showing her best generic smile, the one that couldn't possibly be confused with anything more than a friendly gesture, Tory absently kept one hand over her bag, which was plastered tightly to her hip. "I'm still waiting for someone. But maybe you could help me. I'm looking for someone named Nick Bello."

The twins shook their head. "Haven't seen him."

She took note. They didn't say, "Never heard of him." Obviously they knew who Bello was. This was his hangout. "Thanks anyway."

Then there was a roar of excitement from the card game. One of the guys was kissing a wad of bills. Tory wandered over and watched them play a hand. There was an impressive pile of money on the table. Only three cards were being used, each tented up in the middle. A squat-looking man was the dealer. With nimble finesse his stubby fingers moved the cards around the table.

"Can I help you, miss?" It was the guy behind the bar, still working on the beer glass, his chin moving more than his lips when he talked.

"Uh, yes," Tory said, moving over to the bar, glancing at the guy in camouflage, once again flashing her generic smile. "Actually," she said, dropping her voice, "I'm looking for some information. Uh, someone who comes in here. A Nick Bello?"

The bartender shook his head. Tory couldn't help but follow the flabby neck that waved back and forth like a loosely tied scarf. "Nope. Don't know him."

"You don't know him?" she asked, repeating herself.

The bartender said to the man in camouflage, "Hey, tell her what I said."

"Save yourself the breath," Camouflage said flatly then turned back to his beer. "I don't know him, either."

"Why don't you ask the boys over there?" the bartender challenged.

Tory looked over at the card game, the money being exchanged, and the squat guy with thick fingers running the show. Timidly, she wandered over.

Half a dozen guys were seated around a table covered with speckled linoleum. A shiny metal strip running around the edge was starting to separate from the table. Two guys were standing, leaning over the sitters to throw their money down.

Politely, Tory stood a few feet away and watched several more hands. The point of the game was immediately obvious. Realizing how ridiculously easy it was to follow the queen, Tory sensed they were putting on a show for her benefit.

Finally, just as a hand finished and the gamblers were gathering their money and the guy with the fat fingers was taking a hit of his beer, Tory took a small step closer. She cleared her throat.

"Looks like someone's got a cold," the dealer said.

"Uh," Tory said, realizing she was going to have to talk louder, "I was wondering if you might help me?"

Now everyone stopped playing. Even the guys with their backs toward her turned around. "Help you?" the dealer asked.

"Hey, Mace, c'mon deal 'em," one of the gamblers half-shouted to the dealer.

Mace ignored him. "And who are you?"

"My name is Tory Welch. I just wanted some information."

"Look, miss, this is a private club. You come in here, I don't know if you're a guest or what. All's I know is, couple of guys over there offer you a friendly drink and you say no. *Now* you want us to stop our game and give you some information. First you don't want their hospitality. Now you want our hospitality. Make up your mind."

Mace was the kind of guy who could turn anything around. No matter how carefully she phrased her request, he would throw it right back in her face. The other guys around the table were loving it, waiting to laugh at her. "Maybe I should go." Tory turned to leave.

"Hey," Mace said, stopping Tory in her tracks. "Be a little social. Sit down and we'll talk." Then he looked at one of the guys across the table from him. "Kelly, show your manners. Make room."

A seat at the table instantly became available.

There was no graceful way out. If she left he'd fire a shotgun of nasty epithets at her. Taking the seat at the table didn't seem much better. Surely Mace had something equally unpleasant in mind. At least if she sat down there was a possibility she might find out something about Nick Bello. Tory quickly glanced around the table, then sat down, placing her leather bag squarely in her lap.

Mace said, "Okay . . . what's your name again?"

"Tory."

"Tory, I'm a little slow. Remind me if I forget, okay? Here's how it works." He picked up one of the three cards. "Queen of hearts. This is the money card." Then he picked up the other two, matter-of-factly showing a six and seven of clubs. "These aren't worth shit. Follow the pretty lady and you win." In an instant, all three were lined up on the table. Each had a crease down the middle and sported a red back with a thin white border.

"Actually," Tory began, trying a segue before things got going, "I was just hoping to ask you about a man named Nick Bello. Maybe you know him."

"Nick Bel-lo," Mace said, speaking slowly. "Bel-lo. Bello, Bello, Bello. Maybe." Then, to the bartender, "Hey, bring the lady a beer." Then to Tory, "Bel-lo. We'll play a couple of hands, then talk."

"You want me to bet?"

"You want me to talk?"

This silenced the room. While Tory fished inside her bag for her wallet and pulled out five ones, no one moved. She placed a single dollar in front of her on the table.

"A buck. Hope we don't get busted," Mace teased and got a good laugh out of the regulars.

Mace showed the queen, held it up for all to see. Moving in deliberate slow motion, he worked the cards around the table for several seconds. No picking up and throwing the cards. No fancy stuff.

When he finished, Mace's fat fingers left the cards alone and drummed the table lightly.

Tory said, "The queen's in the middle."

Mace flipped the queen over and slid one dollar across the table, depositing it right in front of Tory. "You're up a buck."

Almost magically, a beer appeared next to Tory in one of the tiny glasses the bartender had been cleaning.

"That'll be a buck," the bartender said, standing close enough to Tory to lean forward and steal a look down her sweater. He reached out and snatched the dollar Mace had slid across the table.

Now that the machine was in full operation Tory had the uncomfortable feeling they would push her as far as she would let them.

"Let me know when you're ready for another, miss," the bartender said and walked away.

"Okay, you're a buck up on me," Mace said. "Let's go another round."

Tory tapped a dollar on the table indicating how much she intended to wager. "Then, maybe you'll help me find Nick—"

"Yeah, yeah, yeah," Mace said. "But the usual bet is five bucks."

"What a coincidence," Tory said and added four dollars to the one already on the table. Now she expected things to accelerate.

And Mace proved her right.

He showed the queen briefly. Then the cards started moving, slowly at first, letting Tory get comfortable. "You got the queen?"

Tory nodded.

Mace continued to work the cards around the table, sliding them facedown, one card at a time. And when he picked them up—before throwing them back down—he snuck her a tempting little peek at the queen. Suddenly he had two in one hand, one in the other. Quickly, he threw them back down, making a slapping noise. Tory kept her eye on the one she thought was the queen, but Mace had done something sneaky, that much she was certain. His fat little fingers moved more deftly than she would have expected, and when he pulled them away Tory was confused.

The third card, the one on her right, seemed the obvious choice. But she'd been through so many tricks with Merlin that only one thing was certain: the obvious choice was the only card you could be sure was not the queen of hearts. She had just witnessed a well performed magic trick. Mace was waiting, drumming his fingers louder than before.

Trying to think clearly, Tory knew from Merlin's logical explanations on the psychology of magic, the queen had to be one of the other two cards. A fifty-fifty chance. There was no way to improve her odds; she had to make a guess.

Then she remembered a simple device Merlin had taught her for marking cards.

Absently pondering her choice of cards, Tory played with her lower lip, rolling it between her thumb and forefinger. This gave her a helplessly lost-in-thought expression which was not wasted on Mace.

Tory hadn't touched her beer. The way the guys figured it, she was about to be out five bucks. Once she left, they could toast her with her own drink.

"C'mon, we don't have all day," Mace encouraged.

"Well, I think it's"—Tory chose the middle card, tapping it firmly on one of the white corners with her index finger—"this one." Then she turned the card over. "Hey, lucky guess," Tory said with a smile.

Mace showed no expression on his face. Silently he pulled a five out of his shirt pocket and dropped it on the table. "You're a good guesser." Then he slid the fiver across the table.

If she wasn't going to leave with any information she was certainly going out of the Friendship Club with her pride. In one lucky guess she'd turned the tables. Not only was she up five dollars, but she'd marked the corner of the facedown side of the queen with a dab of lipstick.

The idea of getting any help from these men was long gone. No doubt they knew who Nick Bello was, and maybe even knew where he was hiding, but these guys were only interested in taking her money and promising information which would never materialize.

Now she was going to have some fun.

"Can I let it ride?"

Mace picked up a stub of a cigar from an ashtray and started chewing it. "Don't talk about it, put the money down."

A fiver and five ones sat in front of Tory. Mace didn't bother to show the queen. He got right down to business, sliding the cards around, throwing them several times, offering no free peeks. When he was finished Tory put on a good show considering her options. The smudge of pink showed up on the card to her left. But she didn't blurt out her answer. Instead she did some more lip twisting, and when Mace started drumming his fat fingers louder and louder, she said, "I think it's the one on the left."

First Mace hesitated for a second, then he did a little clicking noise with his tongue to let the regulars know he had fooled her. He started to reach for the card on his left. If he couldn't beat her with his manipulation then he would grab the wrong card, claiming that's the one she selected. And he had his loyal band of regulars to back him up.

Before his fat fingers touched it Tory said, "No, I believe that's *your* left. My left is the other side."

So good was Mace at the three-card monte sleight that only he and Tory actually knew which one was the queen. There was an uncomfortable silence as the regulars leaned in closely and watched as Mace snapped the card between his thumb and forefinger, turning it over angrily.

The queen of hearts.

Now Mace had to be careful. Really careful. He wanted to pound his fist on the table and bounce Tory's glass of beer onto her lap, but then he would have lost much more than ten bucks. Finally he said the only thing he could think of to save face. "Nice guess." Maybe the regulars would think he was setting her up for the big one. Maybe he could still salvage things.

Again Mace reached into his shirt pocket and came out with two fives. This time he held out his fist with the two bills sticking out, offering them to Tory. When she took them he held on a little too tightly, not enough for the guys around the table to notice, but Tory took note. Mace was pissed off.

Tory dropped the two fives on her growing pile. Twenty bucks. "You don't have a maximum bet, do you?"

Mace ignored her question. The cards started moving. Sliding. Up in his hand and back down on the table. Sliding some more. It was a frenetic ballet staged by a madman. When Mace finished and the table stopped wiggling, he gave his head one hard nod, challenging her.

Tory noticed he was watching not the cards but her eyes. Again she took some time looking at each of the three cards, but the queen could not have been more obvious even if the hand were played faceup.

"I'm not sure," Tory said, giving Mace a false glimmer of hope. She looked at the card to her left, the one Mace wanted her to choose. She swallowed hard, pretending to think furiously. "I'm gonna go with the middle one."

Mace sat frozen. "Okay, smartie, we're going double or nothing."

Tory could hear him breathing hard, wheezing out as he talked. His tone was different, his reputation on the line. When he reached back into his shirt pocket he pulled out his last two bills. "Kelly, gimme five bucks," he said, crumpling fifteen dollars in his angry fist.

"What?" Kelly said, not certain what the hell was going on.

"I said," Mace demanded in a loud voice, "gimme a fin, you asshole."

Now everyone was uncomfortable. Mace threw the money, crumpled up like a used Kleenex, in Tory's general direction. Kelly pulled a five-dollar bill out of his pocket and dropped it on the table.

"You're the big winner, why'nt you buying a round for the table?" Mace demanded, his tone daring her to say no.

Tory turned toward the bar. "A round for the table, please." Then she unfolded the crumpled ten-dollar bill and placed it off to the side.

And that's when Mace did the switch. While Tory was ordering a round of drinks the queen disappeared into his pocket and the four of spades replaced it. His timing was perfect. Just as Tory looked back at the table he innocently dropped the new card facedown in the middle position, so it would appear he had just flipped the queen over.

Doing an about-face, Mace now seemed relaxed. His plan was simple: first he would wipe Tory out, then give her the there-are-only-two-cards-left-do-you-want-to-go-again routine.

While the bartender filled the small glasses from the tap, Mace started to work the cards, sliding them around, picking them up, one at a time. Everything was slow and relaxed, nothing deceptive.

Just as he pulled his hands away the bartender arrived with the beers on a little round tray. "That'll be nine bucks."

Tory looked at the cards. The corners on all three were clean. No smudges. No lipstick.

"Nine bucks," the bartender reminded her. "For the beers."

"Oh, sorry," Tory said and handed him the ten.

"You don't want change, do you?" the bartender said, walking away.

"Why don't you keep it," Tory said brightly.

"Let's get back to the game," Mace demanded. "We said double or nothing. That ten bucks was part of the bet."

Tory leaned forward. For the first time she went eyeball-to-eyeball with Mace. "I'm good for it," she said with authority.

"As long as we're clear on how much you've put up. Which card?" Mace slammed his beer, opening his gullet and pouring the entire contents of the little glass directly into his stomach.

Tory looked at the cards again. One by one she scanned each of the corners, making sure. All twelve of them were clean.

"C'mon, make up your damn mind. I got other bettors here. Pick one. Pick one. Pick one." Mace smiled. "Always save the good moves for last," he mentioned to no one in particular, but he wanted Tory to know it as much as the regulars.

"All right. I don't choose any. I think the queen is in your pocket or under your leg. Somehow you worked the queen out and this is a sucker bet."

Mace couldn't think of anything to say.

Tory went on. "If any of the three cards is the queen I'll pay you *triple* the bet. Turn 'em over."

Mace reached out for the cards with both hands and crumpled them up, then stuffed them in his pocket. "No one—especially no bitch—is gonna accuse me of cheating. The game's over. Take your money and git."

Tory dug through the pile and retrieved her five ones. Leaving the rest of the money right on the table, she walked out of the Friendship Club.

"This was a bust," Tory mumbled to herself as she headed down the street toward her Saab.

The wind had picked up, and she wished she had worn warmer clothes. Before she unlocked her car door she turned back toward the Friendship Club, just to make sure Mace wasn't coming after her. The street was empty.

Sliding into the front seat, Tory locked the doors and dropped her bag on the passenger seat.

The engine made a soft purring sound unique to Saabs. Pulling away from the curb Tory heard a rustling sound coming from the backseat. She turned her head and caught the camouflage coat coming to life.

The man who had been at the bar sat up.

Tory's fear started in her stomach, then spread throughout her body, paralyzing every muscle.

"Now you found me. Just so you know, I've got a knife." With his left hand Nick Bello waved a knife in Tory's face. It was nothing more than a cheap steak knife with a pointed blade and plastic handle. This was obviously a last minute decision, just before he snuck out of the Friendship Club, but it didn't matter. At close range, any knife could be lethal.

"What do you want?"

"There's a question. You go to all that trouble finding me and you say, 'What do you want?' Drive."

Tory started down the street, but her arms didn't want to cooperate. Twice the car swerved, almost sideswiping one of the pickup trucks parked across the street. *The gun. The gun. The gun.* All Tory could think about was the Beretta. But it was at the bottom of her bag, the safety was on, and she'd have to rack the slide before it could be fired. If she could get the gun in her hand, even if it was only a bluff, maybe she could buy enough time to jump out of the car.

"Turn left."

Tory put on her signal and began the turn. The Saab picked up speed, and the Friendship Club disappeared from the rearview mirror.

Nick Bello decided to climb between the front seats. With the knife in his one good hand, this was a difficult operation. Knowing how clumsy he would be, the first thing he did was press the blade of the knife up against Tory's cheek like he was going to shave her with a straight razor. "No funny stuff," he hissed. Immediately she pulled away from the blade, the car swerving hard to the left.

The horrible sound of metal scraping on metal filled their ears as the Saab sideswiped a parked car.

"Shit! Watch it," Bello screamed as Tory struggled to regain control of the car. For several seconds the car swerved wildly. But that was exactly what Nick Bello wanted. Terror. As he eased up on the knife slightly, the car straightened out. Satisfied that he had Tory so frightened she couldn't possibly try anything, he put one leg through the space between the front seats. Working his trunk through the narrow opening took some effort, but he shimmied himself back and forth, ultimately heaving himself forward, his rear end landing on Tory's bag.

"Get this outta here!" he yelled angrily, lifting himself up, pulling the knife away from Tory's cheek long enough to yank the leather bag from beneath him and dump it on Tory's lap. "We're taking the bridge. Get on 28 south, to 279. Now, who the hell are you?"

"Tory Welch."

"The lawyer. Merlin's girl."

"You used to work with Jack Merlin."

"Used to," he reiterated wistfully. Bello looked out the window. "You wanted to talk to me so badly. Talk."

"Well, a couple of guys broke into our house to scare us away from what's been going on at the Medical Center. Unfortunately one of 'em— Leo—told us about the rubbers they delivered to you with bacteria to kill people." Subtly, Tory slipped her left hand into her bag, worming her fingers toward the bottom, searching for the Beretta.

"He gave you my name? Fuckin' asshole."

"That's right. He named you."

"Merlin know?"

"Of course."

"Then why isn't he here?"

"He went to your house," Tory lied, keeping the conversation going until she could find the Beretta.

"Goddamn it. This thing started out good, you know, putting people out of their misery. Like that guy Kevorkian."

"That's what this was all about? Assisted suicide?"

"Sort of. That's what I thought, anyway . . . Hey!!" Bello looked down at Tory's lap and noticed the soft leather of her bag moving as she did a blind search. Once again he held the knife to Tory's cheek, pressing the blade into her skin. "What the hell do you think you're doing? I got nothing to lose. I'll cut you like they cut me. Don't make me cut you!" Tory was paralyzed with fear. Not being able to use two hands was pissing Bello off. "Shit!" Suddenly he pulled his hand away from Tory's face and grabbed her leather bag. "What the fuck are you looking for?" Bello dumped the contents of the bag on his lap. All too quickly he had the Beretta in his hand and the steak knife was thrown on the floor. Although racking the slide was a two-handed maneuver, the former scrub nurse was determined. First he rested the handle of the gun on his knee, pulling the slide back hard. The metal dug into his skin. Harder and harder he pulled until the slide chambered a round and clicked back into position.

Bello fumbled with the gun, finding the safety on the side. He snapped it off.

The Beretta was now ready to fire. Tory gave him the look of terror he was desperate to see.

For the past several days Nick Bello had felt like a small game animal being hunted. Dashing here and there, he hadn't stayed very long in any one location. Suddenly, the Beretta in hand and firmly in command of the terrified woman, he felt as if he could breathe again. The feeling grew, and he became euphoric. Bello even reached beneath his seat, working the lever so he could push himself all the way back. What a wonderful feeling to be in control.

The icing on the cake, the ultimate I'm-running-the-show-and-feeling-good move, was when he put his right foot up on the dash, like he was ready to get comfortable.

Of course Tory noticed. How the hell could she not? Bello leaned way back, the sole of his untied hiking boot almost touching the windshield, but she kept her eyes steadfast on the road. And on the speed-ometer.

Forty miles an hour.

"Since we got some time, lemme tell you about a patient. Twenty-year-old guy, driving his cycle without a helmet. Crashes. Hits some gravel and goes into a pole. He's got a brain like a fuckin' zucchini. And of course he doesn't have diddly squat when it comes to insurance. Fuckin' dirtball, you know what I mean? I mean the best this guy can possibly hope for is tube feedings in some institution 'til he gets a pneumonia. He doesn't even know he's alive, for crissake. But you know what he gets? Six surgeries. Six! And he's still a fuckin' vege-table. And who the hell do you think paid for it? Who do you think?''

The timing was not right for a philosophical discussion of the merits of a society that paid for the health care needs of those less fortunate. Or the even more controversial subject of when to pull the plug.

Many times Tory had heard Merlin joke about dying a Harvard Death. Doctors at some venerated medical institutions were so involved with the disease process they forgot they were playing with lives. They kept ordering blood tests and adjusting the sodium and potassium levels long after hope was lost. When the patient finally succumbed, the doctors took an absurd pride when the final lab values on the deceased were as normal as a healthy twenty-year-old.

Despite her disgust with his methods, Tory probably agreed with Nick Bello more than she disagreed. Of course Tory knew who paid for the medically indigent. Who didn't? But Nick Bello was holding court and wasn't about to relinquish the floor.

"I don't know." *That* was the only correct answer.

"You do, lady. You'n me. And I was getting pretty sick about it. That's when I decided to get involved. Take a right here.''

As they headed up the ramp to Route 279, the traffic thinned out and Tory urged the Saab to go faster.

"Yep, that's when I got involved. Too many people who had no goddamned business being in the hospital. People I didn't want to pay for. And you can be sure as shit many of 'em would've sat up and shaken my hand if they weren't so gorked out.''

The Saab was up to fifty-five. Bello had turned himself in his seat, just a little, so he could look at Tory while he lectured.

"You know what 'gork' means?'' Bello asked.

"Uh-uh.''

"God Only Really Knows. These people had no chance. I was doing 'em a favor.''

"What about me, Nick? I wasn't a gork, but you had it in for me.''

Tory looked briefly at Bello, wondering if he would try to justify what he had planned for her. More importantly, she was buying time for an opportunity. Up ahead, maybe a quarter mile away, was a concrete bridge spanning the highway. Traffic was light. Tory figured maybe it was now or never.

"I ain't gonna lie to you, lady. Things got out of control. But that wasn't my fault. No way. Too many people were poisoned. Listen to me, I didn't know it was gonna be you 'til I saw you. But everyone else I felt okay with. I didn't do nothing wrong. Shit, somebody with no life to—"

The bridge was fast approaching. Tory had an excellent view of its sturdy infrastructure. Picking out a target was easy: the very first support column. She timed it perfectly, turning the wheel hard, almost losing control as the car swerved to the right. Like all accidents, this one happened in the blink of an eye. Nick Bello didn't even try to use his gun or grab on to something. His foot was still up on the dash where it had been for the last ten minutes.

Tory hit the support column just off center, more on Bello's side than hers, and there were two powerful noises, although neither of the occupants could distinguish them. First the horrible sound of the collision. Then, a microsecond later, the explosion of twin air bags deploying. A chemical reaction within each air bag occurred, releasing a powerful burst of hot gas, shooting the air bag out of its container at a speed well in excess of the rate at which the car was traveling at the time of impact.

Luckily, Tory's air bag hit her squarely in the chest. Her abdominal stitches survived impact, although it knocked her back into her seat very hard for a second or two.

As soon as the air bag was fully deployed, small holes immediately allowed the hot gas to escape. That way the victim of a crash was not pinned inside the car.

Bello, on the other hand, was not so fortunate. His air bag, packed inside the dashboard, caught his foot and pushed his outstretched leg back toward his shoulder so violently that his hip joint ripped apart. The Teflon-smooth ball at the top of his femur formerly fit neatly into a socket in the pelvis. Now the socket was teeming with blood, and the ball of the femur was six inches out of place, crammed up against the various muscles that control the leg.

Actually he looked quite absurd, one foot on the floor, the other jammed up against the roof. If not for the screaming he could have been the star of some ridiculous sideshow in the circus. And the pain was enough to make him forget about Leo and the tin-snips. He wanted to commit suicide. He would have used the Beretta, first on Tory, then on himself, if she hadn't already wrested it from his hand.

Initially Bello thought his leg had been torn off. He screamed, grabbing at it with both hands, the layers of soft bandage coming loose from his bad hand. He didn't give a shit that Tory was pointing the Beretta at him. "Help me! Goddamn it! Please help me." Writhing in pain, Bello whipped his head back and forth, desperately trying to find a more comfortable position.

"Was this whole thing about weeding out people who would be better off dead?"

Even though the air bag had deflated, hanging limply on Bello's lap like a pillowcase, his leg was still pointing up toward the ceiling, his toes aimed sideways, and every time he exhaled he let out a scream.

"Bello, listen to me. Was this thing about Kevorkian?"

She was getting nowhere. The front end of the Saab was pretty much destroyed, but Tory tried the key in the ignition anyway. Instantly the Saab purred to life. Despite a loud scraping noise as the wheels started rolling, the car pulled back from the support column. It was in no condition to drive on the road. The bulky air bag flowing from the center of the steering column made steering almost impossible. But it was moving. When she had the car about six feet from the pole she hit the brakes hard, jerking them to a halt.

"AHHHHHHHHHH!" Bello screamed as he was forced back into the seat, his leg shifting, jerking his dislocated hip into a new, even more painful position. "No! Don't move the car."

"Why were you killing patients?" Tory said in a voice loud enough to get Bello's attention. "Why?"

"In the beginning . . . AHHHHHHHHH . . . in the beginning I thought it was about Kevorkian. But there were too many. I was getting . . . suspicious. That little girl—"

"How did you do it?" Tory asked, suspecting she and Merlin already knew the answer.

"They gave me the bacteria. You know that. I injected—" Bello stopped for a painful breather. "I injected the bacteria into the gauze packs."

"Who was behind it?"

"They'll kill me."

Tory put the transmission into drive and stepped on the accelerator. Bello screamed.

The Saab hit the support column, and Bello lurched forward.

"Stop! Stop it! I'll tell you what you want. Please—" Bello pleaded and started to cry.

"Who is behind this?"

"Tommy, the guy who broke into your house."

"Was this his operation?"

"No. He worked for some people."

"What were their names?"

"I don't know. They never told me."

"Who were these people? Tell me!!"

Bello was breathing hard, like he'd just finished running a race.

"Nick, I'm gonna pull back and ram it again! Who was running the show?" Tory screamed as she jammed the car in reverse.

"A doctor. Some doc at an insurance company."

"What company?"

"WIP. Some big shot doc . . . I . . . I can't think of his name . . . he worked at WIP."

Tory picked up her cellular phone and called 911.

16

"Dr. Silverman, a Sandy Keller is here to see you," the stodgy, unattractive secretary monotoned, directing her voice into a small intercom on her desk.

Sandy Keller stood off to one side, near the door with the medical director's name in case Silverman tried to shoot past her. Her cameraman already had the heavy camera up on his shoulder, filming the closed door.

The news reporter's ears were still unadorned. Evidently of the belief that the sum total of all her jewelry had to add up to a certain weight, Sandy wore a necklace of huge white beads that gave her a Wilma Flintstone look. As she waited she wiped her front teeth with a Kleenex, knowing from past experience that her generous use of lipstick certainly left a smudge on her toothy smile.

In no time at all the door flew open. Leonard Silverman stood in the doorway, putting on his suit coat as he straightened his tie and smoothed his shirt. He looked quite frazzled. Initially, Sandy thought she was going to lose him so she went for it. "Dr. Silverman, I wonder if you would care to comment on reports I've received—"

"Of course I will. Won't you come in?" As he made the final adjustments of his jacket, Leonard Silverman stepped aside, allowing Sandy, followed by her cameraman, into his office. To his secretary he directed, "Coffee. I guess just two cups," feeling no need to feed a cameraman. "Maybe some cookies, if you can find them. And hold all calls." Then he smiled as he whispered, "It's show time."

Silverman closed the door behind himself, waiting patiently while Sandy stood by his wall of pictures, getting to know the man by the company he was proud to keep. One photo showed Silverman on a fishing boat standing next to a huge sailfish. Another of him shaking hands with Franco Harris. Another of him in one of those auto-racing suits festooned with too many advertising patches, perched on the hood of a red Porsche. The Stanley-Cup-hoisted-over-his-head-in-a-bar picture came next, followed by a bunch of guys spilling out of a frat house onto the front steps. And finally a photograph of Leonard Silverman's head digitally placed on the powerful body of King Kong.

Conspicuously absent was his family. Sandy knew he had been married and divorced, but there was no evidence of children anywhere. His desk was nearby. She looked over but saw no knickknacks made by a preschooler's hands.

She knew relatively little about Leonard Silverman. Checking the archives of the *Post Gazette* she'd found two articles on WIP that mentioned him. He had attended Pitt Medical School and then had been in private practice fourteen years before coming to WIP as its medical director.

"Well, why don't we sit down, Sandy," he said, motioning her to the sofa with her back to the window so that he could sit across from her and capture the good light on his face. The cameraman got into position behind Sandy but fiddled with his camera for several seconds. Silverman waited quietly, not wanting to talk and spoil the spontaneity of the moment while some video jockey was loading his film.

Looking across the small coffee table at him, Sandy was surprised by what she saw. Expecting a man tightly wound, she found Silverman was anything but. He had an easy smile, and it was obvious how other women might find him attractive. Guessing him to be about forty-five, she admired his dark hair that was styled fashionably long and the prominent nose that made him look strong. In view of the situation, though, his confidence shocked her. Somehow she found herself admiring his bravado: the way he sat back on the sofa, leaning his six foot frame into the cushions, letting his jacket open wide, showing off a little of what he paid a personal trainer to tighten up. "Dr. Silverman—" Sandy began.

"Lenny," he offered with a smile. Before Sandy could start again, the door opened and two cups of coffee and a small plate of cookies were placed on the coffee table.

Silverman picked up the coffee, not intending to drink any, but wanting to look relaxed and comfortable when talking about the buyout. "Coffee?"

Sandy shook her head and realized what the situation felt like—an in home celebrity interview. Like Diane Sawyer sitting in Tom Cruise's living room about to start one of those syrupy interviews that always began with a question like, What is it that makes you connect so well with your audience?

"So," Silverman said, encouraging Sandy to begin.

The reporter turned around and got a nod from the cameraman. "Dr. Silverman," she said, opting for formality, "I appreciate your talking with me on such short notice."

"Actually hadn't expected the interviews to start until next week. I guess news travels, although good news a bit slower than bad. I hope you'll accept my personal invitation to attend the formal announcement at the Duquesne Club next Thursday."

Sandy looked confused but decided not to get off track. "What can you tell me about the Kevorkian Society?"

Silverman wrinkled his brow. "You've got me."

"You've never heard of it?"

"No. Why should I? What's this about?"

"The Medical Center."

"The Medical Center?" He thought for a second. "Isn't this about our buyout?"

"No," Sandy said. Her tone of voice changed as she bore down on him. "Dr. Silverman, I have it confirmed that Nick Bello—"

"Nick who?" Silverman questioned, leaning forward, wondering what the hell was going on. Abruptly it hit him. His mouth opened slightly as his hand came up to his lips. The cameraman eased in for a close-up that would eventually be turned into a still photograph for the front page of the *Post Gazette.*

"You don't know," Sandy said, the words slipping out of her mouth in a whisper of astonishment. This was an unbelievable situation. Sandy couldn't believe her good fortune. *That's why he invited me into his office.* Silverman had no idea why she had shown up. More importantly, no matter what happened she couldn't lose. If he bolted from the room, it was on tape. If he freaked out and started ranting, it was on film. And if he admitted everything that Nick Bello had accused him of, then that would be the lead story at six.

The local news, hungry for the most graphic reports, was peppered on a nightly basis with stories of greed and corruption, robberies and rape, fires and fraud. Ratings paid the bills, and the more graphic the lead story, the better. But few lead stories were as effective as murder, and when the killer was a rich big shot, it was the ultimate.

"Nick Bello is an operating room nurse employed by the Medical Center. He just got out of surgery to repair his hip, which came apart in an auto accident. He had kidnapped an assistant district attorney named Tory Welch. Anyway, now he's talking. He's told the police that you were the mastermind of a plan to kill certain patients with powerful bacteria introduced while they were under surgery. And, apparently, Bello is hoping for immunity from prosecution.''

His priorities of an hour ago—calling his travel agent for tickets to Bimini and sending his latest girlfriend several dozen long-stemmed roses—seemed in another lifetime. Everything he had worked for seemed to disappear and self-survival became the only thing that mattered. Not once had he ever considered the possibility of getting caught. Every detail had been carefully planned. He'd insulated himself from Nick Bello quite effectively, but something had gone horribly wrong.

His first reaction was to scream out how unfair it was that everything he had worked for was about to be taken away from him.

Sitting absolutely still, Leonard Silverman concentrated on many things at once. First priority was maintaining a stone-faced expression. Then he put his trembling hands in his lap and willed them to be still. Finally he tried to think of something to say. *There is absolutely no truth to that. That's a lie. I don't have any idea what you're talking about. Would you excuse me a moment?* But he said nothing, just sat there and concentrated.

"When is the last time you had any contact with Nick Bello?''

Silverman didn't move, looking out the window in lieu of Sandy, terrified of what he might see in her eyes.

"Dr. Silverman, in the interest of being fair, I offer you a forum to speak out on behalf of yourself."

"Okay, let's work out some ground rules. Turn off the camera. Go ahead."

The cameraman did not move.

"Turn off the camera. Thirty seconds is all I request. At that point you may do as you like. But I will say nothing more as long as he's filming.''

Sandy turned around and nodded. "Give us a minute," she said with a subtle wink.

Her cameraman knew exactly what she wanted. He gave her a nod and lowered the camera, holding it in one hand as if it were a heavy briefcase. Slowly he walked over toward the desk and leaned against it, never taking his eyes, or the camera with the glowing little red light, off Silverman.

Silverman sat forward, clenching his hands together. "Listen, I don't have any idea what you're talking about. You've got me in a have-you-stopped-beating-your-wife-yes-or-no situation. Of course I am innocent of any charges, but I don't want to start babbling in front of the camera and look like a guilty fool.''

"There are no charges. The DA's office hasn't filed any yet. Already checked."

"Let's not get into semantics. I am innocent of any wrongdoing. Is that better? And I resent any implication otherwise. If I am to be wrongly accused I don't want to be trapped into saying something that will come back to haunt me."

"So what are you proposing?"

"You put that film away. Lock it up safe. Give me twenty-four hours to talk with my lawyer, find out who's accusing me of what, and then I'll sit down with you, and you *alone,* right here, live if you want, and set the record straight."

"I get you before anyone else?"

"Absolutely."

Sandy looked at her cameraman. Maybe she could win twice. First she could break the story about Nick Bello and the murders at the Medical Center. Then, while everyone else was playing catch-up, she could do a live interview with Silverman and scoop everyone again. "Okay. Twenty-four hours."

"And if I renege you can pull what film you have and use it."

"Don't worry. I will," Sandy said, knowing that she already had enough for a good story.

17

Tommy was letting Leo drive. At first it seemed as if his shoulder was getting better, but after a few days it had started to swell. And throb. By the fourth day the small hole where the bullet had entered was dripping pus. Most of the time he felt hot. Walking up a flight of stairs left him all sweaty. Maybe something really bad was wrong with his arm.

"You okay?" Leo asked after they'd driven in silence for ten minutes.

"I said I'm fine. Quit asking," Tommy snapped back. The Chrysler was getting hot again so he hunched forward, slipping his left arm out of the jacket then using it to ease the right one free.

Ever since dark they'd been going, driving the main roads. Once in a while they pulled off, taking a detour on some randomly picked country road until they came to a bar or tavern. So far they'd hit six bars.

"You gonna tell me what you're so pissed off about, or what?" Leo asked, frustrated he was always the last to know.

"We fucked up big time. That make you happy?" Tommy answered. Leo looked at him like he was speaking a foreign language. "Nicky. The fucker talked."

"What? Who'd he talk to?"

"The police," Tommy bemoaned. "We shoulda fuckin' killed him when we had the chance."

"I *wanted* to kill that asshole."

"Goddamn it!" Tommy yelled in frustration. He slammed his good fist on the dash. "We had him behind that bar and coulda put one in his head."

"Why'd he talk?"

"Member that doc's girlfriend? The one who shot me? Well, somehow she'n Nicky were in a car accident, and he started talkin' big time." Tommy winced from a bolt of pain that started in his shoulder and shot down his back, contorting him into a spastic creature.

"Man, you gotta see a doc."

"I saw Silverman this afternoon. He says it's infected. I need a surgeon to take out the bullet. Gave me some pills to kill the infection."

"Why don't we go to Cleveland or something? See a surgeon there."

"It's no different than Pittsburgh. You go in with a gunshot, they ask a lot of questions."

"There was nothing in the paper. They don't know you got hit."

"Forget it. Silverman said he'd set me up with someone who'd keep his mouth shut. Hey, try this exit."

"Someone like Nicky," Leo said sarcastically. He was driving too fast. Tommy had to use his right arm to catch himself.

"Shit! Take it easy!"

"Sorry. So what makes this surgeon someone we can trust?"

"Don't know. Maybe it's someone he knows."

"Hope he don't pull a Bello."

"There are ways. Believe me, there are ways a lot better than cutting off a guy's finger."

They were in a small town fifty miles from Pittsburgh. It was late, nearly midnight, when they stopped for gas. While he was waiting for change, Leo asked the kid behind the register where he could grab a quick beer and got directions to the only bar in town.

Country music blared from a jukebox. Even this late things were hopping. Tommy and Leo stood in the doorway for almost a minute looking around, sizing up the place. Being from the big city, Tommy thought country music was for hicks, but right now he felt a little like a cowboy walking through the bat-wing doors of a saloon, looking for a fight.

A bleached blond waitress was weaving through the crowd, serving beers and peeling guys' hands off her ass. Couples were dancing on a tiny wooden floor. The only space at the bar was squeeze-in.

Guarding his shoulder, Tommy took a slow walk around, giving people one hell of a look if they got anywhere near his right side. Most everyone was youthful, out late on a Friday night knowing they could sleep in on Saturday.

Suddenly Tommy spotted a guy at the bar all spiffed up in a colorful cowboy shirt and black jeans. He even had a cowboy hat on. As a pretty lady walked by, Cowboy made quite an obnoxious deal of taking off

the hat so he could show off his thick head of hair. Eventually the pretty
lady joined him at the bar. Once he replaced the hat, he ran his finger
around the brim in an ostentatious cowboy salute.

Asshole. Tommy hated guys like this. The jerk was practically asking
for it. The icing on the cake was when Cowboy held up two fingers to
the barkeep, just like a seventies peace sign, and ordered a couple of
beers. That's when Tommy nudged Leo and pointed out the guy in the
cowboy shirt.

"Leo, check out the jerk in the cowboy shirt, over by the bar. Big
nose. Standing with the broad . . . see him? Medium build, wearing that
stupid Stetson, next to the little bald guy. He's perfect."

"I like the chest on the chick," Leo said, getting into it.

"Let's see how well that tattoo of yours really works. You're on."

Of the many techniques for working oneself right up to a crowded
bar, Leo favored the wedge. By placing both hands out in front of him,
fingertips touching, he could weasel himself into the smallest of spaces.
Then it was a question of moving his hands apart, never backing off
even if someone got nasty. Maybe he would mumble something like
"Outta my way. Watch yourself." If that didn't work he just pushed
enough people to give him a belly up to the bar and enough breathing
room to turn sideways and crash somebody's conversation.

The little bald guy was a featherweight. His face knocked into his
girlfriend's breasts, and they both scowled at Leo, then wisely took up
residence several feet downstream.

The guy in the cowboy shirt took a bit more effort. He was heavily
into conversation with his new lady friend. Leo needed a little shoulder
action to move him out of the way.

"Hey, watch it," Cowboy said, lifting his beer way up to avoid spilling it on himself.

"Quit hogging the goddamn bar," Leo said and stood nose to nose
with the guy. "Man, you got a nose on you."

Cowboy did his best to ignore the comment, turning away quickly,
giving Leo an eyeful of the fancy stitching on the back of his shirt.

"Hey, bartender. Couple of beers here," Leo demanded and grabbed
a handful of salty nuts from a small bowl. He cupped them in his fist
so that he could pop them into his mouth one at a time. Grabbing the
beers in one hand, he wedged his way between Cowboy and the bar.
Pumping his hand several times, Leo flipped a series of crunchy nuts
into his mouth, then took a slug of beer and jumped right into their
conversation.

"Nice scoops," Leo said, eyeing the lady friend's chest. "What's
your name?"

"Uh . . . Linda," she said reluctantly, looking to Cowboy to handle the situation.

Cowboy said, "Hey, pal, we're having a friendly conversation."

"I'm friendly."

"We don't want any trouble. We'll move."

"Yeah, let's go, it's too crowded around here anyway," Leo said to Cowboy. Then he turned to Linda, who made the mistake of reading Leo's biceps. "You need to borrow a pen?"

"No, thank you."

"You seem pretty uptight. What say you'n me hit the dance floor?"

"Do you mind?" A hefty dose of annoyance crept into Cowboy's voice.

Leo acted as if Cowboy wasn't there. "You know what you need?" Without waiting for an answer Leo said, "A good *stiff* to drink."

"You're gross," Linda said between clenched teeth.

Now Leo turned back to Cowboy. "So, what's the story? You two just meet or what?"

"Something like that. Look, this is the last time I'm gonna ask you nice. Please leave us alone."

"The last time *you're* gonna ask me nice? That sounds like an invitation to step outside."

Cowboy was sweating. "Look, I don't want any trouble." He sounded like a eunuch.

Linda was looking across the crowded room, distancing herself from both men.

"Tell you what. You'n me had the same idea about Linda. What say you'n me wrestle for her?"

"What?" Cowboy was starting to wheeze. "Are you crazy?"

Leo took a feel of Cowboy's arm. "I see what you mean."

Unbeknownst to Cowboy, Linda was waving at some imaginary friends across the room, trying to find an excuse to leave these two alone.

"Okay, you don't like the physical stuff. Hey, I know—lemme see if I can guess your height and weight. You know, like they do at the amusement park. Winner takes Linda home."

"I don't make bets like—"

Very subtly, Linda was stepping backwards, disengaging herself from the inflammatory situation.

"Five eleven, a hundred sixty pounds."

Cowboy did a double take. Before he had the chance to call off the wager, he realized he'd won. "No." He smiled, looking around, unaware of Linda's disappearance. "Six feet, one ninety. Now beat it."

Before Leo walked away, he took one finger and gave Cowboy a poke in the chest. "You're perfect, pal, exactly what I was looking for. You'n me're gonna go around sometime."

When Leo finally got back to the Chrysler, Tommy was waiting for him. People were starting to leave the bar. Every time the front door of the bar pushed open, they squinted their eyes until they got a good look at whoever was on his way out.

"There he is. All alone. Six foot, one ninety," Leo mused, saying it with the same intonation Cowboy had used. "Like hitting the fucking jackpot." Leo opened the car door.

"Careful," Tommy warned.

"Just watch me." Leo skulked across the gravel lot, timing it perfectly so that he got to Cowboy's car just as he did. Cowboy looked around. When he realized they were alone, he reached for his wallet. Then Leo pointed a finger at the guy, poking him in the chest some more until Cowboy's back was up against his car. Leo kept poking, Cowboy flattening himself out as best he could, mindful not to raise his arms lest Leo pop him one.

Suddenly, without provocation, Leo put one hand on Cowboy's chest, pulled his other arm back, and let his fist go, catching him on the cheek, turning his head hard to the side so he looked right at Tommy for about two seconds before he went down.

Tommy slid over to the driver's seat and started the engine.

18

Tory's first day back at work turned out to be a whole lot busier than expected.

She'd taken a late morning walk in the park, felt so great when she got home she decided to go in to the office. Her quick recovery took everyone by surprise. When the district attorney, a hands-on prosecutor who had visited Tory several times at home, happened by her open office door, he walked in, went directly for the phone, and had Merlin on the line within three minutes. While the DA stood at her desk, Tory was forced to sit in her chair like a naughty little girl while her mother was telephoned. Although Merlin was just as surprised by her presence, both men knew she was going to be impossible to contain. A deal was struck whereby Tory could start back at work but with significantly truncated hours. Officially Tory became a ten-to-four lawyer, smiling all the while because she'd never dreamed she'd get that much.

Her first task was lobbying to handle the case of the Medical Center murders. All her efforts were a waste of time. Multiple murders were just too juicy for an assistant district attorney two years out of law school. This was a case for the DA himself.

As a consolation Tory was made part of the team, entrusted with research. First on the agenda was the corporate structure of WIP. By mid-afternoon, diligently working the phone, Tory discovered that a large insurance company in Connecticut was planning a buyout of the much smaller WIP. An announcement of the buyout was imminent.

One call to Connecticut and Tory was told that, although the deal was not yet finalized, things were proceeding very quickly. Connecticut Insurance Brokers was anticipating a strong presence in Pittsburgh.

Time seemed to fly, and the afternoon soon slipped away. Tory reviewed a series of newspaper articles. At five, an hour after curfew, she started to pack her briefcase. The phone rang. It was the DA's secretary asking her to drop what she was doing and come down to his office.

District Attorney Frank LaBove was, at forty-four, young for the top job. Although Pittsburgh was full of legal talent, Frank had been the cream that floated above everyone else. He'd amassed an amazing conviction rate. The press loved to photograph him. And he attended church regularly with his family. Naturally, every few months, there was talk that District Attorney Frank LaBove would eventually become Mayor Frank LaBove. After that happened who knew where he was headed. The more rumors circulated about his political future, the more Frank was romanced into believing them. But for now he micromanaged his department, taking an active role in every major case pending.

His office was huge, off by itself with a private secretary. Tory patiently bided her time until she was shown into the impressive office. The office was divided into two parts diagonally from one corner to the other. A massive mahogany desk, teeming with papers, a computer, and several phones, sat heavily on one side of the room. Occupying the other half was a large sofa set at an angle to view a large-screen television. As Tory entered she looked first to the desk. The secretary discreetly pointed toward the sofa where Frank was sitting, elbows on knees, mesmerized by what was on television.

With a quick wave of his hand he motioned for Tory to join him. Immediately, Tory recognized Sandy Keller's voice and watched as the flamboyantly dressed newscaster stood in front of the Medical Center, its logo clearly visible on the emergency room sign behind her.

"—under police guard at the Pittsburgh University Medical Center. Sources there inform me that Mr. Bello was in an auto accident last evening with Assistant District Attorney Tory Welch and suffered a severely dislocated hip. Apparently after the accident Mr. Bello, who was employed as a scrub nurse in the operating rooms at the Medical Center, admitted to being part of a plot involving the murder of selected patients having surgery. All that is known is that Bello infected a series of patients with dangerous bacteria during routine surgical procedures. As yet we do not know whether he acted alone or if this was part of a conspiracy. As this dramatic story develops, KDKA will be here to cover it. I'm Sandy Keller, reporting live from the Pittsburgh University Medical Center. Back to you, Alan."

The scene on the television shifted back to the studio where a blue-blazered Alan sat at the news desk, looking over his shoulder at the monitor, watching Sandy's hair blowing softly in the breeze.

"Sandy, one question," Alan said, in a phony prearranged question and answer session. "How many deaths have there been?"

"Alan, at least four, possibly five that we know of. Officials are checking into hospital records, but as you can imagine in a situation like this, everyone is reluctant to talk with me."

"I'm sure you'll stay with it. Good story," Alan announced. It was hard for Tory to tell whether Alan was happy with the quality of the reporting or the fact that there had been a series of murders that would be good for ratings.

KDKA immediately went to a story about a fire, prompting Frank to shut off the TV. "How the hell does she do it?"

"I heard she pays for information. Probably had an orderly on the payroll. At least she doesn't know about WIP or Silverman."

"She'll know within twenty-four hours. What have you got on Silverman?"

"Forty-seven years old. Left a private practice six years ago to become the medical director of Western Insurance. Apparently he's got some clause in his contract that will make him a bundle in the next several weeks when WIP gets sold to Connecticut Insurance Brokers. That's important because Silverman has a ton of debt. Divorced. Six hundred thousand dollar mortgage, credit cards maxed out. The guy's a spender."

"So why is he behind these murders?"

"Bello mentioned something about Kevorkian. Maybe Silverman is weeding out the infirm. Assisted suicide for the twenty-first century."

"No way. This guy is a capitalist. If he's weeding out the infirm it's got to be with the bottom line in mind. Tory, are you comfortable with an indictment?"

"As long as Bello's talking."

"What about the CEO? Frederick Graham?"

"Boring. Nice home. Two sons. Church on Sunday. He could be the mastermind, but all Bello talks about is Silverman."

"Okay. We go for Silverman. We'll hand down an indictment tomorrow. And in case anybody asks, Bello is cooperating. Of course we'll take that into account regarding sentencing, but he will have to stand trial. And no leaks about Silverman. I want him fresh."

"I wouldn't expect anything less from you," Tory said.

By the time Tory got back to her office, her secretary and fellow ADAs were gone. This was the time of day when the phones slowed down and it became quiet to the point of being lonely.

Unexpectedly, the phone rang. It was Merlin. "I'm almost ready to leave, Merlin. Before you ask, I feel great. No pain. I even thought I might run home."

Tory giggled while Merlin said, "Ha, ha," sarcastically. Then he reminded her, "Don't forget it's your night for dinner," and went on about all the delicacies he would like to have prepared.

There was a noise from the hallway. Tory turned sharply. The hallway was empty. Unexpectedly she felt the urge to get out on the street and blend in with the crowd. "Look, Merlin, watch it or you're gonna get Ragu on elbow macaroni or a fried baloney sandwich. I'll be home in forty-five minutes."

After she hung up, Tory heard the noise again, this time much louder. All she could think about was the squeaking noise that had heralded Leo's arrival in their kitchen. Her mind raced, suddenly frightened that Leo was about to descend upon her again.

"Hello," Tory said confidently as though she were expecting someone. The office was far from empty. Maybe if she screamed . . .

The doorway filled with a figure who was reading the nameplate on her door. Although Tory had never met the handsome man in the expensive suit, she had spent the entire day reading about him. The photocopies of the news photos didn't do him justice.

Tory Welch knew exactly who this man was. There was absolutely no doubt.

"Tory Welch? I'm Leonard Silverman."

"I know who you are."

"We've never met."

"I know. I've seen your picture."

"May I assume that you've seen it today?"

Tory was not going to let him control the conversation. "How did you get in here?"

"The receptionist must have gone to the bathroom or something. His desk was empty."

"If you know we have a male receptionist you obviously timed your entrance, waiting for him to leave. What is it that you want?"

"I'd like to offer to help you."

Help me? "Be more specific."

"I've become aware there is a man named Nick Bello who has spent a considerable amount of time in the past twenty-four hours detailing skullduggery at Western Insurance. I understand he has named me as the mastermind of the scheme to kill selected patients at the Medical Center."

Silverman looked at Tory, expecting her to say something. Instead she maintained her posture, holding him in her gaze, offering him nothing.

"I have it on good authority that within the next day or so I will be arrested."

"And you are offering to cooperate."

"Exactly."

Tory thought for a moment, worried that Silverman might be setting a trap for her. "Are you here to turn state's evidence without the advice of your personal attorney?"

"How'd you know?" Silverman asked, wrinkling his brow, taking her perceptiveness as an invitation to sit down in an uncomfortable straight-back chair.

"Without your attorney I cannot talk to you. As of this moment you've been accused of nothing."

"There's writing on the wall."

"Are you telling me you are guilty of the crimes you say Mr. Bello has accused you of?"

"Absolutely not!" He seemed shocked at the implication.

"Then why are you here to turn state's evidence?"

"Well, maybe I have the terminology wrong, so I don't want to get hung up in semantics. I absolutely do not want to come under the scrutiny of your department, nor do I want to be fried by the press. And I certainly do not want my reputation sullied."

"You believe yourself to be innocent?"

"Yes."

"Talk with your attorney. Besides, this isn't my case to prosecute."

"Frank LaBove is handling the case. I know. I hoped you'd be— let's just say, more approachable."

"Any decision would be Frank's."

"Of course." Silverman paused to find the right words. "Of course there are . . . levels of involvement."

Tory frowned at the prospect of some upcoming bullshit.

"Guilty of murder, no," Silverman continued. "Guilty of looking the other way, ignoring what others were doing . . . maybe."

"State's evidence is usually reserved for an individual who has little prospect for a successful defense *and* who has the ability to help make a case for successful prosecution of more significantly involved individuals. David bringing down Goliath."

"Well, I'm David."

"Nick Bello is David."

"Okay, Miss Welch, bottom line. I come back tomorrow and give you a full accounting. Names, dates, places. I point fingers up," he paused, "and down. I accept blame for not knowing what the hell was happening in my own organization. But my conscience is clean. I am not a murderer."

"Again, talk with your attorney if you want. Sometimes we strike deals. But in this case I can't imagine that we would gain significantly more by cutting a deal than we would prosecuting."

"For example—"

"Stop. I am not going to have this conversation with you. There are legal issues which I'm not going to get tangled up with. When a suspect is arrested—"

"So, I am to be arrested?"

"Mr. Silverman, when a suspect is arrested and has been informed of his rights, then it is appropriate to discuss what the suspect knows and explore the possibility of any deal."

"At least tell me this, Miss Welch. If you were me, would you be talking with your attorney?"

"Good night, Dr. Silverman."

19

The Lexus drove around the graceful loop of a long circular driveway. As it came toward them, powerful beams lit their Chrysler through the pines. Pausing for a moment just before pulling onto the quiet road, it motored slowly away from Leo and Tommy.

Leo squinted. "That's his plate. B-1-S-R-M-1-Y. Must be his initials or something. Betcha it means something." Careful not to let Tommy think he was rushing, Leo had his hand on the key but didn't turn it until the Lexus disappeared around a bend.

They'd had the windows down so the inside wouldn't fog while they waited in the chilly October air. Rolling up his window, Tommy said flatly, "You remember what to do?"

"Yeah, give him a little tap."

"Enough to get him out of the car. Then tell him it's your shoulder and—"

"I put my gun in his ribs."

"That's the part you like. Don't forget why we're doing this. Hey, he's turning. Maybe he's headed into town."

Leo watched his speed, taking his foot off the accelerator every time he got close enough to read the license plate. "What do you think that means? B-1-S-R-M-1-Y?"

"Careful," Tommy warned, ignoring the question. "Take it slow."

The Lexus was waiting at a stop sign for several cars to clear the intersection. "I say we do it now," Leo said and looked at Tommy expectantly.

"I don't want to do it on such a busy street. Let's keep our business private. Wait'll there's no one around."

*   *   *

"Hey, Tory, you'd better turn the TV on," Merlin called toward the living room.

Dinner was over and Merlin was doing the dishes, watching the evening news on the tiny Panasonic that sat near the sink.

By the time she'd put down the paper and zapped the television on, she caught the news anchor's teaser that Sandy Keller would be interviewing the medical director of Western Insurance about the Medical Center murders.

"Shit, what's he doing talking to her?"

"She's got some exclusive interview."

"He showed up in my office, wanted to turn state's evidence today."

"And you said no."

"Of course. That weasel is up to something. Why the hell would a guilty person want to talk to the press?"

"You tell LaBove?"

"No, I was in such a rush to get home. When Silverman left he had no doubt I said no."

The Chrysler followed the Lexus through one of several tunnels that led into the city of Pittsburgh. Several minutes later they pulled into an outdoor lot several blocks from the Civic Arena.

Tommy leaned across Leo and handed the attendant a ten-dollar bill. "Tell him to keep it!" Tommy grumbled. After the Chrysler entered the gravel lot, the attendant set up a bright orange cone that signified the lot was closed.

"Get right on his tail," Tommy said and sat up just a little to get the best view. "Now! Do it now!"

Leo sped up to position himself right behind the Lexus. As the luxury import came to a rolling stop before turning into a tight parking space, Leo hit the accelerator and drove right into the very expensive rear bumper.

The damage to the Lexus, even at parking lot speed, could be well over a thousand dollars. Obviously the driver knew it when he angrily threw his door open and jumped out of the car. In a leather, black and gold Penguins jacket, he was a striking figure. One look at the way Leo was dressed and the well-turned hockey fan whined, "Great. Tell me you don't have insurance."

"You stopped short, pal," Leo said, holding his shoulder.

"What the hell were you tailgating me in a parking lot for?" He was bending over his bumper, looking at it sadly. Then he knelt down for a closer look.

"You going to the Pens game?" Leo asked.

The guy driving the Lexus stood to his full height and looked down his nose at Leo. "Not now," he said sarcastically. "I've got to see about this bumper."

"You're not going anywhere, buddy. You stopped short and I think my shoulder's broke." Then he winced at the pain and grabbed his shoulder much the same way Tommy had been doing the last couple of days.

"I didn't stop short," the guy in the Lexus said, ignoring Leo's pain. "And this is a brand-new car."

"So your car is more important than my shoulder."

Then the other door of the Lexus opened.

When the camera finally cut to Sandy, she was seated on a sofa in a richly appointed office. Her makeup was thickly applied. Deep red lipstick contrasted nicely with her cosmetically whitened teeth.

"In the last twenty-four hours I brought to you the dramatic story of Nick Bello, a surgical nurse at the Pittsburgh University Medical Center. Ironically, Mr. Bello is currently a patient at the Medical Center, having suffered a broken hip in an auto accident. He has described for the police a conspiracy whereby certain patients undergoing surgical procedures were murdered. Each of those patients had one thing in common: they were all insured by Western Insurance Company of Pennsylvania.

"I have it on excellent sources that Dr. Leonard Silverman, the medical director of WIP, is to be indicted by the DA's office in the morning." Then, turning her gaze from the camera to Dr. Silverman seated next to her, she continued. "First, Dr. Silverman, explain if you will what the medical director does at an insurance company like WIP."

Silverman was wearing a dark suit, no vest. He looked relaxed, stopping just short of smug. "Well, Sandy, as medical director I help set medical policy so that the quality of care meets very strict standards. I also take an active role in assuring that the physicians working for WIP take care of their patients in a cost-effective manner. We proudly offer the highest quality medical services in the most economical way in the tri-state area."

"Is it true, as Nicholas Bello claims, that it is not a coincidence that all of the patients dying at the medical center were insured by WIP?"

Silverman shifted in his seat and pulled his upper lip between his teeth in a photographically pensive pose. "I wish I could answer otherwise. But having reviewed the various cases I'd have to say that, yes, WIP insurance was somehow involved." When he finished talking, his index finger went up to one eye, wiping gently at something in the corner.

"What was your role in the Medical Center murders?"

"I had no active role in the murders. Period."

Sandy licked her lips with the tip of her tongue. "You emphasized 'active.' Did you have some other kind of involvement?"

"Regrettably . . . yes. There were things I overheard, memos I accidentally saw that should have pushed me to investigate. Instead," his voice got thick as if he were overcome with emotion, "I went about my duties as the medical director."

"Then you knew."

Silverman sniffed. "Unfortunately." He cleared his throat. "I knew."

"And you did nothing."

"I'm embarrassed that I didn't act sooner."

"Dr. Silverman, who at WIP was involved?"

"Under agreement with the district attorney's office I cannot tell you."

"What agreement?"

"Today I met with Assistant District Attorney Tory Welch and agreed to a deposition tomorrow with full disclosure of everyone who is involved." Silverman's voice became stronger as he said, "I've got my courage now. I will name names. And with the strength God has given me I will point fingers at everyone involved in this tragedy." For emphasis, Silverman pointed his index finger right at the camera.

Blaine Huffman was too mad to sit down. Cynthia was clutching her needlepoint on the chintz covered sofa. She knew better than to try to calm her husband. The more Silverman said, the more Huffman wanted to know exactly what the hell was going on. When the camera framed a close-up of Silverman pointing his finger at Sandy Keller, the billionaire almost lost control.

Several minutes later he couldn't take it anymore and stormed out of the family room, retreating to his paneled study. After pacing some more he looked up an address in the phone book, then picked up the phone. He soon thought better of it and slammed the receiver back in its cradle.

Before he realized what he was doing, he had changed his clothes and strode out of the house.

"Blaine, dear, where are you going? Blaine? Blaine?"

The phone rang. Tory went to get it, certain it was for her.

"Hello? . . . No, Frank, of course not. Why would I agree to any of it?" Tory looked over at Merlin and frowned. "He was in my office wanting to strike a deal. I refused. He left. . . . I'm sorry, Frank. I should have come to you afterwards. But he surprised me, just sort of arrived after I was in your office. . . . I assume he's trying to bully us into cutting some kind of deal. . . . Of course it won't work. Frank, how about if you call a press conference first thing in the morning and I set the record straight. . . . Okay, bye.'' Tory hung up.

A child got out of the Lexus wearing a number 68 Penguins jersey. ''Dad, the game's gonna start.''

''Get back in the car,'' his father said harshly, turning his attention back to Leo.

Tommy watched the scene unfolding from inside the car and realized he'd better get out.

''I think you broke my shoulder,'' Leo said again.

The guy looked at his watch, worried about the time. They could hear the sound of other car doors slamming. Penguins fans in black and gold jackets were hurrying toward the arena. The parking lot was nearly empty of people. ''Your shoulder's not broken.''

''How do you know? You a doc?''

''As a matter of fact, yes. I'm an orthopedic surgeon, and you don't break your shoulder going ten miles an hour.''

''Well, it hurts,'' Leo said, rubbing.

The other door of the Lexus opened again. For the second time the kid got out.

''Danny, I'm not going to tell you again. Get back in the car!''

After some heavy-duty pouting, Danny disappeared.

''Let me take a look. It could be your clavicle.'' And when he stepped forward to put his hand just inside Leo's jacket he felt the barrel of Leo's gun in his side.

Tommy had joined Leo, whose mouth was only inches from the doctor's face. ''Now, listen carefully, Dr. Stone. We got a little work for you to do.''

Dr. Stone swallowed hard. There was something about a stranger knowing more about you than you knew about him that really got your attention. ''How did you know my name?'' His voice was thick, but he was too scared to clear his throat.

''You're supposed to be the best. That's what I hear anyway. My friend over here,'' he said and gave his head a little movement to indicate Tommy, ''got shot and has a bullet in his shoulder that's infected. Dripping pus. Looks pretty gross.''

For a moment Dr. Stone felt a whiff of relief. ''Look, I mostly do hands.'' Desperately trying to break the heavy tension, he pointed toward his license plate and said, ''See? Bones Are Money. It's a joke. Ha ha ha. That's where the money is. *Hands.* I never do shoulders.''

"Don't make me shoot you in the kneecap," Leo threatened.

Dr. Stone was frightened. "Okay, let's stay calm. I'll help you. We'll have to go to the hospital, though."

"No hospital."

"Well, to the ER then."

"You're not listening. ERs are in hospitals. We go to the hospital, and they ask a lot of questions—"

"Not if I'm with you. There won't be—"

"C'mon, Doc. If you're half as fast as I've heard, then you'll be back for the second half." Leo knew damned well there was no second half in hockey, but he wanted the cocky asshole to correct him just so he could shove the gun a little harder in his side.

Worried too much about his safety, Dr. Stone ignored the comment. "Look, I'm with my son."

That's when Tommy stepped in. "How old is he?"

"Eleven."

"Give him his ticket. He'll be okay. Keep yours, and we'll bring you back. Promise."

"You're kidnapping me."

"Borrowing you," Tommy corrected.

"How do I know you're gonna let me go when I'm done?"

"I told you to keep your ticket, didn't I?"

Dr. Stone was silent.

"If you give us a hard time I take your ticket and pick up Danny. Am I making myself clear?"

Dr. Stone nodded.

"Okay," Tommy continued. "Give Danny his ticket, then park the car and we're off. The sooner we get going, the sooner we get back."

Walking around to Danny's side of the car, Dr. Stone opened the door and told his son he had a medical emergency. Of course Leo and Tommy hovered close by listening to every word. As Danny was handed the ticket they expected him to whine and complain about having to go to the game by himself. Evidently Danny was used to his father's medical emergencies because he hopped out of the car and barely looked at the two men as he headed out of the parking lot. He hardly said goodbye to his dad.

"Hey, Doc," Tommy said, "you must get called away on emergencies a lot."

"Afraid so."

Danny'll be okay if he has to grow up without you. Tommy got behind the wheel of the Chrysler, tightly tailgating the Lexus as he pulled into the parking space. Then the three of them loaded into the Chrysler, left-handed Tommy at the wheel, Leo and Dr. Stone in the back. "So what's your first name, Doc?"

"Paul."

"So, Paul," Tommy said, checking out his doctor in the rearview, "how're you at removing bullets?"

"I told you, I do mostly hand injuries."

"Popping a bullet out of my shoulder should be a piece of cake."

"I'll need equipment, local anesthesia."

"We'll find everything you need at your office on Center Avenue."

"Why me?"

"You're the best."

"Who told you that?"

"Leonard Silverman."

"Silverman!" Stone blurted out. "What's he got to do with your bullet wound?" For reasons Dr. Paul Stone would never understand, a profound feeling of doom choked off any other words from forming.

"You know Lenny, don't you?"

Dr. Stone nodded his head.

"He said you'd want to thank him for the referral."

Dr. Stone nodded his head weakly.

Leo leaned over the seat and fiddled with the dial on the radio. Mike Lange's voice filled the car with the play-by-play as the puck was dropped. Tommy carefully steered the car through the last remains of Civic Arena traffic on his way to Dr. Stone's office.

20

It was a matter of good timing and luck, nothing more, that Blaine Huffman was able to squeeze himself into the narrow space between the huge rhododendron bush and the two-car garage just before the cops arrived. At first he crouched low to the ground, hoping he would be there only a short while, his leather aviator jacket scraping up against the bricks, making a soft scratching noise. Soon his knees burned so he sat down cross-legged on the dirt, sacrificing himself to the cold.

Dark brown LL Bean GumShoes and thick, hunter green corduroy pants completed his outfit, giving him an urbane Indiana Jones look. A dark figure on a dark night hiding in the bushes.

Forty-five minutes earlier, Huffman had made a frantic dash out of his house, his mind painfully cluttered with the image of Cynthia sitting in the family room crying. For what he intended to do that night it was important that his thoughts be narrowly focused. Trying to slow things down, he took extra time in the garage deciding which car to take. Not for a second did he consider that he might get caught, or that he could get hurt, but Cynthia was such a part of what they'd been through, he couldn't wrest her out of his mind. Finally he cried out, "Damn!" furious that he could fall prey to such petty emotions and quickly walked back to the house, going straight to the family room. Looking absolutely wretched, Cynthia was standing there just as he expected, arms crossed over her chest, pallid cheeks streaked with tears. He hugged her for a good long while, holding her just as tight as the day Kit passed, then said he was off to a meeting and promised not to be late.

The only words Cynthia could muster were, "Be careful," which was such an odd thing to say to someone running out to an evening meeting, but with the way her husband was dressed she knew he was about to put himself in harm's way.

Huffman ultimately chose the Jaguar, not one of those pointy XKEs but the more refined XJS. It wasn't because he enjoyed driving it, but that the XJS didn't stand out quite so much as the big Mercedes or his 911. From the beginning he kept his eyes on the speedometer, watching the needle carefully, rigidly keeping himself a couple of miles over the limit. *Over* the speed limit. That subtlety pleased him. An amateur, he figured, would creep along, the slowpoke on the road. Huffman was too smart for that. The cops practically expected an expensive car to push the envelope a little. Driving too slow might attract some unwanted attention.

Now he felt totally focused. No longer was he a husband or the CEO of a powerful conglomerate. Blaine Huffman was a man seeking revenge. All four burners were going at once, everything was tightly focused on his mission.

This was so different from his meeting with Dr. Merlin. That had been planned very carefully, every detail attended to. He'd even enjoyed a dry run when Merlin hadn't shown up the first time.

Tonight was dangerous, totally by the seat-of-the-pants, and Huffman felt prepared to improvise as the situation demanded.

Strangely enough it felt positively terrific.

The radio, softly in the background, went to the news. He had to endure a second helping of Leonard Silverman describing how he was going to point some fingers at the other people involved in the Medical Center murders. Fortunately the windows were closed because Huffman let out a piercing primal scream that left him drained. "YOU LYING BASTARD! I'LL BREAK YOUR FUCKING FINGERS!" he hollered, knowing Silverman was his only pathway to peace. Some spittle formed at the corner of his mouth which he backhanded away. Focusing more and more, he began to talk to himself, planning out every move. "I'll shoot him in the foot. No, the knee, *both* knees. Yeah, that'll do it. Then he won't go anywhere, and I'll call the meeting to order. If he says 'finger' one more time I'll . . . I'll break it. I'll twist it. I'll twist it until it falls off. Then I'll kill him." Huffman patted his coat pocket, reassuring himself the weapon was still there. "Shit," he said, banging his hand on the steering wheel. Suddenly braking hard, he searched for a telephone.

At the first gas station off the parkway he found a pay phone. There was no answer after four rings, just a machine that instructed him to leave a message. Just to be careful he dialed two more times, in case someone at home was more than four rings from the phone. *Perfect. No one home.*

When he finally got to Squirrel Hill, a peaceful upper-middle-class community within the city limits, he promptly got lost, driving up and down the tree-lined streets filled with expensive homes until he happened by Woodmont Street. That's when he encountered his first problem.

All along he'd planned to circle the block a couple of times. But there on the corner, standing sentry, was a bright yellow No Outlet sign. In some communities Woodmont would be termed a dead end or a blind alley. But this was Squirrel Hill. Woodmont was a cul-de-sac.

He debated driving right up to the house and parking in front, ducking down until Silverman arrived home, though this wasn't the kind of community where one could do that. Someone would notice. So he kept on going, hardly even slowing down, finding a suitable place to park a block and a half away.

As he walked back toward Woodmont, he wished he'd brought gloves. A cold mist had begun to fall, and he kept opening and closing his hands to keep the blood flowing through his fingers. A couple of cars went by. Just before reaching Woodmont, he spotted the rack of lights on a squad car. He kept going, easing himself into a relaxed stroll as the squad car cruised by. Fifty more steps, disciplining himself to count them down, Huffman continued beyond Woodmont. Only then did he allow himself to turn around and head back toward Silverman's street.

Woodmont was a street of large brick homes that sat heavily on great lawns, expensively landscaped with bushes that would provide ample hiding places. He walked confidently, consciously avoiding looking back, only casually glancing at the numbers on the front doors until he arrived at number 15, a two-story home with a small front porch that, at best, might keep a single person dry. Around back, off to the left, was a separate garage.

The street was empty. No one walking a dog. Not a single car parked at the curb. Confidently, in case anyone happened to be looking out a window, Huffman marched right up the front walk as if he were expected and rang the bell. The four chimes played familiarly, E-C-D-G-G-D-E-C.

No answer. No lights came on.

Another push of the button. E-C-D-G-G-D-E-C.

His phone call was confirmed. This was an empty house.

Perfect.

Of course it was never Huffman's intent to break into Silverman's house. He just wanted to be certain there wasn't a Mrs. Silverman at home. Or a Junior Silverman. His meeting was with the doctor, and he had no business with anyone else who might live there. Now all there was to do was wait until Silverman arrived home, ring the bell, and when he came to the door shove the gun in his face and push his way in. He just needed a place to wait.

First he cupped his hands around his eyes peering through one of the windows. It looked like a formal living room.

He continued around to the side where the driveway skirted the house on its way to the garage and cupped his hands to the glass for another peek into Silverman's world. All of these windows were draped.

Abruptly, a car came up Woodmont. The headlights briefly caught Huffman, throwing his giant shadow on the bricks. He turned around, momentarily frozen in the brightness, certain Leonard Silverman was about to pull into the driveway and recognize him. He dropped to all fours, looking like a middle-aged sprinter, ready to take off through the bushes if the car turned into the driveway. Instead it turned away from him and slipped silently into a driveway across the street. Huffman stayed low, never taking his eyes off the car. From his vantage point he had an excellent view of a man slowly emerging from the car and opening the rear door to retrieve what looked like a briefcase. Just when Huffman expected him to walk to the front door, the man paused and turned to look directly toward the Silverman house for longer than Huffman expected.

Huffman swallowed hard. *Don't move. Don't move. If he spotted me in the headlights he doesn't see me now.* Every muscle in his body tightened. *Maybe he thought I was Silverman.*

It was easy to make himself crazy.

Eventually the man tired of looking across the way and proceeded up the front steps, silently disappearing into the house. Not in a rush as though he couldn't wait to call the police. Just an ordinary, end-of-a-long-day walk. As if he needed a two cherry Manhattan.

Huffman didn't dare move for a long time. Finally chancing it, he pushed up on his knees to get himself standing again. *He probably heard the news on the radio and was just looking to see if anything was going on. That's all.*

Moving more quickly now, Huffman continued around to the back. The darkness was a welcome relief. With a quick scan of the backyard, he spotted the huge rhododendron. Deciding to take up residence behind it, he secured himself an excellent view of the route Silverman would likely take from the garage to his house.

He checked his right jacket pocket again. The gun hadn't moved. Then he checked the left pocket for his silencer. And he waited. And got cold. And waited some more.

Finally his knees couldn't take it and he muttered, "What the hell," sitting himself on the wet dirt. The cold immediately seeped through his corduroys.

A second set of headlights drove up Woodmont. This time the car was moving slowly, briefly stopping a couple of times as if the driver were looking for a house number. Eventually the car made it to Silverman's driveway and came to a complete stop. The door opened but the headlights remained on. Huffman could still make out the purr of the engine.

Whoever was driving the car got out and looked around. It was a man. Huffman was certain of that by the silhouette, a dark figure against the bright porch lights from across the street. The flashlight he snapped on must have been one of those six battery models, because he held it up to his shoulder like a bazooka.

After looking this way and that, the man started up the driveway. Every three or four steps he stopped to work the light around Silverman's house. Huffman suspected who it was, but not until a flash of light bounced off a window and lit up the figure could he be certain.

It was a cop. Someone had called the police. Maybe the guy across the street. Or was it a precautionary thing because of what Silverman had said in the TV interview? Huffman didn't care. All he knew was that he was hiding in Silverman's rhododendron bush with an unregistered handgun in his pocket, a silencer, and no goddamned explanation why he was there.

He was trapped. Any attempt to make a break for it would likely get him arrested. Or shot. Quietly Huffman rolled on his side, flattening himself against the cold ground. He controlled his breathing and waited. Soon the brightness of the flashlight swept around the garage. For an instant it shone right in his face, hurting his night eyes as if he'd looked at the sun. But the cop didn't go for his gun or sweep the light back and forth where Huffman hid. Instead, he went up to the back door and tried the handle, eventually satisfying himself there was no sign of a break-in.

It seemed to take forever, but the cop worked his way around the entire house, ending up back at his cruiser. First he backed the car into the driveway, then slowly headed down Woodmont.

*   *   *

Time lost all perspective. Seconds turned into minutes. Before Huffman could steel the nerve to sit himself up, more lights came up Woodmont. This time a car turned into Leonard Silverman's driveway and parked right in front of the garage.

21

Tory awoke suddenly, taking a full minute to convince herself the day really had begun.

Gradually the sounds of morning filtered into the room. Car engines straining to come to life. Merlin in the shower. The bark of Pepper next door. Tory pulled up the covers, enjoying their bed for another minute. Suddenly her clock radio turned itself on, intruding rudely on her reverie by blaring an obnoxious commercial for a furniture store. This was followed by the anonymous voice of an A.M. talk jock, with Leonard Silverman sound bites cleverly woven into the top story, lambasting the district attorney's office for cutting a deal.

Sandy Keller had really stirred things up. Tory felt the acids churn in her stomach, knowing full well she'd be waking up to her own sound bites in a mere twenty-four hours.

Reluctantly, she forced herself from bed. The countdown to her press conference had begun.

By now Merlin was out of the shower, racing about the bedroom getting dressed. "You ready for today?" he asked, giving her a quick hug.

"I have a very bad feeling." Tory trudged off toward the bathroom.

The morning routines seemed to take forever. Soaping herself in the shower. *Yes, I met with Dr. Silverman several hours before his television interview.* Toweling off. *But he walked into my office and I turned him down flat when he offered a deal.* Brushing her teeth. *Regardless of what Dr. Silverman claimed to Sandy Keller, this office is not making any deal.* Getting dressed. *Even as we speak, Dr. Silverman is being arrested and will be indicted later today.* Making coffee. *Didn't you hear me? Of course I'd stake my reputation on it.*

Finally, just before heading out the door, she caught her reflection in the window. *Of course I'd stake my reputation on it.* She liked the sound of that and smiled.

The small media room was actually a conference room where the secretaries congregated with their bag lunches each day at noon. The centerpiece of the room was a long rectangular table, constructed of a single piece of darkly stained oak. Every time fresh blood in the secretarial department was invited for lunch, it was only a matter of time before the question was asked, "How did they get this in here?"

With the chairs set straight and spaced evenly around the long table, the blue screen emblazoned with the seal of the district attorney's office pulled down from the ceiling, and the little podium set up at one end, the conference room was convincingly transformed into something very official.

At nine A.M. the press assembled. Sandy Keller raced around the table in order to grab the seat closest to the podium. Wasting no time, she quickly busied herself reviewing a series of questions she had prepared. Every once in a while she fluffed her hair or adjusted her necklace, generally ignoring everyone else in the room except her cameraman. She shot brusque glances his way every couple of minutes. He was expected to be attentive, and whenever Sandy couldn't catch his eye immediately she would frown.

Of course she was aware of the rest of the media in the room, the lukewarm coffee sippers whom she regularly ignored. After all, she was on fire, with two major stories in as many days with more to follow. As far as she was concerned these people were the extras in the ongoing Sandy Keller story.

The room was filling quickly. A fat reporter with stringy hair covering his bald spot and a tie that made it almost halfway to his belt took the last seat across from Sandy. In addition to his sixteen ounces of coffee he had a cinnamon roll with sticky white icing that preferred the cellophane wrapping. As he began the messy process of smearing the icing back on the roll, he noticed Sandy sitting across from him. "Morning," he mumbled with a mouth full of doughy cinnamon.

"Good morning," Sandy countered, enunciating her words carefully, as if she were a speech therapist talking to a child with a terrible lisp, "Sandy Keller." *Go ahead, say it. "I know who you are. Kudos on your Silverman interview." But swallow your breakfast first.*

"Yeah, Earl Pickering. I know who you are. We been introduced a couple, three times."

"Of course, I'm sorry, Earl."

"Last time we met you said the same thing. 'Of course, I'm sorry, Earl.' What do I gotta do to get remembered?" Without giving Sandy any time to offer a suggestion, Earl went on. "Hey, you want a bite?" he asked, holding up the cinnamon bun, and poked—not figuratively but quite literally—his tongue deep in his cheek, making it go in and out several times, letting the other reporters know that he was having some fun at her expense.

"Now I remember, Earl. It was an Italian hoagie last time, wasn't it?" Sandy cocked her head slightly, satisfied to be dazzling the room with her command of detail.

"Yeah, with the hot peppers. You ever get the oil outta your blouse? The dry cleaning bill was more'n I expected. I like that kind of silk, though, very smooth. But a bitch to get stains outta."

By now Sandy and Earl had the rapt attention of everyone in the room. Instead of hearing how terrific her interview with Leonard Silverman was and getting to play coy about her sources, she was engaged in an inane conversation with a corpulent reporter named Earl.

"I did *not* eat your Italian hoagie." And with that, Sandy reached into her Coach briefcase and pulled out a sleek flip-phone.

"I'm just kidding with you, Sandy. You're not taking it seriously, are you?"

"I doubt if anyone takes anything you say seriously, Earl."

"Hey, if I'm out of line, sorry."

"You're out of line but apology accepted," Sandy mumbled as her fingers tap-danced across the keypads, dialing up the newsroom.

"It's just that the 'Hi, I'm Sandy Keller' routine is old. Hey, I got a good one for you to use next time—"

Before Earl could go on, before he could really embarrass her with whatever petty jealousies he harbored, the call went through. Grateful to every promise James Earl Jones had ever made about prompt telephone connections, Sandy turned toward the privacy of the empty podium, whispering, "It looks like we're starting late. What about a live remote from here at noon?" While she listened she fluffed her hair and gently touched her earlobe where the tiny stitches had been up until late yesterday. "Of course this is a waste of time. I'm sure Frank will sidestep everything. I think the story's with Tory Welch. Lots going on there." Then she looked at her cameraman, carefully avoiding any eye contact with her extras, and sent him a nod. "I'm way ahead of you. Got the police report. Betcha didn't know she shot at them."

That comment was the reportorial equivalent of a stripper pulling down her G-string and showing some shrubbery. Just enough to get the juices flowing. Scooping her colleagues twice in the last two days wasn't enough. Sandy wanted to tease them with the big news she was going to break at lunchtime, knowing they would still be dutifully reporting how Frank LaBove denied blowing the case.

At four minutes after nine Tory sat nervously in Frank LaBove's office, an empty coffee mug balanced on one knee. She was keenly aware of the time, checking her watch more frequently the later it got.

"Okay, last time," Frank began but was interrupted when the door opened. He was in shirtsleeves, his thinking mode, using the entire office as his doodle pad, pacing here and there, unaware Tory's neck was expected to rotate like an owl's. Already he'd opened the door three times, grabbing a quick glance at his secretary's unoccupied desk, each time making a face and pushing the door closed a little louder.

Now his secretary was looking for him. "They're ready when you are, Mr. LaBove. And she's there, right where you said she'd be."

"Thanks." He put his outstretched hands together as if to pray and brought them to his face, covering his nose and mouth in a contemplative mode.

"Need anything else? More coffee?" the secretary asked, waiting to be dismissed.

"No, no, we're fine," Frank said reflexively.

As unobtrusively as she had entered the room, Frank's secretary withdrew, closing the door silently behind her.

"Sandy Keller," Frank remarked in a tone that bordered on reverential.

"You're not surprised," Tory added.

"No, but she may know more than we do."

"What do you mean?"

"She broke the story on Nick Bello. Who the hell tipped her off? Now this crap with Leonard Silverman. How the hell did she get him on camera so quickly?"

"Maybe *he* wanted to be on camera. You know, act like I set up a deal. Force our backs to the wall."

"You mean to push us into the deal."

"Exactly. Notice he came to me, not you. That was no accident. I bet his first plan was to see if I jumped at the opportunity to reel in a big fish. Then when I said no, he figured he could just as easily act like I did say something stupid. Suddenly our conversation is the issue rather than the murders themselves."

"At this point it doesn't matter," Frank said. "Sandy's got sources. That's why we've got to be in synch about everything. I don't want her to be finding little discrepancies between my version of what happened yesterday and yours." He was standing still for the first time. "Let's go through what happened yesterday one more time, step-by-step."

"All right." Tory began, "Last evening, after—"

"After you left my office you went back to your office. Silverman was waiting for you."

"No, actually—"

"Yeah, he was waiting," Frank stated with a tone of finality. "It doesn't really change what happened, but it makes it seem more like he set a trap."

"Fine," Tory agreed. So far this didn't compromise her ethics. "He offered a deal—to cooperate in exchange for immunity—and I said no, that he must consult with his lawyer. The whole thing didn't take more than a minute or two. Then he left."

"And you immediately came to my office to inform me, but I had already left, and by the time you got home he was on the air."

Tory tucked her hair behind her ear. "Frank, I—" Tory hesitated.

"That's the way I remember it." Then Frank noticed the expression on Tory's face and realized he had to go a bit more slowly. "Okay, okay," he said quietly, easing down on the throttle, making a show of just how relaxed he was by sitting himself in a chair directly across from Tory, his buttocks barely indenting the thickly stuffed cushions. "Let's start over. I want to focus on the real issues of the case. It's too easy to let someone like Sandy Keller get us sidetracked. First of all, a little history lesson. I got elected for a second term because I stay involved with my cases. That's what I'm known for. Staying involved. What's Sandy Keller going to focus on? Not the merits of the case. No way. This will all come down to whether I knew what the hell was happening with a capital case."

"You didn't do anything wrong, Frank. I did."

"Okay, suppose we do it your way. You screwed up. I have no choice but to pull you from the case. If there's a screwup, someone has to be responsible."

"I don't want that."

"So we spin things just a little."

Tory didn't know what to say. Was Frank protecting her? Or was he securing his next election?

Frank continued, "Look, I would never ask you to do anything you feel uncomfortable with. Are we on the same wavelength?" This time Tory nodded. "I don't want to walk in there and get blindsided. We've got to be on the offensive with Sandy Keller." The DA got up and paced some more, silently rehearsing.

Tory was a quick study. "So when I couldn't find you in your office I headed home with every intention of calling you. Better?"

"Exactly. Look, Tory, I have total confidence you did nothing improper last night. I wouldn't dare fiddle with what he said to you or you said back to him. It just makes for a stronger case when the press sees that it was business as usual. You comfortable?"

"Sure."

A smile eased across Frank's face. He walked toward the door taking long confident strides and held it open for Tory. As they walked down the long hallway, past the watercooler and a series of offices, Frank continued, "I'll start, say a few words about what happened, and then introduce you. I'll be right there the entire time if you get in trouble."

In a matter of seconds they were at the door. Tory went numb, her fingertips tingled as if asleep, and she felt like a dog on a leash.

Without hesitation, Frank pulled open the heavy wooden door and walked in confidently, first greeting several of the reporters by name, then taking his place behind the small podium. As cameras were hoisted onto shoulders and the room quieted, Tory stood off to one side, trying to meld with the wall. Nervously, she looked about the room, feeling like a dateless girl at a cotillion, anxiously waiting for the evening to be over. Every time one of the reporters looked at her she focused her attention on Frank for a few seconds.

She spotted Sandy Keller sitting directly across the room, staring right at her. This time Tory refused to look away. Her eyes bore into Sandy's, announcing she was no pushover.

"Thank you all for coming. Last night Miss Keller," Frank began as Sandy immediately abandoned the staring contest in favor of a professional nod toward Frank, "interviewed Dr. Leonard Silverman, the medical director of Western Insurance. Indeed it was quite an interview, but there were grave inaccuracies in the content of Dr. Silverman's statements that need to be addressed—"

For the second time this morning Frank LaBove was interrupted when his secretary opened the door. Only this time she scurried across the carpeted floor, wasting no time getting to her boss. Frank stopped talking and leaned away from the podium. For several seconds she whispered something into his ear. Without hesitation he said to her, "I'll be right there." That sent his secretary back toward the door, giving him a second or two to poise himself. "Uh, if you will excuse me, there is some urgent business I must attend to. Tory Welch is here." Frank looked over to his ADA briefly. "She will address the inaccuracies raised in the Leonard Silverman interview last night."

This was exactly how Tory's dad had taught his daughter to ride a bicycle. *Okay, Tory, once more around the block. I'll hold the seat. Don't worry, I won't let go.* Two skinned knees later, Tory was officially a two-wheel rider.

Frank didn't wait for Tory to react before he headed for the door. Whatever it was apparently couldn't wait.

Although it was only about five steps from where Tory waited by the wall to the podium, the walk seemed to take forever, all eyes watching her. "Thank you for coming," she began. "Yesterday afternoon I watched the first of Miss Keller's reports from Mr. LaBove's office. When I got back to my office Dr. Silverman was waiting for me. Evidently he eluded the formality of checking in with our receptionist and found my office on his own."

"Miss Welch." It was Sandy, interested only in her own agenda. "How long did you meet with Dr. Silverman?"

"We talked less than five minutes. Dr. Silverman asked to cooperate with our office in exchange for immunity from prosecution. But no such deal was made. He accepted my—"

"And was Mr. LaBove consulted?"

A dozen thoughts flew through Tory's mind. "During the exchange, no. Dr. Silverman was without counsel. This was an offer—"

Sandy jumped on Tory's words. "Who is in charge of the case?"

How did Frank know?

Someone's beeper went off, but the tone was muted. Earl shoved his Bic pen into a shirt pocket decorated with several coffee stains and struggled to extricate his beeper from his belt. But the beeping continued, muffled by a roll of fat that hung over it like a thick blanket.

Sandy shot a glance across the table, glaring at her obese colleague. "Can you shut that thing up?"

He fiddled some more, finally releasing the beeper's clip from his overextended belt, and squinted to see the tiny message on the beeper.

"Earl," Sandy said, "what's it say, two-for-one lunch buffet at Ponderosa?"

"Miss Keller," Tory cut in, wresting control from Sandy, "I'm happy to answer every question any of you might have. But you have to allow me the opportunity to answer one question before I'm hit with another. Frank LaBove is in charge of the investigation."

"Did you consult with Mr. LaBove before you turned Dr. Silverman down?"

"No," Tory said.

Two more beepers sounded. This time several reporters grabbed at their beepers, straining to read the callback numbers in the poorly lit room.

Something was going on. First Frank did the unthinkable, walking out on a press conference, now the beepers.

Sandy ignored the possibilities and glared at her colleagues. If she couldn't get a little momentum going, she was just wasting her time. "Miss Welch, are you in charge of this case?"

"I already told you, no. Mr. LaBo—"

"At what point did you apprise Mr. LaBove—"

"Enough." Tory glared at the pushy reporter. "Is this how you get your exclusives? By jumping down people's throats, not letting them think? You ask the questions, I'll answer them, but give me the courtesy of listening to my answers. I don't want anything taken out of context. Criminal Law 101. Without legal representation I would be a fool to offer Dr. Silverman a deal of any kind. The notion is ridiculous. I don't need anyone's permission to enforce that, okay? Frank LaBove is in on every substantive decision made in this department."

Sandy was not put off. "Then why do you think Dr. Silverman made the statements aired last night?"

Ring. Ring. Ring. No ordinary beeper for Sandy Keller.

"I think it's obvious. And, before you ask, I *have* conferred with Frank on this. Miss Keller, you were used last night by Leonard Silverman in a failed attempt to bully or embarrass this department into saving him. We are building a strong case. We don't need his cooperation. And for the record, this department will never be bullied into offering a deal to someone who manipulates us through the media. Period."

Sandy's flip-phone, sitting in front of her, rang out again.

Tory looked at it. Earl looked at it. The *other* reporters looked at it. And without a moment's hesitation, Sandy quieted the ringing, shook her head gently so that her hair moved away from her ear, and smoothly brought the phone up without so much as a strand of hair tangled in the process.

"Hello," she said very quietly, then paused to listen.

No one knew quite what to do. Somehow it seemed rude to go on with questions and answers, yet Sandy's behavior was so unprecedented everyone was caught by surprise. Cameras came down. Earl took a bite of his cinnamon bun. Eyes were rolled, smirks exchanged.

Tory Welch stood at the podium, listening to one side of a conversation.

Sandy continued in hushed tones. "Where, his office? . . . His house, oh. I can be there in"—she looked at her watch—"fifteen, twenty minutes. Meet me there with a remote team. I'll go live. Gotcha." And Sandy snapped the phone closed.

In an instant Sandy figured out her priorities. A bone thrown to the dogs would occupy them and keep them away from the feast.

"Miss Welch, you still live with Dr. Jack Merlin, a surgeon at the Medical Center?"

Tory felt a terrible panic coming on. Something was fluttering in her belly, threatening to make a horrible noise. *Miss Welch, did you offer immunity to Leonard Silverman to protect your boyfriend?* It was coming, she could feel it. "Yes, I do, but I don't see how—"

"One last question. Is it true that two men broke into your home approximately one week ago and a weapon registered to Jack Merlin was discharged by you?"

To keep from smiling Tory had to bite her lower lip. "Yes, it's true. Check the police record. A man broke into our home in Aspinwall in an attempt to rob us. Jack Merlin surprised him, subdued him, and while we waited for the police, his partner busted in with a gun, and I discharged my weapon, scaring the intruders away."

Papers rustled, chairs squeaked, and the room came alive.

Earl was the first to speak. "Uh, Miss Welch, do you think there was any relationship between the murders in the hospital and the break-in at your home?"

If he wasn't so disgusting, Sandy could have kissed him.

"No, I do not," Tory said emphatically. "The man told us he was looking for money. We believed—"

Seeing that she had produced a little kinetic energy, Sandy Keller stood and gave a wave to her cameraman. Grabbing her notebook, she surveyed the room, considering which route she would take. The long way around the table would take her sidestepping behind chairs, risking someone asking her what was up. So she chose the shortcut, the ballsy path. Ducking down just a little—as if it were somehow less obnoxious to walk out if you acknowledged your rudeness by making yourself shorter—she tiptoed right behind Tory.

Of course Tory paused in mid-sentence as the reporter scooted behind her. When Sandy neared the door, just in case anyone didn't notice she was leaving, she added, "Excuse me."

Seizing the opportunity, knowing Sandy was creating the perfect diversion, Earl also sped toward the door, his shirt coming untucked in the process on a quest for a phone.

Finally, when Sandy and Earl had disappeared into the hallway, leaving the reporters in the room recovering from the little drama, Tory tried to refocus the direction of the press conference. "It is our intention that Dr. Silverman will be indicted for the murders of—" and Tory read a series of names from a small note card. The last name she read was Kit Huffman's.

Beep. Beep. Beep.

Something big was going on. Another reporter was squinting at his beeper.

"And for the record, not only was Leonard Silverman not offered immunity, Nick Bello, who *has* been indicted for the murders at the Medical Center, will stand trial, although consideration will be given in light of his testimony."

The door opened once again. Earl hustled back into the room. He was trying to tuck his shirt in, shoving a handful of cloth into his pants so that his shirt bunched up. Walking much more rapidly than he was used to, a whiny wheeze could be heard with each breath. As soon as he reached the table Earl leaned in close to another reporter and talked quietly in his ear, the sibilant sounds of his whispers distracting Tory. Once again she was relegated to standing silently at the small podium, shifting her weight from one foot to another.

"Pssst," Earl said loudly to his cameraman, pointing toward the doorway. Then he sloppily gathered his papers from the conference table and grabbed what was left of his cinnamon bun. Before he turned to leave, Earl put his fat hand on the table and leaned over it.

He couldn't resist sharing the news, even if it was only to create a stampede on Sandy Keller's exclusive turf. In his best stage whisper he went on about Silverman to yet another reporter sitting across the table. Now three of them were shoving notebooks back into briefcases and pens into pockets, making quite a bit of noise in the process.

"Sir," Tory said.

Earl didn't hear a word she was saying. He was grabbing his coat from the back of his chair in such a hurry something caught the back of the seat and the chair flipped over, crashing loudly on the carpet. Hastily he righted the chair and headed for the door, more interested in getting the hell out of there than apologizing for the show he was putting on.

"Sir!" Tory demanded in a confident voice. "You are being very rude. If you need to leave, please go."

"My apologies," he said. "Let me clue you in on what's going on, Miss Welch. The maid found Leonard Silverman's house messed up this morning. Blood everywhere."

"Is he dead?" Tory asked timidly, almost afraid to hear the answer. Strangely enough she almost felt guilty. A ridiculous thought, but somehow the way she had been described by Silverman as his conduit for ratting out his accomplices made her feel a tiny bit responsible.

Earl wheezed out, "Sounds like it, but there's no body. Just a weapon and blood." Then he rushed for the door.

"No body," Tory whispered.

Pandemonium hit. Several more chairs were flipped over in the process of emptying the room in the next several seconds.

Five minutes later Tory was in her car driving out of the city.

22

Tory's rental was a relatively new Chevy, already marred by cigarette burns on the dashboard. Even before she turned the key in the ignition she was on her cell phone getting the address from one of the office secretaries. The street meant nothing to her, but getting to Squirrel Hill meant taking the parkway. As she headed off in that direction the secretary called the police, got directions, and called Tory back.

The entire trip took twenty-three minutes, giving Tory a chance to think. *Who wanted to kill Silverman?* The answer seemed fairly obvious: it had to be someone involved with the murders at the Medical Center who thought he would be the target of Silverman's finger-pointing.

Part of her wanted to blame Leonard Silverman. If he was guilty of masterminding the conspiracy, then he'd certainly got what he deserved. Arranging the Sandy Keller interview and bragging how he was going to point his finger at those who were guilty was a foolish thing to do, especially when the DA's office had not agreed to anything.

But Tory felt so involved that she also questioned her own actions. What if Silverman was guilty of nothing more than ignoring what was going on around him? What if he was a hapless wimp grinding away, minding his own business, and in a panic turned to the DA's office for protection?

Then she would have been wrong to turn him down so quickly.

But Leonard Silverman was obviously not some callow Dilbert stuck in a cubicle. When Tory refused to be Silverman's stooge he tried to embarrass her into acquiescing. Not for a second was his behavior that of a helpless innocent caught in a vortex.

And where was Silverman's lawyer all this time? For that question Tory had only one reasonable explanation: Leonard Silverman had the unbridled arrogance to believe he was still in total control of the situation.

After parking her Chevy at the bottom of Woodmont—the road was closed off by a blockade manned by two uniformed officers—Tory showed her credentials. Her arrival did not go unnoticed by the media. The very same group of reporters and cameramen who had dumped her a half hour earlier for a better party were standing in little groups passing the time until someone told them what the hell was going on. Tory's arrival stopped their conversations cold. Immediately, they started toward her, walking slowly, like relentless zombies in a George Romero movie. Earl was there, too, right in front, chewing on a chipped ham sandwich.

There was one reporter who was conspicuously absent.

Not wanting to get into an impromptu press conference, Tory headed straight up Woodmont. Cops were everywhere. A cluster of white squad cars was parked haphazardly in front of number 15 as if the police had raced to the scene of some rapidly developing crisis where time was critical.

It was a beautiful fall day, the air crisp, the sun standing solo in a cloudless sky. Silverman's home shone brilliantly, the sunlight hitting it straight on. There was a great oak tree getting ready to drop its colorful leaves on a lawn that wouldn't need mowing until spring.

Somehow everything looked so pristine that it made Tory shudder. How could this pretty picture be hiding such terrible secrets? It was a beautiful present, wrapped to perfection with ribbons and bows, with a dead rat inside.

For more than a minute Tory lingered on the sidewalk searching for some clue, some tip-off to what might be inside. All she could see was a young police officer examining the front door. He opened and closed it several times, then got down on one knee, checking the locking mechanism closely.

Eventually Tory walked up to him and showed her identification.

Reading the words "District Attorney" on the laminated card bearing Tory's photograph, he suppressed a smile. "You with the DA?" he asked quietly.

"Yes, I'm Tory Welch."

"Glenn Curtis," he said, looking around. When he was satisfied they were indeed having a conversation that wasn't being overheard, he continued, "Lemme fill you in. Same thing I told them," the young officer said, pointing inside the house with his thumb. "Got a call last night from a neighbor, nosy type who thought she saw a burglar walking around the house."

Tory stood on the small porch listening to the story. Crime lab techs kept coming back and forth, squeezing around them as they went out to their van for supplies.

Curtis lowered his voice with each interruption. "So I drove up," the officer continued, modulating his voice in a *Dragnet* sort of way, proud to be bringing the district attorney up to speed, "maybe eight o'clock, maybe a little later, and walked around. Checked the doors, front and back. Windows, too. No sign of a break-in. I mean, if my grandmother lived here I couldn't have been more thorough—"

"Any sign of a break-in this morning?" Tory asked matter-of-factly.

"No way," the officer said confidently, bending over to take a quick look at the latch to double-check. "No scratches on the wood or metal. This ain't been messed with," Curtis said with a tone of finality, inserting the word "ain't" into his vocabulary for effect. "I went all the way around the house with my flashlight, even checked the garage. If there was somebody here I woulda seen him. Whoever it was must've got the hell outta here when I drove up. Once they bolt, ninety-nine times out of a hundred, they don't come back. Unfortunately for Dr. Silverman, someone came back."

"You worked last night and again this morning. Why so soon?"

The front door was opened a crack and Curtis closed it, not saying another word until the locking mechanism clicked audibly. "Got a call from my captain. This is Squirrel Hill, you know what I mean? Murders just don't happen here. When one does we jump on it pretty damn hard."

"Murder? I thought there wasn't a body."

Curtis's face reddened. "Trust me. Someone got worked over real bad. Not a pretty sight, if you know what I mean. Ninety-nine times outta a hundred when you got blood all over the place—"

"I understand," Tory said softly, realizing Officer Curtis had nothing further to offer. "I guess I'd better get inside and check things out for myself."

"You been to one of these crime scenes before?"

Tory felt embarrassed. "No."

"I hear this one's pretty bad."

"You mean you haven't—" Tory caught herself before completing the thought, suddenly feeling embarrassed for Officer Curtis. It was obvious that the young officer was not in the loop.

"Listen, Miss Welch, I gotta get back. Detective wants me to check around the outside a second time. I'll be around if you want to ask me anything."

Tory sucked in her breath. Going to the morgue was tolerable. At least everything was out in the open. This was going to be a new experience, she anticipated, like going into a fun house at Halloween. When you least expected it something would jump out and scare the crap out of you.

Waiting until Officer Curtis headed around to the back of the house, Tory opened the front door and carefully stepped inside, instinctively clutching her bag to her side lest it accidentally touch something.

The front hallway was impressive. Black and white marble tiles, a curved staircase leading up to the second floor, and a crystal chandelier. No blood. No bullet holes in the silk wallpaper. It was a place where guests could say, even before they saw the rest of the house, "My, you've got a beautiful home."

To the right was a sunken living room, two steps down. The furnishing were ostentatious, probably the result of an interior designer acting on the orders, "I don't care what it costs, I want something people will remember." Draperies swirled around the windows like icing on a wedding cake. Black wall-to-wall carpeting was cut out in a variety of places and filled in with bold slashes of white carpeting that intersected with one another like giant Japanese lettering. A glass coffee table, in the center of the room, was supported by wrought iron snakes writhing up from the carpet. Finally, separated by the serpents, were two huge flowery sofas, steroidally stuffed, and excessively fanned with decorative pillows. And sitting stiffly on the sofas, unsure about the etiquette of actually leaning against the pillows, were two uniformed police officers, carefully drinking coffee. They seemed properly impressed with the room, looking from one expensive furnishing to another, until one of them happened to notice Tory. "The family room. In back."

Tory mumbled her gratitude and walked down a short hallway, momentarily pausing as she went by the dining room and kitchen before she reached the back of the house. Next to the kitchen was a small mudroom with a door leading out toward the garage. Through the window Tory could see Officer Curtis giving a large rhododendron the once-over. A series of jackets hung from wooden pegs. A pair of rubber boots stood waiting next to the back door.

No blood. The only thing Tory noticed that wasn't perfect was an eight-inch long black scuff mark on the hardwood floor.

Finally, only a few steps away from the mudroom, was a doorway. Standing solidly in that doorway, blocking any sort of meaningful view, was a uniformed officer.

"Sorry, only the crime unit is allowed," he said politely.

"I'm with the DA's office, Tory Welch." Tory held out her ID. "Who's in charge?"

The officer turned around, trying his best not to allow Tory a look and signaled to a man in a dark suit. "Harry, someone from the DA."

Tory peered around the officer's shoulder as best she could, enjoying the kind of view a child gets when peeking through a crack in a door. At the far end of the room was a massive television set. Several black speakers were mounted on the wall. A small cluster of people stood to one side of the room.

The uniformed officer stepped aside. At once Tory got the full view. It was more a home theater than a family room. The centerpiece of the room, and what seemed to have the attention of four members of the crime unit, was a twelve-foot L-shaped sofa, dark green, arranged for maximal viewing pleasure.

Harry, a middle-aged, balding detective wearing a knockoff blue-gray Harris Tweed sport coat, broke away from the crime unit. He had a scowl on his wrinkled face that looked as if it were on permanent display. The only thing missing from the gnarled cop persona was the chewed-up cigar hanging from his mouth. But he'd certainly mastered the I've-seen-it-all walk, crossing the cream-colored carpet very slowly.

"LaBove not coming?" was all Harry said by way of greeting.

"No. I'm Tory Welch."

"He never comes."

"I'm sorry I didn't catch your—"

"Don't touch anything," Harry snapped.

In some relationships the chemistry was either there from the beginning or it wasn't. Men like Harry could only tolerate truly attractive women when they were on a movie screen. It was a self-fulfilling prophecy that he wasn't going to like her. "Look, would you mind telling me what you hope to accomplish coming onto a crime scene like this? Should I clear the room now that the gawkers are here?"

Tory was taken aback. "Look, Detective, an indictment for Dr. Silverman was issued today. If something happened to him, our office needs to know."

"Who said that something happened to him?" Harry raised his eyebrows.

Harry was going to throw whatever she said right back at her. "Look, Detective, it's a lot easier if we cooperate. I didn't even get your name."

"Gallagher," he said, and kept his big mouth open for a couple of seconds like he was going to let out a belly laugh.

"Okay, Detective Gallagher, if you'd just give me a quick run-through I'll get out of your hair." She didn't prolong the word or smile when she said it. Her eyebrows went up ever so slightly to remind the detective that her choice of words was no accident. It was supremely effective at closing Detective Gallagher's big mouth.

Reflexively, one of the detective's hands came up to his head and touched the hair growing around his ear. "You want blood, we got blood. That what you're into?" Gallagher snarled, sweeping his hand grandly, like a docent in a museum.

"Not really," Tory answered honestly. "I just don't want to hear what happened from Sandy Keller live at five."

Just as Tory said the name "Sandy Keller," Detective Gallagher looked out one of the windows toward the back and spotted the reporter entering the yard, tramping through the bushes, having parked one street over and taken the sylvan route. "Fuck! Fuck, fuck, fuck." Gallagher looked at Tory to see if he had offended her.

"That's the best you can do? I thought you cops had more colorful words than that."

" 'Scuse me." Gallagher pushed past Tory toward the mudroom door, yanked it open, and leaned out like a mother calling her kids in for dinner. "Hold it right there. Yeah, you. I'm talking to you, sister. Would you mind telling me just what the hell you think you're doing?"

"Are you in charge?" Sandy asked sweetly. "I'm Sandy Keller—"

"Turn around, miss, and leave the same way you came in," Gallagher commanded.

"I just want to ask you a question or two, then I'll—"

"Officer!" Gallagher yelled, spotting Curtis wedged in between the big rhododendron bush and the two-car garage. "Please escort Miss Keller from the premises. Now. Do not communicate with her in any way. Do it double-time!"

Officer Curtis stood abruptly. The leathery oblong leaves slapped him repeatedly in the face. "Detective, I got something!" Curtis called out, holding up a lone branch sprouting several leaves.

"Get her outta here!" Gallagher screamed.

Curtis squeezed from behind the bush and approached Sandy, who was standing in the middle of the grassy yard, up on tiptoes so her high heels wouldn't sink into the soft soil.

"Take her arm. No, grab her by the arm," Gallagher directed.

Curtis gingerly tried to obey, but Sandy yanked her arm away from him and swung her pocketbook at his face, causing him to stumble. "Touch me and I'll press charges, you little shit," Sandy hissed as she awkwardly tiptoed toward the driveway where the footing was better and she could walk normally.

Poor Officer Curtis. He had absolutely no idea how to handle the sticky situation. Like a child, he followed several steps behind Keller, clutching his precious rhododendron branch.

Gallagher came out of the house and watched until Sandy was all the way to the sidewalk. Curtis turned to head back toward the rhododendron but spotted the detective making a hurry-up motion with his hand. The young officer broke into a run.

By now Tory was standing in the doorway of the mudroom closely watching the Sandy Keller show. Officer Curtis proudly handed what he must have thought was an olive branch to Gallagher. Breathlessly he sprung into an explanation. "I found this behind that big rhododendron over there. See? The end is all ragged and twisted. Someone tore it off. There's also a footprint in the mulch. Someone was hiding there."

Gallagher started walking toward the rhododendron, grabbing the branch from Officer Curtis. Over his shoulder he yelled, "All right, Counselor, you wanted to see something, come along. We'll get to the blood later."

As Tory walked quickly to catch up, Curtis followed. When they got to the bush Curtis said, "It's back there," and moved around the rhododendron as if leading an expedition.

"Didn't you respond to a call last night that there was a burglar or something?"

"Yessir," Curtis answered crisply as if part of an elite military operation.

"Well, was someone waiting in the bushes?"

"No, sir. Absolutely not, sir. I shined my light in these bushes, there was nothing."

"You did a full and thorough job?"

"Yessir, if my grandmother—"

"And didn't I send you around the house forty-five minutes ago looking for signs of an intruder?"

"Yessir," Curtis said, a bit less confidently.

"Then remind me, Officer Curtis, what did you tell me you found?"

"Uhh. Nothing . . . sir."

"Did you do a thorough search?"

"Yes . . . well, I thought so."

"So in the last forty-five minutes some intruder hid in these rhododendron bushes, broke off a branch, and left a footprint."

"Well—" Officer Curtis began, having no idea what to say.

"Better get your eyes checked. That'll be all, Officer."

"Yessir, you'll have my report—"

"Yeah, yeah, yeah. On my desk in the morning."

"Excuse me," Tory said. "Before Officer Curtis leaves, should we get a look at his footprint next to the one he found just to make sure it isn't one of his?''

"Yeah," Detective Gallagher said, once again his big mouth opening like he was gonna roar with laughter. "That's not a bad idea, Counselor. Curtis—"

"Yessir," Curtis answered brightly, understanding what was wanted from him and moving around toward the back of the bush, intending to place his own foot next to the footprint he had discovered.

"Curtis, stay the hell away from what is now part of the crime scene. Take off your shoes, leave them on the ground, and get the hell outta here. You're dismissed."

Tory's eyes widened. Curtis hesitated for a second, hoping he was the butt of a joke, that no way would the detective actually expect him to take off his shoes and walk out in stocking feet.

"Look, Officer," Detective Gallagher began, "you may think you did an adequate search of this yard last night, but as far as I'm concerned you did a shit-ass job. And maybe you got Silverman killed. How do you feel about that? So don't waste any more of my time. Take your goddamned clodhoppers off, and if you so much as look at Sandy Keller on your way out of here I'll personally rip your eyes out."

Curtis brought his right foot up and tried to pull the shoe off as he balanced on the left. Now he was scared silly, not paying attention to what he was doing and, of course, started to lose his balance. That got him hopping around on one foot while he struggled pathetically with his shoe.

Tory averted her eyes, embarrassed once again for Curtis. As she followed Detective Gallagher back toward the house, the young officer walked toward the driveway on his heels, desperately trying to keep at least some of his socks dry.

Just before Gallagher opened the door he turned back to face Tory. "I'll say this one time. What you see me do and hear me say, you keep to yourself. I'm dealing with idiots like Curtis every day." Then he yanked the back door open and banged it loudly.

As they entered the family room, Detective Gallagher saw the flashes from the police photographer and gruffly commanded, "Okay, you got to play detective. Why don't you park it in the kitchen while the pros finish up and then you'll get your little tour."

Gallagher walked away, leaving Tory to feel as useful as Officer Curtis.

The kitchen was small but quite modern. Tory nosed around casually, finally stopping in front of the refrigerator. Before snooping she took a quick look toward the doorway. Gallagher was nowhere to be seen. Going up on tiptoes, she grabbed the freezer handle through her jacket to avoid embarrassing fingerprints. An automatic ice dispenser, TV dinners, and boxes of frozen crabmeat hors d'oeuvres. Two frosty beer mugs and a bottle of Stolichnaya. Definitely a bachelor's freezer.

Then she checked the refrigerator. Of course she expected the half-full bottle of Diet Coke and white cardboard containers of Chinese food. Even the bowl of fruit. But there was a surprise. Nine little round dishes of red Jell-O, all on one shelf. Somehow Leonard Silverman did not seem the Jell-O type.

The real surprise was how much of the jiggly red stuff was in each little dish. These weren't dessert portions. Each dish had less than a half inch of the gelatin inside. Momentarily, Tory forgot about what was going on in the family room and reached in, selecting one of the little dishes. *Why fill so many dishes with such skimpy portions?*

Immediately, dessert dish in hand, she opened several of the cabinets.

"I said wait in the kitchen, not help yourself to a snack, goddamn it."

It was Gallagher.

"Here's something odd," Tory stated. She walked toward the detective.

"Jell-O. What are you, Curtis's twin sister?"

"Look at how much is in the bowl."

Gallagher took a quick look, less time than he spent on the rhododendron branch. "So. Maybe he was on a diet." Gallagher took out the little leather wallet that contained his shield. "This is typical. There're about thirty-nine steps I gotta go through to solve a typical murder. I'm on about step three and you're in the kitchen getting all hot and bothered over a stupid bowl of Jell-O. Here. You want to be the detective, you carry it."

"May I go into the crime scene now? I'm wasting way too much of your time." Tory walked past Detective Gallagher, handing him the little dish with the red gelatin, finally entering Silverman's family room.

Gallagher sniffed the Jell-O, even touched it one time. "Hmm, strawberry." It felt leathery, like it had been prepared a while ago and forgotten. "Fuckin' DA," he muttered and flipped the dish on the granite counter so that it rolled around like a child's top about to fall.

Any time she wanted, Tory could summon that awful feeling she had entering the county morgue the first time. Cold impersonal surroundings. Unpleasant odors. Almost as though everything in the morgue was part of the corpse. But at least, she reminded herself, everything was out in the open. No hidden surprises.

By contrast, on first view, the Silverman family room looked like any other expensively appointed family room. The big-screen television sat silently against the far wall. From her vantage behind the sofa, Tory could get no hint of the crime that had been committed here.

Aside from a woman in a white lab coat taking fingerprints from various surfaces, the room was otherwise empty. Each time she'd gotten a glimpse of the room the action had seemed to be taking place at the right-most area of the sofa, so Tory headed in that direction.

The room was very masculine. Heavy oak wainscoting ran a third of the way up toward the ceiling. Only when Tory got close to the couch did she realize the wood had been splattered with something very dark.

The wallpaper above it, a dark green that Silverman's decorator surely called "bottle green," had also been splashed.

Was it blood?

Of course that was the logical conclusion, although Tory had never seen blood splattered on a dark surface before. In the movies it was always a white wall. Or if Quentin Tarantino had anything to do with it, a windshield. Dark surfaces weren't dramatic. It could have been Coca-Cola for all she knew, but the closer Tory looked, the more she suspected that indeed the wall had been sprayed with blood.

Then she saw the bullet hole, and everything became frighteningly real.

As bullet holes go, this one was small, punching a black circle in the dark wallpaper rimmed with the white of the drywall. Less than a quarter inch or so in diameter, no wider than a child's fingertip, it could easily be missed.

There was a small wooden table next to the leather sofa. Before Tory dared a look at the front of the sofa she noticed two items on the table. Each was sealed in a clear plastic baggie.

The first was a hatchet. Even though it was bloody, it looked new, probably because the few areas of the blade that weren't stained crimson looked polished. The edge of the blade had a perfect, even margin where it had been machine sharpened. The handle was wrapped in a blue rubbery material full of tiny holes that were supposed to improve the grip.

The second baggie was a welcome respite from the bloody hatchet. It contained a small rectangular box of kitchen-size Hefty bags. No blood or bloody fingerprints on the box. Tory couldn't quite imagine how the Hefty bags might be involved.

Once Tory was finished with exhibit A and exhibit B she turned her attention to the sofa, moving next to it, careful not to let her clothing touch the leather. When she got her first view of the cushions she almost passed out. Quickly averting her eyes, she blinked several times, placing one hand to the back of her neck and squeezing hard to create some pain in lieu of a container of smelling salts.

All she had seen was blood, but imagining how all that blood came to be puddled on the couch was what nearly caused her to faint. Taking slow, controlled breaths, Tory was ready for a second look.

Blood. Two large, sticky puddles of crimson, separated from one another by a random fold in the leather.

Then her eyes moved to the armrest and she saw a smear of blood and a deep gash in the leather. It was four inches long, the edges of the leather puckered up toward her like the lips of an empty mouth screaming out in pain.

Unaware how wide her own mouth hung open, Tory stood there silently, clutching her leather bag, frozen in horror. Back and forth. Back and forth. Her eyes went from the hatchet to the bloody gash. Hatchet. Bloody gash.

"You're not going down, are you? You wanted to see it."

"I'm fine."

"I wonder what the hell Silverman looked like when they got through with him?" Gallagher said jovially. He'd obviously waited at the door to the family room long enough to let Tory's imagination kick into high gear. Now he was ready to have some fun.

Tory was determined not to let him. "Listen, Detective," Tory blurted out, flashing her temper, "I've had enough of your crap. I'm fine. I'm not going to swoon, so let's get on with what happened. Is there anything else to see?"

"You see both gashes, Counselor? Come around front."

Walking the long way around the sofa, Gallagher pointed out a second bloody gash on the seat cushion on the other side of the twin puddles of blood. This one wasn't quite so bad, as it was the second one she'd seen. Besides, it didn't look anything like an open mouth.

"The gashes, I assume, are roughly the same length as the hatchet blade," Tory offered.

"Roughly. The blade's three and a half inches. The cuts measure a quarter inch or so bigger; the ends probably ripped a little. Check out the carpet."

Tory stepped back when she realized she was practically standing on one of two side-by-side crimson stains, each about eighteen inches out from the sofa, appearing like two giant eyes staring up at her from the carpet.

Spotting something, Tory knelt down. Carpeting didn't gash the way leather did, but at the center of each stain was a linear depression where the carpet was cut.

Tory looked back at the two gashes in the leather, then again at the carpet, finally at the spray of blood on the wall and the single bullet hole.

"You can only imagine what it was like," the detective said.

"What *what* was like?"

"Getting his arms and legs chopped off." Gallagher chortled to himself. "Probably took 'em out in a Hefty bag."

"I don't know," Tory said thoughtfully. Absently, she massaged one of her wrists.

"Oh, *you're* gonna figure this one out, are you, dearie?"

Tory stood silently, examining the scene. "Was he already dead when they used the hatchet?"

"Huh?" Detective Gallagher said, surprised by what Tory said.

"It almost looks as if he cooperated. I mean look at the four bloodstains. Two for the arms and two for the legs. Four neat bloodstains."

"What are you, Jessica Fletcher? They shot him then chopped him, huh?"

"I don't know how they killed him, but he sure as hell wasn't fighting." Detective Gallagher was silent. "Any fingerprints?" Tory asked.

"Yeah. We got prints. Lots of 'em. Bloody prints around the couch that match prints from Silverman's bedroom, bathroom, kitchen. I know, I know, they're just prelims, Mrs. Fletcher, but if you doubt their accuracy we'll get a few more from his office. Believe me, they're Silverman's. Hey, betcha we get some of you, too, on the fridge."

"What about the blood type?"

"Try the crime lab in a couple of hours."

"I guess I'd feel less confused if there was a body to go along with the blood and fingerprints."

"We'll have one, unless they chopped him up into teensy little pieces and carried him out in a bunch of Hefty Bags."

"You don't think that's a possibility, do you?" Tory asked, horrified at the thought.

Gallagher let out a belly laugh. "Hell no. He'll show up. Lookee over here, Counselor." Gallagher stepped back and pointed to a large rectangular area of the carpet that was a shade brighter than the rest. "Maid informs us . . . by the way, you want to talk to her, be my guest. Hysterical broad. Anyway, the maid says somebody stole some expensive oriental carpet that sat on *top* of the wall-to-wall. Imagine that. Someone so rich he has carpet *on* the carpet. So my guess is he went out of here wrapped up like a burrito. Look, Miss . . . what's your name again?''

"Tory Welch.''

"This guy was asking for it, Miss Welch. I don't know if you saw the broadcast last night, but if I was one of the other parties involved in those murders up the Medical Center I woulda thought about popping him myself, the way he was flapping his mouth. What the Jews call chutzpah.''

"You know what he said in the broadcast was a bunch of lies,'' Tory said definitively.

"So?''

"So first he showed up in my office wanting immunity in exchange for information. I said no. A couple of hours later he goes live with Sandy Keller—the one you had Officer Curtis hustle out of here—and claims we're cozy. Now this.''

"As I said, he got what he deserved.''

"Then where's the body?'' Tory asked.

"Who the fuck knows?''

"Detective, help me out. Why would the killer remove the body yet leave such a mess?''

"Maybe they wanted to throw him off a bridge. How the hell should I know?''

"You didn't find anything else?''

"Goddamn. You're not going back to that Jell-O, are you? That is exactly why women can't focus on the facts of the crime. You want to know why the fuck he puts this much or that much Jell-O in a bowl.''

"I'm not hung up on the Jell-O, okay? I want to know if your crime team checked every nook and cranny in this house.''

"Yes, ma'am, we did. And if you don't believe we did a job worthy of your approval—and I don't give a flying fuck whether or not you do approve—then do it yourself.'' Gallagher was red in the face.

Tory struck the same pose that seemed to be Detective Gallagher's trademark, mouth held open like she was going to burst out in laughter.

Gallagher walked out of the room.

"Maybe I will look around a little,'' she said to herself. "That is, if you don't mind.''

23

The call came in after lunch. A body had been found in a small park in Aspinwall, mutilated beyond recognition. The deputy who brought in the body even joked that it might not be human. This was the kind of case Julian Plesser, the medical examiner for Allegheny County, loved. Meaty. One of God's puzzles.

At first telling it seemed like an incredible coincidence: a little girl walking a dog and one of the assistant district attorneys had come across the body. That in itself was a chuckle. Dead bodies were discovered by hunters traipsing through the woods. Or lovers looking for an out-of-the-way place to put down a blanket. Not ADAs going for a run in a public park.

But when Julian found out that the ADA was his friend, Tory Welch, he smiled, knowing she would probably be on her way over before he finished.

Julian was a stout fireplug of a man who kept himself in excellent shape for a fifty-two-year-old, running six miles a day, every day, in perpetual training for Pittsburgh's Great Race.

He had first met Tory when she was a couple weeks out of law school and was dragged to the morgue for her first view of a dead body. Since then they had become friends, although not discovering their mutual love of running until spotting one another at lunchtime one day running through the park where the Allegheny and the Monongahela meet to form the Ohio.

At least once a week Tory joined Julian for a noontime run. All too often he would ask the same nagging matrimonial questions about Merlin that her father might. That's when she would take the pace from a comfortable six-and-a-half-minute mile down to five-forty-five, leaving her avuncular—and nosy—friend huffing as she tore away from him.

Each Monday Julian started the week with a freshly laundered, four button lab coat. Keen observers of the coroner's office could probably guess it was Thursday by the dinginess of the white fabric when Julian entered the autopsy room to meet John Doe. The armpits were the worst, discolored with huge yellow stains from Julian's gloved hands taking axillary respite whenever he stopped to think.

Before Julian Plesser even started on John Doe, his hands found themselves tucked into his armpits, the sine qua non that this would prove to be a tough one.

The autopsy room was on the second floor of the coroner's office, a short walk from the County Courthouse. The decor never changed: gray cinder block walls the sad color of a Friday lab coat, the artificial glare of fluorescent lights, and the three stainless steel dissection tables. There was one new addition to the drab room. A framed feature article from the *Pittsburgh Post Gazette,* dry mounted, with the title "Solving God's Puzzle." It had been written almost two years earlier about the medical examiner and was presented to him by Tory at the start of their friendship.

John Doe was a member of a unique group of autopsy room denizens. Only rarely did someone take up residence on two of the three stainless steel tables at the same time. Each table was set at a slight angle so that a constant trickle of water would wash away the fluids as they spilled out of the body. The first table held John Doe's clothes, sticky with blood, folded up inside a large plastic bag, waiting for someone from the crime lab to collect them. The only bit of useful information that could be garnered from the clothing were the initials L.D.S. They were sewn on the inside of the jacket in one-and-one-half-inch rectangular letters, like a name tag in camp clothing, as though someone who bought his clothing at J. Press could actually lose a jacket.

On the middle table, Julian's main workstation, was the naked body of John Doe, supine, skin the color of moldy bread, a face transformed by a beating into a Picasso painting come to life. His four truncated extremities suggested an era when thalidomide was prescribed for pregnant women. For lack of the appropriate place, sitting on John Doe's abdomen was the toe tag, bearing the number 89 in black grease pencil. Each corpse had to be identified. Without a securely affixed ID tag Julian knew he could be accused of sloppy work, so he donned gloves as he debated how to attach the toe tag. First he considered making a couple of punch incisions somewhere in the lower extremity so he could feed the string from the toe tag through. But toe tags were always tied around something, so he looped it around John Doe's penis and knotted the string securely.

Now he was officially John Doe number 89.

On the third table, behind Julian, was the finger that had been dangling like a stogie from John Doe's mouth, sitting in a little metal bowl. There was also the police report, sitting next to the finger bowl, soaking up some liquid that probably shouldn't have been there.

Julian often spent a long time examining the outside of a body. His gloved hands would explore every part of John Doe before a scalpel was taken to him.

It was impossible not to do the extremities first. Julian had a sequence that he followed, but when something caught his eye he could not resist. One by one he picked up the arms and legs, wiping away the clotted gelatinous blood, examining the radius and ulna, the tibia and fibula, the tendons and muscles, seeing them in cross section like a picture in an anatomy book. With the aid of a powerful magnifying glass, he carefully inspected the edges and concluded each had been created by an anterior-posterior blow by something very sharp.

Even for a big city medical examiner it was difficult to look at the face of John Doe. It appeared to have been beaten by a blunt object. A baseball bat was what everyone thought of, but over the years Julian had seen crowbars, table legs, and one time an icicle used to pummel someone to death. When he palpated the skull it had the feel of a melon that was ripe two weeks ago. Soft and squishy, the bones were broken and broken again until the skin of the face and the scalp were all that held things in place. Where the epidermis had burst apart chunks of muscle, bone, and even some grayish material that could have been brain were oozing out.

At the left temple, almost hidden in the skin folds next to a deep laceration, was a small hole, no bigger than Julian's little finger.

A bullet hole.

Now that seemed odd.

Julian turned the head to the left. Rigor mortis, the rigidity of the muscles after death that lasted six to eight hours, had disappeared. John Doe's head was as easy to manipulate as if he were a rag doll. Sure enough, there was a second hole, the exit wound, on the right side of the cranium. Only this was no pinkie-sized hole. The bullet changed shape on its path through the brain and left the body considerably wider than when it entered, taking a quarter-sized chunk of skull with it.

The body's nose was flat, not like a boxer's, but more like a cartoon character who had been hit in the face with a frying pan. Julian went to examine the eyes, but the swelling was too great to see anything, so he had to work the upper lid away from the lower with his fingers. Both orbits had burst in the beating. The lens of the left eye protruded from the pupil sideways.

A mortal bullet wound. A deadly beating. And a mutilation.

Why?

While Julian pondered what would prove to be an unanswerable question he noticed something about the mouth. The lips were swollen but hardly bruised. Amazingly, when he gently worked the mouth open he found it to be almost perfectly intact. Only the right upper central incisor had been traumatized, broken in half.

The rest of the mouth was perfect.

Now there were two sets of "fingerprints" to go on.

Blaine Huffman sat next to his wife in the little study on the second floor of their home. Sandy Keller was doing yet another live broadcast. It had been one of those days when it was impossible to get any work done, the news from Squirrel Hill occupying all his thoughts.

By mid-morning every station with a local news staff was creating bulletins out of tidbits of information they'd pieced together from snippets of conversation heard on their police scanners. Only Sandy had something different to say. Her first broadcast came from the foot of Woodmont. She'd breathlessly described that someone had been hiding in a rhododendron bush behind the house, apparently waiting for Leonard Silverman to arrive home after her broadcast with him.

Of course Huffman was used to hearing his business activities described and analyzed on the news. This was different. Hearing a dramatic description of how he lay in wait behind the rhododendron bush left him breathing hard, a cold glaze of sweat on his forehead. As much as he wanted to call up Sandy Keller and set her straight as to what had really happened, he made no effort to grab the phone.

Sandy was now reporting live from the little park in Aspinwall where the body had been found early that afternoon. The Huffmans sat close together on the love seat, her hand on his leg.

It was getting dark. The wind kept pushing Sandy's hair in her face. Except for some kids who walked back and forth in the background trying to get on camera, the park was empty. Huffman leaned forward, getting a good look at the site as the camera dramatically showed where the tall grass had been pressed to the ground in a crude outline of where the body had been found.

Cynthia's shoulders sagged. Blotches of blue encircled her eyes like sloppily applied makeup. Her dress looked one size too big. Not even the breaking news about the mastermind of the Medical Center murders held her interest. Instead, her eyes drifted to an oil painting of Kit on a wooden bench holding a bouquet of yellow and white flowers.

"Blaine?" Cynthia said, needing some comfort.

He looked at her and saw the tears in her eyes. Slipping his arm around her shoulders, he asked, "You okay?"

"You don't have," she paused, choosing her words, "another meeting tonight, do you?" Her voice wavered, as if she might cry.

The image on the television had changed. Now there was a clip of Tory Welch wearing running gear, turning down an interview with Sandy.

Huffman picked up the remote control and zapped the television into darkness. He wanted to tell her everything, but couldn't.

They sat for a long time in the cozy little room where Cynthia used to read to Kit after dinner. It was impossible for either of them to look at the painting without thinking about what might have happened last night.

Just before Tory pushed through the double doors of the autopsy room she heard Julian's voice coming from down the hallway. She ventured toward his tiny office and stood in the doorway watching the medical examiner standing by his desk, talking on the phone, his back toward her.

"I know the press is saying it's Silverman, Mayor. Let them speculate. But at this point the only concrete thing I've got is his initials sewn into his suit jacket."

Julian turned, spotting Tory, and offered up a friendly little wave. He mouthed the words "the mayor."

Tory nodded and stood in the doorway. She was wearing a blazer and pleated skirt. Julian winked at her playfully, then wrinkled his brow, pointing to her right hand which held a brown-paper lunch bag.

Julian's focus suddenly snapped back to his phone conversation. "In the next hour or so I'll have fingerprint analysis and blood-typing. The forensic dentist's on his way—" Julian was interrupted by the mayor. For more than a minute Julian just listened, getting in only an occasional "Yes, Mayor," finally shrugging his shoulders, letting Tory know he might be tied up for a while.

Tory gave him a little wave and headed for the autopsy room.

If there were other sights and sounds to notice when she pushed through the double doors Tory was completely unaware of them. Immediately she spotted the corpse, lying on the middle table, faceup. He was naked. The expensive clothing that had seemed oversized in the park no longer hid the stumps. The gelatinous blood had been wiped away. Tory now had an unobstructed view of the legs, ending abruptly, just where the ankles should have begun.

She walked closer, aware of her heart beating in her chest and her lungs pulling in air. Briefly she noticed the toe tag. Her eyes immediately worked back down the thighs, over the knobby knees, to the shins, where the amputations occurred. In her mind's eye she could see the hatchet coming down on his leg, cutting through it like a salami. The tibia and smaller fibula, creamy-white circles of bone with crimson-brown centers, were wrapped tightly in slips of silvery-pink tendons.

She placed the brown-paper lunch bag next to the little metal bowl with the finger. Instantly one hand clamped over her mouth. "Oh, my God," she said in a whisper. Shuddering, she looked away, remembering precisely how he'd looked in the park with the finger in his mouth. His stark nakedness made the mutilation seem all the more brutal. She half closed her eyes when she dared a glance at his face, looking through her eyelashes, taming the scene as if it were a grainy photograph.

But even in her fuzzy view, the body had no hands and no feet.

As much as she didn't want to, all she could think of was Leonard Silverman, naked, on his elbows and knees, protecting his bloody stumps from contact with anything, screaming in pain and horror.

Suddenly, the door opened and a man in his early fifties, dressed in a dark suit and somber tie, strode into the autopsy room carrying a large leather attaché case. The first thing Tory noticed was his hair. It was perfect. A crisp part, every strand precisely and perfectly in place, and not a hint of gray.

Of course Tory knew exactly what excessively perfect hair in a fifty-year-old man meant.

The man took one look at the body and shook his head slightly. Although not the least bit overweight, he looked soft, like someone for whom competition meant getting the best parking spot in the lot. Then he looked at Tory and said, "Please tell Julian I'm here," in a condescending tone of voice he probably also used when asking the busboy for more water in a restaurant.

Before Tory could utter a word, before she could say that Julian was on the phone with the mayor, the man walked over to the paper towel dispenser above the sink and pulled, pulled, pulled almost a dozen towels.

"Well?" he said, jutting out his wimpy chin, staring hard at Tory, wondering why she was still standing there. "I don't have all day."

"He's on the phone with the mayor. I'm—"

The man stood there, holding his briefcase in one hand, jerking his other hand away from his body so his watch would appear from under his sleeve, and shaking his head when he saw the time. "He says six o'clock, he should mean six o'clock."

"—Tory Welch. Are you the forensic dentist?"

"Forensic odontologist," he corrected. "Why?"

"I heard him mention you to the mayor."

"The mayor," he said sarcastically.

"I'm certain he'll be here any minute—"

"You know, in real life I'm a reconstructive dentist. I do *everyone*," he said, making it clear that "everyone" was a collective term that referred to his very exclusive patients. "I do the forensics as a . . . community service. Two hundred dollars to come up here. It costs more for my girls to process the check I get. My travel time, parking—" While he talked he was working with the paper towels, placing half of them on Julian's little desk, moving several of them until he was satisfied there were no gaps in the barrier. Only then did he trust his briefcase on what he must have considered a filthy surface. The other towels were draped over the back of the accompanying chair. When he was comfortable that he'd created a sterile enough boundary, he removed his suit jacket, carefully placing it over the towels. Checking his work from several angles, he nodded to himself.

"I'm Tory Welch," she offered for the second time, "from the DA's office."

He paused. "I heard you the first time. Victor Hamburgh." He spoke in an affected manner, as if he traveled abroad often and had picked up some European flair. When he said "Hamburgh" he pronounced it more like "Hahmborg" than the way Ronald McDonald might. He took a second look at his elegant gold watch before he slipped it off his wrist and dropped it into his pocket. "I really can't wait around for Julian." Victor looked at Tory, who was still standing by the third dissection table picking up a manila folder as she read from its label.

Tory opened the folder and pulled out some photocopies. "These must be for you," she said, approaching Victor.

"What is it?" he sounded bored.

"It says these are Leonard D. Silverman's dental records," Tory answered, and offered them to Victor.

"You imbecile," Victor said angrily, turning his head sharply to one side. "If I see those records Julian won't use my testimony and this trip will be an even bigger waste of my time. What's wrong with you?"

Tory recoiled at being talked to so rudely. "You're the forensic odontologist," she answered coldly.

"When you say you're from the DA's office, what are you, a courier?"

"Assistant DA."

"Thank you for nothing," he said curtly. "Look, if I see the dental records *before* I do the exam some hotshot lawyer will accuse me of being biased. My exam is always done cold. Remove them immediately from my line of sight."

Tory took several steps backward, positioning herself near the dissection table where she had found the dental records.

Temporarily Victor busied himself opening his briefcase, the two brass latches snapping loudly. "This the one they found in that park?" he questioned, bringing Tory back into his conversation rather than offering an apology. From the briefcase he produced a crisply laundered lab coat. Holding it by the collar as it unfolded, he then slipped both arms into the sleeves and buttoned it to the neck.

"Yes. This afternoon."

"You suppose he's been dead for more than eight hours?" Victor opened a package of sterile gloves and donned them.

"Well, it's been four hours since he was—"

Victor wanted a yes or no answer. Ignoring Tory, he picked up a pen from the desk—evidently one of Julian's—and went over to John Doe number 89 and used it to push open the mouth. The lower jaw flopped open easily. Victor nodded. "Good. I hate rigor mortis. Like opening an oyster." Then he flipped Julian's pen back on the desk. "Where is he?"

Not waiting for an answer, he went back to his briefcase and carefully removed a piece of equipment that Tory had never seen before. He fiddled with a small metal unit—a halogen light source—which was no bigger than a Kleenex box. Once he'd found a plug near the desk, he set the unit back inside his open attaché case and picked up his headgear. It looked like a high-tech version of a miner's headlamp, but was made of blue plastic and had a knob on the side to adjust its size. Instead of a dim lightbulb, a fiber-optic cable ran from the light source, up Victor's back, and connected with the headset posteriorly, arcing gently over his head, ending in a lens just above his forehead that would focus the intense light wherever he looked.

Victor worked with excessive care placing the gear onto his head. Initially he held it above his cranium, giving it the appearance of a halo, then lowered it precisely so his coiffure remained undisturbed. Comfortable with its position, Victor tightened the knob on the side, flipped the switch on the light source, and swiveled his head back and forth, making certain the light was aimed correctly.

The last thing Victor Hamburgh did before turning his attention to

John Doe was add the additional protection of a second set of surgical gloves.

"Okay, miss, open the dental record."

"Excuse me?" Tory sounded surprised.

"We're going to check his dental fingerprint. I'm going to tell you what I find, you're going to read the chart and confirm or deny a match."

Tory opened the manila folder. Leonard Silverman's entire dental record was summarized in a complicated schematic of the mouth. The outline of each tooth, rendered in order, was displayed on a series of musical staffs. It was a dental symphony, the crowns drawn as empty circled half notes with long roots, lined up neatly just above or below the staff, a monotonous melody of molars and incisors. Many of the teeth had hand-drawn notations, X's, dots, and triangles, all of which meant nothing to Tory.

"All right, miss. Dental 101. Each tooth has a number." Victor pointed just below his right ear. "Starting here, number one, the wisdom tooth." As he moved his finger around his cheek toward his nose he said, "Two, three, four, five, six, seven, eight." Then he touched below his left ear, "Sixteen."

"Also a wisdom tooth."

"Yes . . . also a wisdom tooth. Seventeen is below sixteen, also on the left, running around to thirty-two, right beneath number one."

Tory looked at the schematic of Leonard Silverman's mouth. "I don't know. Let's give Julian another minute or two."

"I've been very generous with my time. What time is it anyway?"

"About two minutes since you checked your watch the last time, which was about three minutes after you walked through the door."

"Then go find him."

Tory hesitated. "Start your exam, Dr. Hamburgh," she said, reducing his name to an all-beef patty.

"I start with the wisdom teeth first."

"That would be one, sixteen, seventeen, and thirty-two."

Victor ignored the comment. He turned to John Doe, but the fiber-optic cable just wouldn't behave. Although designed to run unobtrusively down his back, the cable flopped around and got in the way. He had to hold out one elbow to keep it from touching the dissection table. "This won't work," he complained. He reached into his briefcase. "Here, attach the cable to my back," he said and handed Tory a roll of white adhesive tape. Then he held out a doubly gloved finger and looked Tory in the eye. "And you be careful with the headgear."

Even if Victor was a jerk, there was no reason not to cooperate. As he turned around, Tory ripped off a length of tape. But as she positioned the cable down Hamburgh's spine she gave it a little tug to the right, just enough to shift the headgear.

Victor spun around. "I told you. Be careful!" he snapped. Both hands shot up to his head, but fearing his gloves were contaminated he held them next to the headgear, never actually touching it.

The halogen light shined right in Tory's eyes so that she had to squint to see the results of her handiwork. As the headgear shifted slightly, so did Victor's hairpiece. His toupee bunched up like the battered scalp of John Doe. Now he was sporting a mini-pompadour.

"You done?" he demanded.

"Almost. Turn around," Tory directed and gave the fiber-optic cable one final tug, again moving the headgear, puffing up the pompadour a bit more. *Now all you need is a '57 Chevy and a drive-in restaurant.*

Victor was furious, staring at Tory balefully. Fortunately, Tory tamed her smile. After a long, uncomfortable silence he bent over and opened the mouth of John doe. "Ready?" he demanded.

"Yes."

"One, sixteen, seventeen, and thirty-two are absent."

Tory referred to the schematic. "Each of those teeth has an X through it."

"That means they're absent."

"Sorry, I must have missed the class when you reviewed dental shorthand."

Victor continued. "Three has a temporary filling. Mmmm. Not much wear on it. I'd say less than a month old."

"On number three it says 'temp.' "

"Ooooh," Victor said sarcastically. "Do you think that could be short for 'temporary'?"

The door opened. Julian Plesser walked into the room reading from a piece of paper in his hand. When he spotted Tory and Victor working together he observed, "I see you two've met."

"And it's been lovely," Victor said, not even looking at Tory. "We've established the wisdom teeth are absent. Can *we* get started, Julian?"

"Nice to see you, too, Victor."

Victor, who until now had remained bent over, stood to his full height, showing off his new hairstyle in the process. Julian glanced at Tory, who shook her head subtly as she winked.

"And one more thing," Victor whined. "You've got that . . . that digit sitting over there."

"Ah, yes, you spotted my finger bowl."

Tory laughed. Victor did not.

"Look, Julian, if you knew who the hell this guy was well enough to subpoena his dental records, why didn't you just run his prints for God's sake?"

"Simple," Tory said, stepping forward to join the conversation. "The finger could have been damaged. Right now we don't even know if the finger and the body go together."

Victor recoiled.

Julian beamed. "Lovely, yes, but brilliant."

Tory looked right at Victor when she said, "Forensics 101." With a triumphant smile she handed Silverman's dental records to Julian.

Victor's delicate complexion had reddened considerably. Controlling his emotions was an effort. "Are we ready?"

"Hit it, Elvis." Julian chuckled, and Tory had to bite her lip.

Once again Victor bent over the corpse's mouth. "One, sixteen, seventeen, thirty-two: missing."

"I already confirmed that," Tory chided.

Julian looked at the dental schematic. "Yep, yep, yep, yep."

"You mentioned on the phone a Class Three fracture of number eight. Of course it's acute. Rough edges, definitely happened during the beating," Victor stated. "Next, number three: occlusal temporary."

Julian used his finger to find what he was looking for on the page. "Got it."

"Number twelve: occlusal amalgam. Number nineteen: buccal pit amalgam."

"Got it. Got it," Julian said, touching two separate points on the page.

"And number thirty: gold crown."

"That, too," Julian said.

"Guy took care of his teeth," Victor concluded. "The work on the crown is first-rate."

"Anything else?"

This time Victor took his time answering, checking the upper and lower teeth, shining his halogen headlight all around John Doe's mouth. "No. That's it. You have anything else?"

"A match," Julian said, pulling a sheet of paper from his lab coat pocket. "Wanna see the fingerprint analysis?"

"You *have* the fingerprint analysis?" Victor wailed, shaking his head furiously, dancing the halogen light about the autopsy room.

"Blood-typing, too."

"Good Lord, Julian. Why don't you and Miss Snippy here go to hell.'' Victor snapped off his gloves, loosened the knob on the headgear, and carefully removed it from his head. His hair resettled, taking most of the pomp out of his pompadour. While the lighted headgear dangled from the back of his lab coat, he unbuttoned it, detached the fiber-optic cable with a loud ripping noise, and quickly repacked his briefcase. Victor Hamburgh stormed out without another word.

Before the doors had fully closed Julian took one hand and ran it over an imaginary pompadour on his own head and shared a good laugh with Tory. Finally Tory said, ''So it's Silverman, isn't it?''

''The dentals are a match. It's Silverman.''

''What about the fingerprint analysis?''

''The fingerprint from the one digit we have—probably his index finger—matches prints taken from his house—television, hairbrush, a book jacket on his bedside table, his car—and several sources from his office.''

''That settles it.''

''I also wanted to link the body to the finger. I sent off a PCR test. Won't be available for days, so I ran a blood type on the body and the finger. Both AB positive.''

''The same.''

''But AB positive is four percent of the population.''

''So the blood type's not unique enough to firmly link the body and the finger.''

''Exactly, there's a four percent chance it could be a coincidence. I always run a simple blood-typing first to see if the samples are *grossly different*. Since they matched I have to narrow it down considerably, so I called a buddy at Central Blood Bank and had him run a minor antigen panel. Actually there are dozens of less well-known antigens which are proteins on the red blood cells. Some are quite rare. The exact combination of minor blood types an individual has creates a fairly specific blood fingerprint.''

''In other words you can tell if the blood from the finger and the body are one and the same.''

''Right. First I checked the entire panel of Rh antigens. His particular Rh pattern is a rare one, present in less than one tenth of a percent of the population. From there I checked the Kell, Duffy, Kidd, Lewis, MNS, P and Lutheran antigens. For every antigen I checked, the blood from the body and the finger matched perfectly. The chance of this being a coincidence is less than one in a million. The blood from the finger and the blood from the body are one and the same.''

''So that's it. Silverman's dentals, Silverman's index finger, and blood analysis that confirm the link between the body and the finger.''

"Of course, there are two other questions that need to be answered. First, why was he shot?"

"I wondered about that," Tory agreed.

"Incidentally, he was shot *before* he was beaten. The wounds have incredibly sharp margins and there's precise symmetry between the amputation site from left to right. Too hard to do with someone struggling. Toxicology shows he wasn't drugged. I saw the crime photos. There was an impressive spray of blood on the wall, probably from a severed artery. So, why shoot him?" Julian asked again.

"Maybe the symmetry was important to the killer. You know, obsessive-compulsive."

"Could be," Julian agreed. "Why do you think he was moved? That's the big one."

"Simple," Tory began, speaking calmly. "It was no coincidence that I found him. He's a calling card. Didn't you see the interview with Sandy Keller the other night?"

"Yeah, the finger in the mouth. I already thought about it. He said he was going to point his finger at the guilty parties. Somebody being cute."

"He was threatening to talk, so he was silenced and his finger was shoved in his mouth. Not exactly subtle symbolism."

"Why you?"

"A warning. Scare me off the case. Since Silverman bragged that I was dealing in immunity for testimony, the warning was for me."

"And we all know what that means," Julian said ironically.

"Don't start with me, Julian." Tory decided it was time to change the subject. She picked up the brown lunch bag from the third autopsy table. "I want your opinion." Tory opened the bag and pulled out one of the little glass dessert dishes containing the skimpy portion of red Jell-O. Only this one had a light coating of what looked like off-white frosting.

Julian took one look at it and said, "What's that, a culture plate?"

"I think it's Jell-O."

"Where'd you get it?"

"Silverman's basement. He had a slew of them in his kitchen refrigerator without the stuff growing on top. This one was on a workbench in the basement."

Julian smelled it. "Once upon a time it was strawberry." He sniffed again. "It's covered with mold and bacteria. It looks like he was making his own culture medium. Whenever Jell-O has hardened in the refrigerator it becomes quite stable at room temperature."

"Tell me what this is." Tory reached back into the bag and brought out a small spray bottle labeled 1:10. She unscrewed the cap and offered it to Julian, who sniffed it.

"An antibiotic. Maybe one of the penicillins." He read the label. "One to ten. Hmmm. He was making antibiotic dilutions."

"Why?"

Julian leaned against his autopsy table and pondered. Finally his eyes brightened. "It fits. He was culturing bacteria in his basement, exposing them to increasing amounts of antibiotics, creating super bacteria that were used to kill the patients at the Medical Center."

"On Jell-O?"

"Well, I bet it's doctored up a bit. He probably had to add some baking soda to make it less acidic. Maybe some extra protein. But Jell-O would work. Actually it's very clever. He didn't want to keep ordering culture plates from a supply house all the time and create a paper trail. The start-up colonies could have been obtained years ago, but the culture plates would have to be ordered over and over."

"So Silverman's the mastermind, not an innocent bystander. But he's not the only one involved. Whoever did this wants his secret buried with Leonard Silverman. And I know just where to start."

24

"Sandy Keller," the news reporter spoke crisply into her cell phone. This morning she was standing on the steps of the City-County Building, waiting to go live, a good two hours before the noon news. After the usual "Who are you?" and "How did you come by this information?" Sandy listened intently for more than a minute. Several times she nodded. Once she smiled broadly. When she'd heard everything the caller had to say she giggled once, then asked, "Really, what flavor?" Finally she snapped the tiny phone closed, slipping it back into the side pocket of her bright red blazer as she whispered to herself, "Hmmm. Strawberry."

Holding one hand above her eyes to block out the brilliant sun, Sandy bragged to her cameraman, "It's like a winning streak at Vegas. I'm hot. You want to know how I know?"

It was cold outside, and the cameraman really didn't give a shit, but he shrugged, knowing damn well he was going to hear anyway.

Sandy was dressed for style not comfort. Trying to keep warm, she shifted her weight back and forth from one foot to the other. "When someone's got a tip—not some crap that'll take three weeks to ferret out—but something you can sink your teeth into—and"—Sandy slowed down dramatically—"they choose you over every other reporter in the city. That's brand name. And brand name is hot, baby." Now she knew about the Jell-O, not from Julian Plesser, but from a friend of a friend of his secretary. If anyone asked, and Sandy hoped they would, she'd play coy and talk about her sources as if there was a vast network she had cultivated. There was no way she could resist mentioning the Jell-O. For now it would be a teaser.

"Sandy, we're on in fifteen seconds," her cameraman said, hoisting his heavy camera to his shoulder.

A small crowd had gathered around Sandy, watching her every move. She fussed with her hair, putting on a good show. These were her fans, middle-aged women in drab clothing, the little people against whom Sandy positively sparkled.

Suddenly something caught her eye: a chubby woman smiling broadly. But what Sandy could not resist was what she held in her hand: a small notepad, opened to a clean page, and a pen. There was only one thing this could mean.

Now her cameraman said, "Okay, Sandy, in five—"

Sandy quickly stepped over to the woman—

"—four—"

—stowing the microphone under her arm—

"—three—"

—smiling as she scribbled her signature—

"—two—"

—underlining her name with a squiggle as she smoothly handed the notebook and pen back to the plump lady.

"—and one—"

Sandy started speaking while strolling back to her mark, affecting the air of a busy news reporter just torn away from a breaking investigation. "I'm standing in front of the City-County Building where yesterday lawyers for billionaire businessman Blaine Huffman filed a lawsuit in excess of one-hundred million dollars against Western Insurance Co. of Pennsylvania. Mr. Huffman's daughter Kit, who died recently following routine surgery at the Pittsburgh University Medical Center, is believed to have been one of the last persons to have been murdered in what has been dubbed the Kevorkian Society Murders."

The Kevorkian Society Murders. Although Sandy cautiously referred to it in the past tense—as though it were already in vogue—she was attempting to add her own moniker to the lexicon of the city. She had planned this all morning. Nowhere before had anyone called the Medical Center murders the Kevorkian Society Murders, but Sandy was hot.

"With the recent arrest of Nicholas Bello, an operating room nurse at the Medical Center, and the televised statements by recently murdered WIP Medical Director Leonard Silverman, it has become increasingly evident that officials at WIP insurance were responsible for the series of deaths at the Medical Center.

"In related news I've discovered a curious Jell-O connection to the Kevorkian Society Murders. Join me at noon, when I will have this and other stories. This is Sandy Keller, reporting live."

* * *

Tory stepped off the elevator at the executive offices of Western Insurance Company of Pennsylvania and almost bumped into Detective Gallagher.

"Excuse me," she blurted out before recognizing the detective.

"Don't waste your time," he growled. "He's so scared he can't drink his friggin' coffee." The detective was holding a Brannock Device, the classic model used by every shoe salesman to measure foot size, and a pair of brown wing tips, one shoe dangling from each of two fingers. Holding the shoes up momentarily as though he'd beaten Tory to them, Gallagher brushed past her and boarded the elevator. " 'Member I told you we'd find a body? Now I'll predict we'll have an arrest in the next twenty-four hours."

Ding. The elevator doors closed, and Tory realized how quiet it was. Like a cemetery. No one talking. Silent telephones. Three secretaries at three desks, guarding the executive suite of offices, two of them reading, one staring out the window.

Tory tentatively approached the secretary sitting closest to the elevators. She was a middle-aged woman reading a romance novel. Leaving Tory standing in front of the desk as if she were invisible, she refused to look up.

Tory cleared her throat.

The secretary turned the page.

"Excuse me," Tory said.

The secretary turned another page. It was obvious the cold shoulder was deliberate.

"I'm Tory Welch from the district attorney's office." She spoke with authority. "I need to see Mr. Graham. Now." Tory noticed the spotless desk. No work was in progress. Her computer screen was dark. And the mute telephone, without a single line blinking, had been unplugged.

The secretary looked up sadly and said not one word to her. As if she might cry, she covered her mouth and pointed toward the only office with an open door.

Frederick Graham was sitting at his desk in shirtsleeves, his chair pushed back several feet. For the longest time he did not seem to notice Tory standing in his doorway. He was staring down at the floor.

From across the room it was obvious to Tory what Gallagher had been talking about: Graham's white shirt had a huge brown stain on it. There were two cups and saucers on the desk, otherwise it was empty. Tory wondered whether the one closer to Graham had more coffee in the saucer or the cup. "Mr. Graham?" Tory said.

Graham looked up at her with red eyes. "Yes." His voice quavered. "I'm with the DA's office. My name is Tory Welch."

"They were just here." He paused. "The cops. Detective Gallagher." Tory almost smiled. "I know. Saw him at the elevator."

"Had one of those things at a shoe store. You know, for measuring your size. Took my shoes."

"May I sit down?" Tory asked, already crossing the room toward a plush chair facing the desk.

"Why did he take my shoes?" Graham wondered, looking down at his feet.

"Mr. Graham," Tory said a bit louder, trying to get his attention, avoiding any speculation of why the police wanted his shoes.

"How'm I supposed to get home?"

"Mr. Graham!" Tory said, her voice ascending to a sharp crescendo. Graham looked at Tory, his eyes open wide as though he were surprised someone was in his office. "What? What do *you* want?"

Pulling one of her cards from her bag, Tory decided to start over. Placing it on the desk, she repeated, "I'm an assistant district attorney. I have to ask you some questions."

"I didn't have anything to do with it. Would you mind leaving?"

"You didn't have anything to do with what?" Tory asked.

"Anything. The murders. Lenny. Nothing. I knew the numbers looked too good, but Lenny said he was watching the docs in our panel, not letting them do unnecessary tests."

"Did you know Dr. Silverman was doing anything to the patients?"

Graham stared at Tory like she was crazy. "God, no. He scared me sometimes. Talking about sex and everything. But he never said anything about killing people." Graham rubbed his eyes. "I was holding on for the big announcement."

Tory wondered whether he was trying to mix her up. "What announcement?"

"The buyout. A group from Connecticut was going to take us over." Tory sat forward. "Tell me more about it."

"It happens all the time. M and A's. Merger and acquisitions. Believe it or not, the deal's not off yet," he said bitterly. "No way. And I'm their ticket." Graham looked toward his open door. "The board is meeting right now to see if things can be salvaged."

"Don't you usually attend the board meetings?"

Graham laughed. "I used to. I was asked—no told, and not politely— to wait here. Word is someone's gonna get hung out to dry. Guess who?" He pointed to himself. "Doesn't take a genius to figure out the plan. I'm just waiting for the word so I can go home. Of course they'll need to bring in someone immediately to restore the public confidence in WIP." Then quietly he added, "I betcha I know who they're tapping."

"Who?"

Graham shook his head. "No way," he said, clinging to whatever shred of hope he had that this might not be his last day. "Let's just say someone with silver hair and impeccable credentials." Abruptly his voice turned angry. Every muscle in his face tightened, both hands balled up into taut fists, and his dry lips parted to expose tightly clenched teeth. "Forget it." He smacked his fist against his leg.

Graham's breathing was labored, as if he'd just run a mile. For a while he turned his attention to his wet shirt, pulling it away from his chest, fanning it back and forth as if he were expecting it to dry. When he tired of this he shook his head hard, fighting the unseen demons inside.

"You okay?" Tory asked, sliding forward on her chair so she was balanced on the edge.

"Oh, sure, I'm okay. They're in there. I'm in here. Why shouldn't I be okay? You okay?" Graham sniffed loudly. "Look, Lenny was always the darling. I was the damned workhorse."

They sat quietly for almost a minute.

Graham looked at her through pathetic eyes. "What did he say to you?"

"Who?"

"Lenny. I saw that interview he gave. He was gonna blame me, wasn't he?"

"I don't know."

"Didn't he come to deal with you earlier in the day?"

"I didn't offer him a deal."

Graham stared at her. "Yeah, right. Lenny was number one here. I'm the CEO, but he was number one. He had to be blaming me. Christ, two of the board members grilled me last night over the phone. You know what? It doesn't matter. It . . . doesn't . . . matter. They kept saying, 'Why didn't you know what the hell was happening?' "

"Did you have any idea?"

"Of course not." His hand came up to his nose as he sniffed in loudly, thinking about his sad future. "Would *you* hire me?"

Tory sat like a statue.

"Go on, tell me." Freddy began to cry. "If you were hiring, would you hire me?" He waited for a response. When none came he continued. "I've got three kids. The oldest is a sophomore. Wants to go to Michigan. You know how much I have in the bank? Ninety-two thousand, eight hundred, forty-three dollars. Exactly. I *owe* double that on my house.''

"Mr. Graham," Tory said gently.

"Shit! That fucker did me in. He almost ruined my marriage. Got me thinking 'bout sex all the time. And money. God, did I think about money.'' He was talking faster and faster. "You know what I used to do? You wanna know? I used to sit here at night.'' He reached into the drawer for the second time and produced his calculator. "I used to punch a one," he said, giving one of the pads a vicious jab. "Then I'd hit a three and five zeros.'' Jab. Jab. Jab. Jab. Jab. Jab. "That's what I got in the buyout. That's all I thought about. When that Huffman kid died, somehow I knew the zeros were going to disappear. That was the beginning of things getting out of control. I don't know why, but it scared the crap outta me.''

"Why did it scare you so much?''

"Blaine Huffman. Shit, I figured there'd be a big public brouhaha, and the deal with Connecticut Insurance would disappear. I wanted it so badly. All those zeros. Oh, God, I could taste it. Our numbers were always okay. That little girl didn't have to die. She didn't have to die. So what if the buyout was a little less. I mean . . . I coulda lived like a king on seven hundred fifty thousand. Even after taxes.'' Graham stopped babbling and reached for his coffee cup. His hand was shaking so badly he had to steady it with his other one. Coffee was dripping from the bottom of the china, but he didn't seem to notice. The cup approached his puckered lips, and he sucked cold coffee noisily into his mouth.

Moving in slow motion, he wiped his mouth on the back of his hand while he reached for his desk drawer. Just as his fingers disappeared inside the pencil drawer, Tory had a vision of Graham pulling out a gun.

Jumping to her feet, Tory put both hands on the desk and leaned over it. "Goddamn it, don't you dare.''

Graham quickly closed the drawer partway. Whatever his hand was doing, it was now hidden from view. "What? What shouldn't I do?'' he demanded, raising his voice for the first time.

"Right now, you stop. Take your hand out of the drawer!''

"Why?''

"Now! Do it *now*!'' Tory screamed, certain one of the silent secretaries would come running.

"No," he said defiantly, working his hand around the drawer.

"GRAHAM. GET YOUR HAND WHERE I CAN SEE IT!'' Tory

balanced herself on one hand as she reached across the desk for Graham's wrist.

With a single push of his stocking feet on the floor, he rolled his chair away from the desk, pulling his hand from the shallow pencil drawer. Scrunched up between his fingers was a Kleenex which he quickly brought to his nose and blew into. "See? See? Kleenex."

Tory didn't stop. Now she was halfway across the desk, working the drawer open.

Among the pencils, calculator, Lifesavers, and paper clips was a small revolver.

"Leave it alone! I wasn't going to use it on you."

Tory removed the weapon and sat down. "That's not what I was afraid of."

"Check it out. I didn't use it on Silverman, either, if that's what you think. I've never even shot it. What are you gonna do? Call Gallagher? Tell him I threatened you?"

"You didn't threaten me."

Graham paused. "I couldn't have killed Silverman. I was in Cleveland. Cleveland! I drove back into the city early yesterday morning. That's when I heard about what the maid found at his house."

"So if you were in Cleveland, how did you know what he said in the interview?"

"You want to catch me, don't you?"

"How did you find out?"

"My wife called me in my hotel room. Long-distance," he said. Then he looked toward the doorway and raised his voice. "Ellen, Ellen, come in here a minute, will you?"

Immediately a woman hurried into the office. "Yes, Mr. Graham."

"Mr. Graham," Freddy said wistfully as if he had snuck a peek into the future and knew he was going to lose the respectful way people addressed him. He took a cleansing breath. "This is my secretary," he said by way of introduction. "Ellen, two things. First of all, call MCI and have them generate a phone log of all long-distance calls so far this month from my home. Second, please give"—he reached across the desk for the card—"Miss Welch my itinerary for the past forty-eight hours."

"Mr. Graham was attending an insurance conference in Cleveland. Would you care to see his appointment book?"

"And when did I arrive back in Pittsburgh?"

"Yesterday, around eleven, I believe."

"I had an eleven-thirty here in my office. Thanks, Ellen."

"Yes, Mr. Graham." Ellen turned and left as quickly as she had come.

He sighed. "I'm gonna miss her," he said. Then he placed both hands on his desk and rubbed it gently. "Do you believe me?"

"It's easy for me to check on things in Cleveland. I'm certain Ellen will provide me with the hotel information, people who saw you at the conference."

"And if it all checks out, then what?"

"A series of innocent people were killed at the Medical Center. I want to know who killed them. And I want to know why." Tory stood and walked out the door.

25

The whole way down in the elevator Detective Gallagher couldn't get Frederick Graham out of his mind. From the moment Gallagher walked into Graham's office with the Brannock Device saying, "Name's Gallagher. How'd you sleep last night?" he knew Graham had done it. It was in his eyes, guilty eyes that darted everywhere around the room but avoided the detective. When Graham finally cleared his throat, the first thing out of his mouth was a declaration that he wanted to cooperate fully with the police. So Gallagher said, "Why don't you scare up some coffee for us," and waited silently, letting Graham cross and uncross his legs a dozen times, until the secretary brought them each a dainty cup and saucer and poured the hot coffee. He waited for Graham to take his first sip before hitting him with, "So, what's this I hear about you doing Silverman the other night?" He took some perverse pleasure watching Graham spill his coffee all over his nice white shirt. Only then did he bring his own cup to his lips, taking a nice, slow sip. "Mmmmm. Good coffee. You can tell it's fresh brewed."

That's what he always did when he got a little momentum going, said something nice and chatty, letting the perp know he was playing with him.

Initially Graham was defensive; quickly he became angry. Finally he babbled on about spending the night in Cleveland. Gallagher looked at him hard and said, "Look, pal, Cleveland's what, a hundred thirty miles from the 'Burgh? I drove it in an hour forty-seven after a Browns game. *And* I was drunk. So don't you go thinking Cleveland is a lock tight alibi, unless you had someone in your hotel room that you was banging all night long. Shit, you coulda done a back-and-forth for all I know and still had time to check out at seven-thirty."

Then Gallagher grabbed his silver and black Brannock Device. "You know, we got a great print in the mud right outside Silverman's house the morning after. Guy with eleven and a half shoes." Slowly, Gallagher walked around the desk and knelt down on the floor just like a shoe store salesman. "Take one of your shoes off. Now stand up." He measured the foot carefully with the device, then looked up and saw how Graham's nipples were showing through his wet shirt. "Eleven and a half. I better take 'em both." Of course it wasn't necessary to confiscate the wing tips, but it was worth it just to see the color blanch from Graham's face as he slipped off the other shoe.

Everything was fitting together. It was logical that if Silverman was involved with the Medical Center murders, then Graham was in on it also. But other than Silverman's threat to name names and the way Graham behaved, there was no concrete evidence to link Graham to the murder. Yet.

The elevator stopped in the stunning marbled lobby. Although Gallagher was parked right outside in a fire zone, he headed for a bank of pay phones and called the precinct. After he scribbled Graham's plate number on a scrap of paper he got back on the elevator, pushed the button marked Parking Garage, and rode down to one of several basement levels. In less than five minutes he found a series of parking spaces reserved for WIP. Parked in the very first spot, the only car backed in— Gallagher assumed so Graham could make a quick getaway—was an Acura TL. A sign on the wall behind the car declared: Reserved Parking, Western Insurance, F. Graham.

After placing the Brannock Device and the shoes on the hood of a Lincoln in the next space, Gallagher admired the expensive car. A fine patina of highway grime coated the deep blue paint that Gallagher generically thought of as midnight blue, even though Acura wanted it known as Pacific Blue.

As he fished in his trench coat pocket for a small halogen flashlight, Gallagher looked around, making certain he wasn't being watched. Satisfied he was alone he shined the bright light on the doors and windows, looking for smudges or fingerprints. A small red light blinked on and off just inside the driver's window, warning of a security system. The beige seats looked like leather. Not a crimson bloodstain was to be found, only a half-full bottle of windshield wiper fluid that sat on the floor behind the driver's seat.

Gallagher was in no rush. Slowly he worked the light over the blue metallic paint, looking for something, anything, that would send him back up to the twenty-third floor with his Miranda card and handcuffs.

Nothing. The front and sides of the Acura were clean. Finally, after checking everything twice, he carefully squeezed himself into that narrow space between the back of the car and the cement wall. It was tight, too tight for a thirty-eight-inch gut hanging over a thirty-six-inch belt, and Gallagher couldn't squat down without bumping his ass on the concrete and risk putting his own fingerprints on the trunk. So he had to get down on his knees *before* venturing behind the car, knee-walking into position. He confirmed the plate, CLAUAWS, and shined the flashlight all around the trunk. Nothing.

Finally, just when his knees were throbbing and he was starting to breathe heavy, he spotted it, just to the right of the lock. Floating in a midnight-blue sky like a cloud was a small oval discoloration. Gallagher worked his flashlight about, examining his find from various angles, leaning in as close as his hyperopic eyes would allow. No fingerprints. No smudges. No blood. And no road grime. Just a clean, fresh oval discoloration. If he squinted real hard, narrowing the aperture of his eye so that only the light coming straight at him was focused on his retina, Gallagher could see the telltale fine lines that steel wool would make.

As far as Gallagher was concerned, there was only one reason someone would take steel wool to the back of Graham's thirty-five-thousand-dollar car.

Somehow Tory found it extremely difficult to walk away from Graham's office. Something tugged at her, and she lingered near Ellen's desk, staring back at him. He looked pathetic, a broken man waiting for the ax to fall. At the same time she wondered whether he ever intended to use the gun on himself, or if it was just a prop in a pitiful show.

Suddenly a door behind Tory opened. She turned around to witness half a dozen men, all in somber business suits, filing out of the boardroom, each making an obvious effort not to look anywhere near Freddy Graham's office.

"That's the board of directors," Ellen said to Tory.

"Who's the chairman?"

"Mr. Bass. He hasn't come out yet," Ellen observed as the board members solemnly made their way to the elevators.

"I'd like to talk with him."

Ellen stood and walked toward the boardroom door. "I have to give him Detective Gallagher's card, anyway."

Ellen led Tory into a small but well-appointed boardroom. A series of windows looked out at the top of Pittsburgh's tallest buildings. An oval table took up most of the room. In one corner was a small television set, silently tuned to a commercial. Seated at the table, reviewing some paperwork before him, was Norman Bass, Chairman of the Board.

"Excuse me, Mr. Bass," Ellen said, placing the small business card on the table. "A detective was here and asked that you call him as soon as you get a chance."

Bass picked up the card, read it twice, and pocketed it. "Graham still here?"

"Yes, sir."

"Don't let him leave." Then Bass realized Tory was standing behind Ellen.

"Sir, this is Tory Welch," Ellen said, anticipating his next question, "from the DA's office. She'd like to talk with you."

"Not now. I have to meet with Mr. Graham," Bass declared and started to rise from his chair.

"This won't take long, Mr. Bass. Thank you, Ellen." As Tory sat down, Ellen disappeared and closed the door.

Bass dropped his huge frame back in his seat. "I don't have time for this. My guess is you want Freddy Graham."

"Mr. Bass, I need to know—"

"I don't mean to interrupt you, Miss Welch, but I could sure use a drink."

A drink? Tory looked at her watch.

"I've been up all night." His voice trailed off. He walked over to a side bar and poured himself a bourbon from a crystal decanter. Bass proved nimble for such a big man. The morning light coming through the window illuminated his face, showing off a ruddy complexion and bulbous nose that suggested Bass pulled many all-nighters that required a drink at ten A.M. "You've spoken with Graham?"

"I have."

Bass filled his mouth with the amber liquid and swallowed. "What do you think?"

"Mr. Graham is the first I've spoken to. I'll reserve judgment for now."

"That's right, you're here to ask the questions. You realize, of course, I have no choice but to relieve him of his duties."

"He told me as much. Beyond the Leonard Silverman interview, did you ever have reason to suspect he was involved with the murders?"

Bass winced, as if the word murder hurt his ears. "Miss Welch . . . he worked closely with Silverman. It was his show. Hell, if he wasn't involved, I should fire him for letting something like this go on right under his nose."

"Tell me about the buyout."

"Ahh, the buyout," he said sadly. "You'll probably find out sooner or later. We're a privately held company, but we do have shareholders.

I have an obligation to them to do what is in Western Insurance's best interest. Whether you think it's good or bad, the nineties will be the decade marked by the consolidation of the insurance industry. Naturally we explored our options. I instructed both Graham and Silverman to pursue friendly offers, but I insisted on top dollar for the shareholders. You know what a golden parachute is?'' Tory nodded. ''Well, I created what we affectionately called the Golden Clause for each of them. We amended their contracts with a clause that potentially could have made them rich. When the buyout was complete, each of them would have received a lump sum payment equal to eight times their annual salary. Graham and Silverman whipped the company in shape.

''You want to see greed in action? Go take a gander at Graham's license plate. He loved reminding people that 'AU' is the chemical symbol for gold. *Gold* . . . in . . . clause. I'm sure you'll check it out.

''Anyway, he was putting in eighteen-hour days. In twelve months' time our bottom line numbers were among the best in the industry. Suddenly, we were flooded with offers. Silverman played it like a poker game, going from suitor to suitor, upping the ante.

''But now, Freddy Graham is a liability.'' Bass looked up at the ceiling briefly, searching for answers. ''With luck I believe I can restore the confidence of the public. As far as the buyout goes . . . it remains to be seen if it can be salvaged.'' Bass sipped his drink while he looked out the window, lost in his own thoughts. ''The Golden Clause,'' he said quietly.

''Did you or anyone on the board have any idea why the numbers looked so good?''

''We were naive enough to think we had installed a crackerjack team running the day-to-day. But what you really want to know is did we know patients were dying to improve our bottom line?''

''Patients were being *murdered*,'' Tory corrected.

The wince again. ''Don't! Listen to me. You and I have entirely different agendas, Miss Welch. I continue to have an obligation to direct this company wisely. If that means using a euphemistic word like 'dying' then I will do that. Whatever it takes to restore the integrity of this company I will do, whether it involves putting a positive spin on a terrible situation or handling Freddy Graham decisively.''

''What if he was in Cleveland?''

''I was informed last night about his little trip. So now you think I'm one cold sonovabitch, but listen to the truth. It would have been a whole lot easier if Graham hadn't been in Cleveland and was up to his eyeballs in this thing. Real life is never as neat and tidy as you'd like. His innocence or guilt matters not a lick.'' Bass's voice had gotten louder as he made his point. He paused for a moment. "Because of his little trip to Cleveland I'm giving him the option of resigning instead of being fired." Bass crossed back over to the oval table and took his seat. He lit a cigarette and sucked hard on it. "All he's got to do is sign. If this thing ever blows over, at least he can say he wasn't fired."

"Is his the only resignation I should expect?"

"If you're asking if I plan to resign in shame, the answer is no. The members of the board—all respected in the business community—do not run the day-to-day operations of Western Insurance. This is not a working board."

"Do you or any members of the board of directors stand to benefit financially from the sale of this company?"

Bass slammed his fist down on the table. "What? Is that what you think this was about? Absolutely not. I am wealthy, but not from my association with Western Insurance. You ever hear of the Three Rivers Furniture Factory?" Bass pointed to himself. "That's me. Hell, you just missed one of my commercials. It ran right before that goddamn Sandy Keller. For crissake, it looked as though I was sponsoring her. As a board member I get fifteen thousand dollars to attend about fifteen meetings a year. Once we're sold, all of the current board positions will vanish, and I will no longer be involved. My career has been successful. Not one bankruptcy. And I will be goddamned if this company is going to tank on my watch."

"Mr. Bass, when did you find out that WIP was involved with the series of murders at the Medical Center?"

"On the news. All I do anymore is watch Sandy Keller. I didn't know a damned thing until that Bello character was hospitalized." Suddenly Bass had a realization. "Oh. That was you, wasn't it?"

"One more question. With Graham and Silverman gone, who will run WIP's day-to-day operation?"

"You're looking at him. And the first thing I'm gonna do is shake this place up. Miss Welch, my motto has always been, I can turn trouble around. Anything that smells rotten will be out of here. It's my show now. I'm calling the shots."

When Tory stepped off the elevator in the parking garage she immediately spotted the crime lab van.

"Hell-o, Jell-O," Gallagher called, his voice echoing. "I can't promise you any dessert but come and see some real police work." There was a giddy excitement to his voice.

Tory crossed over to where the Acura was parked. The crime lab technicians had set up powerful lamps to illuminate the area around the car and were searching for evidence.

"Whose car is this?" Tory asked, watching one of the techs dusting for fingerprints.

"Frederick Graham's. I got to thinking after I left, maybe Graham made a dumb mistake. So I checked out his car. Found something." Gallagher led Tory to the back of the Acura.

With ease Tory slipped between the car and wall, squatted down, and observed the small oval area where the top layer of paint had been removed. "What happened?"

"Steel wool."

"Steel wool?" Tory asked.

"Yeah. You know he was in Cleveland." Tory nodded. "I figure he found out Silverman was gonna rat him out, drove back that night, killed Silverman, then dumped the body. In the process he got a smudge of blood on the car. Betcha there's more inside."

Tory leaned in for a closer look. "Where's the blood?"

"Gone. Crime guys think it's steel wool also."

Tory looked confused. "Why use steel wool?"

"You know what luminol is?" Gallagher puffed up his chest, ready to launch into an explanation.

"A chemical that glows in the dark when mixed with blood. It's so sensitive that even if the blood has been wiped off, it reacts." Tory examined the small oval area. "If steel wool removed the paint, there would be nothing to react with luminol."

Gallagher frowned. "Exactly," he said sarcastically.

"Have you opened the trunk?"

"Not yet. The car's alarmed. We'll impound it, take it to the police garage, and luminol it to death."

Tory opened her bag and pulled out the weapon she'd confiscated from Graham. "I took this from Graham. It was in his desk."

"We've got him." Gallagher grabbed the gun, putting it to his nose for a quick sniff. He released the cylinder and spilled the bullets out in his hand. Once again he frowned.

"What's wrong?"

Gallagher handed the weapon and bullets to one of the crime lab technicians. "It's not the gun that did Silverman. Wrong caliber."

26

The phone rang just before six, cutting the silence of the night. Tory was still asleep. As Merlin had just stepped in the shower, the phone was ignored for six or seven rings. "Merlin, get the phone," Tory mumbled, opening her eyes just enough to see it was still dark. Since Merlin always received telephone calls from the Medical Center in the middle of the night, Tory had gotten used to the interruptions. The phone rang again. "Merlin?" she asked, a hint of annoyance creeping into her voice. Another ring.

Once she realized she was alone, Tory lifted her head and peered around the room. A yellow sliver of light cut across the carpet, announcing Merlin hadn't closed the bathroom door all the way. Shaking the sleep from her head, Tory rolled over to Merlin's side of the bed and picked up the receiver. "Hullo?" Tory's voice sounded groggy.

"Tory Welch?"

The voice sounded vaguely familiar, but she could not place it. "Yes," Tory said, sitting up.

"Hey, sorry to bother you, what with it being before six and everything."

"Who is this?"

"Detective Gallagher," he answered, sounding surprised he wasn't recognized.

Gallagher. Tory looked at the bedside clock—5:49. "What is it?" Tory mumbled, already suspecting the reason for the call. Gallagher was probably calling to gloat about what he had found in the Acura.

"Got something here, thought you'd better have a look."

"What did you find, the hands and feet?"

"Huh?" Gallagher replied. He sounded confused.

"Oh, God." Tory sat straight up. "It wasn't the hands and feet, was it?"

"Everything but."

"In his trunk?"

"Forget the trunk. We're way beyond that. Jeeze, the trunk was clean," he blurted, giving Tory some attitude, like she was on the wrong page. "Luminol didn't show anything, anywhere. The car was spotless. Forget the car."

In the background she heard a siren. "Then why're you calling? Where are you, anyway?" Tory demanded.

" 'Member that park in Aspinwall, where you found Silverman?"

"Yes." Tory brushed some stray hairs from her face. A sick feeling was developing in her stomach.

"Well, an early morning jogger found something. I'll be here another ten minutes if you wanna come down."

"C'mon, Gallagher, don't play games with me. What is it? The hands? What?"

"No, wait'll the photographer is finished. No, no, get her away from there! I'll be right over," Gallagher said, obviously speaking to someone else at the park. "Listen, I gotta go." Now he was talking to Tory. "You don't want to come, don't come. Consider this a courtesy."

The line went dead.

Tory had a clear image of a dog or raccoon digging up one of Silverman's hands and dropping it when the jogger happened by. This was Gallagher's idea of a courtesy, getting her out of bed and down to the park to see a half eaten, shriveled up hand.

Meanwhile she was pulling on jeans and a Yale sweatshirt, racing around the room, trying to find socks that matched.

Merlin came into the room, bringing with him the warm, soapy smells of the shower. "Where're you going?" he asked.

"The park. Gallagher called, they found something." Tory sat on the bed as she tied her running shoes.

"What?"

"Creep wouldn't tell me. Probably Silverman's hands," Tory called over her shoulder, heading toward the stairs. "I'll call you."

The morning air was cold, too cold for the way she was dressed, but Tory immediately broke into a jog and headed for the park. *Hands and feet. Hands and feet.*

Even before she crossed Center Avenue she could see the flashing lights from the cruisers. Several of the apartments had lights on, silhouetting curious neighbors in the windows.

Then she spotted the glow. Two squad cars, the police crime unit van, and a big Buick sedan were parked like spokes on a wheel, their headlights directed at the far corner of the small park.

Her corner.

Déjà vu. Crime lab technicians in their crouch. The flashing strobe of the forensic photographer. And Detective Gallagher, standing in the middle of the action, one hand absently scratching his belly.

My God, that's right where I found Silverman.

Tory stopped running. From fifty yards away she couldn't determine what the fuss was about, but any thoughts of a chewed-up hand vanished. The acrid taste of vomit burned her throat. She hoped no one would notice her. Suddenly she was caught in the glare of headlights coming from behind. The coroner's van had arrived, stopping briefly as its front wheels touched the curb, then pushed forward, jumping the curb, loudly scraping the muffler on the concrete.

It was no longer a question of what had been found. It was simply *who* had been found. Hesitantly, Tory started toward the little crowd. As people shifted, Tory was able to see the body. Even from a distance the familiarity was remarkable. Lying exactly as Leonard Silverman had been, was a man. Supine. One arm up. One arm down. As if it were waving to her.

"Oh, Miss Welch," a female voice called. Tory had been spotted. A woman broke from the crowd and hurried toward her. She was lighted from behind by the brilliant headlights and impossible to recognize.

Tory stopped walking, waiting for the woman to get close enough to identify.

"I was hoping to talk with you," the woman continued. There was a man behind her carrying a camera on one shoulder.

Oh, no. Sandy Keller. "Sandy, not now."

"You know who they found?"

"No," Tory stated firmly and walked around Sandy and her cameraman.

Instantly, Sandy smelled an opportunity. Stepping aside, allowing Tory easy passage, Sandy made a circular motion with her index finger directing her cameraman to start shooting. Reaction shots. Every reporter's dream. That's what it was all about. Hands going to mouths, eyes filling with tears, heads turning away. Tory would be perfect.

Sandy's cameraman sidestepped, keeping up with Tory's quick pace. This was a practiced routine, a continuous close-up of her face in hopes of capturing the exact moment when reality struck. The light was perfect, more than enough to capture Tory's emotions.

Tory got closer. It was plain to see that there was one glaring difference between this body and Leonard Silverman's. This one still had a face.

It was Frederick Graham. Faceup in the tall grass, both eyes open, staring up into the dark skies, a single digit dangling from his lips like a forgotten cigarette. Not for a moment was his identity in doubt. Except for a deep gash above one eye, this was the same man Tory had interviewed less than twenty-four hours earlier. No fancy dentals or fingerprints would be necessary. Instead of brown coffee stains, his button-down collar shirt was slick with fresh gore. The sleeves and pants of his dark suit, almost black with blood, ended limply where his hands and feet should have been.

Tory was struck with a terrible thought that held rigid in her mind: if she hadn't lunged across the desk and grabbed Graham's weapon he probably would have suffered less. Absently brushing hair from her face, she realized Sandy Keller was standing to her immediate right, the cameraman to her left, capturing her every move.

"Miss Welch." It was Gallagher, coming out from the bushes. "Thought you'd want to see him before we packed him up."

"Everything looks the same as Silverman, except his face."

"Yeah. One blow to the back of the head did it. No bullet holes. Same killer, though. The position, the amputations . . . Hey, will you get the hell outta here before I confiscate your friggin' camera!" Gallagher suddenly barked at Sandy. "When I got something I'll call you, and make sure you get me from the right side, okay?"

Sandy and the cameraman quickly backed away.

"Jesus Christ," Gallagher continued. "I can't even think without them crawling up my ass."

"Was he reported missing?"

"They're never around when you make a collar," Gallagher fumed. Then looking toward Sandy he growled, "How come you show up before we do and photograph us when we don't know shit? Where the hell are you when we make the bust, huh?"

Gallagher turned back to Tory.

"Was he ever reported missing?" Tory asked again.

"You never call us when you arrest someone," Sandy shot back.

Gallagher whirled around. "That's it, sister. Get the fuck outta here!" Once again he shifted his attention to Tory. "Shit, I can't stand that woman." He exhaled loudly. "They're like leeches. I can't even think straight with them around. Now, where was I? Oh, yeah, was he reported missing?" he mumbled, trying to remember her question. "Nope."

"So his car was clean."

"Imagine that, I was wrong." Gallagher chuckled sarcastically. "I'm sure it'll be all over the news."

"So Silverman and Graham were killed by the same person. If Silverman was killed to silence him, then Graham must have been involved, too. He fooled me."

Gallagher sighed loudly and shook his head. "Not me. I had him guilty all along. That's why I checked out his car right after I talked with him. What I don't get is we hit that car with luminol in every nook and cranny. Nothing. I don't know why the hell someone would've taken steel wool to his trunk."

"Someone who knew what he was doing," Tory observed.

Gallagher held up his hands, as if to say, *Enough, I don't need some ADA to tell me that*. "Hey," he said, changing the subject as if a thought had just popped into his head. "You're two for two. First Silverman, now Graham. An interview with you can be hazardous to your health. Anyone else you chatted up yesterday?"

"Funny."

"If there is maybe I'll just hang out here until the killer dumps him and pick him up." Gallagher stood there with his big mouth open for a couple of seconds as if he was going to let out a belly laugh.

Sandy Keller, keeping her distance in the cool darkness, saw Gallagher's good humor. As the drivers from the coroner's office began loading Graham's mutilated body on the narrow, collapsible stretcher, she ventured a bit closer to Detective Gallagher. "Detective, may I ask one question?" Sandy smiled sweetly.

"Yeah, what is it?" His joke had improved his mood.

A cellular phone began to ring.

Sandy briefly waited for her cameraman to get into position. "I know Mr. Graham was considered a prime suspect in Mr. Silverman's death. With his murder—"

Ring. Ring.

"—do you feel the mastermind of the Kevorkian Society—"

Ring. Ring.

"Will someone answer that, goddamn it!" Gallagher demanded.

If the light had been better, Sandy's face would have shown crimson. "Sorry." She put up her hand, indicating the cameraman should find something else to do for a few moments, whipped the phone from her jacket pocket, and snapped into the receiver, "This better be important. What is it?"

"Jesus Christ," Gallagher whispered loud enough for Sandy's caller to hear.

Tory watched Sandy put a finger in one ear so she could hear better.

The reporter listened for several seconds. "Who is this? . . . How did you get my number?" Sandy paused. "Oh, my God!" she exclaimed, and looked right at Gallagher. "What's his license number?" As Sandy wrote a short series of numbers and letters on her palm, she kept saying, "Yes. Yes. Go on. Yes. I see," very quietly urging her caller to continue. "Why me?" Another pause. "Got it." Finally, without so much as a thank-you or a good-bye she snapped the phone closed and slipped it back into her pocket.

Sandy straightened her hair while she took several cleansing breaths to clear her mind. "Excuse me." Then she touched her ear, checking for an earring that wasn't there. "Where was I?"

"Wasting my time," Gallagher stated.

"I'm sorry," Sandy blurted out. "I *am* wasting your time. Thanks anyway."

"What?" Gallagher roared.

"I'm . . . I'm sorry," Sandy said quickly. Looking around for her cameraman, seeing he was catching a quick smoke, she directed, "Let's go."

Tory watched as Sandy sped back to the KDKA minivan, walking too quickly and almost losing her balance as she crossed the lumpy lawn. "I've seen that look before. She knows more than we do."

27

The Three Rivers Furniture Factory was located in a large warehouse near Three Rivers Stadium. Despite its catchy slogan—"From our factory to your home"—not a single piece of furniture had ever been built at the Furniture Factory. For under a thousand bucks a whole living room full of furniture could be purchased, or preferably, financed. "Sofa, love seat, easy chair, coffee table, end table, lamp, and TV stand, seven pieces in all, the whole nine yards. Nine hundred eighty-seven bucks. That's right, nine hundred eighty-seven bucks. And just to sweeten it, I'll pay the sales tax." That was just how the TV persona of Norman Bass said it, as if he was your friendly neighbor inviting you over for a barbecue. Hokey as it was, the Furniture Factory sold furniture. Lots of furniture.

The huge parking lot was nearly empty at 9:15 A.M. The only cars belonged to the employees—Chevys, Fords, and Saturns—all parked about as far from the front door as you could get, making room for the paying customers. Tory parked her Chevy rental twenty feet from the double glass front doors, next to the only reserved space in the lot. A small sign warned: Reserved, Norman Bass.

This morning, the space was empty.

The Furniture Factory would be Tory's second stop of the morning, the first being a worthless trip to the executive offices of Western Insurance where she was told Mr. Bass was not expected until his press conference at noon. She was also informed Detective Gallagher had beaten her by half an hour.

A salesman was on her before her eyes had adjusted to the cheap fluorescent lighting of the huge showroom. "Hi, I'm Eddie, what can I do you for?" he asked, checking out Tory's chest.

"Actually, I'm not looking for furniture, I was hoping to talk with Mr. Bass."

"Not here," Eddie said with a smile. "You work with that cop or something?"

Tory realized Gallagher had also beaten her to the Furniture Factory. "No, actually I'm with the DA's office."

"You a lawyer?"

"Yes."

Now Eddie helped himself to a look at Tory's legs, not trying to be subtle, genuinely showing his surprise a district attorney could be sexy. "Man," he said, taking her in, making no bones about his opinion of her. "Why'nt you try his downtown office," Eddie offered, then dictated the address to Tory. "You know, I didn't tell the cop, seeing how I got a little problem with some speeding tickets and I lost my license. Figured he found this place, he could find the downtown office."

"Thanks. That's nice of you," Tory said and headed for the glass doors. As she was getting into her Chevy, Eddie appeared outside.

"Hey, just wanted to ask you, with those speeding tickets, sure would appreciate some help with them. Fact is, if you could see what you could do, I'd spring for dinner sometime."

Handle him carefully. "I'm sorry," Tory said, rolling down the window before she closed the door in a friendly gesture, "but my department only handles murders."

"Oh."

Tory started the engine and yanked the car in gear before the engine settled down. It made a terrible noise, but she wanted to get out of the parking lot before the next question came.

"Well, I still gotta eat," Eddie said hopefully.

Tory dropped her left hand into her lap. "I'm married."

"Oh," Eddie said again, bending over to look into the window, surprised he could have missed the ring.

Easing her foot on the gas, Tory slowly pulled away from the Furniture Factory, using one hand as if she did it all the time. "Thanks, Eddie."

"I'd like to meet with Mr. Huffman." Sandy Keller and her cameraman were standing in a large room that was thickly carpeted and appointed with splendid chairs and tables. It felt more like someone's living room than a waiting room.

The moment she had entered Blaine Huffman's world Sandy had focused on a very proper-looking secretary seated at an L-shaped teak desk guarding the boss's door. Sandy paused to admire a trio of drawings that decorated one wall, assuming anybody who had any business with Mr. Huffman would immediately recognize the artwork and be compelled to take a closer look. She had even murmured, "Picasso, isn't it?" to the secretary, but couldn't get her attention and continued across the room, casually checking her watch.

"And you are?" the secretary asked when she finally looked up.

"Sandy Keller."

The secretary looked down at Blaine Huffman's schedule, knowing in advance no Sandy Keller was on the books, but she knew how to handle people and played along.

"KDKA," Sandy added, trying to generate a spark of recognition.

"Yes . . . yes, I know," she said, acknowledging the call letters. Then she checked a second time, running her finger down the page very slowly. "I'm sorry."

"Look. Mr. Huffman filed a lawsuit yesterday against Western Insurance—"

The secretary stared up from her desk, her face registering no hint of familiarity with what Sandy was talking about.

"—and I want to talk with him about it. That's all. I want to give him a forum to speak out about what the insurance company did to his family."

"Mr. Huffman is on long-distance."

"Would you at least ask him?"

The secretary looked across the large room, indicating a leather sofa under the drawings.

"Please have a seat . . . under the Miró you were admiring."

"I'll be happy to wait," Sandy said, pushing her sleeve up just so, checking the time again, letting the secretary know she, too, had a schedule to keep. Then she quickly retreated to the sofa, leaving the art gallery perusal to her cameraman.

Of course the secretary took note, studying Sandy as she pulled out a compact and checked her makeup. After a brief conferral with her boss on the telephone, she immediately returned to her word processor, never so much as looking again at Sandy Keller.

It was taking too long to find the car and Gallagher was getting pissed off. An anonymous tip, coming by way of a phone call patched into his car phone, had instantly changed his plans for the day.

One thing about the conversation had seemed strange. Although the caller made an obvious effort to talk in a low raspy voice, Gallagher had the distinct impression he was talking to a woman. There was a certain quality to the voice that made him think skirt, even though the whole dialogue had only been about three sentences long. When the line went dead he had the name of the perp, the make of his car, and the license number: 102THE9.

"Bingo," Gallagher said to himself as he finally stumbled upon the expensive car, a rich burgundy, chamois clean.

Not wasting any time looking through the windows or at the hood of the car, the detective immediately went around to the back, checked the license plate, and saw the blood. A smudge, and a couple of drops, one of which ran a little, so that it made a tiny red line down the bright yellow letter "T."

Gallagher savored the moment. If he had had a cigar he would have lit it. *Where the hell is Sandy Keller when I solve the goddamn murder?* He reached for his handcuffs, making certain they were fastened to his belt at the small of his back. Then he got out his wallet and transferred the little plastic Miranda card to his shirt pocket. His tremendous fatigue lifted. Feeling like he was in the movies, Harry Gallagher whispered, "I hate punks," just like his hero.

The elevator went from the parking garage to the lobby. A second elevator delivered visitors to the various floors. Gallagher was so excited when he bounded into the lobby he never noticed the fabulous marble floor or the huge Calder mobile. The requisite security officer was in place, wearing a blue blazer and charcoal gray pants, the type who always remembered to say good morning to the old ladies and fit in with the opulent furnishings but couldn't stop a kid from stealing candy.

"Gallagher, homicide," he barked, not slowing down for a second as he flashed his badge and stepped onto a waiting car.

"I really appreciate your seeing me on such short notice." Sandy smiled. Her eyes cased the room looking for camera angles.

"No cameras just yet," Huffman warned the cameraman. Then to Sandy, "Is this about my reaction to the body that was found this morning or the lawsuit I filed against Western Insurance?"

"Things are out of control at WIP. I assumed you knew about Graham."

"I heard it on my way in this morning," he said without a trace of emotion in his voice.

"Look, Mr. Huffman, I'll level with you. I want an angle. I'll bet not one other reporter's called you today, right?"

"I'm listening."

A massive grandfather clock chimed on the hour. "Why? They want the blood and guts of two murders. I broke that story two hours ago." Sandy was talking quickly, racing to get the particulars out of the way.

"Now I want to move on. Maybe it's time to bring Pittsburgh back to a certain reality. Innocent families were hurt, and although I wouldn't expect you to say you're overjoyed at these new murders, I hope to balance things by interviewing you and proving some justice was served."

"Human interest."

"Call it that," Sandy agreed.

"I want to see the tape—all of it—before it's aired."

Sandy and the cameraman exchanged quick glances. "I don't see that as a problem."

"Then you won't mind signing a document extending me that right."

Under the circumstances Huffman's request seemed ludicrous, but Sandy nodded her head in agreement. "I can live with that." One of Sandy's hands beat nervously against her thigh.

Huffman picked up his phone, pressed a single button, and spoke quietly. Almost immediately the door opened. His secretary came in with a single sheet of paper.

Sandy studied Huffman. There was a hint of his aftershave lingering in the air. He had the kind of thick hair that could easily become unruly even though his part was perfect. Clear eyes were set in a strong face that held on to a residual tan from a trip to the islands just before Kit had entered the hospital. In fact, he looked very comfortable standing at his desk, thanking his secretary with a smile. For several seconds he held the piece of paper, reading it to himself.

Sandy focused on a single corner of the paper, watching it for extraneous movement, looking for some indication that Huffman's hand was trembling. There was none.

Huffman quickly scribbled in the date and Sandy's name on the appropriate lines. "Sign here," Huffman said as he offered his Mont Blanc.

Checking her watch yet again, Sandy scrawled her name.

"You're not going to read it?"

"I trust you. Now can we get started?" Turning briefly to her cameraman, Sandy directed him to stand in front of a set of bookshelves, halfway between the doorway and the desk.

Suddenly a ruckus developed on the other side of the closed doorway. A man's voice loudly demanded, "Where's Blaine Huffman?" His secretary's shrill voice commanded, "Hold it, you may not go in there!"

That's when Sandy turned to the cameraman, pointed her finger, and shouted, "Go," just as the door burst open.

*   *   *

Tory took the elevator to the fifth floor and quickly found the door marked "The Bass Company." It opened to a waiting room decorated in everything but Furniture Factory items. A male secretary sat sentry to the inner sanctum of Norman Bass.

Tory strode right up to the secretary, who was nattily dressed in a blazer and turtleneck. He was chatting on the phone.

"Excuse me."

The secretary cupped the mouthpiece. "I'll be with you in a moment," he declared, immediately going back to his phone call.

"I'm Tory Welch, with the district attorney's office," she continued, frustrated with her pointless treasure hunt. "I spoke with Mr. Bass yesterday. I need to talk with him now."

"Absolutely not," he said, cupping his hand over the mouthpiece once again, slipping a little acid in his voice. "Mr. Bass is preparing for his press conference. He is seeing no one at this time." Then he put the phone back to his ear, officially dismissing Tory.

Waiting for no more than a couple of seconds, Tory started around the desk toward a series of closed doors. Her action was unprecedented. In the civilized world of downtown business, brush-offs were respected. The secretary's eyes widened and his jaw dropped so that he looked like a kid walking in on his parents doing the twice a weeker. He stood at his seat not knowing quite what to do. "Hold it, hold it right there. You may not go in there," he said, raising his voice loud enough to summon the cavalry.

Tory made it to the first door. Before she could grab the knob the door flew open. Suddenly she was face-to-face with Norman Bass, his tie loosened at the neck, sleeves rolled partway up, and the faint smell of bourbon on his breath. "What the hell . . . oh, it's you."

"I told her not to go back there, Mr. Bass. She wouldn't listen," the secretary said, raising his voice to flex his authority.

"That's okay, Donald, go answer the telephone or something," Bass said. Then to Tory, "You obviously know about Graham. So you want to know my whereabouts. Between you and the press conference I don't know what's going to kill me first." He shook his head several times in disgust. "Last thing I said to Freddy was 'I need you to sign this.' " Bass turned away from the door and slowly retreated to the comfort of a sofa in his handsome office. "He had one hell of a last day. Well . . . God rest. Hey, what about your buddy Gallagher? Never did get around to calling him. I suppose he'll be back to ask about alibis in the last eighteen hours."

After a brief silence Tory seated herself in one of two turn-of-the-century Windsor chairs arranged across from the sofa. She sat quietly.

Bass picked up a remote control from an antique end table and pointed it at a small Sony television perched atop a beautiful dry sink to the left of his desk. Everything was old. Everything was real. "I read Freddy all wrong." A game show was just going to commercial. "Hope you don't mind. I've got a new commercial airing in . . ." he checked his watch, "three minutes."

"Mr. Bass, about the press conference at noon. Is that when you're going to announce your new position with Western Insurance?" asked Tory.

"I am. I've got a good first lieutenant at the Furniture Factory who can handle things so I can take a leave of absence. By the way, one thing I plan to announce is complete cooperation with the police. You guys want it, you got it. Computer records, files. Everything."

A familiar jingle played on the TV. Bass picked up the remote and turned up the volume. They heard his voice filling the room, announcing how his craftsmen had built way too much furniture, forcing them to have a terrific sale. "And you know what? If you buy a roomful of furniture before Thanksgiving, I'll throw in all the fixings for a turkey dinner."

Tory listened patiently, dividing her attention between the TV Bass and the one sitting across the room from her silently mouthing his own words.

"C'mon, Grandma, bring the troops down," blared from the TV. Tory noted that Mr. Bass was leaning forward, obviously enjoying the moment. When it was over Bass smiled, proud of his work, knowing he was leaving behind a healthy business. Once again he aimed the remote at the TV, but Sandy Keller's voice stopped him.

The scene unexpectedly switched to an outdoor shot in front of an office building. Sandy was standing in such a way as to make certain the name of the building, The Huffman Tower, could be read. Rhythmically reflecting off the glass doors was the on-again, off-again strobe light from a City of Pittsburgh police wagon.

"I'm Sandy Keller—"

"She's gonna beat this Graham thing to death," Bass growled, thinking he was sponsoring Sandy Keller once again, not that his choice of words was insensitive.

"—with what we all hope is the final chapter in the Kevorkian Society Murders. In this KDKA exclusive I have dramatic shots of billionaire Blaine Huffman, as he was arrested for the murder of Frederick Graham."

Bass grabbed his chest. "Holy shit!" he blurted out, not taking his eyes off the small screen for a second.

Suddenly, Tory felt like the guest who had overstayed her welcome.
The image on the TV shifted to inside Huffman's office. In footage
shot in that on-the-run jiggly style, a door burst open and Detective
Harry Gallagher raced in, one arm outstretched with his detective's
shield, the other brandishing his service revolver. "Huffman, are you
Huffman? Put your hands on the desk where I can see them. *NOW!*"

The camera whipped over to Huffman before Gallagher could register
a response to Sandy Keller's presence. The billionaire stood at his desk
holding his hands up, mistakenly thinking he had been told to put 'em
up. "What's going on?"

"You're under arrest for the murder of Frederick Graham. Turn
around. You have the right to remain silent—" and he recited the rest
of the Miranda rights. When he finished, Gallagher realized Huffman
had not yet turned around. "I said turn around. You understand English?
I can Mirandisize you in Español . . . that's better." Gallagher looked
right at the camera. His red face filled the screen. "Put your hands on
the wall!" Gallagher produced a pair of handcuffs from the small of his
back and cautiously walked around the desk with the wide based gait
of someone expecting the unexpected. "One hand behind your back.
Now."

Huffman obeyed.

Gallagher snapped a handcuff on one of the arrested's wrists. "The
other. C'mon, I don't have all day." When Gallagher finished securing
Huffman, he said, "Let's go," and gave the camera a single nod.

"Did you know anything about this?" Bass asked.

"Of course not," Tory replied.

Instantly the scene shifted to the front of the Huffman Tower, lingering on the disgraced businessman as he was led away by Detective
Harry Gallagher.

What the camera never showed—Sandy being careful to wait until
the camera was pointed away from the desk—was the star reporter
sneaking over to Huffman's desk and snatching the piece of paper she
had signed several minutes earlier.

Eventually Sandy was back live. "Less than one hour ago police
received an anonymous tip that led them to Huffman's car. Blood was
found on the license plate. As you just saw, a handcuffed Blaine Huffman left for police headquarters minutes ago. More at noon. This is
Sandy Keller—"

Bass silenced the Sony. "My God. What a relief."

Tory sat absolutely still as Bass got up from the sofa and went over
to the dry sink. It looked to be pine, probably early American, trape-
zoidal in shape, the front panel being somewhat narrower than the back.

Bass put a hand on one knee, steadying himself as he bent over, working the white ceramic knob. He snatched a bottle of Jim Beam and held it up by way of an invitation.

"No thanks."

"Yesterday you saw me with a morning drink. The world was falling apart. A little Kentucky Straight also goes a long way to celebrate the beginning of a better day."

"You're still going to have your press conference?"

"Absolutely. We're on our feet again." He smiled.

"I won't take up any more of your time," Tory said, starting to go. "Now that things have worked themselves out, may I ask you a question or two?"

"Sure."

"Graham. Incompetent or guilty?"

"I don't know. I bought his story."

Bass held up his glass in agreement. "Hear. Hear." He spoke reverently. "I'm going to go through the computer files damned carefully."

"I'm certain the police will want to look over your shoulder when you do."

"I'll promise you one thing. If it turns out Graham had nothing to do with the unpleasantness at the Medical Center, I'll personally rip up his resignation and make certain Western takes care of his family forever. One more thing," Bass said solemnly. "I thank God that the police worked this thing through so quickly. If Blaine Huffman is some kind of maniac seeking revenge regardless of who was guilty, then you and I both know who may have been next. Hell, even you thought I was involved. I may be one lucky son of a bitch."

28

Blaine Huffman sat on a metal chair that was bolted to the floor in a narrow holding cell. Iron bars made up one of the four walls, cinder block the other three. Ten feet above his head was a tangle of water pipes and ventilation ducts that needed a new coat of paint. A long, filamentous spiderweb, hanging by only one of its many original anchors, dangled down, moving gently with the breeze any time someone walked past the cell. Already he had undergone fingerprinting, mug shots, and the indescribable indignity of a rubber-gloved cavity search. Finally, when they flipped him a roll of toilet paper to wipe off the Vaseline and told him he could get dressed, his belt and tie were confiscated. His pockets were emptied of his leather billfold, 330 dollars in cash, and a platinum American Express card. As the hours of the day wore on, Blaine Huffman's nightmare took hold. His hair became thick with grease and his armpits began to stink. Of course mirrors were not provided; he could only imagine the transformation. He sneezed, the dusty corridors getting to him, and covered his mouth with manicured fingertips. He mumbled, "Excuse me," his fingers wandering over his face, feeling the stubble. In looks, at least, he had become one of them.

Across the room was a second cell, considerably larger and empty, big enough to hold three or four prisoners. Somewhere off in another room there must have been other prisoners because every once in a while he heard someone scream out.

It was now eleven hours since he had been arrested. Twice already Huffman had been shuttled to a tiny conference room where he was allowed to meet with his lawyer. Meanwhile, the cops raced around, gathering evidence before they would talk with him. A trickle of uniformed cops paraded through the area, happening by his cell, seeing what a billionaire looked like up close, hoping this might be another O.J. and they could say they had seen him the very first night. After each of them had a look at Huffman sitting on the metal chair, leaning forward, elbows on knees as if he was trying to have a bowel movement, they were shooed away by Officer Larry Shirl. Sitting easy spitting distance from Huffman's cell, Officer Shirl manned a heavy wooden desk with a walkie-talkie and a *People* magazine.

Several times Officer Shirl had tried to share an interesting article with his only prisoner. "Hey, it says here that Burt Reynolds is making a comeback." But each attempt was met with, "Will you just tell me why the hell they think I killed Graham?" Over and over Officer Shirl said the same thing, "I don't know anything. They'll be down for you before you know it. I'm sure they'll explain everything."

Huffman felt more and more desperate, and looked more and more guilty.

Eventually, Officer Shirl opened one of the desk drawers and pulled out a brown paper bag. His hand disappeared into the bag six times, pulling out a thirty-two ounce bottle of Coke followed by what looked to be pieces of chicken wrapped in aluminum foil. "You haven't eaten. You want something?" the policeman offered, lining up his meal in front of him.

"I need to use the bathroom."

"You've got a commode," Officer Shirl offered and looked toward the back of Huffman's cell.

"It's broken. Filled with toilet paper. The water's at the top of the bowl."

Noticing the puddle around the base of the toilet, Officer Shirl said, "I see what you mean, but I can't let you out." He took a swig of Coke. "Like I told you, pretty soon they'll send someone to bring you up for questioning." He looked across the room toward a metal door to indicate where Huffman would be going. "You can stop on the way." The officer was huge, more than three hundred pounds of cop squeezed into a uniform that probably fit six months ago but was now tight enough to make bending over impossible. A series of fat rolls, tiered on top of one another, prevented him from getting his chair close enough to the desk to unwrap his roast chicken dinner without stretching his arms out all the way.

"I want to see my lawyer," Huffman stated, standing up and walking over to the bars to plead his case.

"Who's he?" Gallagher wanted to know. The detective was standing in the viewing room as Tory and Merlin entered. It was small, no bigger than a one-man holding cell, and it was dark, the only light heavily filtered as it came through the one-way mirror from the adjoining interrogation room. Aside from a couple of wooden chairs, the kind that used to be in every grade school in the country, the room was empty.

"This is Dr. Merlin, from the Medical—"

"Ahhhh," Gallagher said, eyeing the surgeon up and down, taking note of the white pants and surgical scrub shirt, realizing he had probably come right from the hospital. "The boyfriend." Then he shrugged and added, "Hell if I care, enjoy the show."

Merlin gave Gallagher a crisp nod, sensing this wasn't a handshake situation. He had an excellent view of the interrogation room over the detective's shoulder. Other than a rectangular table and chairs, the only concession to technology was a black tripod mounted with a video camera.

"This isn't voyeurism, Detective. Huffman came to visit Dr. Merlin soon after his daughter was killed."

"Oh, yeah?" Gallagher looked at Merlin. "What happened?"

Merlin looked away from the interrogation room. "He managed to break into my office and surprised me when I walked in at seven A.M. He told me he thought my behavior in the operating room had contributed to Kit's death."

"That's it?" Detective Gallagher asked, sounding disappointed.

"Pretty much."

Gallagher shrugged and went for the door.

"One thing, though," Merlin continued. "He had a weapon with him, some gun he bought in Germany. And he made a point of telling me that he and his wife had spent the night in Cleveland, and that he planned to drive back there before she missed him."

"So you took that as a threat, huh?"

"For a couple of minutes. Then we talked. He was a father sick with grief. Look, he wasn't behaving terribly different from how I would have acted given the same circumstances."

"And you chose not to report this?"

"Before he left my office he shook my hand. I don't know what I would have reported."

"Lemme get this straight. You decided a break-in was hunky-dory. Oh, wait, I remember you now. You're the same guy who kidnapped your girlfriend after emergency surgery and never reported that someone tried to run her over. So why worry too much about a little threat from a grieving billionaire."

Merlin ignored the crack about kidnapping Tory from the hospital.

"Until I heard that Huffman was arrested today, I never thought it was significant. End of story."

Gallagher took a step toward Merlin. The surgeon held his ground.

"No, Doc, not end of the story. Huffman killed two people. Maybe Silverman got what he deserved, but we don't know jack shit about Graham. How 'bout if Huffman killed an innocent man? How'd you feel about that?" No one said anything for a few seconds, Gallagher testing Merlin, waiting for him to apologize. Ultimately, when it was obvious no apology was coming, Gallagher said, "Listen, I gotta hit the can before they bring him up."

This time, when the detective went for the door, he gave one of the wooden chairs a little push so that it squeaked across the floor. Before the door had time to close, Merlin was over by the one-way mirror. His reflected image was superimposed on the view of the interrogation room. "Things are happening too quickly," he said quietly. Tory had seen him like this before, losing himself in thought, his mind clicking away, chipping away at the puzzle.

Officer Shirl had a mouthful of white meat that he quickly swallowed. "Anyway, you already met with your lawyer, don't sweat it. They'll be down for you any minute now." Holding up one of his Reynolds Wrapped chicken parts he asked, "You're sure you don't want some?"

"I need to use the toilet."

"Sorry," Officer Shirl said, then took another mouthful of chicken. "I can get you something to drink if you want. A Coke or something."

"Maybe you could call up to your supervisor," Huffman said in a calm voice. "See what's going on, tell them I need to use the bathroom."

Officer Shirl picked up some papers from his little desk and began reading them. "This here's your file."

"Look, I don't care about that, I just need to empty my bladder."

"Hmmm," Officer Shirl commented. "Smart guy like you, getting blood on your license plate."

"Blood," Huffman whispered, and a terror spread through him, making him dizzy. He grabbed the bars of the door and shook them hard, creating a decent jailhouse rattle.

"Yeah. Says you did some guy, chopped him up pretty good, and got a smudge of blood on your license plate. One-oh-two-T-H-E-nine. What is that, your name or something?"

"Forget it," Huffman stated.

"C'mon, what's it mean? Some secret code?"

Huffman took a deep breath. "Do you have any idea what an exponential function is?"

"No," Officer Shirl said.

"I didn't think so. I want to see my lawyer—now—before this gets out of hand."

"No, you're gonna wait like all the other animals in the zoo," Officer Shirl said, clearly annoyed.

"Look, put the food away, and get me whoever's your supervisor. Do it now, Officer."

Officer Shirl wiped his mouth with a paper napkin. "Hey, I ain't the one in jail, so watch how you talk, Blaine." His use of the word "Blaine" was deliberate. "You want to go to the bathroom, there's the commode. Or piss in your pants. I don't give a damn."

"Officer, I demand you allow—"

"Hey, Blaine, guys in for double murders don't do a lot of demanding around here. Pull out the hog and spray the walls if you like. I don't really care."

"Double murder?" For the first time Huffman realized that he was being charged with two murders. "I need to speak with my attorney."

"Put a lid on it, Blaine," Officer Shirl said, talking through a mouthful of white meat. "You'll wait like all the others."

"You goddamned fat slob!" Huffman shouted, proving he was losing it.

"I hope your bladder explodes."

Huffman was grabbing the iron bars. "I won't be in here forever," he hissed through clenched teeth.

Officer Shirl picked up his *People* magazine and pretended to read.

Huffman sat down on the metal chair, fighting his bladder's best efforts to empty itself.

The door opened and two uniformed police officers walked in. "Larry," one of them said to Officer Shirl, "we're going to escort Mr. Huffman to meet with his lawyer."

"Have you had adequate time to meet with your attorney?" Detective Gallagher asked deferentially.

"Yes," Huffman said, looking for a moment at the mirrored wall, wondering how many others were watching.

"And you understand the Miranda rights I read to you."

"Yes."

"And you understand this conversation is being video recorded."

"Yes."

"Then let's begin. State your name."

"Blaine Huffman. I reside at 7 Bunkerhill Road in Sewickley."

"And the name of your attorney."

The man sitting next to Huffman leaned toward the microphone. "Marvin Freeman."

Huffman looked around the windowless room. Fluorescent lights. Sturdy wooden table. Video camera. And Gallagher alone on his side of the table with his handwritten notes. On the way in, he'd noticed the cardboard box and the Brannock Device next to the detective's chair, but they were hidden from view once he sat down.

"And you understand the charges?"

"Actually no," Freeman said. "Initially I was led to believe the charges related only to the murder of Mr. Graham. Now we're told it includes the murder of Dr. Silverman as well."

"We have solid evidence to link both murders to Mr. Huffman."

"And that is—"

"Not only was there blood on the license plate, but the crime guys found a handprint on the rear bumper. Silverman's."

Huffman shifted in his seat.

"Okay . . . Mr. Huffman, did you know Mr. Frederick Graham?"

"No."

"Ever meet him?"

"No," he said definitively. "Oh, wait, my assistant did talk with him on the phone once."

"When was that?"

"Three, four months ago. My family was insured through Western Insurance. My daughter needed an experimental medication for her liver disease, and we had to contact Mr. Graham for approval."

"And did he give you approval?"

"Eventually."

"Eventually?"

"It had to go to committee and get the medical director's approval. Took almost a month. I finally told the doctors to go ahead, that I'd pay out of pocket. But it worked out."

"Any other contact with Mr. Graham?" Gallagher asked.

"No. Don't even know what he looked like."

"And two nights ago, do you have an alibi for your whereabouts?"

Huffman stared straight at Gallagher. "I was at home with my wife."

"No one else saw you?"

"The housekeeper, Mrs. Rosales. Ask her."

"I already did."

"Did she confirm that I was home?"

"And you did not go out that night?" Gallagher asked, ignoring Huffman's question.

"No."

"Uh, Detective," Freeman asked, "my client's question is a reasonable one. Did the housekeeper confirm Mr. Huffman's statement that he was home?"

"Of course. She has also been in his employment for eleven years."

"And that indicates—" Huffman said.

"It indicates that her entire livelihood depends on you. Why shouldn't she confirm anything you say."

"Detective, you've prejudged my client as guilty. What alibi would you accept?"

Gallagher worked his tongue around his lower gum line, cleaning out some remnant of his dinner. "Maybe we should continue." He looked down at his notes. "You filed a lawsuit against Western Insurance."

"Yes," Huffman said, never looking to his attorney for guidance.

"The day before Graham was killed."

"What was the basis for that lawsuit?"

"As I'm certain you know, my daughter was killed by operatives of Western Insurance, ostensibly to weed out sicker patients who proved too costly to insure."

"And was Frederick Graham specifically named in the suit?"

"He was the president of Western Insurance."

"Mr. Huffman," Gallagher said, pausing long enough to warn everyone what was coming, "did you have anything to do with the murder of Frederick Graham?"

"No."

"How do you explain his blood on your license plate?"

For the first time Huffman looked to his lawyer.

"Mr. Huffman already stated that he had nothing to do with Graham's murder. We have no idea how the blood appeared on the license plate."

"Isn't it obvious what is happening?" Huffman asked. Freeman put his hand on Huffman's wrist to silence him. "No? I'll tell you what happened. First Silverman went on television and bragged that he was going to blow the whistle on what was going on at Western Insurance. Then he was killed, evidently to shut him up. Apparently, Graham was also a liability. When I filed a lawsuit against the company they killed Graham and framed me for it. Hell, not only do I take the blame, but if I'm the murderer of Graham and Silverman then my lawsuit would disappear, wouldn't it?"

Gallagher stared at him hard, trying to imagine him in prison. "October 17. Leonard Silverman was killed at his home. An alibi?"

"Again, I was at home with my wife."

Gallagher nodded. "It was a while ago," he said. "How can you be certain?"

"I sat on the sofa with my wife and watched Leonard Silverman being interviewed by Sandy Keller. He was practically bragging about what he knew." Huffman clenched his fists.

"And you never left your home."

"I did not."

"You were home from the time the interview took place until you left for work in the morning."

"Yes. Let me ask you a question, Detective. Was it a coincidence that Sandy Keller was in my office interviewing me when you arrested me? Or did you plant her there to put your face on TV?"

"We don't work that way. Period."

Huffman put his hand to his chin and stroked his stubble contemplatively. "It wasn't a coincidence, though, was it?"

"Forget it," Gallagher said, annoyed.

"She called you. I had it backwards, didn't I? She tipped you off and waited for you to come busting in. But how did she know—"

"I said forget it. If Mr. Freeman here wants to talk with Sandy Keller, be my guest. God knows she loves to talk. By the way, what size shoe do you wear?"

"Excuse me?"

Gallagher rose from his seat and used his foot to work the Brannock Device out from under his chair. "Stand up." He walked around the table, kicking the Brannock Device like it was a soccer ball.

"This is ridiculous," the lawyer said.

"You got some kind of a problem with me knowing your client's shoe size?"

Turning to his client Freeman asked, "What size are you?"

"Eleven, eleven and a half, depending."

"Lemme see," Gallagher was saying, getting down on one knee, repeating his shoe store salesman routine.

Huffman untied one of his wing tips and slipped his foot out. Then he put his foot in the device, remaining in his seat.

"Size ten. Now let's try it standing."

Huffman looked at Freeman as he stood, his foot remaining in the Brannock Device.

"Ahh, size eleven."

"What's this all about, Detective Gallagher?" Freeman demanded.

"Out at the Silverman house, morning after he was killed, we found a footprint—size eleven—behind a rhododendron bush."

"This really is ridiculous," Huffman said, his voice rising in anger. "There must be fifty thousand men in this city with a size eleven."

"I bet you're right, Mr. Huffman. At least fifty thousand. But how many of them have a pair of LL Bean GumShoes? See, we got a pretty good plaster impression of the print. Turns out to be an LL Bean GumShoe. There was also some kind of a gash in the toe."

Blaine Huffman shifted in his seat.

"In fact, Mr. Huffman, I found these in your garage. Don't worry," he said to Freeman, "we had a search warrant. Every 'I' is dotted. Every 'T' is crossed. No mistakes." As he was saying this he was reaching down next to his chair, pulling up a clear plastic bag with a pair of LL Bean GumShoes inside. He held them up to the light. "See that little gash right at the toe area of the left one? Perfect match. One more thing. We removed a couple of dried up globs of dirt from your shoe. I've got the boys from the crime lab running some tests. We'll know if samples we took from the Silverman garden match the dirt from your shoe. And we'll know by morning."

Gallagher put the clear plastic bag with the GumShoes back in the box under the table and rose from his seat. "I believe we're done," he said, his voice sounding confident. "I'll have them take you to a private room, give you a couple of minutes with your lawyer before they take you back downstairs." As Gallagher rose from the table he took the time to push his seat in, doing it as if he were rising from the dinner table. Without another word, he headed for the door.

"Wait!" Huffman commanded.

"No, let him go." It was Freeman again, clamping his hand on his client's wrist. "We've gotta talk."

Gallagher waited by the door, sensing a confession. He controlled his excitement well, only his trembling hand on the doorknob gave him away.

"No," Huffman said, taking control.

"Listen to me, Blaine, in twenty-four hours I'll have forensic experts going over every piece of evidence. These guys are flying by the seat of their pants. Trust me, they're making mistakes. This isn't your area."

Suddenly aware of the video camera, Gallagher slipped both hands into his pockets. He was already planning the press conference when he heard Huffman say to his lawyer, "I don't want to get off on a miserable technicality. I'm not some O.J. Simpson. These charges are false. Absolutely false. And the last thing I want is some dream team defense that gets me off so I'll be a prisoner of my phony innocence . . . Gallagher, siddown!" Huffman waited until the police officer looked comfortable. The room was very quiet as the billionaire began to speak.

"We're starting over. I've already lied to you. But, bottom line, I did not kill Silverman or Graham. I had nothing to do with their murders. Period." He took a single deep breath. "It was obvious what Silverman was doing in that phony interview with Sandy Keller. He was so damned clever the way he used her, I . . . I went crazy. I couldn't let that murderer get away with it. I told my wife I had a meeting and went to his house to see him. If what he said was true, I knew there was a chance he wouldn't come home after that interview, but I had to go. I had to find out. So I took a gun—it's in my top right desk drawer.

"Anyway, I drove to his house, wearing the shoes I'd purchased from LL Bean. I parked a block away in case I ran into trouble and had to escape through the neighbors' yards. But someone must have spotted me because a squad car arrived several minutes later, and I was forced to hide in the rhododendron bush."

"You were there when the police officer checked around the house?" Gallagher asked, getting swept up in the story.

"I watched him. He practically stepped on me."

"Go on."

"He checked the doors to the house, shined his flashlight around, and eventually left. Before I could sit up, a second car started up the driveway. Silverman's Mercedes. I stayed put as another car followed the Mercedes up the drive."

"What kind of car?"

Huffman shook his head. "Don't know. A sedan, and the engine ran rough like it needed a tune-up. One person got out of the first car. Two got out of the second carrying a guy. I figured it was Silverman, but I didn't have much of a view, mostly a bunch of legs walking up toward the house.

"They were inside for maybe twenty minutes, then came back out, carrying something heavy in a rolled-up carpet. They dumped it in the trunk and left in the second car, leaving the Mercedes."

"Then what did you do?"

"I stayed in the dirt for another twenty minutes. Then I went home and went to bed. The next morning I found out what the hell happened."

"That's a good explanation for the shoes, Mr. Huffman. Anything else you want to straighten me out on?"

"Yeah. One thing you didn't bring up, but I'm gonna tell you about. After Kit died—before anyone knew there was a conspiracy going on— I got a call from Banks Wickford, the president of the Medical Center. He was a real weasel, calling me up to tell me that the surgeon who had operated on Kit screwed around in the OR. I paid an unannounced visit to Dr. Merlin, tried to scare the crap out of him. Haven't seen him since. At least you heard it from me and not from somebody else.''

"It's nice that you're coming clean. But you were at the site of the first murder. There's blood *and* fingerprints on your car . . . and you've got a great motive.''

"I told you. It's a carefully devised frame-up." Gallagher rose for the second time. Before he reached the door Huffman said, "One thing's been bugging me, Detective. Silverman hadn't cut a deal with the DA's office, but he went to a lot of effort setting some kind of a plan into motion. How the hell did he miscalculate so badly?''

29

Huffman bent over and tied his shoe. Coming around the table, he paused by the cardboard box for several seconds, peering at his GumShoes as if they had betrayed him. An incredible fatigue was starting to win the battle with his adrenaline. He put both hands to his face and rubbed his eyes hard. Finally, when he could linger no longer he stood at the doorway staring at the mirrored wall intently, as if it were an ordinary pane of glass and he could see right through it, locking eyes with whomever had been observing him.

All the while Tory and Merlin watched everything that happened in the brightly lit interrogation room. The lingering image that came out of the interview was the haunting look on Huffman's face as he told his version of the rhododendron story, which contrasted nicely with the clenched-jaw mask Freeman had worn.

Immediately the door opened, momentarily filling the dark room with yellow light. Gallagher strode in. He went several steps out of his way to run into the chair again, shoving it noisily out of his way. "You hear that crap?" he snapped, pacing back and forth like an animal.

Tory spun around in her chair. "He was impressive," she commented.

"It was bullshit! The whole thing was a goddamn act." Gallagher raised his voice. "His friggin' lawyer tipped him off. They set the whole thing up."

Merlin continued to look through the mirror as if he were watching an instant replay of the dialogue. *How the hell did he miscalculate so badly?*

"It wasn't an act," Tory countered. "If he knew about the shoes from his lawyer he would have blurted out his rhododendron story right away. Huffman got backed into a corner and had no choice but to tell the truth. We've got to consider other possibilities. Like Norman Bass.''

"Norman Bass? Look, Huffman is guilty.'' Gallagher held up his index finger. "First, he admitted he was at Silverman's. We got it on tape.'' Then a second finger. "Second, we've got blood evidence *and* fingerprints on his car.'' A third finger. "And he's got one hell of a motive.'' He seemed agitated, like he wanted to make a show of how right he was. "Norman Bass,'' he said sardonically.

"Before you go and strap Blaine Huffman in the electric chair, there're a couple things that bother me,'' Tory said, standing now to face Gallagher at eye level.

"Enlighten me, Counselor.''

"For the sake of argument, Detective, let's assume Huffman is guilty. Let's go back to the night he heard the interview and went over to Silverman's house. The coroner confirmed that the first thing he did was shoot the guy and kill him. *Then* he mutilated him beyond recognition.''

"So?''

"If this was crazed revenge, why kill the guy first? Wouldn't he want the pleasure of hurting him?''

"Hey, Counselor, you get Huffman up on the stand and ask him yourself.''

"This brutal beating was done with surgical precision. All the time Huffman was brutally beating Silverman, he somehow neglected to bash in the teeth. Silverman's dentals were nearly perfect,'' Tory added.

"Don't look a gift horse in the mouth,'' Gallagher said, missing his own joke.

"You saw the body. He didn't look human. Brains were leaking out. One of his ears hanging by a thread. You couldn't even tell where his eyes were. Yet his dentals were intact.''

"So?''

"What a coincidence.''

Gallagher didn't hesitate. "Maybe Huffman wanted Graham to know damn well Silverman was dead and that he was coming after him next. Psychological torture. How the hell should I know?'' From his tone of voice, it was clear that the detective didn't like the cross-examination.

"Why did he move the body so *I* would find it? I didn't know anything about Blaine Huffman at that point.''

"Maybe the message was for your boyfriend here. Yeah . . . yeah . . .

maybe the boyfriend was supposed to find the body, letting him know what would have happened to him if he *had* fucked up with the daughter.''

Tory shook her head. "That doesn't make sense. Once Huffman knew who killed his daughter, he couldn't have cared less about Merlin.''

"Why the hell are you giving me a hard time?'' Gallagher demanded, irritated with Tory's logic. "Don't ask me to explain the criminal mind, okay? Hell, the shrinks don't know what's going on half the time. How'm I supposed to know? Everything he did had meaning to him, and that's all that matters. Look, Counselor, I don't give a damn who did it, but we've got Huffman by the balls. Until you give me another killer, I'll stick with the evidence.''

"There's too much that doesn't make sense.''

Gallagher pointed his finger at Tory. "Get off your soapbox, lady.''

"Detective, I'm not trying to give you a hard time.''

"The hell you're not.''

"Just . . . just listen for a moment,'' Tory said calmly, trying to reason with the angry detective. "Why would Huffman file a huge lawsuit—creating a mountain of publicity for himself—the morning *after* killing Silverman? And if he were guilty, he knows damn well a million-dollar defense is a successful defense. Why admit to anything?''

"He's playing us for idiots.''

"Then what about Sandy Keller? Huffman was right, wasn't he? Out of nowhere you get a tip from Sandy Keller.'' Tory snapped her fingers. "The case is solved.''

"Maybe you should get off my back and find out who her source was,'' Gallagher suggested.

"I'm way ahead of you. Remember that call she got when we were in the park? One call to Cellular One confirmed the call came from a pay phone.''

"Big deal. Stick with criminal law for another twenty-seven years. You'll be shocked how many anonymous tips we get that solve crimes.''

"But the tip went to a news reporter, not the police. Was this whole thing staged?''

"Yeah, by a zombie named Leonard Silverman.'' Gallagher's hands were waving about. "No hands or feet, but he did it. Or maybe it was Graham. Or an alien.''

"Or Norman Bass.''

"May I add something?'' Merlin asked.

Gallagher rolled his eyes. "Sure,'' he said impatiently. "What kind of a host am I being? Everyone just jump in. Now we'll hear from the boyfriend.''

"Do the fingerprints on the car bother you at all?" Merlin questioned.

"Noooo," Gallagher said mockingly.

"The prints were on the trunk, right?"

"Yessss, on the trunk. Seven inches from the key entry. We've established that. Where the hell have you been?"

"When they put Silverman in the trunk he didn't have any hands. Doesn't it seem odd that he would leave prints *after* his hands were amputated?"

"Listen, Doc, we don't know if there was some scuffle *before* he was killed, or if one of the amputated hands dropped out of Huffman's pocket and hit the car. And frankly, I don't give a shit. I got a lot of paperwork to do, so you'll have to excuse me."

"Maybe someone came *back* with one of Silverman's hands and put prints on the car to make it look like he'd been in the trunk."

"You two are really starting to piss me off."

"One more thing," Tory said. "If Huffman had mud all over his shoes, why wasn't there any mud on the carpet in the room where he killed Silverman?"

"Maybe he took his shoes off. You know what? That's it. Keep your stupid little thoughts to yourself. We're supposed to be on the same team. There is not one shred of evidence to suggest someone else did it. I'll let Frank LaBove decide what to do." Gallagher gave the wooden chair a good hard kick, sending it across the room. As it crashed off the wall he disappeared into the hallway.

"He knows we're right," Tory said.

Merlin smiled as if he were enjoying himself. "It feels like we've just been treated to an elaborate stage illusion. One of those tricks that goes on for a while, sneaking up on you, letting you feel comfortable with what's going on, then *wham!* You've been had."

"You have a magic allegory for every situation." Tory smiled.

"Huffman is the stooge they picked out of the audience who has everything done to him. Gallagher's the obnoxious guy in the front row who has to know how the trick's done right away or he gets mad. And in every great illusion there's always some key piece of information the magician flaunts right in front of your eyes until you take it for granted. Take levitation. Every woman who has ever been levitated wears some kind of flowing dress. The magician even walks her around on stage, showing us how pretty she looks in her dress. He makes us wait while he gently adjusts it as she lies on the table so she might be more comfortable. Because the magician appears so nonchalant about her dress we buy it. But it's the dress that hides the apparatus that lifts her up.''

"So who's the magician? Norman Bass?'' Tory asked, wondering whether the magician in Merlin already had a clue.

"Whoever is wearing the white gloves.''

30

The following morning Merlin ran teaching rounds while Tory endured a long meeting with Frank LaBove in his office. The district attorney hadn't seen fit to kick any furniture around the room while he explained there wasn't a single piece of exculpatory evidence to exonerate Blaine Huffman. It was common knowledge that two things motivated district attorneys: first, what made legal sense and, second, what pleased the public. Never mind that when it came to the politically savvy DA the order was more often two-one than one-two. Even if there were problems with the case against Huffman, there was no expedient way for a future mayor to ignore the impressive physical evidence the police had collected.

At noon Frank went out to the front steps of the courthouse building, the conference room being too small to announce the indictment of Pittsburgh's wealthiest individual. Tory sat alone in Frank's office with a sandwich, using the remote control to watch him on all three networks. Initially the DA made a brief statement, reviewing the particulars of the case and promising to handle the prosecution himself. Then he opened it up to questions. Tory silenced the television and wandered over to the window. Pressing her nose to the thick pane of glass, she had an overhead view of thirty or forty reporters crowding around a small podium where her boss stood. When the thought of Norman Bass popped into her head, and how he always had a television on wherever he seemed to be, Tory wondered if he was celebrating with Jim Beam. That's when she decided that now might be a good time for a visit.

Back in her office, as she was slipping on her coat, the phone rang. It was Merlin, asking her out for dinner. Evidently he'd seen the press conference and, suspecting what kind of day she was having, insisted on meeting her downtown at five o'clock.

Tory snuck out of a side door to avoid any of the reporters. The sun was trying in vain to break through a shelf of clouds and the air felt warm enough, so Tory decided to walk. Twenty minutes later she rode the elevator up to the executive offices of Western Insurance, having no idea what she was going to say to Norman Bass.

The elevator doors opened. Immediately Tory spotted an off duty cop strolling back and forth, looking bored. "You a reporter?" he wanted to know, unaware the media had set its sights on Blaine Huffman and couldn't care less about what was going on at Western Insurance. Giving Tory's credentials a cursory scan with tired eyes, he motioned her on.

Computer screens glowed and phones rang as Tory entered the executive suite. It was as if nothing out of the ordinary had occurred in the last two weeks. At each desk sat a secretary, diligently going about her work. Tory was especially surprised to see Graham's secretary typing away. "Ellen," Tory said sympathetically, approaching the desk. "I'm sorry about Mr. Graham."

"At least someone is." Ellen spoke quietly, looking about to make certain she wasn't overheard. "Around here it's business as usual."

"Is Mr. Bass in?"

"He's in Connecticut. Flew out last night, trying to patch things up. He'll be back tonight, though. If you want to come back in the morning, I'll pencil you in."

Tory shook her head. "Maybe you could answer a couple of questions for me."

"We're not supposed to talk to anyone without clearing it with him first," she said with a touch of bitterness, dutifully stating the rules but indicating she was fed up with them. "Anyway, I don't know very much."

"How long have you worked here?" Tory asked, noticing their conversation wasn't attracting any unwanted attention.

"Three years."

"Who do you think was really in charge?"

"Mr. Graham," Ellen said loyally, then snatched a Kleenex that had been tucked inside the end of her sleeve, using it to wipe her nose.

"How often did he meet with Mr. Bass?"

Ellen looked toward Graham's office. It was probably a reflex, Tory realized, the way any secretary—especially a loyal one—would check out her boss's office to make certain she wasn't being overheard. "You know," Ellen said, lowering her voice to a whisper, "it was really Dr. Silverman."

"Excuse me?" Tory asked.

"Dr. Silverman. Running the show."

"Oh."

"He was the one who did all the talking. He was always running into Mr. Graham's office—he never knocked or anything—just to tell him some idea. When he was leaving Mr. Graham's office, he would say 'cha-ching, cha-ching'—you know, like a cash register? And sometimes he was impatient with Mr. Graham, saying things like he didn't know how to dress or making him buy some special scotch. He acted like he owned the place."

"Do you think it bothered Mr. Graham that Dr. Silverman told him what to do?"

"I don't know. I was instructed by Mr. Graham to let him know whenever Mr. Bass was on the floor so he could go in to, you know, socialize. Mr. Bass didn't have an office or anything, so he would use the conference room. But Dr. Silverman always beat him to it, and the two of them, Dr. Silverman and Mr. Bass, would be sitting around having a drink, even if it was before lunch." She clicked her tongue in disapproval. "Mr. Graham would only stay about a minute before he would go back to his office, walking real slow, and just sit at his desk looking out toward the conference room."

"It sounds like you didn't like Dr. Silverman very much."

"Don't get me started."

Tory paused a moment to let Ellen know the next question was an important one. "Now that you think back on it, was there any indication Dr. Silverman was involved with anything . . . illegal?"

"No." Then she thought a little more. "Unless you call sleeping with every one of his secretaries illegal." Ellen shook her head.

"What is that about?"

"Well—and this started way before he kicked his wife out—Dr. Silverman was having affairs with his secretaries."

"Secretaries?" Tory asked, surprised there were more than one.

"He hired five. One after another. All sex bombs, if you know what I mean. But they were incompetent and eventually got fired. Not one of them lasted more than three months. Not until Mr. Bass did the hiring," Ellen said, and smiled for the first time.

"Mr. Bass did the hiring? Tell me a little more about the relationship between Mr. Bass and Dr. Silverman."

"You know who you should talk to? Carolyn," Ellen said, pointing to an unattractive woman sitting at a desk across the room. "She was Dr. Silverman's secretary."

Tory immediately understood why Carolyn had lasted more than three months. "Do you think she and I could talk in the conference room?"

"Go ahead."

A kid who had gone through a windshield had been in the hospital almost eight days. He wanted to be called Bill, but the nurses insisted on calling him William when they changed his dressings, which really pissed him off. It wasn't enough that he had long greasy hair and terrible acne. Now he sported two hundred fifty stitches, give or take twenty. Eighty of them were internal, the rest snaked across his face and body like black caterpillars crawling all over him. The closer he got to discharge, the more obnoxious he became, craning his neck to look down the nurses' tops when they did his bandages and saying, "What's up, Doc?" to anyone in a white coat.

How he kept up his supply of cigarettes didn't matter, it just made the nurses mad. Some of them even said things they shouldn't say about patients who were still in the hospital. Bill worked hard at being a pain in the ass, always lighting another cigarette as soon as one was taken away from him.

Finally, they beeped Merlin.

Carolyn seemed surprised that someone wanted to talk with her. As unattractive as she was from across the room, Silverman's former secretary was even more homely up close. Her hair was obviously the victim of multiple color changes. Now it was streaked with highlights of blond, but past efforts with red remained, and everything had grown out enough to show she was really a brunette. Her clothing was as poorly color-coordinated as her tresses.

Before she pushed herself up from her desk, she grabbed a plastic water bottle with a lipstick-stained straw poking out the top. Once in the conference room, Carolyn stood next to the big table, not knowing where to sit. Tory noticed a huge run in her panty hose, creating a sausage-like protuberance of flesh bulging out of her calf.

Eventually the two women sat across from one another. Tory had to wait while Carolyn sucked down a mouthful of water. "I know you've been through a lot," Tory began gently. "I'm sorry to bring up old memories."

"But they got the guy who killed Lenny and Mr. Graham. I heard on the TV."

Tory was surprised that Carolyn had been on a first name basis with her boss. "Yes, they arrested someone."

"I knew something like this was going to happen."

"How did you know?"

Carolyn's eyes misted over. "It was . . . I just had a feeling, that's all."

Tory waited while Carolyn wiped her eyes, smearing her mascara. "What I want to know is a little more about Dr. Silverman. For instance, did he work mostly with Mr. Graham or Mr. Bass?"

Carolyn scrunched up her face while she thought. "I guess you could say he worked more *in* the office with Mr. Graham, but more of the dinner meetings were with Mr. Bass." She took another sip of water.

"Would you say Dr. Silverman got along with Mr. Bass?"

"Got along?" Carolyn said, a tone of suspicion in her voice. "You know Mr. Bass said not to talk with anybody . . ." And with that she got up from her chair.

"No, no, no. Nothing like that," Tory reassured. "Look, I'm just doing routine background. I think Mr. Bass wanted you to stay clear of the reporters. Besides, Ellen said it would be okay to talk."

"Oh," Carolyn said in a tiny voice.

"You okay?" Tory asked. Carolyn nodded and sat back down. "So, did they get along?"

"I guess I don't know. Like I said, most of their meetings were in the evening. Mr. Bass had another job that kept him pretty busy during the day. You ever see one of his commercials?" Carolyn asked brightly, hoping to move to a lighter subject.

"I have, actually. Did you notice Dr. Silverman acting differently the last couple of weeks?"

"He was excited. He was always having me arrange long-distance conference calls to Connecticut. And there must've been a million meetings. He was back and forth between his office and Mr. Graham's a dozen times a day. He was, you know, hyper. Like a little kid on Christmas morning."

"Did you enjoy working for him?"

"Oh, yes," Carolyn said with a smile, and Tory noticed her cheeks flush red. "He was very handsome, you know, quite a ladies' man," she added wistfully.

"And he was nice to you."

"Yes," Carolyn answered hoarsely, then touched her pockmarked face that had hit puberty a dozen years before Accutane was patented. "Lenny was wonderful to me."

For a moment Tory wondered whether Silverman's success rate was one hundred percent with his secretaries. "Were you close to him?"

"Not like you might think," Carolyn said, taking Tory's question as a compliment. "I worked for Lenny for two years. But I was his secretary. He was my boss."

"I noticed you call him Lenny."

Carolyn blushed. "You're right, all the secretaries call the executives Mister. In fact I never called him Lenny once in my life. But that night, when he did the interview, I stayed late, you know, in case anyone needed coffee or anything. And when it was over and I was putting my coat on, Dr. Silverman—uh, Lenny—must have thought I looked upset or something because he did the sweetest thing. He came over and put his hands on my shoulders." While Carolyn spoke she touched her fingertips to her shoulders. "Then he said,"—now Carolyn's voice got thick—" 'Everything will be all right, I promise. Good-bye.' " She started to cry. Her breathing quickened, and Carolyn wiped tears from her eyes. "He hugged me. He *hugged* me. I cried all the way home. You know"—she took a sip of water—"Lenny knew he was in danger. He knew they were after him. He said 'good-bye,' not 'good night,' like he always did. I could see it in his eyes. He knew someone was going to kill him."

Tory sat quietly.

"You know," Carolyn said in a burst of loyalty, "I . . . I never really believed he did anything wrong. He just wouldn't."

"So what's going on here?" Merlin asked casually, as if talking to a neighbor across the hedges. He had been in the middle of afternoon medical student rounds when his beeper had gone off, sending him and a bevy of eager fourth years on a detour to Ten South.

"Hey, what's up, Doc?" Bill said, nodding to the curious little crowd waiting in the hallway, keeping beat to an imaginary rhythm in his head. He was standing over by the window, all skinny in jeans and a T-shirt adorned with some equally emaciated rock star, cupping the remains of a cigarette in his bony hand.

"Bill, you know the rules," Merlin said, slipping a hand into his pocket.

Bill smiled and looked at the wispy smoke emanating from his own fingers. "Not you, too, Doc. What about Sir Walter Raleigh, and history, man?"

While Merlin was pulling his hand out of his pocket, he put the other one out, palm up, to accept the cigarette. Reluctantly Bill handed it over, taking his time, enjoying his outlaw status, showing off his bruised hand with all the black sutures. Some white ashes fell to the floor as Merlin snatched the cigarette between his thumb and forefinger.

Then, instead of walking over to the sink like all the nurses did and running the glowing ember under the water before dropping it in the trash, Merlin held his other hand out, thumb-side up, in a fist. Dramatically he opened his fingers partway. He held the cigarette up, first for Bill to see, then turning sideways for his audience in the hallway. Without a word, Merlin had announced what he intended to do. It was a dramatic performance, holding up a lit cigarette like it was something magical. Everyone knew to pay attention, the medical students jockeying for position, and Bill taking a hiatus from acting like a jerk.

There was always a correct length of time for a magician to hold something like a disgusting cigarette butt in the air, and instinctively Merlin knew when to get on with it. With casual precision, Merlin positioned the cigarette above his fist, paused while the smoke from the burning tobacco steadied itself into a thin blue line, and dropped it, lit end first, into his waiting hand.

It was a magical moment and quite a sight, the wispy smoke streaming every which way from Merlin's hand. Naturally Merlin was cool about it, not like some magicians who waved their hands around like they belonged in the burn unit. He held his hand steady as if he couldn't understand what the big deal was all about.

Finally, Merlin repositioned his other hand above his fist and, one by one, pushed each of his fingers inside, jamming the cigarette down. His thumb was last, and he wiggled it about to make sure the job was done right.

The smoke stopped.

Merlin opened his fist.

No charred flesh. No flaky ash residue. And no cigarette.

By now, Bill was as astounded as if he'd seen a reflection of Tom Cruise when he looked in the mirror. The students were oozing into the room. Someone blurted out the obligatory, "How'd you do that?" but otherwise the room was silent.

It was Bill who spoke first. "Hey, that was cool, Doc!" Then, shedding the facade, he quietly added, "Will you show me?"

"All right." He turned to his medical students. "All you guys grab some coffee and meet me in the ICU in ten minutes." As much as his students wanted to see how the trick was done, the thought of a coffee break was even more tempting. Quickly the room emptied.

And Merlin broke the first rule of magic.

When they were alone, Merlin reached into his pants pocket and retrieved his trusty prop. "It's a thumb-tip," he explained, inverting the small magical device and dumping the crumpled butt into the trash can. "You can hide small things inside."

Bill smiled, obviously pleased to be in the club. "Hey, can I see it?"

Merlin handed it over. "This hasn't been easy for you, has it?"

"No. I can't wait to get the hell out of here," Bill answered, looking inside the thumb-tip at the black burn mark in the plastic.

"It's not every day that I get called for cigarette patrol." Bill looked up and smiled. Merlin continued, "Hey, how 'bout I stop at McDonald's tomorrow and bring in a couple of Egg McMuffins and you and I have breakfast together?"

"Sure."

"Now," Merlin said, "will you do me a favor?"

"I know. I know. Don't smoke in the room." Then Bill went over to his bedside table, opened the drawer, and brought out a pack of Marlboros. "Here," he said, handing them over. "Wait," Bill added. Going over to a small suitcase tucked behind the door, Bill unzipped it and pulled out two more unopened packs. "I guess you'll want these, too."

Merlin was touched, knowing Bill could have gotten away with only turning over a single pack. The other two were a peace offering. "You want to see how to use it? Why don't you try it on?" Merlin had already decided to give the thumb-tip to Bill as a gift.

Bill did as instructed. Although his thumb was still stained brown from the Betadine, and marred by the dozen stitches that laced up a two-inch-long laceration, he slid it into the thumb-tip. One of the sutures caught on the edge of the plastic. Bill winced in pain. Yanking his thumb out, he cried, "Damn," as he examined the damage. One of the stitches had ripped, and there was some blood.

"Hey, let me have a look at that," Merlin said.

For a moment, Bill misunderstood what Merlin meant. Feeling guilty, he looked inside the plastic, readying his automatic apology. "Oh, sorry. I got some of my blood in your thumb. Don't worry, I'll wash it out."

Some of my blood in your thumb.... "Oh no, don't worry about that," Merlin said absently, replaying the exact words Bill had just said in his head. "It's yours."

"What do you mean?"

"It's a gift."

"Huh?" Bill said, trying to figure out why anyone would give him something. Then it hit him. "Hey, I don't got AIDS or nothing."

"No, it's not the blood."

"It's a pretty good deal, Doc. I get a little blood in your plastic thumb thing and it becomes mine. Too bad it's not a car." Bill laughed at his own joke. Carefully he eased his new toy onto his other thumb and bent over to retrieve the cigarette butt from the trash can so he could practice the trick.

As much as Merlin wanted to get the kid's attention and explain that the blood had nothing to do with his generosity, he saw his presence wasn't needed anymore. Musing about the last thing Bill had said to him, Merlin headed back into the busy hallway on his way to the ICU.

31

It was one of those I've-got-something-to-tell-you-No-I've-got-something-to-tell-you situations. Tory and Merlin had just been seated in Billy Shears, a small tavern near the courthouse that had become their downtown favorite. Decent food, half a dozen beers on tap, and enough flannel-shirted construction workers stopping by for a shot and a beer to keep the trendy attorneys from the DA's office away. Invariably, a table in the back was vacant where Tory and Merlin could enjoy a private meal.

First they'd ordered beers, then almost simultaneously jumped into their stories. Tory recounted her visit to Western Insurance and the dynamics she'd uncovered. But mostly she described the story Silverman's secretary related about the last night of his life. "She seemed quite certain of herself," Tory recalled, "calling him Lenny because of the way he hugged her as she was leaving."

"You think he was having an affair with her?"

"No way," Tory answered. "Her feelings were unrequited. Apparently, Silverman had affairs with a string of attractive secretaries until Norman Bass hired this one. Believe me, she was hired as much for her looks as the attractive ones were. Anyway, she said he knew he was in danger. She also made a point to tell me he said good-bye, not good night, as if he knew something was going to happen very soon."

The beers arrived and Merlin gave his rendering of what had transpired with the thumb-tip. "He misunderstood why I was giving him the thumb-tip. He thought it was because of the blood that got into it. So he said, 'I get a little blood in your plastic thumb thing and it becomes mine.' *It ... becomes ... mine.*"

Time seemed to slow down as they sat silently for several minutes.

Some guys with hard hats at the end of the bar laughed loudly at a dirty joke, and the waitress wandered by the table to see if they were ready to order. But the two were digesting what the other had just said, ignoring their beers, staring across the table at one another. Any other night, they might have been two lovers so smitten that words weren't necessary. But tonight their minds were racing to make the pieces of the puzzle fit. Each had information the other needed, and together the picture was slowly becoming complete. *He knew he was in grave danger. He said good-bye. . . . I get some of my blood in your thumb-tip and it becomes mine. Yours becomes mine.* As the information began to work together, the haze that had confused them lifted. Gradually at first, they considered the obvious. *Silverman was running the show. Graham was a puppet. Silverman had proven himself brilliant. He was a physician. Graham had been out of town the night Silverman went down, but his car had that peculiar steel-wooled spot. Huffman had filed a multimillion-dollar lawsuit, drawing a great deal of attention to himself, but also ruining any chance of completing the Connecticut deal. The teeth were nearly perfect. The lawsuit had to be stopped and Huffman silenced. Wait a second, maybe that's why his car had that peculiar steel-wooled spot. The teeth were nearly perfect. It should have been Graham, not Huffman, in the interrogation room. Huffman was a last-minute substitute. And the teeth were nearly perfect. Someone had to be incredibly careful to bash in the face and preserve the teeth. And the finger. Yours becomes mine. Would a killer take the time for poetic metaphor? No. The finger was more important than that. Nothing was left to chance. Nothing was an accident.*

And suddenly, they were struck by a simultaneous epiphany that could never be explained. It needed to be confirmed, but they knew the answer.

By the time the waitress happened by their table to tell them about the specials, they were gone. She shrugged, scooped up the ten-dollar bill, and cleared the table.

Ten minutes later they were taking the steps two at a time toward Julian Plesser's office. It was just after six P.M., the beginning of a long night.

Tory was the first to wonder, "Do you think this will upset Jules?"

"I thought about that. A good coroner is expected to know just about everything. Usually they have the egos to go along with it."

"So the answer is yes."

"When a doctor claims not to care when he makes a mistake he's either a liar or a truly bad doctor. It'll bother Jules, but he'll handle it. If anything, he'll probably admire the brilliance of it.''

Then Tory said, "Let me do the talking. I want to phrase everything right.''

By now they were at the door to Julian's office. There was no light coming through the frosted glass. When Tory tried the knob it was locked.

It was a short walk down the hallway to the autopsy room where they hoped to find the medical examiner in the middle of a case. Just as they were about to push their way through the swinging doors, Julian's secretary walked out. "Just turning out the lights," she said.

"Oh, I'm glad we caught you," Tory said. "Do you know where Julian is?''

"He left over an hour ago. Maybe you can come back in the morning.''

Suddenly the powerful momentum seemed to vanish. Julian's secretary was moving toward the elevator, anxious to go home herself, while Tory and Merlin straggled behind.

"Tory was supposed to pick up some papers he left on his desk," Merlin said quickly.

"Oh, good thing you caught me. Don't worry, I've got a key," the secretary replied, pulling her set from her purse. Several seconds later she had unlocked the door to the coroner's office while reminding Tory and Merlin to close it when they were done because it would lock on its own.

Seeming to be in a hurry, the secretary said her good-nights and immediately headed back toward the elevator. The first thing Tory did once they were alone was to whisper, "I hope we're doing the right thing.''

Merlin was already over at Julian's desk. He looked up and gave one of his reassuring smiles. "This is working out better than I thought. The fewer people who know the better. There's no chance of a leak, and we've got the element of surprise on our side.'' Then he went back to a huge stack of autopsy files, thumbing his way through until he found the one marked LEONARD SILVERMAN. The desk was a mess, so Merlin cleared a space while Tory came around to join him.

The autopsy file contained a series of documents.

First were a series of photographs of the deceased from an endless array of angles, both at the site where Tory found him in the little park and on the stainless steel autopsy table. It was impossible not to pick up the shot of Silverman lying in the tall grass with what looked like a cigar sticking out of his mouth. Ironically, she remembered exactly what she had thought about that afternoon, standing there in her running gear, listening to that little girl screaming as she ran home to her mother. Absently, her hand went to her mouth, just as it had done that afternoon.

After a while she was able to release the photograph. Julian's typed notes from the gross anatomy portion of the autopsy were next, followed by a typed statement from Victor Hamburgh stating the results of his forensic dental exam. Finally there was the thin beige file from Silverman's private dentist, the same one Tory had read from during her brief stint as Hamburgh's assistant. This was what they were after. On the side tab that protruded almost an inch, a typewritten label read, "Silverman, Leonard." On the front of the chart, stamped in blue ink, was the dentist's name and address.

"Eric Michael, DDS," Merlin read aloud.

"Wait a second," Tory said. "I just remembered. He had a temporary filling. The forensic dentist said it was less than a month old."

"Perfect." Merlin opened the chart. The first page of the chart contained the drawings of teeth as they appear in the mouth. He flipped through the pages of office notes—writing on one side of each page, the other blank—until he came to the last entry. Then he read: "September 28. Pain in molar. Gross carious lesion occlusal surface number three."

Tory touched her right cheek. "Third upper tooth from the back."

Merlin smiled.

"Two more credits and I'll have my dental degree," Tory said, her confidence pervading the room.

Merlin continued. "Superficial caries removal. IRM."

"What's IRM?" Tory asked.

"And you only have two more credits?" Merlin asked playfully before explaining, "Intermediate Restorative Material. Dentalspeak for a temporary filling. Now we know he was there recently. If we can crack into Eric Michael's computer we can see if a charge was generated for the visit."

Merlin then spent some time looking through the chart, bending over the handwritten notes, bringing his face quite close to the paper, flipping the pages backward and forward, looking like a spy trying to break a secret code. "Look at this," he said to Tory, showing her the first entries in the chart. "Seven pages of notes altogether. Look at the handwriting." Merlin then turned to the last page. "It changed over the years. Nice and tight in 1989. Big and loopy last month."

Tory thought for a moment. "Maybe over the years the dentist got busier and rushed through his notes."

"Could be," Merlin agreed. He turned back to the first page of written notes, the ones starting in 1989 when Silverman first started seeing Dr. Michael. Instead of examining the written side, he turned the page over, to the blank side. With the soft touch of a blind man reading Braille, Merlin ran his fingers over the page. "Try it," he said to Tory. "Very gently."

Tory did the same. "You can feel the words through the page."

"Exactly, yet they've been squooshed in the chart rack for almost a decade. What do you think?" Merlin asked.

"I'd like to see a few other charts from Dr. Michael's files."

Reading from the front of the chart Merlin said, "And isn't this convenient? Dr. Michael's office is downtown. We can walk."

"Now?" Tory asked, looking at her watch. "There won't be anyone there."

"That didn't stop us from sneaking our way into here."

"How're we going to get inside?"

Merlin snapped his fingers. "I've got to get something from my car." Obviously he had a plan, but it was more fun to tease.

Not wanting Merlin to have the last word, Tory rolled her eyes, opened her bag, and rummaged through it until her hand found the Beretta. Slyly, she pulled it out, released the clip, checked it as she'd seen done countless times in the movies, and smoothly snapped it back inside.

The lock was a Schlage, but Merlin didn't care about brand names. All he worried about were the fancy locks with the weird tubular keys. This one was old and had only five pins, which was tantamount to being easy. He produced a locksmith's pick set, a small leather pouch filled with thin metal tools. He selected two of them. First he took the torsion wrench—a thin five-inch piece of spring steel that looked like a piece of linguini in the shape of an "L"—and fitted the short arm snugly inside the bottom of the keyway. With his left hand, he pulled on the long arm of the "L" to produce a constant rotary torsion on the cylinder of the lock. As soon as the pins became lined up, the torsion would instantly turn the cylinder.

Next he took the second tool, called a double rake pick. Basically it was a straight instrument, also spring steel, comprised of a thick handle with a thinner piece that extended three inches, gradually tapering to a point. The last quarter inch or so of metal was shaped in a graceful zigzag, almost like the smooth loop a Dairy Queen cone has at the very top.

Gently he worked the raking pick into the keyway just above the torsion wrench. There were different techniques for lining up the pins;

some lock pickers pulled the rake back quickly, others worked it in with a gentle finesse. Merlin was from the pull-back-the-rake-hard school of lock picking. After the third try, he felt the cylinder give.

Once they stepped inside Dr. Michael's dental office, Merlin closed the door behind them and found the lights. They were standing in a small waiting room, filled with half a dozen chairs and a magazine rack stocked with heavy plastic folders protecting the copies of *Time* and *Newsweek*. Directly in front of them was the business office complete with a ceiling-to-floor chart rack, computer, and multiline telephone. A waist-high white Formica counter, where the receptionist would sit, separated the two. Off to the right was a door that led around to the business office and exam rooms.

"I'm scared," Tory said, taking a deep breath.

"You want to wait outside?"

"This is breaking and entering."

"Ten minutes. Tops. Then we're outta here," Merlin reassured. Taking Tory's hand, he guided her through the door and into the business office. "See if you can turn the computer on," he directed, grabbing several charts at random from the rack. While he examined the handwriting and gently palpated the back of the pages, Tory wandered over to the reception desk. Before she got to the computer, she spotted Dr. Michael's appointment book and opened it. In no time at all she exclaimed, "I got it! Come here! Remember September 28th, the temporary filling? Well, that entire week Dr. Michael was in Mexico. Not a single patient that whole week, just the word 'Mexico' in big block letters."

Merlin gave Tory a hug. "We were right."

Tory hesitated. "What about the handwriting?"

"Nice and neat. It doesn't matter whether the notes were written this year or in the eighties. He wrote out this file in one sitting and his hand got tired. And you can't feel the old notes through the paper. Silverman's dentals are faked. Everything fits. The bastard's alive."

"Okay, just to be sure, take me through it one more time."

Just then there was the sound of a key turning in the lock. Before they could do much more than duck down, the door opened. The first thing that Tory thought about was that they had been followed by the two men who had broken into their house and now were trapped. But then they heard a man's voice say, "Oh, damn, they left the lights on again."

Dr. Michael. It had to be. If they'd been followed, the last thing the thugs would comment on was whether or not the lights would be on.

Merlin made his hand into a gun, like a child would do playing cops and robbers, and mouthed, "Gimme your gun." While Tory went into her bag Merlin whispered, "You stay down."

Patiently, Merlin waited until he heard the door close, knowing it would be hard for Dr. Michael to make a dash for it. That's when Merlin stood up.

"Who the hell are you?" the dentist demanded while he was backing up toward the door in his horn-rimmed glasses and crested blazer. It was obvious from a distance that his hands were trembling and his face had emptied of color. The guy was terrified. And then he saw the gun. His head started swiveling back and forth, looking for a second hoodlum as he was forced to relive a dream he'd hoped would never come back.

Merlin decided to go for it. "Silverman wants to talk with you."

One, two, three seconds went by. Dr. Michael stood there, unable to speak, his head oscillating faster and faster. "No way. I did everything you guys said—"

Then Merlin brought up the Beretta in a two-handed firing position and pointed it at the terrified dentist. "Silverman says you must be the leak because the police know."

"No, they don't. Oh, God, please, no. They arrested that guy. I think his name's Huffman. I saw it on the news." He was in agony, talking faster and faster.

"Move away from the door," Merlin ordered.

Dr. Michael held his hands out, fingers pointed toward the ceiling. "No problem. Okay? I don't want any trouble." As he stumbled into the waiting room and stood over by the magazine rack, Merlin came around and stood right in front of him.

"You're in trouble. Now let's save some time. What the hell did you tell them?" he demanded again.

"Nothing! I swear to you, nothing. When the sheriff came for the records I didn't even see him. One of my girls turned the file over." He kept his hand out, bobbing it up and down, trying to calm the situation.

"We gotta go take a little ride."

"Where?"

"You know where."

"No, I don't. The two guys never told me anything. I examined that guy like they wanted me to. I did the chart just like they said and . . . and . . . and that was it. I don't know anything." And with that Dr. Michael covered both eyes with his hands and began to whimper. Merlin came close and gave him a little push backward, right in the middle of his chest. The dentist collapsed into one of the comfortable seats in his little waiting room.

"The records weren't perfect," Merlin said.

"What?"

"The handwriting—it got sloppy toward the end."

"I couldn't help it. I had to do it all at once. I . . . I did my best. Please believe me! Tell Dr. Silverman."

"You can tell him yourself. And don't forget to mention why you wrote that you put a temporary filling in him September 28th."

"What?" Dr. Michael said. "I had to. It was a temporary filling. If I didn't put in a recent appointment, it would have looked phony."

"Listen, you idiot, you were south of the border September 28th."

"Mexico," he whispered. "Oh, God. It's not my fault. I was at that apartment when I wrote the notes."

"What apartment?" Merlin asked.

"Where they had that guy. I don't know where I was! I was blind-folded."

"Shit," Merlin hissed. "You don't know anything. Hey, Tory."

Dr. Michael sat up straight. "Who are you?" he asked for the second time.

Merlin stood over the dentist. "We're gonna make this simple. You faked dental records."

Tory came around to the waiting room, holding up her identification. "Dr. Michael, I'm Tory Welch with the district attorney's office."

"Wait. No one was dead. The guy was sedated. He was alive, I swear to you."

"How do you know Silverman?" Tory asked.

"I'm his dentist."

"Okay, slowly from the beginning, what happened?"

"My God, I almost had a heart attack just now. Do you think I want those thugs to come back for real?"

Tory spoke in a voice purged of emotion. "With what you've just told us you are an accomplice to murder—"

"Don't you understand? These guys are serious!"

"Sir, do you want to go to jail?"

"Of course not." He looked around nervously. "Look, what about a deal? Yeah, a deal. They'll kill me! What about if the DA keeps my name out of it entirely? What about that?"

"Sometimes that can be arranged."

"Look, they got me in a little indiscretion. Something bad. I don't want my wife to know."

"Okay." Tory smelled victory. "Here's the deal. And it's nonne-gotiable. You level with us right here, right now—everything. I'll rec-ommend to the DA to *try* to keep your name out of it. That's it. I can't guarantee anything. Do you understand?" Tory waited for the dentist to nod. "The DA may tell me no way. But your odds are a lot better cooperating than what I'll do if you don't help us."

"Thank you."

"One more thing. If I catch you in a lie, no matter how insignificant, the deal is off and I'll have this place crawling with cops in ten minutes."

Dr. Michael nodded broadly. "Okay." He took several cleansing breaths. "About six weeks ago I hired a new assistant. A pretty girl who . . ." Dr. Michael's voice trailed off and tears flowed from his eyes.

"That's it?"

Dr. Michael's mouth was working but no sounds were coming out.

Tory turned slightly to speak to Merlin. "Call the police."

"No, no, wait," Dr. Michael said. "She seduced me . . . in my own dental chair. Somehow they got it on film. I don't know . . . they must've had a camera in the next building or something. If my wife ever finds out, I don't think I could take it."

"Go on."

"One night they came in here, right when I was getting ready to leave."

"Who came to see you?" Tory wanted to know.

"Two guys. A guy named Tommy—he had his right arm in a sling— and another guy, I don't know his name. Really. He had blond hair. Oh, yes, he wore cowboy boots."

Tory and Merlin looked at each other, knowing exactly who was being described.

Dr. Michael continued, "They had one of those TV-VCR combinations with them. They showed me the video. I had no choice. I mean what could I do? Tommy said I was lucky. Lucky! They said I was lucky because they needed me. You see, if I turned up dead that might seem suspicious because I was already Silverman's dentist. They needed me. Anyway, they took me to this apartment to examine some guy they had there. He was heavily sedated, barely moving. I don't know who he was. He sorta reminded me of Leonard Silverman, but in a country western sort of way. You know, wearing one of those shirts with the fancy stitching. Anyway, I had to examine him and create a fake set of records. Then I destroyed Silverman's records and slipped the new ones into the chart rack. That's all."

Tory said, "You go home now to your wife."

"Really?"

"Tomorrow morning you cancel your patients and show up at my office," Tory handed him one of her cards. "Ten A.M."

Dr. Michael read the card. After swallowing hard he spoke, "Let me ask you one thing. What would you have done if you were me?"

"If you're not at my office—"

"Don't worry," he said, realizing he wasn't going to get an answer. "I'll be there."

32

"It's Bass. It's gotta be," Merlin said as soon as they hit the elevator.

"Let's go through it together." Tory tucked her hair behind one ear.

Merlin punched the button for the lobby. "Okay. Silverman organized the murders at the Medical Center. But he was smart. Some part of him knew he might get caught, so he devised a back door escape. As soon as he found out Bello talked, he came to you knowing damn well you wouldn't cut a deal. Then he went on TV and did his pointing fingers speech for Sandy Keller. Meanwhile, his hoodlums—Leo and whoever that other guy was at our house—found some innocent Joe who was the same height and weight as Silverman."

The elevator stopped and the two hurried out to the street and headed back toward the courthouse.

Tory continued the story, "So what Huffman described watching from the rhododendron bush was this guy being brought into Silverman's house. The reason they shot him was to make certain he wouldn't move around and risk destroying the dental evidence. Is there any way to check the finger?"

"They can do tissue typing. There's no way to change the antigens in the tissues themselves, but that takes time, probably two weeks. Julian was probably under pressure to make an identification, and with all the minor antigens he checked matching exactly and the perfect set of dentals, tissue typing probably didn't seem necessary."

"So, who did the amputation?"

"Maybe there's some surgeon who hired a pretty nurse and got the Eric Michael treatment, video and all."

"Oh, Merlin!" Tory blurted out, as they waited for a traffic light to change. "Remember—on the news—the day after I found Silverman, that story about the orthopedic surgeon they found in his car."

Merlin hit himself in the forehead. "Right, the one who killed himself. I didn't pay any attention to it."

Stepping off the curb, Tory thought back on what she could remember about the suicide. "He had a computer printout from some medical lab that diagnosed him as having AIDS. No one questioned it. Eric Michael had to be kept alive. After all, he was the family dentist. But who would notice if some orthopedist killed himself?"

"Then they framed Huffman—"

"No," Tory said, "I bet they framed Graham first. He was so freaked out the day I saw him. He didn't have a clue what the hell was going on. And when they found out he had a great alibi, they cleaned off his car and looked for someone else."

Merlin smiled. "Enter Blaine Huffman."

They arrived back at the Allegheny County Courthouse and headed directly up to Tory's office.

"What about Bass?" Tory asked as she was unlocking her office door. Immediately she went to her desk and pulled out the accordion folder filled with documents concerning Western Insurance. She scanned through them until she located the chairman's home address.

Merlin scratched his chin. "If Silverman was masterminding this whole thing alone, and all he cared about was disappearing, he would have done exactly that. Disappeared. And we wouldn't find him in a million years. But first he framed Graham, then Huffman. Why? Why go to all that trouble?" He quickly answered his own question. "Because Western Insurance didn't want a shroud of suspicion hanging over it. Too much money at stake. Silverman's murder needed a solution. As long as you and the police were poking around, Bass wouldn't be able to finish off the deal in Connecticut."

"And even though Bass said he wouldn't benefit from the sale of WIP, he was probably a principal in some limited partnership that would have profited handsomely."

"Exactly. Bass was much closer to Silverman than Graham was. You heard that yourself. It's odd that the medical director was more in the loop than the president. Even in death Silverman engineered the deal to go through. And if he couldn't be there personally, he had to trust someone."

"Bass," Tory whispered. After one mandatory phone call, they were gone.

* * *

Norman Bass lived well. Not that they could see much of his brick Tudor from the street, but there was a small gatehouse at the end of the driveway that was magnificent. A hanging light off the side of the gatehouse showed off the splendid herringbone brickwork of the winding driveway. By now they didn't feel in so much of a rush so Merlin drove back and forth several times, finally pulling up to the curb at one corner of the huge property. Through the trees and bushes they could see lights downstairs. Twice they spotted someone walking past one of the windows.

A pair of headlights came up the street in front of them. Tory and Merlin scrunched down as the car drove past. By the time Merlin sat up and looked in the rearview mirror, the car was gone.

Tory checked her watch. "It's getting late. What do you think?"

"Look," Merlin whispered, his eyes locked on the house, "I see two people."

There was one window that was particularly big. One figure could be seen standing in front of it while a second figure walked past. "You think Silverman's there?"

Suddenly there was a loud rapping on the passenger window and Tory jumped. It was Gallagher, smiling through the window. He made a little circular motion with his hand, instructing Tory to roll down the window. Bending over at the waist he said, "You shoulda seen yourself. You must really be into this cops and robbers stuff."

"Where'd you come from?"

"When I saw how much fun you two were having as I drove by, I parked down the street and decided to give you a little scare." Then he tried the back door but it was locked, so he kept working the handle while Tory turned around in her seat to unlock the door. "This better be good," Gallagher said as he got in. He rubbed his face as he would first thing in the morning. "You said you got proof, right?"

Tory answered, "Of course. We went to the dental office and got a full confession from the dentist. The records were faked."

"So Silverman's alive," Gallagher muttered, still having trouble with the story.

"If he faked the dentals, he must be alive," Merlin added.

"That is one hell of a story, cutting his finger off. Jesus Christ."

"Ready to go?" Tory asked and opened her car door.

"Gimme the skinny on why you're so damned sure Bass is working with Silverman."

Tory pulled the door closed, but it was Merlin who spoke next. " 'Cause if Silverman's only intention was to escape, he wouldn't have needed to create such an elaborate frame-up."

"Hold it, boyfriend," Gallagher interrupted. "Her, not you."

Merlin didn't say another word, just leaned back against his door and waited for Tory to speak.

"Silverman had a close relationship with Bass. If Silverman set up Blaine Huffman it was to pull scrutiny away from Western Insurance and to derail the lawsuit. If he's doing all that, he's involved. No way he's acting like a guardian angel. He's involved and working with Bass, who cleverly situated himself in the role of CEO."

"So you want me to go in there and arrest Bass."

"Yes."

"This is too fuckin' crazy," Gallagher said emphatically. "You can't arrest him because your little scenario says the two are working together."

"Right now we've got the element of surprise on our side. If Silverman finds out what we know, then he might disappear for good."

Gallagher put his hand out as if he'd had enough of this bullshit. He leaned back and pulled at his trench coat, which was bunched up under him. "All right, Miss Welch. Whaddya say we sleep on it. I'll come up to your office in the A.M. and go through this scenario one more time. Then if we agree—"

Tory knew she could force the issue, but instead decided on a compromise. "Okay, Detective. How 'bout this? We go in there now and talk to him. Tell him what we know about Silverman, push him just a little. Same as if you questioned him in his office the other day. Then it'll be your decision what to do."

Gallagher rubbed his neck as if it might be sweaty. "And if I say no, you and boyfriend pull some magistrate out of bed and file a criminal complaint. No way. Let's go."

Merlin and Tory opened their car doors simultaneously.

Gallagher grabbed the backs of the two front seats and yanked himself forward. "This ain't no Kennywood fun house. He stays in the car."

"What?" Tory exclaimed. "He figured this whole damn thing out."

"Then thank him now, 'cause he's waiting in the car."

Tory looked over at Merlin as he pulled his door closed.

"Forget it," Merlin said calmly, "go." Silently, he watched as Tory angrily got out of the car and slammed the door.

The walk to the house took several minutes. At one point Gallagher commented about the fancy driveway costing more than his whole goddamn house, but Tory was realizing that in her anger she had forgotten her bag and didn't hear a word he said. Abruptly she stopped walking, more as a reflex than an attempt to go back to the car. But Gallagher was eyeing the house, trying to figure out what it cost, and didn't notice she'd fallen behind. Tory had to double-time it just to catch up.

The front door was massive, something you might find on an old church. Great iron strap hinges reached halfway across the wood. A heavy black knocker, set just below a small rectangular window, must have looked too imposing because Gallagher looked around for a doorbell. There was none, so he picked up the knocker and used it to tap lightly on the door.

Almost immediately footsteps could be heard and then the sound of the latch working. Slowly, as if it might be as heavy as it looked, the door opened. Norman Bass stood there, a drink in one hand. If he was surprised to have these two visitors so late at night he hid it well. Wearing a V-neck sweater over a dress shirt, the first thing he did was look at his watch. "I was just on my way upstairs."

"I know it's late, Mr. Bass," Gallagher said, choosing a tone more obsequious than Tory expected. "We haven't met. I'm Detective Gallagher. We never did get to talk the other day. I wonder if we might have a brief word with you now."

"You know, I just got back from Connecticut and I have a board meeting first thing in the morning. Perhaps we could get together—"

Before Bass could finish getting rid of his late night guests a woman's voice called from some distant part of the house. "Norman, who is it?" By her tone it was evident she really didn't care who it was.

Bass drained his drink, leaving only the ice cubes swirling around the bottom of the glass. Reluctantly, he turned toward the stairs and did one of those civilized calls that poorly camouflaged what he really wanted to say. "It's nothing, dear. I'll be up in a few minutes."

"Do your visitors know what time it is?" the woman's voice went on, sounding increasingly annoyed.

"I'll handle it, Donna," Bass called, shaking his head in frustration. He then pulled the door open all the way to invite his guests in. "All right. You might as well come in now." He stepped aside and waited as his guests stepped into the grand foyer. "This way," Bass said, walking past his guests as he led the way into a heavily decorated den. The lights were already on. Bass played host for a moment, using the glass in his hand to motion toward twin love seats set at right angles to one another. The ice cubes bounced and tinkled around in his glass. Bass chose a high-back chair for himself. Once they were all seated he said, "When I said to you, Miss Welch, that I wanted to cooperate I meant it." He placed the tumbler on a small table next to his chair. "But not in my home, and certainly not in the middle of the night."

Gallagher shifted uncomfortably in his seat and adjusted his trench coat.

"Mr. Bass—" Tory started to say.

"You have your man. Western Insurance is clean. And I have a company to run. Or should I say, sell. Now, tell me . . . what pressing business do you have that couldn't wait until morning?"

Gallagher turned to Tory. "Counselor."

Deciding on the direct approach, Tory said, "We have evidence that Dr. Silverman is alive and faked his own death."

"What?" Bass said and leaned forward in shock.

"Tonight we discovered his dental records were faked. He planned his own death very cleverly."

"Faked," the chairman said, but the words barely made it past his lips. With this stunning news Tory expected Bass to find a bottle of Jim Beam, and he did not disappoint her. With both hands he pushed himself out of his chair and stumbled across the carpet as if he were a much older man. He found his bottle in a built-in bar and held it up by way of invitation. Knowing his guests weren't over for drinks, he didn't bother looking for a response. Never mind putting ice in the short glass he favored for his Jim Beam. Bass grabbed a tall glass—probably one he used for serving gin and tonics to his guests all summer long—and filled it halfway. "What about . . . what about the fingerprints and the finger?" he stammered while dosing himself with two gulps.

Gallagher looked at Tory as if he, too, would like to hear the explanation once more.

"First of all, the fingerprints were real. They were checked with prints Silverman left in his bathroom, office, car—"

Bass held out the glass and moved it around, encouraging Tory to continue.

"—and everything matched. So the finger belonged to Leonard Silverman."

"But I read something about some blood tests the coroner did," Bass said hoarsely.

"Exactly," Tory acknowledged. "The blood from the body and the blood from the finger matched perfectly."

"So how the hell did that happen?" Bass demanded.

Donna's voice wafted down from the upper reaches of the house. "Norman? Norman!" Tory waited for Bass to answer. As if he had not heard his wife's bleating cries, he repeated the question. "So how the hell did the blood type of the finger and body match?"

"As I understand it, blood was drawn from the dead man into a syringe. When the finger was surgically removed from Silverman, the blood in the syringe was immediately squirted through the arteries in the finger, washing out Silverman's blood and replacing it with the same blood of the dead man.''

Bass slowly worked his way back to his seat and sat down heavily. "My God. Do you have any idea what this means? The Connecticut deal, which finally got back on track today, is going to fall apart.'' Bass rubbed his eyes. "God-fuckin'-damn it! I am *sick* of this crap he dumped on us.'' His show of temper surprised Tory. "All right. Now, we have different agendas, and I'll work with you every inch of the way. But I've gotta consider damage control. I mean, can I expect Sandy Keller any minute?'' Bass looked across at his two visitors, not once looking up as Leo appeared in a doorway behind the two love seats. Slowly, silently he crept into the room, the thick carpet absorbing any noise his feet made.

Gallagher leaned forward as he spoke. "No. The press has not been notified.''

"Well,'' Bass continued sarcastically, "I applaud you for not putting this on the news like your last arrest.''

Leo stood still for a moment, equidistant from Tory and Gallagher, the three of them forming an isosceles triangle. His gun, the very same Russian roulette revolver, was in his right hand, waist high.

Bass had no idea what Leo intended to do, but he kept the conversation going. "Who else knows?''

Leo took another step. He raised the revolver above his head, moving his hand slowly so as not to let his clothing rustle. Bass wanted to turn his head and close his eyes but forced himself to hold his gaze.

"Norman? Norman,'' came Donna's voice from upstairs. This time it was a welcomed intrusion.

Abruptly Bass turned in his chair toward the doorway to listen more closely.

"Well, actually,'' Gallagher said, "this is information that Miss Welch here came to me with just tonight.''

"Ahh tonight,'' Bass said, looking out toward the stairway as if Donna was about to appear. "So, no one else knows?''

"No one,'' Tory said. As her words reached Leo's ears, the revolver came down with a powerful stroke, the blunt end of the grip squarely meeting its mark.

THWACK. It was the sickest of sounds, much louder than he had expected. Bass could not help but whip his head around in time to see Detective Gallagher slump forward and roll off the love seat onto the floor.

"Oh, shit,'' Bass whispered as he leaned forward in his seat to see if any blood had gotten on his expensive carpet. Tory pressed herself into the armrest at the horrible sight of Gallagher sprawled out on the floor.

When she saw Leo standing behind the love seat, Tory sucked her breath in loudly.

"Long time no see, huh, sweet lips?" He held the gun waist high and aimed it at Tory.

"Merlin knows everything," she blurted out. "Forget about this."

Bass quickly walked over to the door and closed it quietly. "Oh, Miss Welch," he said, "you really will have to be quiet, otherwise Leo will put you in dreamland just like the good detective." Then he turned to Leo and said, "You couldn't wait to hit him, could you?"

"There's no blood," Leo said. "I hit him perfectly." They both looked down at the cream-colored carpet. "I waited until she said no one else knows," Leo was saying while he walked around and sat right next to Tory on the love seat. Using the gun to slide Tory's skirt up her thigh, he went on, "You'n me have some unfinished business. I jus' wish lover boy was here, 'cause I'd blow his fucking head off as soon as I could squeeze the trigger." Then he aimed the gun at Tory's head and pretended to shoot the gun, kicking his hand back at the imaginary recoil. "Pow."

"Enough, Leo," Bass said. "I don't want Donna coming down here and seeing the detective. You'd better get his gun."

Leo nodded and got up. He used his foot to roll Gallagher on his back, the detective's trench coat and sport jacket opening conveniently to expose his shoulder harness. Leo plucked out the service revolver and flipped it to Bass.

"Careful with that thing," Bass snapped, arranging his hand on the pistol grip. "Okay, miss, let's go."

Leo slipped the Smith and Wesson into his pocket and bent over to heave Gallagher over his shoulder. Bass stood there, absently pointing the gun more in Leo's direction than Tory's as he watched. Gallagher was heavy. Leo wasn't strong enough to do a clean and jerk with him, so he worked the unconscious detective into a sitting position on the floor leaning against the sofa. Then, holding Gallagher's hands all the while, Leo walked around the sofa, leaning over the cushiony back so as not to release his grip. When he was behind the love seat, he pulled the detective up onto the seat like a sack of beans. Coming around to face a very limp Gallagher, Leo was then able to get down on one knee and roll the detective onto his shoulder.

"See that, Miss Welch?" Bass said with a smirk. "Leo's not as dumb as you thought he was when he stopped by your house." He directed

Tory through the first floor of his residence, past a powder room, a formal dining room, a sunroom, and a darkened office. Eventually they reached the back door. Louder and louder, Leo's faltering footsteps slapped on the floor as his breathing became labored.

The small group approached the big black Mercedes parked a short walk across the lawn, Leo struggling, hunched over like he was going to drop his load. Hearing the noisy breathing, Bass sped up and beat everyone to the car so he could open the cavernous trunk. The moment Leo reached the car, he dropped the detective inside with a thud that caused the car to rock back and forth gently, like a boat on a lake.

"Get his keys," Bass ordered.

"Why?" Leo said between gasps.

"How the hell will it look when they find his car parked out front, or," he said, eyeing Tory, "did you two come in your car?"

"He picked me up. It's down the street." Tory knew the general direction of Gallagher's car, but she had no idea what he drove.

"See?" Bass said to Leo. "You gotta think." He looked at his watch then at a second-floor window while Leo reached inside the trunk, rolled Gallagher onto his back, and went pocket to pocket until he found the key ring.

Finally Leo stepped back while he caught his breath. His hand slipped deep into the pocket of his jeans and worked his fingers around the pistol grip. Having his gun in hand felt good.

Tory was in a panic. What if she couldn't identify Gallagher's car? What then? Would it dawn on Bass that they hadn't come together? It terrified her to think what Leo would do to Merlin.

Satisfied that the unconscious detective was without gun or keys, Bass closed the trunk lid, taking care to touch the glossy paint job with nothing more than his fingertips. Automatically Bass rubbed his hands together as if he had just changed the oil.

"ELBUORT," Leo said, reading the license plate in the scattered light from the house.

Bass headed around the car.

"What is that, anyway? ELBUORT. Some kind of nickname?" Leo wondered.

"Let's go," Bass said to Leo.

But Leo was still mumbling to himself, "ELBUORT. ELBUORT," repeating the word as if it would eventually come to him.

"Leo!" Bass said, raising his voice sharply. "You're gonna drive Gallagher's car. You want some rope to tie her up?"

"Nah, throw her in the trunk," Leo said.

"We don't know which car they came in, Leo."

"So, she points out Gallagher's wheels and we pop her in the trunk with the cop." Then Leo opened one of the back doors and waited for Tory to get in. "ELBUORT," he was still saying as he slid in next to Tory.

Slowly the car started to move, Bass barely giving it any gas.

Ring. Ring. Ring. "Goddamn it," Bass moaned, knowing who it was. He looked at the phone and ignored it. *Ring. Ring. Ring.* Now he worked the pedal and gained some speed coming around to the front. *Ring. Ring. Ring.* It wasn't going to stop, and it seemed to be getting louder. "Which way?"

Tory could hear the bricks mumbling under the tires.

"Which way?" Bass screamed. "Which way is the car, goddamn it?"

"Left," Tory said, hoping the incessant ringing would distract Bass enough to drive right past Merlin. "At the next house."

Ring. Ring. Ring.

Bass gave it some gas and the mumbling of the bricks became more of a stutter.

Ring. Ring. Ring.

Now Bass was looking down at the phone, cursing under his breath. Tory was looking out the window. *Don't stop ringing. Keep ringing.*

Suddenly Bass hit the brakes. The big Mercedes jerked to a halt, and he grabbed the cellular phone from its cradle. "What, Donna? What is so important that you can't leave me alone for ten seconds?"

Keep driving. Tory could spot the dark outline of Merlin's car through the branches of naked bushes.

"Look, Donna, why don't you go to bed! I've got a quick errand to run and I'll be back after midnight."

"Turn left out of the driveway. It's at the next house," Tory said.

The Mercedes didn't move. Bass was going to sit there at the end of the driveway until his domestic crisis was solved. "Look, I gotta go, Donna," Bass said. Not waiting for a response he said, "Good night, Donna," with that singsongy voice parents resort to after saying good night to their child one time too many.

The Mercedes started to roll again. "Which way was that?" Bass asked, his voice considerably calmer.

"Take a left. Down about a hundred yards."

"ELBUORT," Leo whispered, still working on the license plate.

The car bounced gently as it left the drive and hit the road.

Tory looked out the front window and saw Merlin's dark silhouette looking at them. *Do something. Do something, quick.* "Try spelling it backward," she said to Leo.

"Huh?"

"Spell ELBUORT backward."

"Ohhhh," he said as if he'd figured it out himself.

"T-R-U."

They were moving down the road. Merlin's car was on the left. Tory assumed Gallagher had parked on the right. "Down on the right. You can . . . you can see it." Then to Leo: "T-R-*O*-*U*-B-L-E. Trouble."

"So?"

"If I recall our conversation, Mr. Bass," Tory said, as they were parallel with Merlin, "you told me you can always turn trouble around. Isn't that right?"

Bass craned his head to see Tory in the rearview. He smiled at the fact that someone else appreciated his own cleverness.

The ride to Gallagher's car was very short. Mercifully, there was only one car parked in front of the next house. Bass pulled up to the curb right behind a late model Buick. "I'm sorry, Miss Welch, but you're going to have to join your friend in the trunk. I can't very well hold a gun on you while we drive up to Butler, now can I?" he said as he popped open the trunk lid. He waited in the car while Leo hopped out and nudged Tory around to the trunk.

Gallagher just lay there. Tory was starting to wonder if he was dead. "Hop in," Leo ordered, reaching in and giving the detective a cruel shove to move him deeper into the trunk.

One of Gallagher's arms moved and he groaned.

Getting into the trunk of a car, even a car as big and roomy as a Mercedes, was awkward. Tory turned sideways, putting one leg into the trunk, resting her knee on the clean carpet. As she shifted her weight, she started to bring the other leg into the trunk. Leo lifted up her skirt and treated himself to an eyeful of thigh.

"Fuck you," Tory hissed, pulling herself inside the car and flattening down so the lid would close.

Merlin was going crazy. He had spotted the Mercedes in the driveway and watched it come to an abrupt stop at the end of the driveway. There was no doubt in his mind that Tory was in the backseat. Something had gone terribly wrong—that much was obvious. As he turned around in his seat he watched Tory climbing into the trunk of the Mercedes. In desperation he grabbed Tory's bag from the floor in front of the passenger seat and dumped it out, looking for the Beretta. *Why the hell don't I have a cell phone?* His head rotated back and forth, watching for the Mercedes to pull away one second, then rummaging through a pile of junk on the seat. The Mercedes. The contents of her bag.

The red brake lights on the Mercedes came on, and then the car backed up, just as Merlin found the Beretta. A few seconds later the lights came on in Gallagher's car and both cars pulled away from the curb.

That's when Merlin started his car, did a U-turn without the benefit of headlights, and began the pursuit. Two blocks later Merlin turned on the headlights, keeping as much distance between them as possible.

33

"All right, get out of the car, both of you," Leo commanded as the trunk lid swung open. For a moment Tory stared up at him, curled up in the dark trunk like a frightened animal, which made Leo angry. "Now! Get the hell outta there." He emphasized the words by banging his pistol grip on the back of the car, which marked up the paint, but Leo didn't care; Bass was already on his way to the house.

The ride had taken over forty minutes, long enough for Gallagher to start moaning incoherently. For the last several minutes the Mercedes had driven slowly down a rutted road, bouncing its passengers around wildly. Tory climbed out first, then it was Gallagher's turn. His movements were clumsy, as if he were half asleep. One of his pant legs caught on something and he tumbled out of the car and onto the ground. Leo gave the detective a kick in the ribs to hurry him up.

Tory looked around. They were in dense woods that smelled heavily of pine. No lights from neighboring houses could be seen. Tucked into the woods, beautifully lighted from tree-mounted floodlights, was an Adirondack lodge. Whether it was for hunting or fishing, this was a place for rich men to come and play. Rustically constructed of stone and logs, the lodge had a steeply sloped roof and several large masonry chimneys. Cords of wood were stacked along one of the side walls. In the distance, Norman Bass could be seen reaching the front door.

"Get up," Leo said to Gallagher, giving him another sharp kick in the side.

Slowly Gallagher got to his knees, grabbing hold of the bumper while he stood. He rubbed the back of his head and looked around, surprised to see his own car parked next to the big Mercedes.

"Okay, let's go. To the house." The three of them set off, Leo holding his Smith and Wesson, Tory and Gallagher several steps in front. "And don't try nothing," Leo reminded them, figuring he was supposed to say something like that.

It was now getting close to midnight. Before they reached the lodge, Tory chanced a quick look around, hoping to see some headlights or any sign that Merlin had followed them.

There was nothing. The view through the pines was black and barren. A voice inside her head foolishly screamed at her to run. As they got close to the front door they walked on a flagstone pathway. Ironically the air smelled wonderful, like burning oak and cherry. Even before reaching the front door, before they could hear any voices, the sound of a crackling fire greeted them.

The door was open partway. Timidly, Tory pushed it all the way and the three of them entered a great room. Most of the front wall was filled with a huge stone fireplace throwing off enough heat to warm the oversized room against the chilly autumn night. There was a large moose head with a mature set of antlers mounted above the mantel. An open stairway led from the front door to the second floor, and there were closed doors at either end of the room. On one wall was a gun rack stacked full of shotguns and rifles, and a bearskin was tacked up on the back wall. Three large chandeliers, complicated-looking fixtures constructed of antlers, hung from a series of rough beams in the ceiling.

But it was the seating area that caught their attention. One long saddle-brown leather sofa, inlaid with an Indian print across the back cushions, faced the fire. It was flanked by two similar chairs. In front of the sofa was a low table, a cross section of a large oak, mounted on sturdy legs that were nothing more than logs taken from the same tree.

Norman Bass was already comfortably ensconced in one of the leather chairs, a glass of Jim Beam in one hand. Seated on one end of the sofa, close enough to Bass for intimate conversation, was Leonard Silverman. He looked grand, wearing a smoking jacket over a pair of corduroy trousers, regarding a fat cigar, as if contemplating the smoke rising from the burning ember was the only care he had in the world.

Tory and Gallagher stood silently together trading looks with Norman Bass until Silverman finally noticed he had company.

"Ah, Miss Welch, we meet again," Silverman said warmly as if he fully intended to serve drinks and have a nice long chat. He brought the cigar to his lips and drew in the heavenly smoke. "H. Upmann, Habana," he said, blowing out a thin stream of smoke as if he were with his poker buddies showing off what he'd smuggled across the border.

That's when Tory noticed his left hand was heavily bandaged in layers of white gauze, enough dressing to make it look as if he was wearing an enormous white glove.

"Ah, you noticed," Silverman said, lifting his left hand to show it off. "So how's my digit doing?" When Tory didn't answer he continued, "Well, you've seen it more recently than I. How is the little fella?"

"You're not nearly as clever as you think."

"Oh, if we must. You're right. Eric Michael was a mistake," Silverman admitted. "Did he tell you about the video?"

Leo laughed, happy to be in on the joke.

"We didn't need him," Tory said confidently.

"Oh? Well, that's good. Then we don't have to take care of him tonight, do we? Well, no matter. You found the Jell-O, I'm told. You taste it?"

"No."

"I had to doctor it up with some crap I got at the health food store." Then he looked at Detective Gallagher. "Where are my manners? I'm Leonard Silverman."

"Fuck you," the detective snapped.

"Now, now, Officer. Let's be civil. Take a seat. You, too, Miss Welch."

Leo used the short barrel of his revolver to give Tory a painful jab in the small of her back, pushing her toward the leather chair so she would be seated opposite Norman Bass.

"Thanks anyway, I'll stand," Gallagher said and pushed his trench coat back so he could slip both hands in his pockets.

Leo eased himself back behind the detective, then took his foot and placed it on Gallagher's ass, giving him a shove toward the sofa. The detective stumbled forward, banging his knees on the slab of oak. Before Gallagher could get pissed off, before he could even realize what was happening, Leo came at him and slugged him in the back of the head with the pistol grip.

Harry Gallagher went down over the table, his head somehow landing on one of the leather cushions of the sofa.

"Fuckin' cop," Leo muttered.

"Well, it's like a party," Silverman said brightly, assuming the role of the resourceful host who knows how to get a social occasion back on track. "I know I could use another drink. How 'bout you, Miss Welch. Scotch? Maybe some cream sherry?"

It was sickening to look at Detective Gallagher, but Tory couldn't pull her eyes from the man. His head was turned sharply to one side, forced so deeply into the cushion it looked as if his mouth couldn't possibly exchange any air.

Seeing his guest otherwise occupied, Silverman looked at the hired help. "Leo, a scotch, and maybe a refill for Mr. Bass. The usual. Get yourself a soft drink, if you like."

Merlin left his car at the road, a two-minute walk past the dirt drive where he saw the two cars turn. Not for a second did Merlin consider finding a phone and calling for help. He was terrified that time was running out, so he stumbled his way through the woods, clutching Tory's Beretta so tightly the muscles in his hand kept cramping. Twice he fell when he tripped over an exposed root. His sweater was covered in pine needles, but he could see the lights through the woods and that kept him going. When he was a hundred yards from the house, he spotted the Mercedes and Buick parked side by side.

He crouched behind a large rock and studied the two cars until he was certain no one was lingering around them. Most of the rooms of the house were lighted. Methodically his eyes searched room by room looking for signs of life. No one was walking around. The only useful bit of information was the thin line of light outlining most of the front door.

He stayed in his crouch as he crept closer to the lodge, the woods providing cover until he was less than fifty yards away. Everything seemed to make too much noise. His feet crunching the tiny pebbles. His breathing, coming and going harshly from his lungs. Even the way his ears crackled when he swallowed. Then the wind picked up and he could smell the fireplace. He moved closer, stopping to take a look around. Closer still, and another rest. His heart was going crazy in his chest. The hammering of his own pulse grew louder and louder in his head until he couldn't tell if there were any noises coming from the house.

Finally, he worked his way to the log siding that made up the front of the lodge, and he rested, wedged safely in the little corner made by the chimney, vainly trying to get control of the tremendous fear that clouded his thinking. His back up against the unfinished timber, Merlin looked left toward the front door, then leaned forward and looked around the protruding masonry. Suddenly the sound of laughter drifted from the crack where the front door was left open. Laughter. Goddamned laughter, like someone was having a swell time. What the hell was someone laughing at? He brought the Beretta up and checked the safety three times, making sure it was off.

Taking several deep breaths he found the nerve to inch himself toward the window, first ducking beneath it, then slowly pushing up until he was able to peek over the sash.

The view was perfect. Tory sat stiffly in one chair. Gallagher was at one end of the long sofa, slumped across the oak table as if he were a rag doll thrown across the room. There was Silverman, not six feet from the detective, working on a cigar as he held court. And finally, legs crossed comfortably, drink in one hand, enjoying the comfort of the other chair, was Norman Bass.

No one else was in the room.

And no one was holding a gun. Of course that seemed odd, but Merlin didn't dwell on it. Carefully he lowered himself back down and once again crouched as he approached the front door.

Push the door open. If Silverman or Bass makes a move, shoot.

At the front door Merlin hesitated as he took several deep cleansing breaths. Over and over he reviewed in his mind where everybody had been sitting in the room. Tory on the left, then Gallagher and Silverman, finally Bass on the right. Playing the odds, Merlin figured Bass probably had the gun. How else could he have kidnapped Tory and Gallagher? It was probably in his lap. Merlin inched toward the door, grasping his right wrist with his left hand, holding the Beretta out in front of him, ready to kick the door open.

Click. Click.

The first click was louder than the second, and Merlin knew it to be the unmistakable sound of a gun being cocked, a trigger being pulled back in anticipation of firing. Merlin lowered his weapon and turned his head just enough to see Leo's blond hair. "Hello, Leo," he said with a false confidence. "You're a sore for sighted eyes."

"Turn around, asshole. You'n me got some unfinished business. If I see your face I might just blow your head clean off your shoulders."

Merlin straightened. Even though he had the Beretta down at his side, Leo's gun was inches from his head. He had no choice but to go along with whatever he was told to do.

"Now, Doc—and you go real slow so I don't have to kill you—walk through the door. That's it, nice and slow."

Merlin pushed the door open and walked into the great room.

"Check out what I found sneaking up to the house," Leo said proudly and stepped back from Merlin so he could haul off and give him a kick in the rear with his cowboy boot. "The doc—and he's all mine."

"Leo," Silverman said, looking quite comfortable in his smoking jacket. "What's that in Dr. Merlin's hand?"

Spotting the Beretta, Leo grabbed it. "Gimme that. Where'd this come from? He didn't have it on him outside." He looked at the gun with disdain, turning the puny weapon over in his hand several times. "What's this little thing?" Leo asked, "some kind of toy?" Then he walked over near where Tory was sitting and said, "This what you shot at me?"

Tory didn't answer.

"I said," Leo continued, raising his voice, "this what you shot at me?" Leo shoved the Beretta in the waist of his pants for safekeeping.

"Yes." Tory looked up at him boldly. "Too bad I missed."

Leonard Silverman stood now. "All right, boys and girls. Knock it off, everyone." Then to Merlin, who remained several feet away from Norman Bass, he said, "So, while you're here maybe I can have you check the wound."

"You got quite a sharp kid working for you," Merlin teased. "Didn't even frisk me. Hey, Leo. Is that the same gun we played Russian roulette with?"

Leo looked at the Smith and Wesson briefly, remembering the ordeal. "You shoulda never come here."

"Still looks new. Betcha you never used it once since that night."

Leo looked at his gun. "You don't know shit."

"I know everything about you, Leo. I remember how you gagged and cried like a baby when I stuck that thing down your throat."

Bass sipped his drink, watching Leo get red in the face, wondering why the hell anyone would give someone with a gun such shit.

Silverman rolled the cigar between his thumb and fingers, letting Leo run with it, seeing how he handled himself. "Dr. Merlin, I wouldn't push ol' Leo here too far. He's quite a dangerous man," Silverman said casually, giving the nod to his boy to handle it.

Leo's hand was shaking with anticipation, but he managed to release the cylinder from the gun and show off all the shiny brass cartridges waiting to go.

"Him? Leo?" Merlin went on, acting shocked by what Silverman had said. "He cried like a baby when I had him. He's not even tough *with* a gun. Lookit him, Silverman. Look at his hands. Shaking like a leaf. He's a pussy. What are you paying him?" Without waiting for a response, Merlin turned back to Leo. "Whatever it is I'll double it."

Suddenly, Tory felt as if she were in a bizarre dream. Merlin was talking crazy, out of his head, trying to provoke a man with a gun. As well as she knew Merlin, it seemed as if he had lost touch with reality.

Leo took several steps closer to Merlin. The surgeon held his ground.

"Ooooh, cowboy boots," Merlin mocked. "You got cowboy boots on. You ride one of those toy horses outside the Giant Eagle? Hey, I know, why don't you give me the Beretta and we'll go back-to-back and take twenty paces. That is, if you're a man."

"Shut up, asshole! Quit your talking. I know what that is. Trash talk. But I'm the one with the gun, so shut your fuckin' mouth."

"Go ahead, Leo. Instead of putting the barrel in your mouth, why don't you shove it up your ass."

"I mean it! Shut up!"

"See, Silverman. I told you. What a baby. I bet he's really annoying if you run out of diet soda. You hired a wimp."

"Shut . . . your . . . fucking . . . mouth!" Then to Silverman, "He's asking for it. He says one more thing I'm taking him out."

Before Silverman could intervene, Merlin jumped in, chiding him. "One more thing. One more thing. See, you showed your boss good restraint. Maybe you'll get a raise. Did you have the balls to tell Silverman about blabbing about delivering the rubbers with the bacteria in it? 'Cause without you telling us that, we would've never figured this thing out. No way." Merlin looked at the revolver in Leo's hand, double-checking to be sure. He remembered holding it up to the light that night Leo broke in and seeing nothing but darkness when he sighted down the barrel.

"That's it. You're dead!" Leo screamed, clearly out of control.

Every muscle in Leo's body tightened as he began to squeeze the trigger. Everything went into slow motion.

BANG!

The first scream was Tory's as she winced from the report of the Smith and Wesson.

The second was Leo's, a desperate cry of pain.

The revolver had exploded in Leo's hand, the quick set Epoxy having blocked any exit from the chamber. As the hammer struck the .38 Special plus P bullet there was no place for the bullet to go; Leo was left with his hand wrapped around a grenade.

The last sound before anyone spoke was the noise made when the revolver dropped to the floor with Leo's right index finger still wrapped around the trigger.

"My finger!" Leo screamed. "My finger!"

Blood was squirting out of Leo's hand in pulses. Flailing about, he sprayed Bass and Silverman in the face with red dots.

Merlin wasted no time. In the confusion, he took several steps forward and snatched the Beretta from Leo's pants. "Here," he called to Tory and flipped the Beretta to her. "You're the marksman."

Leo was now on the floor, his blue jeans soaking up the puddle of blood, examining the damage. "Where's my finger? Oh, God, where's my finger?"

Tory stood up. "Hands on your heads, men."

Silverman and Bass put their hands on their heads.

"Okay, everybody. Let's stay calm," Silverman said.

"Yes," Bass agreed, his voice shaking. "We don't want anyone to get hurt."

At that very moment, Tommy entered in from the kitchen, appearing in a doorway behind Merlin, aiming his big Sig Saurer .45 with the laser sight at Merlin. "Trust me, Miss Welch, I will not hesitate to shoot Dr. Merlin. Drop your gun." Merlin whipped his head around to watch Tommy slowly walk toward him. "I said, drop it, Miss Welch."

Silverman and Bass had lowered their hands by now.

"Hold it," Merlin said, but it was too late. Tommy had reached him and the Sig Saurer was jammed against Merlin's head. Although his right arm still moved stiffly, it had recovered enough to hold the weapon. He wrapped his left arm around Merlin's chest, pulling him in close.

"Don't do nothing to get him killed," Tommy said to Tory.

Tory took several steps forward so that she was only a couple of yards from Merlin and Tommy. The two men were standing so close together that Tommy's head looked as though it was growing out of Merlin's right shoulder.

Slowly Tory's left hand came up and formed the saucer. She said nothing, but turned on a gaze that let Tommy know she meant business.

"That bullet you shot at Leo that night. Caught me in the shoulder. Don't think I won't use this."

"And if I shot you once don't think I'll hesitate to do it again."

"You'll hit lover boy, here. I don't care, give it your best shot. C'mon, let's be smart, put the gun down, and we sit down and talk."

"I'm going to count to five," Tory said confidently. Her hand was incredibly steady. "If you haven't put your gun down, then I'm going to assume we can't settle this quietly. One."

"You better tell her not to shoot," Tommy said right in Merlin's ear.

"Fuck you," Merlin said.

"Two."

"Just three to go," Tommy said to no one in particular, but he tightened his grip on Merlin just the same, ready to whip him around in the event Tory got to five and was stupid enough to pull the trigger.

"Three."

Silverman erupted in a smile. This was getting good.

Bass shifted in his seat to get a better view. His hand reached for the detective's gun, which was stowed in his pocket.

"Four," Tommy said right back at her. "Go ahead, shoot now, Miss Welch. If you had the balls you would've already done it."

Merlin seemed to disappear. *Poof!* It was as if he had left the room. As far as Tory was concerned Tommy's head floated all by itself in space like a toy balloon. Merlin was no longer part of the equation. "Five."

Bang!

Bang!

Two shots went off.

The first bullet from the Beretta struck Tommy squarely in the right eye, piercing the orbit and entering the skull where it ricocheted back and forth, liquefying a path of cerebral cortex in the process. Tommy's head snapped back, and he was instantly dead.

The second bullet also came from Tory's gun. This one caught Norman Bass in the right shoulder. He had made a sudden move. Maybe a startled reflex or maybe he was going for his gun. It didn't really matter.

Merlin and Tory embraced for several seconds, Tory keeping one eye on Leonard Silverman.

As Tory went to the phone to call the police, Merlin tended to the wounded, his first patient being Harry Gallagher, who remained slumped on the couch with a nasty laceration to the head.

EPILOGUE

The locker room at Sparrow Run Country Club was nearly empty. It was late enough in the day that most of the eager attendants had served their last drinks and were busy buffing the golf shoes of members who had gone off to dinner in the grill room.

Banks Wickford's locker was on the second floor. This was no ordinary locker room. No cement floors. No metal lockers. At Sparrow Run each member had an elegant oak locker and the floor was covered with plush blue carpeting emblazoned with the club logo repeated over and over. Banks had come out of the shower room with an oversized towel wrapped around his waist, a second one draped over his shoulders. As he finished drying himself he lingered by a small window at the end of his row of lockers, admiring the way the brilliant green of the first fairway shone in the waning sunlight. Suddenly he remembered the time and dropped both towels to the floor, making the effort to drop them close enough to one another so that the attendant would only have to bend over once to collect them. Naked, he turned toward his locker.

That's when he saw Blaine Huffman looking crisp and businesslike in a handsome brown suit, white shirt, and red tie. He had positioned himself directly in front of Banks's locker.

"Blaine, I, uh . . . didn't hear you—" Banks stammered, feeling so incredibly naked as he looked down at himself.

"We've got to talk," Huffman said flatly, never letting his eyes wander south of the equator.

Banks's first instinct was to grab one of the towels from the floor and cover himself. But this was the men's locker room and you were supposed to be naked here. Interlacing his fingers, Banks used them like fig leaves. "My last round of the year. Such a beautiful day. It's so depressing to put the sticks away for the winter. You play today?"

"No. We're having dinner. I was told I might catch you here."

"Oh," Banks said, not liking the sound of what Huffman had just said. "I was sick about the way they treated you, arresting you that way." Huffman said nothing. "So . . . uh . . . I take it you saw they handed down indictments for Bass and Silverman this morning?" he asked, reminding Huffman that they had always been on the same team. "I think the Medical Center has weathered the storm quite well, considering."

"Actually, it's Jack Merlin I wanted to talk to you about."

Banks smiled weakly. "You mean that he and Tory announced their engagement?" he said hopefully. "We were all pleased."

"He told me about it."

Shit. Merlin's in with Huffman. "He's really something, isn't he? I mean figuring that whole thing out."

"He figured you out, too. Let's go back to that phone call you made to me."

There was an awful silence for the few seconds it took Banks to collect his thoughts. "You know, looking back, I feel terrible about that . . . I mean what a terrible misunderstanding . . . trust me, Blaine, I took Katherine's death just as seriously as—" Banks caught himself before he said "you." "What I mean to say is I personally interviewed everyone in the OR that day. We read him all wrong."

"We?" Huffman asked.

"I," Banks said softly.

"Listen, Banks, you caught me in a vulnerable position that night you called. Christ, I was insane with grief. You knew damned well when I hung up the phone I believed Merlin was responsible for what happened to my daughter."

"That wasn't it at all. I was just trying to let you know I was handling things."

"You wanted me to blame Jack Merlin so I wouldn't sue the Medical Center."

"Oh, no, no . . . it's—"

Huffman stared Banks down, showing him no hope of escape. "When you barged in on us that morning in Merlin's office I had already drawn a gun on him." Banks sucked in his breath audibly. "My God, I could have done something crazy."

"Blaine, if I misread the information I was given, then . . . I apologize. I was wrong, absolutely, positively wrong, and I'm deeply sorry.

It's just that things were happening so quickly. I was trying to do right by you.''

"You're a calculating bastard.''

Banks swallowed, afraid to say anything.

Huffman continued, "I have a meeting tomorrow morning with Carter Forsythe. I intend to inform him that I plan to donate ten million dollars to the hospital's endowment.''

"What? Oh, my God,'' Banks gushed, an overwhelming sense of relief lifting his spirits. "That's wonderful . . . absolutely wonderful. We've got to do something. Celebrate.''

"Not so fast. There's one string. In any deal there's always a string. You know what I mean?'' The smile disappeared from Banks's face as quickly as it had come. "You must resign as CEO of the Medical Center. If you don't I will meet with Carter and the board anyway and inform them you blew a ten-million-dollar gift. Imagine what will happen next.''

"You don't understand . . . my God . . . they put me up to that phone call . . . *they* wanted me to do it . . . it wasn't my idea—''

"Don't whine. It's unbecoming.''

"Let me sit down with you and Carter.'' Banks placed his thumb and forefinger on either side of his nose, right between his eyes, and squeezed hard. "I know we can straighten this mess out.''

"In fact, I don't want to see you here anymore. Sparrow Run is a haven for me and running into you will spoil it. You're through here.''

"You can't do that. You don't own Sparrow Run,'' Banks whispered.

"No, but I do business with a lot of people. Anyone who plays golf with you will find out quickly that I will never do business with them again. A round of golf with you will be the kiss of death.''

Banks put his hand to his chest. He was breathing loudly, taking his breath in like a child about to cry. "You're being unfair. I was acting on Katherine's behalf. You can't do this to me. Where will I go?''

"Quit sniveling, Banks. You're embarrassing yourself.''

"I love my job. There must be something that I can say, something that I can do.''

"No. Show up here again and I'll do my best to make sure you don't find work again. Got it?''

"Couldn't I at least talk to Merlin, make things right?''

Huffman turned to leave. "I'll tell Merlin you wanted to make things right. By the way, Banks, we called our little girl Kit.''